T0283529

STORM
FURIES

BAEN BOOKS by WEN SPENCER

THE ELFHOME SERIES

Tinker

Wolf Who Rules

Elfhome

Wood Sprites

Project Elfhome

Harbinger

Storm Furies

ALSO BY WEN SPENCER

Endless Blue

Eight Million Gods

The Black Wolves of Boston

To purchase any of these titles in e-book form,
please go to www.baen.com.

STORM FURIES

WEN SPENCER

Copyright © 2024 by Wen Spencer

A Baen Books Original

Baen Publishing Enterprises
P.O. Box 1403
Riverdale, NY 10471
www.baen.com

ISBN: 978-1-9821-9354-6

Cover art by Dominic Harman

First printing, August 2024

Distributed by Simon & Schuster
1230 Avenue of the Americas
New York, NY 10020

Library of Congress Cataloging-in-Publication Data

Names: Spencer, Wen, author.
Title: Storm furies / Wen Spencer.
Description: Riverdale, NY : Baen Books, 2024. | Series: Elfhome ; 7
Identifiers: LCCN 2024011070 (print) | LCCN 2024011071 (ebook) | ISBN 9781982193546 (hardcover) | ISBN 9781625799715 (ebook)
Subjects: LCSH: Elves—Fiction. | LCGFT: Fantasy fiction. | Novels.
Classification: LCC PS3619.P4665 S76 2024 (print) | LCC PS3619.P4665 (ebook) | DDC 813/.6—dc23/eng/20240318
LC record available at https://lccn.loc.gov/2024011070
LC ebook record available at https://lccn.loc.gov/2024011071

Printed in the United States of America

10 9 8 7 6 5 4 3 2 1

This book is dedicated to my wonderful patrons on Patreon. It is through their support that I am able to do what I do.

Special thanks to

Marti Garner
Roger A. Josephson
Andrew Riley Prest
Mary Sithe
Torsten Steinert
Elisabeth Waters

And

Alisha
Kathy Brann
Andrew Hart
Jacquelyn L. Jacobs
Richard Jamison
Anders Ljungquist
Alice Ma
Albert McCann
Clemens Ladisch
William Wagner
Robert Williamson

And an Extra-Special Thank-You to

Dr. Hope Ring
Dr. Nan Nueslle
Ellen McMicking

STORM FURIES

1: AFTERMATH

"Right." Tinker bounced in place, thinking frantically. "Change of plans."

She'd been woken up in the middle of the night with the news that she had somehow acquired six siblings, four of which hadn't been born yet. Nevertheless, said unborn babies were terrorizing the neighborhood as talking mice. How? She hadn't a clue although a certain pocket-sized dragon was certainly involved. The day had gone downhill from there. Currently an unknown number of oni warriors were attacking Oakland and all the *domana* elves might be dead.

She was at the Tinker Domi Computer and Research Center with all five of the *sekasha* warriors who made up her Hand. Rainlily had left in the morning to take a message to Windwolf but had caught back up with her on Stormsong's Delta. It meant for vehicles that they had a Rolls-Royce, a hoverbike, and whatever Tinker could commandeer from the EIA. The research center sat at the edge of the North Side, meaning that they would need to cross the Allegheny River to reach Oakland. There were seven bridges that they could take—more if they made a wide enough circle—but that would eat up time. The Veterans Bridge was the most logical place to cross—but the oni had ambushed her on it once this summer already. Dusk was falling; they only had another hour or so of daylight left, but it also meant that they would soon have the cover of darkness. A storm was blowing in.

The white canvas tent over the casting circle billowed, threatening to be torn from its stakes. The towering line of windmills hummed loudly, changing the pitch of their blades to keep them from spinning too fast. Judging by the strength of the wind, Pittsburgh was in for a fierce thunderstorm. She might be able to work the storm to her advantage but it meant that using the hoverbike would be risky.

"We had a plan?" Only Stormsong dared to ask.

The other four *sekasha* warriors looked confused but they weren't questioning Tinker. Bless them: she really didn't have any good answers at the moment.

"Yes, I had a plan." Tinker had learned when fighting against people who could see the future, it was best not to talk about what she was doing. She hadn't told her Hand what she planned just in case someone was "listening in." "I was going to hide away and be clever." Said aloud, it wasn't much of a plan. "There was a little more than that. I was going to make some...things." If the EIA came through, she still might make something unexpected, so she'd better not talk about it. "I thought I would have more time."

Tooloo had said that it could be a matter of minutes before the spell would go off, but at first, Tinker hadn't believed her. Why did the crazy old elf have to talk in riddles? What did the chicken and weird mismatched chess pieces have to do with the mess Pittsburgh was in now? How bad of a mess was it?

Up to a minute ago, Tinker had felt rapid-fire calls to all three Spell Stones that she could tap. Windwolf, Prince True Blood, and the Stone Clan had been fighting deep in the forest to the east. Forge and Jewel Tear had been scoping out the oni forces attacking Oakland. Everything had stopped so abruptly that she was afraid that the oni's attack spell had killed the others. She, Oilcan, and the twins had been safe within a shield when the spell hit. All the other elves in Pittsburgh had been unprotected.

"I'm not sure what the oni's spell did but the other *domana* seem...incapacitated," Tinker said as she waited for the other *domana* to act; to prove that they were still alive. "What did the oni do? Did they kill all the other elves?"

"They could not, not without great risk to themselves," Pony said. "The 'greater blood oni' are in truth nothing but Skin Clan elves hiding behind a façade. In ancient times, before we were immortal, the Skin Clan would test their spell working on their slaves and then interbreed with the successes to bring the desired result into their bloodlines. They are largely as we are. Any spell aimed at the masses will strike them too."

Tinker nodded, clinging tight to the logic of it. The fear that Windwolf and the others were dead lurked deep within her chest. It was a dark, painful thing and she was desperate to ignore it. "So the oni could have just...broken the *domana*'s link to the Spell Stones? It would explain why the others stopped casting. The *domana* use a genetic key to create a link. But each clan has a different genetic key. How could the oni have taken out the Fire Clan and the Stone Clan in one shot?"

"It has always been a closely guarded secret as to how the wood sprites created the *domana* link to the various Spell Stones." Pony glanced at Stormsong. "You were trained by the Wyverns. Did they know anything about the genetic key?"

Stormsong clicked her tongue in the equivalent of an elven shrug. "Only that the clans insisted that they alone would be able to access their Spell Stones. Even before the end of the Rebellion, the seeds of the Clan War were growing. Whatever the wood sprites used as their key, it is very dominant. I have never heard of any *domana* who could not access their clan's *esva*."

She paused a moment, tilting her head in confusion. "Although, now that I think of it, Wolf has been the only one that ever had access to two *esva*. Not even his siblings could tap both sets of Spell Stones. It was so singular that there was no precedence for how he would be trained. There was a great debate over whether he would be trained on both *esva*; there were many who said that he only should be given access to the Spell Stones of the clan that he chose to join. My mother—"

"Your mother what?" Tinker asked when Stormsong stopped abruptly, mouth open, her eyes scanning quickly as if reading ancient text a second time.

"My mother...my mother is Pure Radiance, head of the *intanyai seyosa* caste, greatest ever born after the legendary Vision—"

"Yes, I know who your mother is," Tinker said, cutting her off impatiently.

"My mother was the author of the marriages between the head of the Clans and King Ashfall's children. She insisted that Wolf be trained on both *esva* and martial arts." Stormsong swore softly in English before falling back to Elvish. "She was the one who encouraged Flame Heart to bear ten children until one was born being able to use both *esva*."

In other words, Pure Radiance arranged to have a specific child born, trained in war, and then shipped across the ocean to fight the oni because she foresaw the need of someone like Windwolf.

"Shit," Tinker whispered. "If she set Windwolf up for this, then he might have been immune to the spell. But if that's true, why isn't he tapping the Spell Stones?"

"He could still be in shock," Pony said. "Remember that you slept for days after your transformation. Even if he was not changed, he could be unconscious."

Unconscious in the middle of a battle. Tinker swore softly. She wanted to race to Windwolf's side but she didn't even know where to find him. The troops had left by train the day before and planned to march into the virgin forest after disembarking at some vague spot alongside the track. Rainlily could get her to the spot where the troops camped. Surely it wouldn't be too hard to find Windwolf's trail as the army cut through the woods. Prince True Flame had emptied Pittsburgh of royal marines. They had taken thousands of the red coated soldiers with them.

"Your responsibility lies with the enclaves," Pony said as if guessing her thoughts. "Wolf has sworn to protect his Beholden. As his *domi*, it falls to you to protect them when he cannot. You cannot abandon them."

"Right." Tinker grabbed hold of her hair, resisting the urge to pull it out in frustration. "How long can the shields on the enclaves stand against the oni?"

"The shields were designed to be effective against the dangers which are common to our world: spell arrows, force strike, black willows and the like," Pony said. "Sparrow was to oversee improving the enclave shields to work against human weapons but there were always delays in the effort."

Sparrow had been a Skin Clan mole. Of course she would have kept the shields from being improved. It stood to reason that the oni had a means to breach the shields. It meant that no matter what, she needed to go to Oakland and defend the enclaves.

"We have a new plan?" Stormsong prodded.

Tinker held up a hand to hold off questions. She was still

thinking furiously. The six of them couldn't take on an army. What could they do? What *should* she do? Tooloo seemed to think Tinker could fix everything if she just…just…just what?

"I know you're clever," Tooloo had said. *"You can figure this out without me showing you how the pieces are arrayed in this deadly game and reminding you how they move."*

Tinker took out her datapad and looked at the pictures of Tooloo's chessboard. Tooloo had set up a Queen's Gambit with Tinker as the black player. It would suggest that, in terms of a game, the oni had moved first. What was Tooloo considering the first move? The start of Vision's ancient feud with her creator? The Skin Clan's invasion of Pittsburgh after the first Shutdown? Or was it the attack on Windwolf that Tinker blocked by saving him?

The white pawn had been a small plastic monkey figurine with both hands clapped over its mouth. Lain and Esme Shenske had nicknamed their younger half brothers "Flying Monkey Four and Five." Tinker wasn't sure who One, Two, and Three were—their stepbrother Yves Desmarais and themselves? Chloe Polanski could be considered "Flying Monkey Number Six" since she was Lain and Esme's younger half sister. It felt right to say that the little plastic monkey statue represented Chloe.

It suggested that when Tinker killed Chloe, she accepted the Queen's Gambit. The tactic in chess meant that she had traded the ability to control the center of the board for greater mobility of her pieces. But what did that mean in the real world? What did Tooloo expect her to do? Should Tinker even be considering doing anything that Tooloo wanted her to do? Who knew if Tooloo's desired outcome was even morally correct? Did Tooloo want all the *domana* dead? She certainly acted like they were evil incarnate. Tooloo had tried to keep Tinker from interacting with Windwolf, lying to her about the possible outcome.

Sort of lied.

Tooloo was correct that the human child she helped raise no longer existed; Tinker had been transformed into an elf with all the *domana* bells and whistles. Tooloo said by becoming Windwolf's *domi*, Tinker had allowed Pure Radiance to get the upper hand. Her daughter used Tinker as poisoned bait in a trap for the oni. Most of the summer had gone—not as Tooloo wanted, but as she had foreseen.

Vision and her daughter had some kind of running war that

had spanned thousands of years. Which one did Tinker want to win? How could Tinker know when both weren't telling her the stakes?

Tinker started to walk fast toward the computer lab while thinking furiously. She didn't have time for chessboard riddles. If the oni had broken the *domanas'* link to the Spell Stones, then she and Oilcan were the only heavy hitters left. She didn't want Oilcan fighting a horde of oni—Iron Mace's death already weighed heavily on him. Nor did she want to wade into battle alone. The chances of her messing up and getting everyone killed were too high. She needed more people.

She pulled out her phone and swore. It had no signal. "Oh, no, not now!"

"What is it, *domi*?" Pony asked.

"I need Jin Wong to call the Flock. I need the tengu in Oakland en masse. He's probably still in the city—someplace."

Out of the corner of her eye, she saw Pony and Stormsong flash through blade talk and then Stormsong dashed off, toward her hoverbike. Tinker nodded in agreement with her Hand's decision. It wouldn't take Stormsong long to find a tengu scout; she was Pure Radiance's daughter. It might take longer to path her way to Jin but he could use his "calling all tengu" ability to marshal them in the city.

Tinker spotted Captain Roger Josephson across the compound, talking to three of his men. She veered toward him. "Captain! Captain!"

"*Domi*, I was just coming to find you." He handed her a piece of paper that showed what his people had managed to collect for her. "We found most of the things on your list—at least, everything in the storage unit. The only thing my men couldn't locate was the slab saw. You didn't give a location. We're not even sure what it is. Do you mean one that cuts wood or stone?"

Tinker waved aside the question. She had added the slab saw to confuse anyone who got hold of the list and tried to figure out what she intended to do with the various pieces. If Josephson's men had found one, she would have only used the twelve-foot-long, chain-driven sawblade as a psychological warfare weapon. She didn't plan on getting close enough to the oni to engage in sword versus chainsaw combat. Josephson must have sent out an entire squadron of trucks to comb the city to have found as much as they did. "Good. Good. Cool, you got the electric-to-magic converters. Oh, you found my eight-inch pipes! Fantastic!"

"We're glad to help," Josephson said. "The whelping pens were a clarification of the issues for us. Whatever our relationship is with the elves, it's at least civilized, peaceful, and humane. We have no fears—being stranded on Elfhome—that the elves will not treat us with honor."

Tinker nodded, glad that she could count on unwavering support from Captain Josephson and his men. They were, though, only a small fraction of the EIA forces in Pittsburgh. "Where's Maynard?"

"He's been on the move all day. He started on the South Side dealing with the morgue overflow. Then someone drove a car into the Oakland power substation. He started a work crew there and moved to our communication center downtown. Do you need to talk to him?"

"My phone doesn't have a signal," Tinker said.

"We have a system separate from the civilian network."

Tinker indicated that Josephson was to follow her. Time was wasting. She didn't want to get stuck updating both Josephson and Maynard. "The oni just used a massive magical bioweapon that targeted the *domana*. That's why I'm here: I needed a casting circle to erect a countermeasure spell to shield myself." It sounded so selfish, but it would take too much time to explain that she'd made the bad assumption that Oilcan was in Oakland. At the last minute she realized that he was in McKees Rocks. "There's a good possibility that all of the other *domana* are currently unconscious."

"Does this include the Viceroy and Prince True Flame?" Josephson asked.

"Magic operates on a one-*mei* range—which is nearly a thousand miles. Even *domana* on the East Coast were hit." She pointed at the nearby large military cargo trucks. "I need those trucks, with all the things on my lists loaded into them, and every man you can muster for combat in Oakland as soon as possible."

To his credit, Captain Josephson only reacted with a slight widening of eyes. "Say again?"

"The oni are launching an attack on the enclaves. I need to counterattack with everything I can pull together—which means I need you to come with me. We'll leave as soon as I pick up the printouts that I queued earlier. Get hold of Maynard and tell him to send what he can. I've put the word out to gather the tengu, so tell your men not to shoot at any that show up."

"Yes, *domi*. Understood." Captain Josephson walked off, barking orders to his men.

Tinker needed more than just the tengu and the EIA if she was going to take on an army.

"Are there any Wyverns or royal marines left in the city?" Tinker was under the impression that Prince True Flame took all of the elves with him to face off against what had seemed to be the bulk of the oni army. She hadn't seen any of the royal forces all day but she hadn't been paying close attention. Pony would know—he kept track of that kind of information.

"Prince True Flame left behind one Hand of Wyverns and three platoons of royal marines," Pony said. "The Wyverns were at his camp."

Said camp was in a large clearing beyond the enclaves where Windwolf had planned to build a palace. Tinker only vaguely remembered the place as a shadowy collection of tents where Sparrow ambushed her. Tinker had been avoiding the place, partially because of the bad memories, but mostly because she didn't want Prince True Flame blocking her more questionable activities.

"They probably could hear any outbreak of fighting in Oakland," Tinker said. "Would they defend the enclaves or stay at the camp?"

"The Wyverns would definitely engage the enemy," Pony said. "One platoon of marines are currently guarding over Forest Moss's *domi*. They could be anywhere in the city and perhaps unaware of what is going on."

"Oh! Yeah!" Tinker had totally forgotten about the teenager. The girl was two or three years younger than she was and questionable at making good life choices. "It's fine if they stay out of the fight."

"The other platoons are guarding the train station as there are royal forces incoming from Brotherly Love." Pony named Windwolf's East Coast holding that was connected via the railroad to Pittsburgh. "One of us should be able to recruit them to join the fight."

By "one of us," Pony meant one of the five "holy" warriors

who made up her Hand. Tinker had commandeered a platoon of Fire Clan royal marines earlier but they had been standing by, awaiting orders from Prince True Flame. Pony was implying that she wouldn't be able to repeat the trick on a platoon with direct orders to guard a specific point. The *sekasha*, however, were considered holy and were to be obeyed without question.

It was a part of elf society that Tinker couldn't totally wrap her head around. The *sekasha* were thought to be perfect but the *domana* were running the show. Everyone would wait for her to lead—even when she didn't know what she was doing. Since June, Tinker had learned that she needed to give the order before Pony would act. The problem was that she didn't always have all the data.

"Since the derailment, the trains are only running during the daylight." She worked through the logic aloud. "There shouldn't be another train until dawn. Penn Station is the control center for the trains but the rails coming in have dozens of weak points elsewhere that the oni could sabotage more easily if they want to mess with the trains. The royal marines are basically just guarding an empty shell."

She considered logistics. Stormsong was the only one of Tinker's Hand who spoke fluent English. The others were trying to learn and picking it up at incredible speed, but it was still rough. "Captain Josephson!"

"Yes, *domi*?" Captain Josephson came trotting back to her side.

"Do you have anyone here who speaks Elvish?"

"Private Clemente," Captain said. "The rest of us have been trying to pick it up as we go."

"I need Clemente and two of these trucks to go to Penn Station to pick up some royal marines."

"Understood." Josephson peeled off, calling out names of men who were going to be drivers for the royal marines.

Tinker turned to Pony. "Pull all the royal marines from the train station. Load them into the trucks. Have them head to Oakland via Forbes Avenue. Oh, and make sure to tell the marines that the tengu are allies."

That should get the marines to Oakland without colliding with the oni army with no backup.

Pony nodded. Blade talk happened and Little Egret strode off toward the trucks.

Rainlily moved forward, carrying a wyvern-scale vest in Wind Clan Blue.

"*Domi*," Pony said. "Please, put this on."

"Me?" Tinker said.

"It would be best, if we're going into combat, that you take every precaution against being wounded."

Yeah. Right. She pulled it over her head as her stomach flip-flopped with fear. She had marched into the whelping pens and had blasted her way through Ginger Wine's but still, the upcoming fight terrified her. Those were different—she could have pulled out of those fights if things had gone badly. There was going to be no retreat from this battle.

Should she try for other humans? Were there other humans? She had no real pull with the police, especially after Nathan's death. She couldn't contact Team Tinker with the cell phone system down nor would they be particularly helpful. Yes, they all had guns: they were Pittsburghers. A few were decent shots. Some—like Andy Roach—were a little dangerous with anything sharp or fragile. Carl Moser had a *laedin* or two at his art commune but they had joined him because they wanted to be something more than meat shields.

Regular Pittsburghers might not be aware of what was going on in Oakland. Even if the three television stations still had the ability to broadcast, all the TV sets in the city were currently dead. Some of the smaller radio stations—the ones that young people listened to—were probably off the air. There was no way to spread the word, calling for help.

Tinker wasn't sure if Pittsburghers would even care what happened to the elves. Chloe Polanski had been poisoning humans against the elves for a decade or more. Until Tinker saved Windwolf, there were very few elves who she interacted with: Gin Blossom on Team Tinker and the handful who belonged to Moser's art commune. Those males and females were rebels against their own society; they had few nice things to say about *domana*. Between them and Tooloo, Tinker had thought of the *domana* as aristocratic snobs. She had to assume that the EIA were going to be the only humans who joined her in the defense of the enclaves.

She gathered up everything that she had queued to the computer center's various printers. It was a hodgepodge of spells and magical whizzbangs. She wasn't sure how she was going to use them all. Her lack of preparation was the most terrifying part of this whole mission. What the hell did she know about going to war?

She felt the spark of power that was Jin Wong calling on his Flock. It was like a drop of dark water into a still pool, a sudden break that rippled out over the city. As it spread, there were tiny motes of replies, thousands of them.

Stormsong had found the tengu then and should be on her way back to Tinker.

Far out east, she felt Windwolf call on the Wind Clan Stones.

Relief flooded through her. She closed her eyes and focused on him. He'd set up a shield spell but nothing else. Did he still have access to the Fire Clan *esva*? Was he alone or had Prince True Flame and the others survived?

Gods, she wanted to ignore the situation in Oakland and go to him. She knew, though, that his heart would echo what her Hand told her: He would want her to protect the enclaves. All their people—some whom he had known for a hundred years or more—were in harm's way. People who had welcomed her in, watched over her when she was hurt, obeyed her without question even when she made the most impossible requests. They had accepted her wholly when she probably was the last thing that they expected. She owned them.

"*Domi*?" Pony said softly.

"I'm thinking." Could she let anyone know that Windwolf could still access the Wind Clan *esva*? The talking mice suggested that anything spoken aloud might be overheard by a member of her family—evil aunts and all.

She was going to strain their resources just to counter the oni in Oakland. Could she send Windwolf any help at all?

She handed her bag to Pony and walked out in the stormy dusk. She cocked her fingers, brought them to her mouth, and spoke the trigger word that would let her set up a resonance between her and the Wind Clan Spell Stones. She held it for a long minute and then cast a scry spell, sensing the movement of the winds around her. It reported the incoming storm winds, the quickening spin of the windmills, and a large flock of tengu heading toward her.

There. She had let Windwolf know that she was alive and

kicking. Hopefully he would find it as comforting as she had found proof of his survival. It was all that she could send him.

It made her feel helpless, though, and the feeling enraged her.

Captain Josephson came jogging over to her. "*Domi*, we're ready."

She nodded. "When the tengu get here, we'll head out."

She should also let Oilcan know that she was okay. She had felt him set up the new shield in McKees Rocks just before the oni spell hit. Oilcan must have used Geoffrey Kryskill's casting circle. She'd forgotten all about it or she might have gone there. She didn't want him in the middle of the insanity she was about to throw herself into. She flashed through the morse code: GE OB LVG NS AS MR AR. *Good evening. Old boy. Leaving North Side. Stand by McKees Rocks. End of message.*

NS and MR was their own personal code for locations around Pittsburgh.

Oilcan tapped the Spell Stones and signaled back: VE AR. *Understood. End of message.*

As lightning flashed on the western horizon, the tengu came swooping in on massive crow-black wings. They settled around her, kneeling. It was Riki and a hundred of his people, faces painted for war.

"*Domi*, the Flock is yours to command," Riki said. "Jin Wong is leading our main force to Oakland. I am here to coordinate our efforts."

Thunder rolled over them.

Tinker pointed toward the gate. "We go."

2: LOST IN THE WOODS

Wolf Who Rules Wind was deep in the forest, surrounded by oni forces, when the transformation spell hit. It washed over him like fire. Every nerve and cell within his body recoiled with pain. His senses went to white, overloaded. He lost all awareness of the world around him. Surely he wasn't dead—death wouldn't hurt so much. Time stopped in a sea of white fire. His hearing leaked back as the white started to recede.

"Wolf! Wolf!" Wraith Arrow's voice called to him.

"Some-some-something hit me." Wolf struggled to push the words out into the whiteness. His voice sounded distant and frail.

"Get your shield up!" Wraith Arrow urged, seemingly at a great distance.

Wolf guessed that he'd lost his connection to the Spell Stones. He couldn't feel the link but then he couldn't feel his body. Two hundred years of training allowed Wolf to twist phantom fingers into the correct shape, bring them to the mouth that he couldn't feel and say the word that reconnected him to the Spell Stones. The low thrum of power flooded into him, pushing back the whiteness.

He grew aware of the swamp first. The dank earthy smell. The dampness under him as he lay on his back. Somewhere close by, a pitched battle still raged. He could hear the enemy drums beating out commands. The thin whistle of spell arrows cutting through the air. The screams of pain. It was too quiet; he couldn't hear the roar of True Flame's fire spells nor the rumble of the Stone Clan's force strikes. Had the other *domana* been struck down like he had been?

Wolf staggered to his feet, blinking again and again, trying to force his vision to return. The world slowly came into focus. The sun was setting behind the steep wooded hillside at their back. Heavy rain clouds filled the sky, whipped by storm winds. They stood on the edge of a wide marshy meadow, full of denuded stumps and thick clumps of cattail reeds. On the far eastern side of the marsh, the land sloped up to an enemy fort.

His three Hands—all fifteen of his personal guard—stood alert around him. Where were the rest of his people? Oh yes, he'd sent the *laedin*-caste warriors to Sunder because he wouldn't have been able to protect them from the phoenix scorpion. The corpse of that massive horror loomed behind the *sekasha*. There was no sign, though, that the other *domana* were alive beyond the fact that the oni were fighting *something*. Darkness of Stone had been at the center of the camp, protecting his *sekasha* and *laedin* warriors after jumping out of Cana Lily's gossamer. Said airship was drifting over the oni trying to flee to the east, pouring war fire down out of its machicolations. Tall ironwood trees in and around the fort kept him from seeing the gossamer clearly.

Wraith Arrow studied Wolf with concern. "Can you fight?"

Wolf flexed his free hand, taking stock of his own health. Ignoring the fact that his legs felt like they were made of soft noodles, he seemed sound. "I can."

He considered the battlefield. His *sekasha* seemed unaffected by whatever hit him. The three clans had split up in four directions. Prince True Flame, two score of Wyverns, and several thousand royal marines were north of the camp. Sunder and Forest Moss had paired up, attacking from the south with a small number of Stone Clan warriors. Wolf had held the west side while Darkness and Cana Lily staged an airborne assault. Until moments ago, all the *domana* had been holding protective shields over their people while casting scrys and offensive spells. Wolf was the only one currently maintaining an active spell. Even the shield on the Stone Clan gossamer was down, making the great beast vulnerable to enemy fire.

"The oni must have used the weapon that *domi* warned me about," Wolf said. "They must have targeted the *domana*. Either

I'm the first to recover or the others were hit harder for some reason."

His Hands had divided into Shields and Blades. Half of them had cancelled their protective spell to conserve local magic. It was a common tactic for when a *domana* was too wounded to protect their people. It reminded Wolf that the valley had only a handful of weak ley lines and no *fiutana*—which was odd. Yes, the swampy ground provided the oni with black willows but otherwise the valley offered no advantages.

The lack of magic meant that the oni couldn't create strong defensive spells like those protecting his enclaves. It would also mean that if the *domana* were unconscious or dead, the elves wouldn't be able to set up a strong fallback position.

"We need to push through the camp to Prince True Flame's position," Wolf said. "If the others were more incapacitated by the spell, then we should consolidate our forces."

Wraith Arrow nodded at this. "The Harbinger's people are all veterans of the Rebellion; they will be on familiar grounds. Prince True Flame's forces are younger; they only know how to fight with a *domana* at their back."

The same could be said of his people in Pittsburgh. Fear lanced through him as he realized that all the *domana* within a *mei* would have been hit by the spell. What of his beloved? *Trust your domi to be strong,* he'd told Forest Moss. Glib words when Tinker had three *esva* to call on. She needed to be conscious to use them.

She has Little Horse and Discord to keep her safe until she regains consciousness, he told himself.

Tinker was everything he could hope for in a *domi*. More. He had not known his secret heart until the turbulent summer made his feelings undeniable. He had no inkling of how much he wanted someone who was so separated from the normal social expectations that they would freely accept all of him. His odd parentage. His unusual upbringing that saw him trained as a *sekasha* as well as a *domana*. His little blade brother and his first love—so often seen as lowly mutts. His quirky personal household that was a mix of young elves barely past their majority and his grandfather's people who were all born during the Rebellion. The city full of humans. Even the half-oni and tengu who had quickly proved how worthy they were of being part of his society. Tinker had opened her heart and taken them in and protected them with fierce cunning.

My beloved is clever beyond words. She has already proved herself brave and resourceful.

Then—almost like a reward for his trust in his *domi*—he felt someone nearby call on the Wind Stones. It could only be his beloved. Relief poured through him.

Much as he wished he could fly to her side, he had tens of thousands here who needed his strength. He could not abandon them in the middle of a battle that he started. He turned his attention back to his own problems.

All the horrors within this camp were dead or safely contained underground. The camp's crude defenses had been breached when Darkness dropped into the middle of it. The oni within it seemed to be focused on disorderly retreat.

"A straight line will be the shortest path," Wolf said. "We will cut through the camp. We can see how Darkness fares as we head to Prince True Flame."

Wraith Arrow nodded agreement to the plan.

A simple plan in words. In deed, it proved to be more complicated, as the swampy meadow had a meandering stream that fed unexpectedly deep pools. They moved from one damp grassy hummock to the next, sometimes taking large steps, other times jumping.

As they picked their way across the meadow, the whistling call of the tengu scout sounded nearby.

Wraith Arrow glanced to Wolf and then waved the hidden scout forward. The male glided down from the edge of the clearing to land silently before Wraith Arrow.

"The oni have fled the immediate area," the male said as he knelt. "There is a massive force on their way from the other camps. It is a force in the thousands. It is traveling slower than we expected. They have cages that appear to contain some type of horrors. It seems as if transporting them is what is setting their pace. We believe that the oni from this camp are retreating to meet the reinforcements."

"What of the Stone Clan?"

"Sunder and Forest Moss seem to be unconscious. Sunder's people would not reply to our call, so we could not confer with them. The Wyverns that were guarding Forest Moss are moving to True Flame's position—probably to report on the status of Sunder's group."

"The Stone Clan would not want outsiders near their unconscious *domou*," Wraith Arrow murmured. "Wyvern or tengu."

If all the other *domana* were unconscious, then they could not stand against the incoming force. They might need to retreat, at least until the others regained consciousness—assuming that they weren't somehow permanently harmed by whatever hit them.

The tengu suddenly glanced toward the west, peering into the darkness. "Jin Wong calls the Flock! *Domi* wants all who can fight to head for Oakland immediately. She's is angry and goes to fight."

All? His beloved would only call for all twenty thousand of the tengu if she expected a serious invasion.

"Go to her," Wolf said. "She will need all that she can gather to her side. Tell Maynard to send trains—we will send what we can to Oakland."

The tengu nodded and took off.

On the far eastern side of the marsh, the land sloped up to a stockade of rough-hewn logs placed side by side, their ends sharpened. The oni had dug a trench before the wall—too wide to safely jump—and filled it with wood spikes coated with something organic that was no doubt poisonous. The sound of fighting had grown louder even as the rumble of thunder heralded the approaching thunderstorm.

"Smash it in?" Wraith Arrow suggested a course of action.

Windwolf shook his head. While that was the easiest route, he might hit the already besieged Stone Clan forces. They were without *domana* shields. "I'll bring it down toward us. Stand ready."

He hit the far side of the wall with a force strike. The logs sheared off and fell outward, bridging the trench. The stench of feces and blood flooded out of the camp, smelling like sewage running through a slaughter yard. Chaos reigned inside the high walled area with some oni standing and fighting while others were trying to flee.

Darkness had dropped from a gossamer into the camp with nine Hands of *sekasha* and a full company of *laedin* warriors. His people were gathered into a tight knot against the eastern wall. The *sekasha* stood shoulder to shoulder in a half circle. The *laedin* fought from behind them, protected by the overlapping shields of the holy warriors. There was no sign of Darkness. Wolf could only assume that the male lay on the ground behind his people. All attacks against them were ineffective. Direct attacks by the oni were dealt with either by the *sekasha*'s magically sharp swords or *laedin* spell arrows.

Darkness's grizzled First sheathed his sword as Wolf approached; it signaled that the holy warrior expected the Wind Clan to honor their vows of peace for the duration of the war. The male was a legend of the Rebellion whom Wolf never thought he would meet: Ruin of Stone. Of the Stone Clan *sekasha*, only Tempered Steel was more highly thought of. He had the same unbending calm as Tempered Steel. Deep in enemy territory, literally back to the wall, his *domana* wounded or dead—and Ruin seemed unfazed. His face was splattered with blood but none of it seemed to be his own.

Intimidating as Ruin might be, Wolf was glad to be facing him instead of Jewel Tear's proud and untested First, Tiger Eye.

"Something struck down Darkness," Ruin said in greeting. "He seems unharmed but he is not conscious."

"I believe it was the magical device that I showed Sunder. I was incapacitated for some time." Wolf wasn't sure how long that he had been unaware. It seemed only a few moments to him but it might have been several minutes. "The tengu report that Sunder and Forest Moss seem to be unconscious."

He added in the information on the oni movement in the area.

"Darkness did not detect any *nactka* within the camp," Ruin said. "But that matters little, given the range that the device could reach. We've cast a healing spell on Darkness to speed his recovery. He will be awake within the hour. Sunder's Hands will do the same if hir was struck down."

"I am joining Prince True Flame's forces to give them protection," Windwolf stated, leaving it open to the Stone Clan to choose what they would do.

Ruin nodded. "It would be wise. We will need to change our attack plan to deal with the loss of power. We should see that the prince is protected. His people have never fought without a *domana* at their back."

Wolf had been alarmed that the Harbingers had been sent to Pittsburgh. He wondered now if the choice was orchestrated by Pure Radiance, who knew that the forces sent to fight the oni would need to be able to do it without the strength of *domana*. The Wyvern's First would have been the one with final say but Sword Strike had always been guided by Pure Radiance.

Wolf would consider it all for the best if it did not make him wonder why Pure Radiance had allowed the Stone Clan to send Earth Son, Forest Moss, and Jewel Tear to Pittsburgh first. It seemed unlikely that the female had been outmaneuvered on something so important. She had come to the Westernlands just to meet his new *domi*. Or had her visit been a ploy to lure the oni out and force them to make a move before they were fully prepared?

The heavens opened up, pouring down rain.

Now was not the time to distract himself with conjecture.

Wolf recast his shield, this time so it protected Darkness and his people. The rain cascaded down his shield. The Stone Clan gathered up their unconscious *domana* and their wounded. When they signaled that they were ready to move, Wolf headed north toward the Fire Clan. All the *sekasha* canceled their personal shields, conserving the local ambient magic for their brethren without a *domana* to protect them.

"Cana Lily is down," Wraith Arrow said from Wolf's flank. He was watching the gossamer that now hung over the southern flank of the battle. "His people are signaling Sunder, asking for orders. They're rattled. I cannot see what they're being told."

"They will be told to withdraw north," Ruin stated firmly. "Cana Lily was born after the Rebellion. His people will not know how to get him up. The gossamer is a means of evacuating wounded. They are our first priority."

That statement surprised Wolf. He would have thought that the older warriors would have been fixated on wiping out the oni, given how fast the enemy could spawn. He knew that the basic principle of their society was those who obeyed were to be protected at all cost. He knew most of his people, born during the Clan Wars, would have believed that the *laedin*'s protection took precedence over the oni. He hadn't realized that the mindset started prior to the end of the Rebellion.

"Aye, the gossamer is turning north," Wraith Arrow reported.

The rain grew heavier, pouring down his shield. Between the falling darkness and the heavy rain, Wolf could barely see beyond the edge of his shield. He picked his way carefully northward through the open gate of the oni camp.

"Sunder's people will follow," Ruin predicted. "It is the logical tactic given the situation."

True Flame had reduced much of the forest north of the camp to fire and ash. The force of his flame strikes had shattered branches and splintered the upper trunks of the towering ironwood. The forest-floor bracken had vaporized in the blasts, so only cinders lay underfoot. Here and there, broken timbers still burned brightly, lighting the area. The land sizzled as the heavy rain fell on hot embers. Smoke and steam drifted over the burnt landscape, partially hiding the blackened lumps of dead. Some were clearly wargs. Others were oni that had been humanoid in build. A few could have been elves. A handful of the burned were still alive, too burnt to move, groaning in pain as Wolf's party neared. His people paused to check on the wounded. When it was clear that it wasn't an elf in pain, they gave mercy to the dying.

It was nothing like any battle that Wolf had been part of before. Nothing had been this massive, grim, and brutal. It rattled him. He struggled not to let it show. All of his people—those here on the battlefield and others back in Oakland—were counting on him.

A wall of red emerged out of the dark and smoke where the royal marines held a defensive line around a pocket of green. The marines looked startled and unsure by the appearance of Wolf and his people. They apparently had no warning that the battle plan had been changed.

"Let us pass," Wraith Arrow ordered.

The royal marines made an opening. One turned and whistled, "Ally commanders in camp." A "Confirm" sounded faintly out of the darkness behind the Fire Clan troops.

"Our people will scout." Ruin pointed to three of the Stone Clan *sekasha* and flashed through blade talk to order them to sweep the surrounding area. "They will assess what the oni forces stand at in the immediate vicinity."

Three Hands of the holy warriors peeled away, disappearing into the dark rain.

There had been five thousand royal marines with Prince True Flame. It seemed as if most survived the initial attack unscathed. There were only a handful of wounded near the back of the line. Judging where they'd seen the oni undead lying, it seemed as if the enemy hadn't gotten close enough to engage the Fire Clan hand to hand.

The marines took note that Wolf had Stone Clan mixed with his own people and their gaze went fearful. They realized that the other *domana* must be down for the Stone Clan to be inside Wolf's shield.

Red Knife came jogging up to meet them. If True Flame's First was coming to greet them alone, then Wolf's cousin was truly unconscious.

"We have set up a base on a stone outcropping just before another marsh." Red Knife pointed into the darkness. "The oni in the immediate area are dead. What survived our initial attack has fallen back. We were going to pursue but True Flame suddenly dropped unconscious."

"If you allow it, we can cast a recovery spell on the prince," Ruin said.

Like Cana Lily, True Flame had been born after the Rebellion. His people were too young to know the spell.

Red Knife nodded. "I will permit it."

Ruin signaled to his Second then turned to Wolf.

The three *sekasha* stood waiting for Wolf to speak. As the only *domana* standing, it fell to Wolf to decide their course of action. The problem was that all three of the holy warriors were painfully aware that he was only two hundred and fourteen years old. Wraith Arrow would support Wolf regardless of his decision. A good First would never undermine their *domana*'s ability to command, especially in front of other clans. Red Knife had helped to train Wolf in combat tactics; he might still see Wolf as a student, not a commander. Ruin was over thirty times Wolf's age, a legendary warrior who had fought in two wars that spanned centuries. The males, however, represented three different clans. Ruin most likely would not bow to the much younger Wyvern. Wraith Arrow had battled for ultimate leadership of the *sekasha* caste and lost by a single sword blow. He gave the younger Red Knife the respect due to his status but only because of Wraith Arrow's failure to protect Howling.

Wolf took a deep breath, collecting his thoughts. They had neutralized the nearest oni camp. The tengu stated that the collective contents of the other three were converging on their location—although not at a fast march. It meant that they had a little over an hour before thousands of oni flooded over them.

It was clear to Wolf now that the camps had been set up as

a trap for the elves. The oni had been in disarray during their attack; there had been no clear high commander in their ranks. It seemed that the camp, despite having more than a thousand oni, wargs, and horrors, had been stripped of its top leader. While Pony noticed that the oni were slipshod when compared to elves, Lord Tomtom had been brutally efficient. It made no sense to have no high-ranking officer within the camp—unless everything within it was just poisoned bait.

Tinker had warned him that the oni had eleven of the magical devices. She had mobilized her people to find the *nactka*, but obviously she hadn't found them yet. Kajo had used one to do something to the *domana*—most likely make it so that both the Fire Clan and Stone Clan couldn't call magic from their Spell Stones. It meant that the enclaves had lost their two trained defenders and Oilcan, leaving only Tinker. She, like Wolf, was able to use more than one *esva*. The spell had definitely touched Wolf; so their immunity was limited. He wanted to rush back to Tinker, keep her safe, but with the other ten *nactka* still in play, Wolf could lose all his powers once the oni realized he had escaped their first attack. He couldn't allow the massive force within the forest to follow him back to Pittsburgh. He needed to deal with them now.

"Oakland most likely will come under attack shortly," Wolf said. "The lack of high-ranking officers here means that they are elsewhere. The logical target would be the enclaves. If the attack had come earlier, the Stone Clan *domana* would have noticed Forge and Jewel Tear tapping the Spell Stones. The oni waited until we were engaged here to spring their trap. We will split our forces. I will hold here with a bare minimum while the rest return to Oakland."

Wraith Arrow stiffened but allowed nothing to show on his face. It was the *sekasha* way to hide one's feelings from their enemies.

Red Knife glanced at Ruin to see if the Stone Clan agreed to this tactic. There was nothing to read on Ruin's face. Red Knife voiced the doubt that the others refused to show. "What about the horrors? Can you take them alone?"

Lighting flickered across the sky as the wind kicked up.

"The night is ripe for violence," Wolf said. "The goddess of war rides, heralded by the storm furies. She blesses me with this raging tempest. I will take her blessing and use it against the oni."

3: PLEASE STAND BY

Leaving North Side. Stand by in McKees Rocks.

Tinker's Morse code message to Oilcan was at once completely clear while extremely vague. Where was she heading? To Oakland? If she was, she didn't want him there to help her.

Oilcan wasn't sure what to do. He didn't want to fight but he knew from experience that if he did nothing, and Tinker was killed, he would never be able to live with himself. It still haunted him that he had hidden in a closet while his father killed his mother. He'd only crept out of hiding after his father's rage had turned to grief. He'd stood in the kitchen as his mother's blood pooled around his bare toes.

It didn't matter that he'd been only a ten-year-old boy, built small like the rest of his mother's family. His father had been a wild bear of a man filled with alcohol, self-importance, and rage that simple hard work wasn't bringing him the success he thought he should have earned. His mother had been smart and resourceful and could have fled Boston at any time over the years as his father became more and more violent. None of it ever mattered deep in his heart.

He'd done nothing to save his mother. He lived with crushing guilt since that night.

He needed to head to Oakland. Thorne Scratch would not leave him; the *sekasha* protected the *domana* from capture as well as from harm. Moon Dog would probably also stay with him for the same reason. He couldn't take the kids with him.

His five kids had no combat training or weapons. Rustle had a broken arm. The four who had been rescued from the whelping pens were trying to be brave but there was terror in their eyes. Spot was only eight or nine. Until a few days ago, the boy had never left the half-oni compound because of his puppy dog looks. The tengu girl, Rebecca Brotman, had been stung multiple times by giant hornets. She was barely conscious. Blue Sky Montana had spent the last month or so learning how to fight from the *sekasha* but Oilcan knew from experience that the little half-elf would want to wade into the thick of things—heedless of danger. That worked at the racetrack where no one dared to use brute force on a child. It wouldn't work against the oni. Roach's little brother, Andy, was a klutz who lacked any common sense. There was a reason Team Tinker never allowed Andy to handle anything that could be dangerous or easily broken.

Andy's younger cousin, Guy Kryskill, had two rifles in his pickup's gun rack. The Kryskills were local legends at shooting. Like his brothers, Guy was tall, broad shouldered, and levelheaded, but he was only sixteen. Besides, Oilcan wanted Guy to watch over the others.

Oilcan knew also that he couldn't leave the kids at Geoffrey Kryskill's workshop. Storm clouds blanketed the sky. Thunder rumbled with the approach of heavy rain. Night was falling. The power was out. His kids were already terrified. The cavernous warehouse had no creature comforts nor was it particularly safe.

"Guy, Andy, Blue Sky," Oilcan named them all despite the fact that he thought of Guy as the one he was leaving in charge. "I'm not sure if it's safe to stay here. The oni already jumped us on the South Side. They might come here, looking for me. You need to find someplace else."

"My brother's not home," Blue Sky said.

Oilcan nodded even though he'd already mentally eliminated the gas station. The oni must have had someone spying on them in Oakland because Oilcan didn't know he was going shopping until Tinker told him about her little sisters. Yes, he planned to go sometime for everything his kids needed. It was the panic of being guardian to two preteen copies of Tinker that had made the trip today and not later, after the *domana* returned to Pittsburgh.

He had to assume that the oni knew who was with him. Blue Sky had arrived at Sacred Heart by hoverbike, probably traveling at near Mach speed like normal. A Roach Refuse dumpster hauler had been sitting at the front gate—complete with door lettering advertising the landfill's address.

Where else would the kids be safely hidden?

"Tooloo's place was closed," Blue Sky said. "She might not be home. She keeps everything tightly locked when she's out."

"My mom's house is bad," Guy said without elaborating.

"We could go to the clubhouse," Andy said.

They stared at Andy for a minute, surprised.

"What?" Andy said.

"That's a good idea," Oilcan said.

When Roach decided he wasn't leaving Pittsburgh to go to college, he laid claim to a flashy, prefabricated, modular "log cabin" mansion. The home was on a remote country road, ten miles from his parents' place. It was a party house with all the bells and whistles: five bedrooms, five bathrooms, a massive combined kitchen and living room, a walkout finished basement, a two-story deck, an inground swimming pool, an oversized two-car garage, and a second detached garage with three more bays.

Roach ran Team Tinker's merchandising business out of the basement. The team had pooled money to buy tools, hoverbikes, and other racing gear. The mansion provided space enough to store it all. People started to stock favorite food and drinks in the pantry, refrigerator, and the big industrial-size freezer. Someone found a billiard table and moved it in. Team members hunted down old pinball machines abandoned around the city to refurbish. Slowly the place became where Team Tinker would hang out, strategize, and play all hours of the day.

After two years of living with the chaos, Roach had moved closer to his parents and donated the log mansion to the team. Despite its official status as their clubhouse, the team kept its remote location quiet. It stood empty too much. They didn't want someone breaking in and ransacking it. Neither Tinker nor Oilcan had been out to it since May. None of the team had used it much this summer, what with the war breaking out and shutting down racing. The oni probably didn't know that it existed.

It would be a good place for the kids to stay. The mansion had beds and couches enough to sleep a score of people, a well-stocked pantry, and an emergency generator for power.

"Blue, take my pickup truck again." Oilcan wanted to be sure that Blue didn't balk at running and hiding. "I need you to protect the others. Guy, you and Andy take lead. There's not going to be any patrols of royal marines out this far."

Guy nodded. "You're not coming with us." It was a statement, not a question.

"Of course he is!" Andy said. "You are—aren't you?"

"He's going to Oakland." Blue Sky pouted as if Oilcan was going to a party without him.

"I need to," Oilcan told the boys. "The oni grabbed my kids once. I'm asking you to keep them safe while I go deal with whatever is in Oakland."

"Geoffrey's in Oakland," Guy said. "So is Roach. Both of them would tell us to go home if we showed up there. The joy of being the baby brother of the family: everyone treats you like you're still eight years old."

Andy nodded to this as the cousins were both the youngest of their respective family branches. Guy used to have a little sister but she had vanished without a trace when they were all just little kids. It made both families more protective of their remaining siblings.

"You've got keys to the clubhouse?" Guy asked because with Andy you needed to check things like that.

Andy patted his pockets until he found a large key ring. "Yeah, I have keys."

Which was good because Oilcan's set was at Sacred Heart.

There was a sudden loud rumble of thunder as the storm hit the river valley.

"It's going to rain." Baby Duck whimpered.

There wasn't room enough for all ten kids in the two cabs. Rustle and Rebecca were both wounded and couldn't be jammed in tight with others. There was also the possibility that they might get into a running fight.

"I'll get a rain cover." Guy headed to his brother's storage lockers. He came back with green canvas tarps and some nylon rope. "We can tie one end down and let them hold onto the other end so they're not pinned in."

Lightning struck someplace nearby with a loud crack, lighting up the skylights, followed instantly with a boom of thunder. His kids and Spot all yelped.

"Should we be going out in the storm?" Cattail Reeds asked what they were all obviously thinking.

"It will be okay," Guy said as he cut the rope into one-yard lengths. He handed four to Blue Sky to fasten to the corners of his tarp. "We don't have that far to go—we'll be there in twenty minutes or so. We can stick to back roads. We probably won't see another vehicle. Blue and I both know the way so even if we lose sight of each other, we can get there easy."

They secured one end of the tarp to the tie-down anchors. On the other end, they created looped handles that could be threaded through the tie-down and held taunt. After a short debate, it was decided that if it came to a running fight, it would be better to have Andy in the cab than wounded Rebecca. Guy found some quilted moving blankets to make her more comfortable in the bare metal bed of his pickup.

His kids surprised Oilcan by hugging not only him goodbye but also Thorne Scratch. They had been terrified of her just days ago. He could see that it also startled her in that she set her face to the warrior's neutral mask, but she warmly embraced each child.

"Listen to Blue Sky," Thorne murmured as she pressed her cheek to Cattail Reeds. "He is true *sekasha*, even as small as he is. He knows these males and this city. He would not lead you into danger."

It hadn't occurred to Oilcan that Thorne Scratch wouldn't automatically trust Andy and Guy. It was Blue Sky's judgment that swayed her.

Spot hovered near Baby Duck, looking as if he was worried that he'd be left behind.

"It's going to be okay." Oilcan lifted Spot into the back of the pickup that Blue Sky would be driving.

"I want Tommy," Spot whispered as he huddled alone in the truck bed.

"We'll get you back home as soon as the fighting is over," Oilcan promised. Wherever that might be; he wasn't sure where the half-oni lived. Every time he brought up the subject, Tommy growled something like "we're not staying."

Spot nodded dolefully. The little boy obviously wanted to believe Oilcan but knew the oni too well.

Oilcan lifted Baby Duck up into the pickup's high bed. The little female was quacking out of nervousness. She and Spot clung to each other. The elfhound puppy, Repeat, leapt up to settle on the other side of Baby Duck. Merry helped Rustle up into the cab and scrambled into the back. Oilcan realized that the kids were splitting up in the same way as when they left the enclave. It put all the younger kids together—which shouldn't be a problem if Guy was leading in his pickup.

"What about him?" Blue Sky glanced at Moon Dog. The look was more worried than hostile—the fight with the oni must have changed Blue's opinion of the male.

Oilcan still wasn't sure how Moon Dog ended up on their shopping trip or even how he got to Pittsburgh, since he hadn't been on the official list of newly arrived Stone Clan *sekasha*.

The male must have wandered into Sacred Heart just as Blue Sky described the ice cream shop. The decision to come along with them seemed so utterly random—especially for one of the holy warriors. Nor was Oilcan sure that Moon Dog had followed the developments since they fled South Side. Did he understand that the oni were invading Oakland and that the other *domana* were dead or injured? The conversation had flowed in and out of English and Elvish. If Blue Sky no longer distrusted the male, sending Moon Dog with the kids was an option.

But it really wasn't Oilcan's choice to make. Moon Dog wasn't his Beholden.

"I'm going back to the enclaves," Oilcan told Moon Dog after explaining the situation.

"*Waya!*" Moon Dog said. "The little ones are going on to someplace safe while we stand and fight! Wonderful! It will be just and honorable battle."

We. That sounded like the warrior intended to come with Oilcan, no matter how bad the odds were. Thorne Scratch had said that the warrior monks from Cold Mountain Temple saw the war with the oni as "a chance of a lifetime for glorious battle without any stain on their honor." Perhaps that was why Moon Dog was in Pittsburgh. But why, then, had he come with them for ice cream?

Cattail Reeds and Barley had gotten settled into the back of Guy's truck with Rebecca and Andy's two big elfhounds. The kids were ready to go. Still it felt so wrong, covering the kids up with a piece of cloth and sending them into the stormy night alone. The tarp might protect them from the rain but not the oni. Even if Oilcan went with them, there wasn't enough space in the flatbed's cab for more people. If he was going to ask Thorne Scratch and Moon Dog to fight an entire army, he couldn't soak them to the skin for an hour beforehand.

And fight an entire army was exactly what they might be doing. Prince True Flame had emptied the city of almost all of the royal forces. The expectation had been that Forge and Jewel Tear could effectively protect Oakland.

"You'll get there when you get there," Oilcan told Guy. "There's no reason to rush. Just be careful."

Guy snorted. "I've got the easy job. You're the one who needs to be careful."

4: THE EYES HAVE IT

"Our baby sisters can't read minds," Lucien had warned Tristan before their family descended on their forest encampment. *"But I've found it's best not to think of things you don't want them to know about. Thoughts are the precursor of actions. When you create a plan, it's as if you've set up vibrations in the likely outcome to your actions. The Eyes sense those vibrations, just like sharks can detect the thrashing of a swimmer."*

The *fiutana* had seemed "deep within virgin forest" but in truth it was only sixteen miles from downtown Pittsburgh. On a hoverbike, full throttle, piloted by his fearless sister Adele, it took less than ten minutes to weave their way through the trees, across the Rim into empty urban sprawl, and rocket down the highway. Tristan clung tight to Adele and tried to keep his mind focused on his official duty. Lucien had volunteered Tristan to investigate how things stood in Pittsburgh now that the battle was being waged in earnest. Since Tristan looked like a human child, he should be able to move freely through the city.

The mission, however, was just an excuse to get Tristan out from under their father's thumb and into the city. Lucien wanted Tristan to find his runaway love: Carla "Boo" Kryskill.

Tristan had done similar jobs for their father. Humans rarely suspected children of being enemy spies, but there were always awkward questions: Who are your parents? Where do they work? Do you live in our neighborhood? Are you an official resident of our school district? Who is your family doctor? Why aren't you in school? Won't your parents be worried that you're out so late? Alone?

They were questions that always filled Tristan with existential despair if he had to think about them too long. It had been one thing when he thought he was a human adult with a rare medical condition. It was quite another knowing that he was a half-elf and still truly a child. Should he be doing such work for his father? Shouldn't he be home with his loving mother? Would he be better off grabbing as much money as possible and disappearing? How angry would his father really be?

Tristan would normally spend up to a month prior to any assignment setting up a false identity with all the possible loose ends nailed down. Birth certificate. Social Security card. School transcripts. Medical records. The works. He would have answers scripted for any awkward question.

Lucien had waited until their baby sisters were distracted. It meant that Tristan didn't have his normal prep time. He couldn't use his real name in case Lucien or one of his people had slipped up sometime in the last eight years and told Boo about Tristan. Since Marc Kryskill was a police officer, a fake name without supporting paperwork wouldn't work. Nor could Tristan safely borrow the identity of a local boy. With the Kryskills' sprawling family connections, any randomly picked name might be well known to one of them. Tristan had noticed that none of them had close interactions with off-worlders. It would mean that they would be unfamiliar with any family on Elfhome via a work visa. He had searched through Lucien's copy of the EIA visa database. He found an American family who had arrived in Pittsburgh at the end of last year. The father held a high-level accounting position with an import company and the mother worked at the University of Pittsburgh. Their son Liam Davis was fifteen years old. It would be a struggle to pass as fifteen but it gave him a paper trail.

He decided that his excuse for latching onto the Kryskills would be a simple "made a mistake with the mass transit and got lost while trying to find an alternate way home." It was nicely vague, working for any location that he might end up at. He could use it coming from or going to any place in the city. "I'd gotten on the wrong bus (or light rail train) and I guess that I walked for blocks in the wrong direction once I'd gotten off." Since the Davis family had been on Elfhome for only a few months and Liam was only fifteen, it was believable that, on his first outing, Liam had gotten completely lost.

Tristan had a borrowed name, a readied excuse, and a backpack filled with random props that might be helpful but little else. No paperwork to back up his borrowed name. No answers to the questions he would most likely be asked. What could he say to get the Kryskills to take him in, or at least keep him long enough for him to dig through their private lives?

He couldn't even use his travel time to create credible lies—not while riding behind Adele. He forced his mind onto another problem. No matter how his game of hide-and-seek played out, he would still need to furnish their father with some kind of report.

"What should I know about our plans—like the strike on Midas?" Tristan shouted over the roar of the hoverbike's engine. He wasn't sure who or what Midas was. Tristan didn't know the finer details of their attack. He knew, for example, that moles scattered across the city were going to take out Pittsburgh's power and communication hubs but he didn't know in what way. How was he supposed to report that the humans were ineffectively or successfully countering their plans if he didn't know what those plans were?

"Someone found out that Midas was trying to build a gate back to Earth," Adele called back. "Either that or the mice belong to them. I'm not sure which. I took a peek at the shipyard before we left camp and it was nothing but mice."

Ah! The shipyard! That explained much. When Tristan first arrived in Pittsburgh, he and Lucien had several conversations about a multinational corporation that recently modernized the shipyard on Neville Island. Lucien hadn't told Tristan the company's name; in the grand scheme of things, the name made little difference. The brothers' focus had been on the massive 3D printer that could print out an entire tugboat in the matter of hours—engine and all. Lucien wanted control of the facility. A fleet of boats would greatly expand their ability to use the Ohio and Mississippi Rivers. Buying Midas would have been the simplest and most effective method of taking over the printer but their technophobic father refused to give Lucien the funds. Seizing the printing facility by brute force wouldn't work as the machines were too complex for Lucien's people to run. Ancient elves and most oni were hopeless when dealing with technology. The tengu could not be trusted. Tristan and Lucien brainstormed how they could seize control of the company without buying it or endangering key technical personnel.

The changeling, however, proceeded to wreak havoc with all of their plans. Important personnel like Lord Tomtom and his best warriors had been killed. Resources like the tengu, the Turtle Creek facility, and Malice were lost. All discussions about the shipyard were dropped as Lucien focused on damage control.

That explained what "Midas" was but it left a dozen more questions. How was Midas building a gate to Earth? With their 3D printer? How did they figure out the science that stumped the best minds of Earth for decades? Had someone leaked them the design of the gate that Lord Tomtom forced Tinker to build? There been countless true bloods working on the project as carpenters. They understood casting magic well enough to work with ironwood. Or was the leak to Midas from the tengu before they fell under the changeling's protection? It might even be someone working with Tinker herself. Obviously the Eyes would have raced to take control of any gate building activities but it sounded like someone beat them to the punch. Who? And what were the "mice"?

Adele had been roaring down the Parkway East. She suddenly dropped all power into the lift engine and popped up onto the Liberty Bridge on-ramp. Tristan tightened his hold out of fear and she laughed.

"Where are we going?" Tristan asked as the bridge took them across the river, away from Downtown. He'd planned on going to the coffee shop that Boo's mother owned. He figured that a woman with seven children would have a hyper mothering instinct.

"The joy of being first born is that Father had Yves tweak me the least," Adele called back. "Standing at the center of the casting circle—knowing that you're going to be forever changed? I'm happy about not being fiddled with any more than I have been. It always made me feel like a hollowed egg—empty on the inside, painfully fragile on the out. It means, though, that every time the others were improved, it got harder and harder to win against them in practice battles. Harder—but not impossible. I just needed to be really sneaky."

Did this mean that Adele knew that he had a secret mission? Had he just made a mistake in asking?

"How does this relate to Midas?" Tristan asked cautiously.

"We thought that we only had Pure Radiance to dance around. We thought we were being so clever. We used all the little tricks that worked on each other. Using disposal tools. Manipulating things remotely. Never letting underlings know who we were or what we were trying to do. Keeping our distance from Pure Radiance's instruments. It turns out that there is more than just Pure Radiance pulling strings."

"Esme?" Tristan guessed.

"Her. The changeling. Pure Radiance's mongrel of a daughter. The tengu's dream crow. Lain is her mother's daughter—she probably still catches glimpses of what is to be. We're suddenly ankle deep in those who sow the future."

It was a rough translation of the term "*intanyai seyosa*," indicating that Pure Radiance and her ilk were farmers, carefully tending seeds that they had planted.

"That does make things more tricky," Tristan said as he realized that it might be the true reason that Lucien had kept him in the dark. Not because of their little sisters but the other "Eyes" in the city. Tristan was not only related to Lain and Esme but also spent half his life living with them. His *nuenae* partially overlapped theirs—it would allow their older half sisters to dream of Tristan's activities. It was likely they could "see" Lucien too. Was that why Lucien wore his demon-like mask? His oni name was "White Snake": a creature so deadly that it didn't need to camouflage itself. It was oddly comforting to think that Lucien might wear his mask more to protect Lain than instill fear in his followers.

"Esme and the dream crow were lost in space until August," Adele said. "Sparrow had taken Pure Radiance's mongrel to Earth in May. The changeling did not seem to awaken to her nature until after the wolf child remade her on Midsummer's Eve. None of them should have been able to block our assassination attempt in early June."

Tristan had heard enough about the failed effort to know that it had gone mysteriously wrong. All of the underlings assigned to the mission had vanished that night. From what Lucien was able to piece together, his operatives had stopped Windwolf's

car, killed his guard, started to give chase but never reached the
changeling's junkyard. The obvious answer was that someone
intercepted the assassination squad and killed them. "You think
there's an enemy *intanyai seyosa* operating in Pittsburgh?"

"We've all felt watched—from time to time," Adele said. "I
always assumed that it was one of the other Eyes. Fefe is sure
that it's someone else—someone close by. She's the most tweaked
of us. If she is sure, then the threat is real. Danni has a plan to
catch the enemy *intanyai seyosa* out."

Danni had been with Lucien downstream on the Ohio River.
Originally Yves was going to use their Turtle Creek camp to cast
the transformation spell while Lucien led the troops into Oakland. Yves had been MIA and the changeling had parked Esme's
spaceship on top of their casting circle. Their father refused to
change their plans as the loss of the orbital gate meant that they
were running with a limited supply of food and ammo for their
troops. Lucien needed to take over Yves's duties and find an
intact casting circle. Danni and one of Lucien's underlings took
over moving the troops upriver to Herrs Island, from which they
would launch the attack on Oakland. It sounded like Danni was
going to deviate from their original plan even more.

Being in the dark to the Eyes' plot was going to make both
of Tristian's missions—official and unofficial—a hundred times
harder.

"Danni and Fefe are confident." Adele took the right turn
off of Liberty Bridge to climb up Mount Washington. "But I am
not so sure. I know what it's like to be the less gifted one in a
showdown."

Like his baby sisters, the enemy would be able to feel the vibrations of thought preceding action. This might be the true reason
Lucien had told him nothing about the family's plans. Tristan
wasn't sure why Adele was telling him this. If their enemy could
pick up the same vibrations, wouldn't the less said the better?
Perhaps she believed he knew so little that he couldn't forewarn
their opponent with his thoughts.

They shot down Grandview Avenue to the upper station of
the Monongahela Incline. The building was dark and the incline
tram wasn't moving. The city's power was off already.

"While Father was at Shikaakwa, you could stay out of the
fray," Adele said. "You've been on Earth without magic your

whole life. You might have the same inborn ability to dance on the edge of danger. Lucien has a little of it, so you might too. You've had no time, though, to hone it like the rest of us. We all felt it would be better if you stayed back out of the line of fire. Father won't allow that, so into the mix you must go."

That surprised him. His baby sisters had been little girls when he last saw Adele or Fefe. Chloe had been like a rogue moon all summer, communicating only via cryptic notes carried by Lucien's operatives. If Chloe had known that he was on Elfhome before she was killed, her reports gave no indication of it. Danni had been at the forest camp. She alternated between coldly snubbing him and ambushing him with knives drawn. He had thin cuts all over his body from the attacks. The few times that they actually spoke, their conversation had been laced with snide, hurtful comments. He had figured that Danni hated him, yet Adele seemed to be implying that the sisters agreed to protect Tristan for as long as they could.

"I understand," Tristan said even though he didn't. Yes, he knew that their father fully expected Tristan to be useful to the cause. Emperor Heaven's Blessing always viewed his children as tools to regain his empire. What Tristan didn't understand was Danni: if she liked him, why had she continually attacked him? Maybe Danni thought she was forcing Tristan to exercise what little precognitive power he had inherited from his mother.

"We've got fires to light all over the city," Adele said. "I thought about having you deal with the trains, but that's going to need someone who looks more intimidating than you. We still have some operatives that can pass as human; I'll throw one of them at that."

Their father had given all his slaves pointed ears to make it obvious which of his subjects were free born and which were property. Heaven's Blessing and his supporters could pass as humans with their rounded ears. Since the first Startup, a growing number of them had been embedded into Pittsburgh's infrastructure. The EIA had only been able to weed the magically disguised oni moles out of their ranks, leaving the ancient elves embedded.

"I've got to go pick up some troops and search out a nest of troublemakers on Mount Oliver." Adele stopped in front of a small one-story clapboard building painted cream yellow with a sign stating MONONGAHELA INCLINE 1870.

On a normal day, the historic funicular railway would give him access to Station Square at the foot of Mount Washington. There was no way to walk down from the cliff top—at least as far as Tristan knew of. Someone more familiar with the area might know of one. With the power off, Adele was effectively stranding him on Mount Washington.

Was it because she knew of his mission for Lucien and disapproved?

When they were little, his baby sisters wouldn't back down once they had decided a course of action. They were sure that they knew better than anyone. If Lucien felt the need to sneak behind the back of the Eyes, then age had not changed that mindset. Tristan had no hope of challenging Adele's decision.

"This isn't Mount Oliver." Tristan let his confusion bleed into his voice. He pointed toward the neighborhood that bordered— somehow—Mount Washington. While he knew general locations, he didn't know how to find his way eastward through a maze of hilltop streets and across the deep uninhabited valleys.

"Doh!" Adele said. "Hop off."

Tristan reluctantly slid off the back of the hoverbike. "Why are you dropping me here?"

"It seems like the least dangerous hot spot." Adele nodded toward the radio tower a block from the incline. "WESA is my favorite station; it's what the cool kids listen to. It caters to bands that mix rock music with traditional elf instruments. None of our other siblings like it. WESA was broadcasting some weird stuff all day—maybe longer. I've been stuck in a cave, so I have no idea how long it's been going on. There's so many fingers pulling strings, I can't get a handle on it. Maybe it's nothing. It seems safe enough for you to poke around."

WESA? Chloe's reports hadn't included it beyond an early mention that National Public Radio had pulled its funding. WESA stopped broadcasting within three years of the first Startup. No new license had been issued, so it wasn't the case of a new owner. Someone must be using the old equipment to run a pirate station. Chloe must have considered that beneath her notice. Her arrogance killed her. It might kill them all. What else had she stupidly missed?

But it wouldn't be wise to speak ill of the recently dead. Not when her twin sister was there, in front of him, looking unhappy. The Eyes might fight with each other like a howling pack of wild monkeys but they had a fierce "us against the world" bond. Tristan suspected it came from how aloof and impersonal their caretakers had been.

"I'll look into it," Tristan said instead.

Adele nodded, dismounting her hoverbike to rummage through its seat storage compartment. "Sitting around in the cave, waiting for visions of Yves to come to me, gave me time to think. About Yves. About you and Lucien. About...about this war."

He wasn't sure but he suspected that she almost said something painfully open and honest about their father. It was sad that she deemed it too dangerous to complain about him on this dark and desolate street corner.

"I'm tired of this war," she said instead. "Always hiding. The months of living in the woods with the man-eating plants and animals. Sending people out to kill. Sending people out to be killed. I want it to be over. I want us to get to our happily ever after."

"Happily ever after?" Tristan echoed in surprise.

"We're the children of an emperor," Adele said bitterly. "When we were young, we thought that made us princesses. We thought we would live in a palace and wear fairy silk gowns and eat those dainty little cakes that you used to bring for your silly tea parties. We all did."

"Petit fours." He gave the name of the treats. He'd nearly forgotten about the tea parties that he held for the girls as he tried to recreate the happiness of his own childhood. The desserts were all part of the mystical formula. His five baby sisters were not his mother and two older sisters; his tea parties were not the tranquil joy that he remembered. It was like trying to entertain wild monkeys that were armed with forks. He'd learned not to give them silverware.

"Yeah, those." Adele took out a lightweight rain jacket stuffed into a carrying pouch. "You were always so sweet to us when we were little. I think you're the only reason we understand the word 'love.' Anyhow, princesses are supposed to live happily ever after. That's how all the stories end."

He didn't know what to say. She was no longer a child nor did she have long to live. The gray mixed in her buzz-cut pale blond hair was testament to that. Unless she allowed herself to be "tweaked" by Lucien, she would have only a few more decades left.

She was, though, still his little sister.

He wanted to say that the war would end soon, that she would have her happy ending—but that would be a lie.

If their assassination attempt had worked, then Sparrow would have taken up the reins of power. It would have been a simple matter to cut the Pittsburgh-based enclaves off from the East Coast holdings, take out the Wind Clan Spell Stones, and then aggressively import backup from Earth with humans being none the wiser that a coup had taken place. They could have built up power in the Westernlands without fear of reprisal from the Easternlands. All of it had failed in the worst way. The Viceroy survived. Their presence had been revealed. Pure Radiance had come to the Westernlands to set the changeling into motion. After that, the changeling had careened out of control, doing crazy, impossible things that unraveled decades of planning.

They had no choice now. They were isolated and outnumbered by millions of elves who were very aware of their existence. After they captured Pittsburgh, they would have to rush to take out the Spell Stones of both the Wind Clan and the Stone Clan before the crown could send more *domana*.

If they succeeded, they had the rest of the world to beat down and enslave. It could take hundreds of years; he might even live to see it to the end. His baby sisters would not.

Adele handed him the jacket. "It's going to rain cats and dogs soon."

She had on waterproof camo coveralls. She must have packed the rain jacket especially for him. It warmed his heart to think that she cared that much for him.

"Thanks," Tristan put the jacket into his backpack.

"Don't let Father ever see this." She handed him a phone. "Lucien set up our own private network so we can stay in contact with each other even with the Pittsburgh system down. You know how much Father hates us using technology but it's better than stumbling around in the dark, not knowing what everyone else is doing."

He checked its address book. It showed only three numbers entered, labeled: Dad, Mom, Sissy. If he had to guess, Lucien was "Dad" and Adele was "Mom" and Danni was "Sissy." Odd that there were no entries for Bethany, Chloe, and Fefe. Had Adele only set up the phone after Chloe was killed? Was Bethany not on Elfhome? Was Fefe too close to their father to risk the phone?

"Be careful." Adele swung onto her hoverbike and revved its engine. The machine lifted up off the pavement. "I've lost one brother this summer—not that I particularly liked Yves. I really don't want to lose you too."

Tristan had changed out of his "oni warlord" clothes at the encampment, putting on a disguise of "normal human boy." Lucien had provided the clothes; they felt oddly exotic. The blue jeans had baggier legs than he was used to. There were heavy boots that weren't Doc Martens. The T-shirt advertised an elf fusion rock band named Naekanain. The graphic had a stylized outline of the castlelike headquarters of the EIA done in Pittsburgh gold and the elf runes for "I don't know" in Wind Clan Blue.

Lucien had shoved things into the bag while Tristan changed clothes. Tristan dug through his backpack to find out what exactly his brother had given him. There was a Swiss Army knife with twelve different "blades," a September bus pass, a half-filled loyalty punch card from a place called Ellen's Tiny Deli, a house key with no indication where the matching lock might be located, and a wallet with a dozen worn dollar bills of different denominations. Cash! Tristan hadn't had to deal with real currency for years. There was no real weapon beyond the pocketknife. That might prove annoying. He was trained in unarmed combat but that was only good for certain situations.

He wondered about the loyalty card. If the shop had been one of their cover businesses, Lucien wouldn't have needed a card to get free food. Was the deli food so good that Lucien sought it out despite the risk? Pittsburgh wasn't New York City with every type of food delivered to the door all hours of the day. Two months in the forest and Tristan was desperately wanting pizza and tacos. Or had Lucien known that Tristan might need all the little flourishes that went into a good cover?

As Tristan tucked away the card, he caught sight of his reflection in the station's window. He'd forgotten—deep in the forest without any mirrors—how much he looked like Lucien. When they were younger, people had trouble telling them apart. They shared their mother's pale blond hair and their father's sharp cheekbones, elegant nose, and vaguely almond eyes.

Boo might take one look at him and know that he was Lucien's brother.

How could he change his looks in a matter of minutes? He could punch himself in the face; it wouldn't be the first time he used that tactic to get out of a tight space. A pair of eyeglasses would be less painful. Did he grab a pair from his disguise kit? Yes. He'd packed the chunky black "Clark Kent" frames. He frowned at his reflection. If he had the time, he would color his pale blond hair to something darker. Because their father forbid them from cutting their hair, Lucien's was down to his waist. A quick messy haircut would make their father angry but would help disguise Tristan.

He found a hiding spot around the corner from the incline station so no one could see him hack at his shoulder-length hair with the Swiss Army knife. He found his kit's mirror to check his reflection again. The haircut and glasses helped slightly. There was nothing more he could do about how he looked. He would have to rely on tone of voice and word choice. Lucien had a deeper voice as he was closer to puberty and still had his New Yorker accent despite years in Pittsburgh.

Tristan put away the mirror, considering what he should tackle next. He had planned to go to the coffee shop but he'd reach it long after its closing time. With the power off, Boo's mother probably closed early. If she stuck to her normal pattern, she would head to the South Hills where she lived with her two teenage sons, Guy and Duff.

He would need to catch up with her later. For now, he would check on the radio station.

5: MURDER HOUSE

"What the hell happened here?" Law Monroe whispered.

It was the fourth warehouse that Law and Bare Snow had been to since they started chasing after the *nactka*. All four buildings had appeared abandoned on the outside. This one on Thirty-fourth Street at the edge of the Strip District looked like a slaughterhouse.

Law crouched on the loading dock, cautiously peering through the open bay door. The interior was lit only by the last rays of daylight through high narrow windows. The smell of carnage hung thick in the air. A mist of blood coated everything. There were dead bodies littering the floor, still leaking out bodily fluids. She cautiously rolled the nearest body over. It was limp and warm; rigor mortis hadn't set in yet. The male was one of Kajo's pack bearers that she'd been following all afternoon. She'd seen him and the others alive just thirty minutes earlier. Now, in this nondescript warehouse at the edge of the Strip District, the pack bearers were all mysteriously dead. There were no bullet shells on the ground, nor the smell of gun smoke in the air. The exit wounds weren't the ragged holes made by high-powered guns. The holes were perfectly neat circles, like those made by spell arrows, only much too small. The bodies looked like they had been used as pincushions.

"I think someone set off a puffball," Bare Snow whispered, crouching beside Law to examine the body. "His fingers are

43

starting to go stiff. In this heat, I'd say that the puffball was triggered minutes after they arrived."

"A what?" Law collected puffball mushrooms to sell to the enclaves. She'd never heard of a variety that filled people with holes.

"It is an ancient type of magical trap; a sphere made of clay that looks like a puffball mushroom." Bare Snow pointed to curved shards of red clay scattered across the top of a cardboard box near the door. "It's filled with small darts etched with a version of the spell-arrow spell. When the puffball is triggered—either by a specific sound or a key word—a concussion spell on its core goes off, spraying the darts into the air to activate. They will pierce almost everything: flesh, leather, wyvern-scale armor, and ironwood. It has been one of the forbidden magics since the end of the Rebellion. They can sit armed and forgotten for centuries before accidently being triggered. The *sekasha* thought them dishonorable and thus banned them even as the Clan War started. No elf born after the Rebellion would even know how to create one."

"How do you know about them?"

"My mother thought I should know all the forbidden magic since our enemy were the ones that developed them."

A forbidden spell? One that normal elves wouldn't use and humans couldn't know as no one would teach it to them? Either the Skin Clan just fumbled a trap or something had gone south within the enemy's ranks. Maybe Kajo had cleansed his ranks again, killing the pack bearers like he had killed the tengu within his camp. Was this the entire contingent of pack bearers that they had been following?

Law did a quick head count and then counted again. The dead seemed to be the entire work party that they had followed all day. Who had driven away their big yellow truck? Did the mystery driver have the *nactka* now?

Law and Bare Snow had stumbled across two identical oni warlords that morning. It had been a combination of keen observation of the native wildlife, clever tracking, and pure dumb luck. Two nearly identical warlords, dozens of warriors, and a score of pack bearers had been camping a few miles beyond the Rim. After breaking camp, the war party headed to the edge of Oakland.

By that point, it was early afternoon with the sun just starting its slide down to the west. The taller of the two warlords had used a monster call to send black willows toward the back end of the enclaves. In Law's mind, that probably meant that he was Kajo and the shorter masked oni was the body double, meant to confuse possible assassins—like Bare Snow.

Kajo then split his party into two groups.

He kept his body double, eighty heavily armed warriors, and a score of wargs. Law knew from experience that the magically enhanced wolves had a keen sense of smell. Bare Snow's invisibility spell didn't erase her scent. It would be insane to try and kill Kajo. Besides, their target was the egglike *nactka*.

Kajo took almost nothing else with him in terms of luggage. Twenty brutish red-skinned pack bearers headed off with the small mountain of camping equipment. Tents and bedrolls comprised much of the gear but there were several large mystery duffel bags. Any one of them could hold ostrich eggs of mass destruction. While the pack bearers were all armed with rifles, they didn't take any of the wargs with them.

It was a complete no-brainer as to which group Law and Bare Snow should follow.

Law had called Alton Kryskill, dumped the whole problem of the incoming black willows into his lap, and then chased after Kajo's camping gear.

They had followed the pack bearers on foot for about a mile up Braddock Avenue. As they neared the great wall of trees at the Rim, the oni turned onto Lincoln Highway and stopped at a gas station where a bright yellow box truck waited. The vehicle looked like an old Penske moving van with all the company logos painted out in a dull tan. Such trucks were common in Pittsburgh. Someone must have gotten a deal on retired equipment and imported them in bulk. They were such a common sight that Law had never considered that they might be all owned by one organization.

By the end of the day, she would lay money on it.

As Law took a head count through her binoculars, the pack bearers stripped away all that was oni. Their leather clothes. Their face paint. And finally, using some kind of written spells, their red skin and brutish bodies. While their ears were not pointed, they had the tall, willowy figures of elves.

"They're all Skin Clan!" Bare Skin had whispered fiercely.

Law nodded as she committed the newly revealed faces to memory.

The only time she and Bare Snow had encountered the human-looking elves was when they were overseeing complex espionage missions. There had been Skin Clan operatives embedded in the EIA hunting for Windwolf and within the train offices to set up the strike on Station Square but there had been none on the train itself. It meant that the equipment that the pack bearers were loading onto the yellow truck must be important. Kajo would have probably used normal, true blood oni otherwise.

Law had also realized that the pack bearers wouldn't have bothered to strip off their disguises if they were going to head back into the forest. The group was going to drive into the city. She and Bare Snow weren't going to be able to keep up with a truck on foot.

Law moved back to make a phone call to Widget Bunny. The girl had a backdoor into the city's traffic camera system, set up when she had helped Law save Windwolf from an assassination attempt. She might be able to use it to track the pack bearers while Law backtracked for her Dodge.

"Hey-o!" Widget answered.

"Hi, it's . . ." Law paused before saying her name as the morning conversation replayed in her mind.

"We don't know what level of technology that they're operating at," Widget had said. *"We have to assume that anything we say might be overheard."*

"It's me," Law said. "I need a favor. You know that backdoor that we talked about this morning?"

"Back. Door," Widget murmured, sounding mystified.

A male voice murmured in the background. "The backdoor to . . . to that special computer system?"

"Ohhhh," Widget said as understanding dawned.

"Are you with that boy that you have crush on?" Law asked.

"Sh-sh-sh-sh." Widget made a funny hushing sound in panic. "Yes, I am. He has a problem with some trees—among other things. I think you know which ones I mean, Bam-Bam."

That had been Law's nickname in high school, something only locals like the Kryskills would know. Alton must have told Duff about her phone call regarding the incoming black willows.

"Okay," Law said. "Can you peek through that door that we talked about and see if you can spot a box truck located at the intersection of Braddock Avenue and Lincoln Highway?"

"Lincoln Highway?" Widget echoed in confusion. It wasn't surprising that Widget didn't recognize the street names—it was on the opposite end of town from where the Bunnies lived. "Oh! Oh! That door! What was the other street? Braddock?"

"Lincoln runs along the Rim." Duff sounded a lot like his older brother. The whole family had broadcaster quality voices. "From the Allegheny to the Parkway. Braddock should be right about here."

"Can you see the box truck?" Law said.

"Maaayyybe. Give me a second." Widget typed on a keyboard on her end. "And what's a box truck? Is it a certain type of truck or is it simply a truck carrying boxes? What am I looking for?"

"It's a big truck with a cab on the front," Duff said. "It has a separate cargo area in the back that's square like a box."

"It's yellow," Law added.

"Why didn't you say that it was yellow first?" Widget said. "Okay, I'm looking at the intersection . . . and . . . there's the *yellow* truck. It's under the gas station marquee. Right? Blast it all! Who are all those people? Bad guys?"

"Yes, very bad guys," Law said. "Can you keep eyes on them?"

Widget snorted. "In that big yellow thing? Easy peasy lemon squeezy. They're not going to be sneaking around on little back-streets or off-roading in that."

While Widget had tracked the yellow truck through the city, Law and Bare Snow had doubled back to where they'd left her Dodge. By the time they had caught back up with the truck, it had driven to an equally abandoned area on the North Side. It had parked on a short, dead-end street with the unlikely name of Riversea Road.

Law tucked the Dodge into a nearby alley called Drovers Way. She and Bare Snow picked their way over to a spot where they could spy on the Skin Clan "movers." Like a line of ants, the elves were carrying the camping gear into the building and boxes out of it to be loaded onto the truck. Law did another head count to be sure that the numbers hadn't changed on them.

"What do you think is in those boxes?" Bare Snow whispered as they watched from the shadows.

Law blew out her breath; she didn't have a clue.

The Riversea Road building had elaborate redbrick architecture that dated it back to the middle eighteen hundreds. There was an ancient electrical grid on the façade, looking like it connected up to old knob-and-tube wiring, which suggested that the warehouse hadn't been used for almost a hundred years. Nothing about it gave a clue as to what the oni might have stored within the building.

The elves could be loading anything from apples to weapons onto the truck. The boxes were made of corrugated cardboard without any logos or labels—something almost unheard of in Pittsburgh. The city had a monthly flood of containers of all types. None of it was unmarked: it seemed like the people on Earth were obsessed with labels. Pittsburghers reused old cardboard boxes with no regard for their origin. Newcomers often used the sturdiest containers for dressers and pantries. They made bookshelves and tables from the second most common shipping material in the city: the pallets that the boxes were transported in on.

It was weirdly intimidating that the Skin Clan had a warehouse stocked with plain boxes. It spoke of unimaginable connections on Earth, deep pockets, and mind-boggling foresight.

What did Law know for sure? Kajo had camped out last night. His pack bearers had packed up the camping gear and taken it to the truck. If this was a group of humans, Law would assume that they were done sleeping outside.

"Kajo must have ditched his tents because he's not going to be camping in the woods tonight," Law said slowly as she felt her way through the logic. "That would mean that he plans to sleep indoors. A house or warehouse or office building—somewhere in the Pittsburgh area. Someplace that can shelter a hundred warriors."

It still gave Kajo almost two thousand square miles to pick from.

"I don't blame Kajo," Bare Snow murmured. "The way the wind is blowing, it's going to storm big soon."

Law nodded as she added this to her calculations. The weather report had called for heavy evening thunderstorms. Kajo probably knew this; he had moles in nearly every institution in the city. "If he plans to be at his new camp for more than a day, he would need things like food and bedding."

It was just a wild guess but it felt right. Kajo had eighty warriors and twenty wargs with him. That was a lot of mouths to feed. Traveling light would make sense if he planned on taking shelter within the city proper. The pack bearers could gather supplies quickly and move to a new location via the moving van. It would allow Kajo to travel unencumbered.

Just because it felt right, didn't make her guess correct. She didn't know enough. She really needed to know what was in the warehouse and the unmarked boxes. You could only build a trap for an animal if you knew where it slept and what it liked to eat. What little information that the tengu *yamabushi* Yumiko had given her about Kajo wasn't enough to guess where the warlord had stored the *nactka*.

Law decided that she and Bare Snow would search the building after the elves left. She called Widget to tell her to continue keeping an eye on the yellow truck.

When Law was a child, she had resisted her grandfather's lessons on all things electrical and mechanical. She saw the training as his way to use her as slave labor. She was glad now that a lot of it had still sunk in despite her resistance to learning it. It meant that she knew how to get around simple security systems and basic door locks.

"I could just go in through a window," Bare Snow whispered from somewhere to Law's right. The female had stripped down and gone invisible in case there were guards inside the building. "There's a lot of ways in other than this door."

Law shook her head as she picked the heavy duty Yale mortise lock on the front door. "This building has a security system." She paused to point out where she'd already attached a heavy-duty magnet to a door sensor. "If we just opened the door without disabling that, it would set off some kind of alarm. That part right there is old and low tech. There might be something more inside—something more sophisticated."

Law wasn't sure how Bare Snow's invisibility spell worked. It seemed to bend light around Bare Snow so that she disappeared from the landscape. Law knew that it didn't cover the female's scent. Law wasn't sure if the spell would work on the motion sensors. Some security systems used infrared energy—body heat—to detect intruders. Would the spell keep Bare Snow invisible at that level? Maybe. Law's grasp of electromagnetic radiation was weak but she was fairly sure that heat was a form of light. Whether or not Bare Snow's spell extended into those spectrums was the main factor.

Even if her invisibility magic worked that way, not all sensors were based on infrared. Some systems used ultrasonic sound waves. Bare Snow was not magically silent when she was invisible. She could move very quietly, even through dead leaves. The problem was that most security systems didn't pick up noise being made by humans. They used ultrasonic sensors that bounced sound to a known object and back. It detected the interruption of the signal by something unknown blocking the reflected wave. Law was fairly sure that such systems could detect Bare Snow even while she was invisible.

"There should be a control panel by the door that will let me override everything," Law said as she worked her lockpicks through the last tumbler. It clicked loudly as the door unlocked. "Okay, this is it. Kill anything that moves while I disable the security system."

It was anticlimactic. There were no oni or monsters within the warehouse. The control panel was as old and low tech as the door sensor. There were window sensors that would be triggered by opening them. There seemed to be no motion sensors or anything else on the inside of the building. Law bypassed all the inputs just to be sure.

Once Law was sure that it was safe to move about, they rifled the warehouse. Kajo's camping gear sat on the shelves nearest to the loading dock. There was no sign of the mystery duffel bags that she thought the *nactka* might be in. The warehouse held shelves upon shelves of canned goods. Big commercial-sized cans of things like carrots, corn, peaches, pears, and sweet potatoes. Smaller tins of luxury food like smoked mussels, wild mackerel, stuffed calamari, a dozen different types of sardines, gourmet cookies, and fancy chocolates. Law had never seen so much food, not even in the Oakland branch of the Giant Eagle supermarket just after Startup. While the pack bearers had carried out dozens of boxes, the shelves were all still full. The elves had left behind enough to feed an army for months.

Across the aisle from the camping gear were cardboard boxes stacked flat with rolls of packing tape beside them. The pack bearers must have taped up boxes and filled them with cans pulled from the shelves. Judging by how much food they'd taken, Kajo was planning to stay in one spot for a long time.

Law went through the camping gear a second time to be sure that the *nactka* weren't among the various tents, folding cots, and sleeping bags.

"Oh! Oh my!" Bare Snow whispered in the next aisle.

Law turned to the corner to find Bare Snow taking big jars of peanut butter off a shelf.

Bare Snow held out the peanut butter to Law. "We should take everything here for the Bunny babies."

It was a tempting idea. Hazel Bunny had said that they were running low on basic food supplies. The Pittsburgh stores were picked bare of imported groceries. All that was left was what the local farms could produce. Law had promised to keep the Bunnies stocked with fresh meat, but the women had a dozen mouths to feed through the winter.

Law should stay focused on the *nactka* but she had no solid proof that the magical bombs had been on the yellow truck. The Bunnies had a real need for food and there were several dozen jars of peanut butter. Kajo probably wouldn't miss a few. "Okay, take three or four but from the back of the shelf."

Bare Snow nodded and set about moving jars forward to disguise the fact that some were taken.

If they were going to take peanut butter, they should go for broke. Were there any bulk staples that they could easily steal? Hazel had specifically mentioned that the Bunnies were low on flour.

In the back of the warehouse, Law found big metal airtight bins holding fifty-pound bags of flour, sugar, rice, and dried beans. She and Bare Snow shifted one bag of each to the big fishing coolers on the back of her Dodge.

"We'll come back later for more," she told Bare Snow.

Looting the food, though, made Law think of Usagi's offer to join her household. It was so unfair that Bare Snow was being held accountable for a crime committed before she was born. If Law understood the timeline correctly, Bare Snow's mother had been an adolescent when someone else in the family assassinated Howling. She'd gone into hiding on an island for close to a century before meeting Bare Snow's father.

Surely any sane person wouldn't hold an unborn child responsible for the acts of her family who were all long dead?

"What needs to happen to get the death sentence lifted?" Law asked.

"God needs to whisper in Wraith Arrow's ear," Bare Snow said.

"Which god?" Law didn't know much about the religion of the elves except that they had an entire pantheon of gods.

"Whichever one he's willing to listen to." Bare Snow clicked her tongue in an elf shrug. "The *sekasha* are born perfect; Wraith Arrow might not even listen to gods."

With Widget guiding Law to the other places where the yellow truck had stopped, it was lather, rinse, and repeat. Law would disarm the security system. She and Bare Snow would slip in and rifle the place. The second stop was a small warehouse on the South Side on Cabot Way. It was another food depot but much smaller with walk-in freezers and refrigerators full of meat, apples, potatoes and onions. By the door was a stack of big YETI Tundra 350 hard-shell ice chests, only available on Elfhome by special order. She would know as she had to order her own big coolers that she used to store fresh fish. These were still in their original cardboard shipping containers. There were empty boxes, Styrofoam end caps, and plastic wrappers that indicated that someone had unboxed four of the ice chests. Beside the remaining chests was an ice machine quietly refilling with ice. Obviously the pack bearers had filled four chests with ice and frozen meat and carried them off.

Law eyed the chests. Could she take one—or two? Oh hell, she was definitely coming back and looting this place down to the studs! The building had an impressive solar array on the roof, which explained why the freezers and refrigerators are all still quietly humming. She didn't have to worry about the food spoiling before she returned—although she was going to have to find someone with a great deal of freezer space almost immediately.

The third warehouse had been nearby on Wharton Street. It had an odd array of goods from toilet paper to bed linen.

The *nactka* weren't in any of the warehouses. If the pack bearers had carried them away for Kajo, they hadn't offloaded them from the truck yet.

✧   ✧   ✧

Law called Widget for an update on the yellow truck after searching the warehouse on Wharton Street. "Where's our target now?"

"Well... I've got some good news and some bad news," Widget said.

Law's stomach went queasy as all the possible things that could go wrong flashed through her mind. "What's the bad news?"

"I lost the truck," Widget said.

Law locked down on a curse. It wasn't Widget's fault; the girl was doing the best that she could. Law should have followed the truck instead of checking out the second and third warehouses. Kajo could go to ground and vanish for weeks with what his people had stocked up on.

Widget expanded on how she lost track of the truck. "Tinker *domi*'s fight with Malice took out some important infrastructure downtown." A lot of stuff had been taken out by the dragon and the massive helicopter that Tinker commandeered from the elves. Widget probably meant the traffic cameras. It wasn't all that surprising that some of the cameras were collateral damage to the fight. "Our target left the South Side via the Birmingham Bridge. I didn't see where it went when it got to the other side. The stupid bridge weaves over and under the Parkway, the Boulevard of the Allies, and Forbes Avenue. It's like a cat's cradle of roads. I couldn't figure out the intersections fast enough to track the target. I only know that it didn't go out toward Oakland, so it either headed into Downtown or went crosstown, toward the North Side."

"What's the good news?"

"It-it-it's a long story but I started out this morning by hacking into a laptop that belonged to the ex-director of the museum," Widget said. "Ex-director as she's now dead. That's why I'm... I'm where I am."

Widget meant with Duff at the bakery. Law frowned, wondering what the museum had to do with anything. Was the director dead because she had been an oni mole? There had been some kind of excitement at the Carnegie in July, but Law had been busy trying to find the oni camp where Tinker was being held captive. "And?"

"My mom used to do this kind of investigative shit all the time," Widget said. "She would always say 'follow the money' so

I dug around until I found this whole section of property taxes and utility bills for buildings that have nothing to do with the museum. All three places that you've been to had their taxes and utilities paid by the museum: Riversea Road, Cabot Way, and Wharton Street. I'm trying to get eyes on the other addresses—maybe the truck is at one of them. Hold on."

Law waited, listening to Widget type and whisper her odd innocent swears like "blast it all!" and "fudge nuggets!"

"Gotcha!" Widget cried with triumphant. "If you were going to hide, you shouldn't have picked something so big and yellow!"

"Where is it?" Law said.

"It's in the Strip District!" Widget said. "It's currently at the intersection of Penn and Butler *and* Thirty-fourth Street. Gah, Pittsburgh intersections are so wonky."

Penn and Butler? That would be Doughboy Square with the bronze statue of a World War One infantry soldier.

"I know where that is," Law said.

"That's right by Moser's place," Duff added in the background.

Widget continued to explain. "Number ten on the museum list is on Thirty-fourth Street. I couldn't get eyes onto the building, but I spotted the truck coming up Thirty-fourth, so it must have just left there. It's on Butler now, heading north."

The truck was going to run out of city fast. Carl Moser could lay claim to an entire block of row houses because of the proximity to the Rim. There were a few blocks of mostly empty houses and the three-hundred-acre sprawl of the Allegheny Cemetery before the city abruptly ended in massive trees.

Law switched to speaker, slotted her phone into its dashboard mount, and headed for the Strip District.

"The truck turned into the Allegheny Cemetery," Widget reported a few minutes later. "Why the hell would it go there? Are the oni robbing graves? Raising the dead? O. M. G. What if they can make zombies with magic?"

"I don't think that's possible," Law said. "What entrance did it use?"

"The one that looks like the front gate of a castle. Normally I'd say it was very cool but right now it's super creepy. Major horror-movie vibe—complete with flickering lightning. According to the maps, the cemetery is huge—like a square mile in size—just with little weird bits taken out so it's not really a square.

I've got eyes on the entrances but the other gates are all chained shut with weeds growing through their bars. If they're coming out, they'll probably use the main gate again. The truck is still in there—doing something."

"I'm going to check the warehouse on Thirty-fourth Street." Law said. "Call me if the truck moves again."

The fourth warehouse had been filled with death and little else. It was the final destination of the pack bearers—in more than one way. The space contained nothing but potential. Subtle modifications had made it into a solid fortress with the river protecting its back. It could easily house eighty warriors and twenty wargs with a separate living space for Kajo.

Someone had killed Kajo's people and stolen the truck filled with everything needed to live comfortably for days if not weeks. Whoever they were—they were currently at the Allegheny Cemetery.

6: THE TIME HAS COME TO TALK OF MANY THINGS

"You'll waste time flipping pages and coming to conclusions already reached," Tooloo said. And the crazy old elf had been right: the twins had already figured out a way to block the oni spell.

Tinker sat in the back of the Rolls-Royce as they headed toward Oakland, flipping through the photos she'd taken of the chessboard. Tooloo said that she'd given Tinker everything she needed. To do what? Not stop the oni from casting the spell. Tooloo hadn't given her time enough to do that. If Tooloo wanted to stop the oni from using the *nactka*, she would have told Tinker about Dufae's box in June when it arrived in Pittsburgh.

Tooloo had bitched about Tinker's demands for the unedited version of the Dufae Codex, saying that Tinker was wasting what little time she had. Tooloo hadn't complained as Tinker took the pictures. Tooloo wanted Tinker to focus energy toward deciphering whatever the gameboard showed.

The Skin Clan was playing White—at least that was what the board's positioning and the little plastic monkeys seemed to suggest. Tooloo had staged a miniature bottle of Heinz ketchup as the Black's king. The Heinz factory was on the North Side, still making condiments for Pittsburgh-only use. It had a huge sign that you could see from most of downtown of a bottle pouring ketchup out into the Heinz logo. It was so symbolic of Pittsburgh that all the University students owned a T-shirt of it. Tinker had assumed that the miniature bottle represented the city but what if Tooloo was indicating the factory itself?

Black's bishop right of the queen was a little Superman action figure. Was that Windwolf? Tinker thought he would be the black king but she couldn't see him as a tomato-based condiment. Nor was Windwolf particularly holy. Was the black bishop Jin Wong? The tengu leader had that spiritual leader vibe and he could fly. It kind of made sense in that Windwolf wasn't in the city currently but Jin Wong was.

Both of her rooks were chicken figurines. Six of her pawns were mice—five Minnie Mouse and one Mickey Mouse to be exact. By the number and sex, she guessed that they represented her newly arrived siblings.

The only swapped pieces on the White's side of the board were the queen, one bishop, and four of the pawns were monkeys. If Chloe had been flying monkey five, who were all the other monkeys? Surely not Esme and Lain. Had Esme's stepfather created an entire swarm of half sisters, or were some of the number Esme's two little half brothers who mysteriously refused to say goodbye to her?

That felt chillingly right.

There were a variety of possible moves for White to make after his Chloe pawn was taken. Which one he chose would be helpful to know but Tooloo's board held no clues that Tinker could see. Nor did she know what a "move" might entail. Certainly White's second pawn didn't look like it was storming Oakland on the chessboard.

If the mice were her younger siblings, that left the mystery of the two chicken rooks. Were they supposed to be tengu? Or real chickens? Tooloo normally didn't let her rooster Box into the house, so maybe that was a clue that "chicken" was literal.

Or was she overthinking this? Why had Tooloo stayed hidden in Pittsburgh for so long, doing nothing to warn anyone about the oni? Why did she let it get to this? What did Tooloo want?

There was so much that Tinker didn't know.

Cloudwalker was driving. Little Egret had gone to the train station to commandeer the royal marines there. Rainlily was following on the Delta in case they needed the mobility that it afforded.

Pony and Stormsong flanked her in the backseat, silently waiting for her to do something brilliant. Tinker didn't have a clue where to even start.

"Do either one of you know how to play chess?" she asked her First and Second.

"I have never seen this 'chess' game before," Pony said. "It is totally unfamiliar to me."

"I do—a little," Stormsong admitted reluctantly. "It is one of the many humans games that Wolf and I learned in order to find out more information about Earth. Chess. Senet. Backgammon. Mehen."

What information about Earth could you get out of a game of chess? That knights were wonky people, never moving straight, always jumping around? Tinker's concept of the game was tainted by her experience with Tooloo. She wondered if that was how all elves played the game.

"I don't understand," Tinker said. "What did chess tell you about Earth?"

"We were questioning *domana* who traveled with trading caravans to Earth. They had an odd reluctance to talk about their time among humans. It's like they had committed some evil perversion that they had to keep secret. Everything about Earth was hidden away like it was tainted. The merchants, though, loved to play human games. They were desperate to play them with someone. Wolf would coax them into a game and then play for hours, plying them with food, wine, and questions."

"What kind of questions?" Tinker said.

"Everything. Anything we didn't know. We wanted to focus on the Westernlands but until Wolf reached his majority and built a strong enough support system—two strong Hands and several solid households of Beholden—he would not be able to petition the queen for land. We were afraid if he asked too many questions about the newly found continents, that others—*domana* older and more established than Wolf—would realize what had been overlooked and claim the best land."

Tinker was still confused. She'd been under the impression that the elves traveled the silk-road routes. "The trading caravans came to North America?"

"No, they traded with the European countries that colonized the western hemisphere. Columbus had discovered the West Indies Islands and within decades the Spanish had explored much of Central and South America. The Dutch, Portuguese, English, and French were soon to follow, each with a different agenda, to claim different parts of the continents. The *domana* merchants traded only with the European country closest to the natural pathway that they had claimed for their clan. Fire Clan dealt with the Italians. Wind Clan traded with the English. So forth and so on, dictated by the pathways and the clan holdings. It meant that all the merchants had different sets of information. It was like a jigsaw puzzle scattered across the Easternlands, totally ignored, waiting for us to put together the pieces. Based on everything we learned and what maps we could gather, we decided to set up our first camp along the Hudson River."

Tinker nodded, understanding Windwolf's strategy.

The French Revolution had been in the late 1700s. Tinker was vague on the exact dates that Dufae first arrived in France and when he was later caught up in the political turmoil. Sometime between him arriving and being executed, his way back home had been blocked off by the oni war.

Tooloo could have been on Elfhome until Dufae fled his parent's home. Her dabbling was the most logical reason that Dufae decided to break into his uncle's spell-locked box. Tooloo might have come to Earth at the same time that he did—although she might have been slipping back and forth between the two worlds. It would be one way to keep Pure Radiance from finding her.

Tooloo was probably the person who took Dufae's infant son, Etienne, from France to Boston. A human in those deeply religious times wouldn't have kept the Codex. Certainly Tooloo would have been the person who taught Dufae's grandchildren how to speak and read Elvish. Etienne had been too young to have learned it from his father. Etienne's daughter had taught her brother's grandchildren, Leonardo and Ada. Oilcan's mother had taught him both High and Low Elvish so that Oilcan could speak it better than Tinker, who had been born on Elfhome.

Two hundred years of babysitting someone else's kids. That was a long time—even for an elf. No one does that without an elaborate plan in place that needed those kids.

"Tooloo—Vision—your grandmother—has a plan. I'm guessing it was one that your mother doesn't like—that's why she had Vision bound hand and foot."

"Perhaps," Stormsong said. "I've been thinking about it since I learned that Tooloo was Vision. It makes me wonder about everything that I know about my mother and Vision."

"You don't think you know the truth?"

"In a manner," Stormsong said. "This what I've been told. The Skin Clan—wishing to be gods—would experiment on their slaves to see what impact changing them would make. There were limits to what they could do. Strong? Tall? Beautiful? Long lived? Yes, that was possible. But true godlike abilities of legend? To know the future? To be able to step between worlds without aid of a natural path? No. That was impossible with what they had to work with. So they started to track down strange and wonderful creatures. The children that they created were often immediately destroyed as monstrosities, having no magical gifts that the Skin Clan wanted for themselves. But then they discovered the dragons. Having met Impatience, I am not sure how they trapped the creatures, but they did. One by one, the Emperor Heaven's Blessing gathered the godlike beings and started his unholy experiments. We know—or I should say 'what I've been told but I have been given no proof of its validity'—that Clarity was the dragon that my mother's bloodline came from. One has to wonder, of all the dragons ensnared, how it was that the one that could see the future had fallen prey to the Skin Clan. She was the last. One could conjecture that, knowing her bloodline and all that happened afterward, Clarity had allowed herself to be captured in order to exact revenge against the Skin Clan."

"Knowing that she would be killed?"

"Rage makes you do strange things if you let it," Stormsong said. "It is the emotion that we *sekasha* are most cautioned against. Rage is the absence of reason. But having heard Providence speak through Jin Wong—I wonder if perhaps that death was not the end of Clarity."

"You think Tooloo might be possessed by Clarity?"

Stormsong nodded slowly. "Something like that."

Riki had come looking for Tinker to see if Impatience had marked her as his Chosen One as Jin Wong had been lost to the tengu. Without their Chosen One, they were lacking a way to speak to their guardian spirit. Riki said it would be a red mark on her breast, roughly above her heart. Tinker had never seen Tooloo naked; the old elf could have such a mark without Tinker knowing.

Riki seemed to think Tinker might have been marked because Impatience had touched her—if nearly chomping off her hand could count as "touching."

"Vision was born after Clarity had died." Tinker pointed out. "Clarity couldn't have marked Vision as her Chosen before being killed."

Stormsong clicked her tongue. "I do not know how she could have accomplished it, but if any being could leap her spirit into a random child made from her genetics—Clarity could. And would. Ruthlessness is one of hallmarks of my mother's bloodline. Arrogance is another."

"I have never considered you arrogant," Tinker said.

"I am my father's child in that regard," Stormsong said. "But there was something that my mother once said to me. She said that her mother was more dragon than elf, and as such, did not act in the best interest of our race."

"Is that why your mother betrayed Vision?" Tinker said.

"I believe it might be. I had heard whispers of how she had helped the Skin Clan bind her own mother and gone to confront her about it. She told me not to be stupid about the motives of people who whisper loudly enough to be heard. I pressed her for an answer. She told me then how her mother had been made differently from the others of our caste—more dragon than elf—or more exactly, a dragon in elf form."

"Tooloo doesn't seem that different from other elves to me." Aside from the fact that she lived alone, seemed to hate the *domana*, resented the *sekasha* for their part in establishing peace between the clans, lied as easily as she breathed, and never pranced around nude in communal baths...

Okay, maybe Tooloo wasn't like all the other elves that Tinker knew. She didn't seem very draconic either. Tinker's sample size on dragons, though, was Impatience (whose name suggested that he was hyperactive) and Providence (who was dead, or perhaps more accurately, mostly dead).

Considering her upbringing, Tinker didn't feel like she was a good judge of "normal" humans either.

"I took my mother at her word because I had not met any dragons," Stormsong said. "I wonder now..."

"About what?" Tinker asked once Stormsong trailed off to silence.

Stormsong sighed, shaking her head. "It is difficult to explain. There is so much my mother has kept from me that I am not even sure where to begin. I have been digging through the layers of debris like an archeologist, looking for the broken pottery to piece together. My mother has never done anything on whim. Every step she has taken is to move our people—all of our people—whether they wanted it or not—toward some idea of a perfect world that my mother has. She planned the Rebellion, ended the Clan Wars, chose who would be our first King, arranged the marriage between Wolf's parents and convinced them to have child after child until one was born with the ability to call both *esva*."

"It was not without dissension. Those who tried to block her found themselves either plowed over or neatly dodged." Stormsong leaned close to whisper, "Some think that Howling's assassination was to keep the Clan War from ending, but it neatly put Longwind into power, who supported my mother's plan."

"You think Pure Radiance had Howling killed?" Tinker whispered once she remembered that he was Windwolf's grandfather.

"No, but she should have been able to prevent it. Such plotting creates massive vibrations in the fabric of the dream world. Howling supported peace between the clans but he did not favor the idea of one clan ruling over the others—unless it was the Wind Clan. He hoped Wraith Arrow would win over Cinder. Howling considered Otter Dance an abomination and had been against Longwind taking her as his First. He would have refused to cooperate in producing a single half-breed on the chance that it could use both *esva*, let alone producing ten such children."

It took Tinker a moment to sort through the names of people that she'd never met but were now essentially her in-laws. Otter Dance was Pony's mother who was half Stone Clan and half Wind Clan. She was First to Longwind, who was Windwolf's father. "So Pure Radiance let Howling die?"

Stormsong shook her head. "I have no proof of it, just suspicions. She would know that someone within Howling's household plotted against him. It was more convenient for Howling to die than to warn him. My mother would do anything to steer us in the direction that she desires the world to go. For that reason, I always ignored the whispers about my birth. I knew that I was never born from a forbidden love or a drunken mistake. My mother carefully and coldly planned my birth—but I never knew why. At least, not until Pony was born. On his naming day, I began to suspect what might be the shape of her plan."

"Which is?"

"There is an ancient myth or a prophecy or perhaps a combination of the two. The goddess of war is said to ride a storm horse across the skies, its hooves the sound of rolling thunder. With her fly the Storm Winds, a thousand winged furies that sing in exaltation. In the goddess's wake, like a flood or a tornado, the landscape is changed by her passage. My mother named Pony: Storm Horse Galloping on Wind."

Stormsong's true name was Singing Storm Wind, which could be seen as one of the singing furies. It would be odd coincidence except Pure Radiance had named both Tinker's First and Second.

"Your mother thinks I'm the Goddess of War?"

Stormsong clicked her tongue. "I do not know. You do a surprising amount of collateral damage for your size."

Tinker frowned at Stormsong. She really wished people would stop saying that! It wasn't like she planned to do so much damage.

"I am sorry, *domi.*" Stormsong dipped her head in an abbreviated bow. "I do not know what my mother believes nor what she hopes to accomplish. I have asked her many times, nearly every day when I was very young. I can only guess. I think that she realized that the Skin Clan had escaped beyond her ability to root them out by fleeing to Earth and Onihida. She knew that they would return someday with the power of two worlds at their beck and call. I think she might have expanded on a myth in order to keep the others of her caste aware that they should be on the lookout for 'the goddess' and her entourage."

Tinker stared at her, slightly horrified by the implication. "You make it seem as if I was fated to be with you and Pony."

"Me, Pony, Cloudwalker, Rainlily and even Wolf," Stormsong said. "There is a second prophecy about the goddess marching across the battlefield with a wolf beside her. Cloudwalker's true name is Walks Among Storm Clouds Looming on Wind, and Rainlily's is Lily That Sways in a Storm Wind."

Once upon a time at Aum Renau, Tinker had been introduced to all the *sekasha* en masse. Since then, she'd been using the English nicknames for many of them. She hadn't realized that of the *sekasha* she had chosen for her Hand, all but one had names that incorporated storms.

"What about Little Egret?"

"I believe he was named by a temple priestess who did not

see his destiny. At least, I hope that is why and not because he is doomed to an early death."

"But—but—but—you're all hundreds of years older than me—and I was a hermit outside of my team. And I wasn't even sure you liked me at first."

"I was still angry with my mother," Stormsong said. "I wanted her to tell me what grand plan she had for me. I think that I am beginning to understand—or at least, I would like to think I am. I would have never agreed to go with Sparrow if I knew that she planned to kill Wolf. If any other *sekasha* spotted your sisters creeping around the museum, they would have killed them but I knew that I needed to let them go. Wolf needed to be badly hurt and to have you save him the way you did, or he would not have fallen in love with you. You needed Pony to be beside you at the oni encampment or your plan would have failed. So many things I would not have allowed. My heart would not have allowed it.

"I suppose it has come in handy that my Second can see the future," Tinker said.

"I think it is something more fundamental. Something that Wolf, I, and Pony share—we're all mutts. Remember how I said that the merchants hid away their connection with Earth? It is because most of our people see outsiders as dangerous—even repulsive. Most of the Fire Clan thinks the Stone Clan people are too short and brown and ugly. Stone Clan calls Fire Clan 'giraffes' and thinks they're too tall and ungainly and ugly. The elves in Pittsburgh are the ones who were willing to follow Wolf despite the fact he is half Fire and half Wind. Wolf was the only one who was willing to offer to me because he thought of us alike—two mutts that everyone despised."

"So by design, all the elves in Pittsburgh are the ones most willing to deal with humans without the automatic fear of the other?"

"Considering my mother, yes, by design."

Tinker handed Stormsong her tablet. "I think Tooloo gave me some secret message in this but I can't figure it out." She explained what she thought the chess pieces represented. "At least I think Tooloo was trying to tell me something. Maybe I'm wrong. Maybe she was just messing with my head."

"I do not think you are wrong. Dream symbology is highly

personal. Your mother borrowed heavily from stories of a girl being lost in an alien world. Alice in Wonderland. Dorothy in Oz. If Vision is like my mother, then she has been training you in the symbology all your life without your knowing it."

"So, if I think the Heinz bottle is probably the city, then it probably is Pittsburgh—because that's how I think of it?"

"Yes," Stormsong said.

"Windwolf is Superman?" Tinker pointed to her bishop. "Or Jin Wong?"

Stormsong winced. "A better question would be: Did Tooloo ever teach you anything about the chess pieces that wasn't cut and dried?"

Tinker blew raspberries at the question. "Playing with her was always about the chessmen acting like they were real people and not game pieces. She'd play both sides at the same time, having them randomly go off on adventures. In a typical game, one queen would fall in love with a knight..."

"Every game?" Stormsong said.

Tinker paused to think. Had any game ever not had that scenario? "Yes, every game. One queen would fall for a knight on the other side. Sometimes my queen. Sometimes her's. Wait. We would switch sides since white usually goes first." Tinker took the tablet back to double-check the photos. Yes, one of the monkeys stood next to the white king. She hadn't played with Tooloo since she was very young. She considered all the games that she could remember. "It was always the white queen that fell in love. I hated playing white because of that. The outcome varies wildly. Sometimes the king orders a pawn to execute his queen. Sometimes she leaves the board, taking the knight with her. Sometimes the knight kills her. Sometimes she just captures the knight and holds him prisoner until the end of the game."

"So," Stormsong said, "one of the other side has fallen in love with one of your allies. The Skin Clan's 'king' does not condone of the affair—nor does your knight return the fervor of the white queen's love. The queen's action and your knight's fate will matter greatly in how the game plays out."

"Oh, you've got to be kidding me! The white queen is one of Chloe's sisters? Who the hell is the knight?"

"You've probably never met him nor is he related to you by blood. The further removed a person is from you, the more generic their dream symbol becomes. What else did Tooloo have the pieces do during your games?"

"Everything. Anything," Tinker complained. "The pawns were the worst. They all went any which way Tooloo wanted them to go. Sometimes they would just leave the board and she'd say that they got bored. The bishops could get wonky but only sometimes. Let me think." Tinker closed her eyes and tried to remember the things that reduced her to tears during the games with Tooloo. "One time my bishop assassinated my king—but I can't remember if I was playing black or white at the time. I really hope I was white."

"What about the rooks?" Stormsong said.

"I have not a clue." Tinker eyed the black rook substitutes. "The rooks always behaved themselves. I'm not sure what these chickens as rooks mean. Tooloo has lots of chickens so she can sell eggs. She easily has over a hundred laying hens at any one time. Her place seems really small from the front of the shop, but it goes all the way up the hillside and back for almost half a mile. She's got all sorts of gardens and orchards and cow pastures with bird coops scattered all among them. A lot of her layers are Rhode Island Reds or little bantams. Those she keeps near her shop so it's easy to collect their eggs. She has Jersey Giants and Freedom Rangers for meat. Their coop is farther out. She has a lot of random other birds: turkeys, ducks, guinea fowl, quail, doves, and a pair of very mean gray geese."

She was rambling, hoping to stumble over some meaning hidden deep in her brain.

"Her place sounds almost like an enclave," Stormsong said.

"One without any walls, but yeah, a lot like one." Not that Tinker realized it growing up. Places like Poppymeadows opened only their dining rooms to humans, barring them from exploring deeper into the walled-off enclave. She and Oilcan had only been to the enclaves a few times as teenagers, spending their own dime to celebrate some special occasion. She never realized that each one was a self-sufficient farm. Tooloo would know that Tinker now had access to enclaves. "Tooloo's place is the only farm that I've ever been to. I know there's lots of others in the South Hills. They supply little ma-and-pa stores all over the city with eggs and milk."

"She would not choose a place that you've never been to,"

Stormsong said. "Symbology is gossamer in nature, it is the stuff of dreams. It is what your gift uses to communicate to the sleeping part of your brain."

Tinker stared at the picture of the rook. What could it mean? What did chickens stand for in her brain? "Chicken. Chick. Chick. Chick. Chicken! Bok-caw! Bok-caw!"

Thus she was making chicken noises when she climbed out of the Rolls-Royce in front of the Wyverns.

7: EVEN MONEY

"Why are we stopping here?" Olivia asked Tommy Chang as she gingerly climbed down out of the cab of the possibly stolen EIA cargo truck. She turned her wide-eyed innocence toward Tommy, looking all of thirteen. He wasn't sure how old Olivia was except that she'd dodged Tinker's question of "how old are you," which usually meant that the person was underage. Olivia seemed to be a normal teenage girl, somewhere between thirteen and seventeen, in a modest gingham sundress and sensible shoes.

Tommy had only known Olivia for a few short hours. He didn't have a lot of experience with teenage girls, but he'd grown sure that Olivia wasn't a "normal" girl.

She'd turned up at Poppymeadows while Tinker was holding a war council. She'd seen Tommy's cat ears. She overheard him talking about his father, Lord Tomtom. She realized that he was half-oni. When they collided later on the North Side, Olivia understood that the royal marines might kill Tommy on sight. They'd killed every half-oni that they found up to that point. It mattered much that Olivia protected Tommy without hesitation. She told the elves that Tommy was to be trusted—that he wasn't to be harmed.

Nor had she done it because she was softhearted. Olivia had hunted Jonnie Be Good down, coldly shot the man in the leg, and then questioned him as he lay bleeding on the ground. She followed that up by leading the attack on Midas Shipyard. Tommy now knew that Olivia was smart, cautious, ruthless, and fiercely loyal to those she considered her friends. With the twenty royal marines in the back of the truck at her beck and call, she was a force to be reckoned with.

Tommy didn't know, though, how much he could trust her with his entire family. He was going to point her in the direction of Oakland and send her on her way. First, though, he was going to get what he wanted off her truck. "I need Knickknack."

He wasn't going to go through all the effort to save the boy and then let Olivia take him away. He should have just put the kid on the back of his hoverbike. He'd grab Knickknack and then shoo Olivia away.

"Me?" Knickknack's voice came from behind the tarp covering the bed of the big truck.

"Yes, you!" Tommy called as he walked toward the back of the military cargo truck stuffed full of royal marines, rescued prostitutes, and one Irish girl who worked for the EIA.

Tommy hoped that the rest of the circus would go away and let him deal with his family. The female prostitutes, though, spilled out after the boy. They jumped up and down, clutching each other, screaming with might have been excitement or fear. Tommy didn't know or understand. Why were they screaming?

"No. No. Just Knickknack," Tommy said but the royal marines were already following. They, at least, had good cause. Some of them were hurt and needed the space and light to tend to their wounds. They eyed the screaming females with the same bewilderment that Tommy felt.

"Why here?" Olivia repeated as she followed Tommy to the back.

"Red!" Peanut Butter Pie shouted. "O! M! G! You rock, girl!'

The prostitutes launched themselves at Olivia, squealing loudly. Why did human females scream like that when they were excited? The females of Tommy's family either had it beaten out of them at a young age or never had anything to celebrate with such abandon. Tommy wasn't sure which. At least Olivia was calm and quiet. If he just left, maybe Olivia would take the hint and go.

While the loud chaos swirled around Olivia, Tommy dragged Knickknack through the bronze front doors of the William Penn Hotel. The massive crystal chandeliers were still all lit up for their paying guests. Their light reflected off the freshly scrubbed marble floors. The odor of a lemon-scented cleaning solution hung in the air.

Tommy paused at the door to scan the hotel's lobby.

He had been afraid that some of his family who couldn't pass as human might be in view. He had also been worried that the area might be filled with random strangers hanging out, waiting for rooms to be cleaned. He'd expected his people guarding the doors and someone manning the desk. There was no one in the lobby.

Where did everyone go? Had the oni already hit it? Everything seemed too neat and clean and orderly.

He reached out with his mind, seeing if he could pick up someone hidden.

Yes, there was someone ducked down behind the main desk. He couldn't tell who it was: family or foe.

"I can see you," Tommy called.

"Tommy!" Trixie popped up from behind the desk just as the royal marines spilled in behind him. She dropped back into hiding. "Tommy?"

The marines seemed to have followed him out of sheer curiosity. They gazed about the lobby, pointing and exclaiming over the fancy coffered ceiling, the big chandeliers, the fancy area rugs and the grand piano. Trixie could pass as human even buck naked; it should be safe for her to show herself.

"It's okay," Tommy said with more confidence than he felt. He dragged Knickknack to the main desk. "They're with me. It's a long story. Where is everyone?"

Trixie rose up to peer over the counter. "Alita said that there's some kind of trouble. She ran through here, talking too fast for me to understand what's wrong. You know how she is. She's upstairs waking Mokoto and Babe."

"Mokoto?" Knickknack echoed with surprise.

Tommy gave the boy a shake to keep him quiet. Olivia and the prostitutes spilled into the lobby behind the marines. Olivia was back to looking about thirteen, doe-eyed and lost, unsure what to do to regain control of the situation. The rescued females seemed unwilling to let Olivia out of their sight but they were still squealing and talking loudly over whatever Olivia was trying to say. Tommy was starting to think "loud" was the normal volume for the streetwalkers.

Trixie ignored the chaos to finish her report. "Housecleaning moved up to the tenth floor in case we get more guests. Eighth floor is full. Ninth floor is half filled. We have over forty guests now."

Tommy wondered if he killed any of their "guests" at the shipyard. He decided that he probably hadn't. All the workers at the shipyard had been lowly grunts in sweat-soaked work clothes. The dead men probably had gone the cheap and reasonable route of finding an abandoned house and squatting in it. The businessmen who had been in the lobby earlier had worn expensive silk suits and reeked of cologne so badly that he could still smell traces of it.

"Half of our guests want room service," Trixie finished up her report. "So anyone who isn't cleaning or babysitting is on kitchen duty."

Tommy's sensitive ears caught the soft ding of the elevator down the hall. The doors slid open to Babe in mid-sentence.

"...not following this at all." Babe ducked as he stepped off the elevator. He was yawning deeply, barely awake, but armed for trouble. He had all his various weapons, from his sawed-off shotgun in his hand to the machete strapped across his back. "Who are these cell people?"

"That's what I want to know too," Mokoto murmured from Babe's shadow.

All of Aunt Amy's kids were small fierce creatures that looked cute and harmless. Mokoto leaned into his cuteness; he was wearing a cutoff jeans jacket over a white-on-white polka dot mini-dress with pink plaid sneakers. Despite the skimpy outfit, he was tucking away his arsenal of small, deadly weapons. He probably was only wearing the short jacket to hide his shoulder holster.

Mokoto's little sister, Alita, wore a knee-length black hoodie to hide away all her cuteness. She absently kicked Babe with her chunky combat boots. Even with a thick three-inch sole, her foot looked tiny next to Babe's. "Cell means a group, like roommates or band members. We're supposed to only know the people in our cell so that the oni can't figure out who is part of the Resistance and, more importantly, who the leaders are."

Zippo ducked out of the elevator last, a younger, smaller version of Babe. He nodded silently to what Alita was saying. Apparently he was part of whatever Alita had gotten mixed up in. He had his ironwood staff across his back and his twin batons at his sides.

"It probably works well on most people," Alita continued, talking at her normal breakneck speed. "If you hadn't just spent the last five years of your life working concession stands all over Pittsburgh—the racetrack and all the little street fairs and Oktoberfest and Midsummer Eve's Faire—you probably don't know who hangs with who and how some of the bigger families are connected. But if you have, like me, it's all kind of obvious—not that I'm going to go around telling anyone. I don't really understand why they call it the Resistance. It's some human thing that happened long ago. I'm not sure I understand it—something to do with the villains of that one Indiana Jones movie—but I always thought all of that was made up because magic doesn't work on Earth. I can't ask too many questions because then the others in our cell get all 'Are you kidding? Didn't you learn this in school? The Second World War!' I stopped asking but it leaves us kind of in the dark on some stuff. Which world is the second one? Earth? Then which one was the first world? Anyhoo, there's this place called Paris that filled up with the guys who were face-melted. The Resistance did all sorts of tricksy-tricksy stuff right under their noses. It's hush-hush James Bond kind of spy stuff."

"Oookay." Babe obviously was struggling to follow what Alita was spilling out in her normal hundred-miles-per-hour way.

"You two joined this spy organization?" Mokoto cut through to the heart of his little sister's information.

"Not really," Alita said. "More milked it for info by pretending to join. We were double agents. Triple agents maybe."

"You shouldn't have gotten Zippo messed up in this." Mokoto rapped his knuckles on his little sister's head. "You're supposed to keep him safe, not get him into trouble."

"I told them Zippo's name was Goemon and that I was Fujiko Mine. I wore my tallest stilettos with a wig and a double-d breastplate. Most of the people in our cell are just kids and they really look at the world at the surface level. They totally bought the idea that I was just doing everything as a lark and that I dragged Zippo in for fun. They kept saying we needed to take it more seriously. They have no idea. They're just babes in the woods."

"It was fun," Zippo said quietly.

Babe gave his little brother a sympathetic look, as he fully understood what it was to be partnered up with someone who could think rings around him. He was clever enough not to say anything aloud.

Knickknack noticed the group for the first time as they reached the lobby. "Mokoto!"

"See!" Babe pointed at the boy as Mokoto froze with surprise. "I told you Tommy would be able to find the Undefended."

Mokoto wasn't the type who cried easily. He struggled to keep all emotions off his face as he closed the distance. He caught hold of Knickknack and hugged him tightly, fingers digging into the boy's back with the strength of his feelings.

"I'm sorry," Knickknack said. "I should have listened to you. I've been stupid all summer."

"Yes," Mokoto growled into Knickknack's shoulder. "You have been."

"Where's Bingo?" Tommy asked the room.

"He's still out," Trixie said simply, giving a meaningful look to Olivia, the royal marines and various others wandering about the lobby. "He's doing what you told him to do."

Tommy had told Bingo to find a safe place to move their family—assuming that Tommy could get them to abandon the hotel.

"Where's Spot?" Trixie asked.

It took Tommy a moment to remember why he should know where Spot was. "Shit! I forgot. He's still with Oilcan's kids."

"In Oakland? Oh, that's not good." Alita took out her phone and whispered a curse at what the screen said. "Very not good!"

"What is it?" Tommy asked as Trixie said, "Is that your spy network?"

"Yeah, we're using messages boards for general updates. It's been going insane since the scouts started to report in. There was a first wave of black willows east of Oakland but the tengu took them out. A second wave of oni warriors was spotted on Herrs Island, heading up Liberty Avenue. *Tā māde niǎo!* We've been hearing about some kind of mega genetic spell bomb that the oni were holding in reserve. Command is saying that the oni are going to pull the trigger and take out the *domana*."

Tinker had just learned about the box that morning. Had the Resistance known about it before that or did the information spread like wildfire from that meeting? The tengu could have connections with the militia.

Olivia cried out. "What? The *domana*?"

"Oh, shit." Alita whispered as she seemed to notice the additional people for the first time. "What the hell are they doing here?"

She meant the royal marines.

Olivia pushed forward, focused intently on Alita. "What did you say?"

If they'd been out on the street, Alita probably wouldn't have given a straight answer, but they were "at work" and their aunts had beaten politeness into them.

"The oni have this spell bomb," Alita said even faster than normal. "It uses dragon bits and pieces to transform large numbers of people with one cast. It's like a magical nuke. It's how the oni merged the tengu's ancestors with crows, making it so the tengu lay eggs and have hollow bones and all the bird stuff. They might look like people but their insides aren't much different from pigeons." Alita quoted one of Lord TomTom's favorite sayings. "Anyhoo, the oni are going to use the bomb to take out the *domana*. Like—right now."

Olivia covered her mouth as if to keep in a scream. Her eyes were wide with horror. "Forest Moss? Tinker? Her cousin? The Viceroy? Will they be killed?"

Her whispered fear spread cold tendrils through Tommy's gut. His family had been outed as monster spawn to the entire city, protected only by Windwolf and Oilcan. If the *domana* all died...

Would Jewel Tear die too?

Alita was shaking her head, still focused on her phone's screen. "Texas Holdem is saying that the oni will just break the *domana*'s ability to call the Spell Stones. The spell won't kill them."

"They won't be able to cast spells?" Olivia whispered in horror. "Forest Moss and others are fighting the oni army in the woods! They'll be helpless."

If all of Alita's information was right, Oakland was about to be royally screwed. Forge and Jewel Tear had been left behind to protect it. If they were as helpless as the *domana* on the front line, then there would be no power hitters protecting the enclaves.

"Who is Texas Holdem?" Tommy asked. "And how do they know what the oni are going to do?"

Alita shrugged. "The message board is the least secure forum that the Resistance uses, so it requires you to use a code name. Texas Holdem could be anyone in the city. I don't know if they really know anything for sure or if they're talking out of their butt."

"What is the little one saying?" one of the marines asked the Irish girl in Elvish as the conversation had been in English up to this point. They looked concerned at the dismay and fear on Olivia's face.

The Irish girl started to fumble through a very condensed version of the discussion, focusing only on the important parts. Olivia stared inwardly as she whispered, "What should I do? What can I do?"

Tommy couldn't answer the questions because he wasn't sure either. Kajo was dancing around the elves the same way he had danced around Lord Tomtom.

The glittering crystal chandeliers went dark.

Tommy pointed up at the lights. "Did someone just turn those off or did the power go out?"

Alita hissed another Chinese curse. "I lost signal. I was at full bars."

Mokoto pulled his phone out of his jacket pocket. "Shit. The oni must have cut the phones as well as the power."

Tommy growled with frustration. His family was scattered throughout the hotel with all of the toddlers and infants way up on the seventeenth floor. There was no way to communicate with the babysitters other than to run the stairs. Nor would he know what message to send upstairs—he had no idea where to move everyone so that they would be safe. He didn't even know in which direction the oni were attacking.

"Mokoto, get everyone off the lower floors until Bingo comes back," Tommy ordered. "Be sure to hit the kitchen, the laundry room, and the swimming pool. Also check that no one was on the elevators when they stopped working."

"There might be a backup generator," Knickknack said. "On Earth, most hotels are required to have one."

"We'll get the generator running, Tommy, if there's one." Mokoto caught Knickknack's arm and dragged him off toward the hotel's kitchen.

Tommy turned to his other cousins. "Trixie, go tell housekeeping to go back to their bedrooms."

That would get all of his family on the highest floor. Hopefully, Mokoto was right that the oni wouldn't climb seventeen floors to regain control over his family.

"What about our guests?" Trixie said. "They might be roaming the halls, pissed off that the power is out."

"So they'll be pissed!" Tommy snapped. "Tell the idiots to get back to their rooms or pack up and leave. They're welcome to find someplace else while the oni are attacking!"

Still, idiots would be idiots. They might take advantage of the chaos to do whatever they wanted, including raping any girl that they stumbled across in the dark. Trixie was armed and dangerous but she didn't look like it. She was another one of Aunt Amy's cute, small, and deadly kids. Dealing with idiots might slow Trixie down. "Babe, go with her."

Even an idiot wouldn't pick a fight with Babe and his six foot three inches of pure muscle.

"What does this mean for us?" Zippo asked Tommy quietly. "What with Oilcan being *domana*? Are we going to be okay if he can't do shit?"

How the hell would Tommy know?

Lord Tomtom had told him more than once that the oni's end goal was to kill or capture all the elves in Pittsburgh. His father had been impatient with Kajo's lack of action. The oni had the numbers and magic to take down the enclaves. Kajo refused to act because the *domana* would easily win back any ground that the oni won. Even if they took out Windwolf, there would be royal forces like Prince True Flame and the Harbingers within a week's travel. Pittsburgh was just the first step in a global conquest. Kajo was willing to be patient.

With the *domana* rendered powerless, it would be a simple thing to storm the enclaves. If the oni wiped out the elves, life in Pittsburgh would become impossible for his family. They were safe only because Windwolf, Tinker, and Oilcan were willing to go to bat for them. There was a full continent of elves a couple thousand miles away and when they reached the city, the gloves would be off. No matter who won the ultimate battle, it would be bad news for the half-oni.

"Command was issuing walkie-talkies to some cell leaders." Alita took a headset out of her pocket. "They didn't have enough to go around as they were rare as hen's teeth even before Tinker yanked the gate out of orbit. I figured that Team Providence might have left gear out at the racecourse after you banned them, so I went and pillaged their lockers."

Jin Wong had executed all of Team Providence so it wasn't surprising that their gear was left behind. The racing teams were the only ones who had voice-activated headsets. Police, paramedics, and others used handheld sets.

"Command says Tinker *domi* is heading to Oakland," Alita reported as she continued to scroll through messages saved on her phone. "Forge and Jewel Tear are out of commission—whatever that means. *Cào!*"

"What? Is Oilcan okay?" Tommy asked as Alita continued to curse in Chinese.

Alita shook her head. "There's no word on Oilcan but the last message posted on the boards was from Texas Holdem. They said that the oni has doped out Storm One's location and is sending a goon squad that way."

"Who is Storm One?" Tommy asked.

"Duff Kryskill." Alita tapped her headset. "He's running the radio communication for the Resistance. With the phones down, radio is the only way we're able to coordinate. Texas Holdem posted seconds before the power went out, so the people checking the board at that exact second—like me—are the only ones who saw it. Command ordered all cells to Oakland and Duff is over on Mount Washington or Mount Oliver—someplace. I'm not sure exactly where. I don't know if anyone else was checking the boards for new posts—everyone else is in the middle of a combat zone."

"Mount Oliver?" Olivia echoed. "Duff is running the Resistance out of the bakery?"

"Say what?" Alita said.

"I worked at the Jenny Lee Bakery for a while," Olivia said. "End of July and the beginning of August. I started at four in the morning, dividing and shaping bread. Duff was my shift manager. He's related somehow to the people who own the bakery. He's been working there for years, usually in the morning before he went to high school. He's got a little cubbyhole office way in the back by itself. The bakery has all sorts of backup power systems so it can keep operating through a blackout. It would be a good base for a communication center."

"But does Texas Holdem actually know what they're talking about?" Tommy asked.

Alita spread her hands to indicate that she had no idea. "They did seem to know that Forge and Jewel Tear would be out of the fight an hour before the fighting kicked off."

"Aoife," Olivia said. "I know the Director told you to stay with me, but it would be safer for you to stay here with Tommy's people. I'm going to the bakery. I'm not sure what I'm going to do—I'm not even sure I know how to get there from here—but I need to do something."

"*Mauryah!*" the Irish girl cried in surprise. "I'm coming with you. I'm not going to miss out because someone thinks I'm some wee colleen that needs protecting."

Alita kicked at Tommy's foot. "Can I go with them? I can get them up to Mount Oliver. I don't want to sit here waiting to see if we're going back to the way it used to be. I'd rather die fighting."

Zippo nodded, silently indicating that he wanted to go with Alita for the same reason.

"Fine, you can go." Tommy pointed at Alita's three-inch soles. "Can you run in those?"

Alita rolled her eyes but jogged slowly in place to demonstrate that she could.

"Fast enough to outrun lesser blood oni?" Tommy pressed.

Alita blew out her breath and kicked off the clunky shoes. She pulled flats out of her hoodie's pocket and put them on.

Tommy turned to Zippo. "You've got a gun?"

Lord Tomtom never provided the half-oni with any weapons. He probably suspected that the half-oni would use them against his warriors. Over the years, Tommy had gathered what he could. Hunting rifles. Shotguns. Compound bows and carbon arrows. Machetes. Modified broom handles. Butcher knives. Bingo and his brothers kept to weapons that played to their brute strength like the machetes and staffs. The pistols were in short supply and usually went to their smaller cousins.

"I've got a twenty-two," Zippo said unhappily, lifting his shirt to show off a kidney holster. It was a small-caliber pistol with not much stopping power but it was better than nothing.

"Good enough." Tommy knew that Alita had a Glock pistol hidden somewhere on her. Mokoto and his cute but fierce younger siblings had gotten first dibs on the smaller weapons. They could be trusted to know when to use lethal force.

Tommy turned to Olivia. "This is Alita and Zippo. They're my cousins. Let them ride shotgun with you. They'll give you directions to Mount Oliver from here."

The back of the truck—packed with royal marines—might be dangerous for Zippo. He didn't completely pass as human, up-close and personal. The boy was shy, though, and might not ride in the front without Alita.

"What are you going to do?" Alita asked.

"I'm going to run out to Oakland," Tommy said. "I'm going to try to find out what's going on with Oilcan, and fetch Spot."

8: A GRAVE MISTAKE

Normally, Law liked Allegheny Cemetery. Her grandparents used to bring her to the graveyard after church. The Monroes had moved into the general area back in 1829 when they purchased the farm that would later be Monroeville. Her branch of the family had moved into Pittsburgh proper before the turn of the twentieth century, exchanging farm work for railroading. She and her grandparents would stroll around the cemetery, visiting the graves of her great-grandparents, great-aunts, great-uncles, and distant cousins. All her memories of the cemetery were of sunshine, green leaves, and a sense of belonging to the land. It was one of the many reasons she never considered moving to Earth.

As dusk neared and a storm thundered in the distance, though, the graveyard was a really creepy place. There were no streetlights on the cemetery grounds. Shadows gathered into growing pools of darkness that could hide any number of enemies. The trees tossed in the wind, shedding autumn leaves that skittered loudly across the narrow paved road that wound its way through the cemetery. The white noise would mask any warning sound of approaching oni.

Law stood in the bed of her Dodge Power Wagon and peered over the ten-foot-tall fieldstone wall that encircled much of the graveyard. The place was huge: three hundred acres of rolling wooded hills with something like fifteen miles of private paved roads winding their way through the cemetery. What would be the smart thing to do? Beside her, Bare Snow was sulking like a twelve-year-old girl who had been told to eat her peas. Her cheeks were puffed up in full-on pouting indignation.

"We should have just gone after Kajo," Bare Snow whispered, twisting the hem of her camo T-shirt. "Kill him. Mount his head on the wall. That's what Emperor Heaven's Blessing did to Scourge."

"Who?"

"Scourge!" Bare Snow whispered fiercely. "He was the greatest warlord who ever lived. He would swoop in on his ship, the *Blood Frenzy*, and capture cargo ships. He would kill any of the crew who were loyal to their Skin Clan masters and free all of the slaves willing to rebel. He used the loot to set up hidden island forts from which we could harass shipping on every ocean and sea. The Water Clan exists because of Scourge."

Kajo had had too many oni warriors and wargs traveling with him. It would have been pure suicide to "swoop in" and kill Kajo. That attempt would have ended in a bloody failure.

Law shook her head. "Kajo wasn't our target. We're after the egg thingies."

Their chase had taken the entire day, bouncing all over Pittsburgh, to end up at the two-hundred-year-old cemetery. It was a brilliant hiding place. It was near the heart of the city, yet there was little chance that someone would try to squat in the "empty" buildings. Pittsburghers might be willing to take on steel spinners and strangle vines but were weirdly terrified of ghosts. After her grandparents had died, even Law never visited the graveyard.

"The *nactka*." Bare Snow supplied the name of the egg-shaped devices. "Though that is not what my mother called them." Her sulking grew deeper. "I do not remember the name exactly. It was a silly name like 'put a cork in it' or something equally childish. The wood sprites invented them while they were still slaves of Emperor Heaven's Blessing. The devices are one of the twenty lesser-forbidden magics outlawed at the end of the Rebellion. My mother told me if I ever stumbled across one, that the holder was sure to be Skin Clan."

"That might have been true this morning," Law said. "Considering everything that we've seen, I don't think that the people that have them now are Skin Clan."

"Who are they?"

"I'm not sure. To make that puffball trap, they would have to know ancient forbidden magic. Considering how many *sekasha* are running around the city, most elves wouldn't touch it with a ten-foot pole. It could have been Kajo getting rid of his Skin Clan masters in the confusion of war. Maybe. Maybe not. Kajo has stayed hidden all these years. That trap feels far too messy for him. It feels more like a double cross against Kajo. Whoever took the *nactka* knew where and, more importantly, when to hit. We weren't that far behind the pack bearers—that was a very narrow window to hit."

"Inside job." Bare Snow whispered one of the English phrases she had learned from watching television with the Bunny children.

A tall fieldstone wall surrounded the parklike grounds, screening the cemetery from the casual passerby and part-time spy. Law didn't think it extended entirely around the graveyard but her knowledge of the backside of the property was hazy. There were other exits than the big castlelike main gate but she'd never seen them actually open. Their wrought iron gates were always chained shut. Her grandparents did say that they used to be open but everything had changed when Pittsburgh was shifted to Elfhome.

Widget had seen the truck go into the cemetery. She hadn't called to say it had come out. It meant that the yellow box truck was still inside—somewhere. The three hundred acres contained lots of places to hide. Business offices. Maintenance buildings. The old groundskeeper residence. A chapel. Crypts. Mausoleums. It was like a little village of the dead.

If the mysterious thief just wanted to hide the *nactka*, stashing them in a crypt would be simple and clever. If the murderous thug was using the cemetery as a camp, then the groundskeeper residence or the business offices would be more logical hiding places.

"Let's split up." Law pointed at the maintenance compound tucked in the northwest corner. "I'll search those buildings." She indicated the winding road leading into the graveyard from the main entrance with the castlelike structures. "Check the—" What was Elvish for chapel? "That stone building there by the gate. Then there's that big building on the hill."

If she remembered correctly, it was filled with the concrete vaults that were buried into the ground into which coffins were then placed.

"Then there's some little stone buildings beyond it." Law

suspected that Elvish didn't have words for *crypts* or *mausoleums*. Elves didn't bury their dead; they cremated them under the open sky, returning the souls to the god that oversaw rebirth. Bare Snow had been both horrified and pleased when she found out that Sparrow had been given a human burial.

"We can meet up there." Law pointed at a distant crypt that would be the end of Bare Snow's counterclockwise search and her own clockwise one.

Law's reasoning was that the maintenance compound might have a human security system while the crypts were surrounded by dead leaves. Bare Snow could move silently and invisibly through the graveyard while Law dealt with cameras and sensors.

"Okey-dokey!" Bare Snow started to strip off her clothes.

Law slung her rifle across her back and then carefully lowered herself down the other side of the wall. A running retreat was going to be difficult but there wasn't a better way.

The maintenance compound had half a dozen structures, separated from the rest of the cemetery via a tan brick wall. She remembered being fascinated by the buildings when she was a kid. The six buildings were different shapes and sizes but all had been built a hundred years ago in the same style out of the same tan brick. They were like nothing she'd ever seen before but all matched each other. The deep inset windows had sills of thick granite slabs. The lower windows and doors had decorative brick arches. The hipped roofs were slate. The buildings ranged from a narrow garage with eight arched bay doors, to a large possible-barn with second-floor hayloft doors and a mysterious narrow roof ridge inset with windows.

Since her grandparents had scheduled their visits on Sundays after church, there hadn't been any employees moving around the compound, giving clues to what the buildings were actually used for. The garage was self-explanatory although it wasn't clear why the graveyard needed eight vehicle bays. Law recognized the smallest building as a salt shed only after it had been filled with road salt one autumn. What were the other structures used for? Two had what seemed to be haylofts, perhaps left over from when the cemetery used horse-drawn vehicles—or maybe not.

She had always thought that the buildings would make the perfect secret lair. The compound was walled off and isolated, accessible only through a place that few people would want to visit. She had never seen other visitors or employees at the cemetery. Even now, there seemed to be no one around. Someone, though, had been taking care of the grounds: the grass was short and there were no weeds in sight.

Someone had painted elfshine lures all over the maintenance compound. The L-shaped driveway and the interior of the garage bays and salt shed gleamed dimly from the drifting swarm of glowing insects. There didn't seem to be anyone—elf, human, or oni—within earshot.

Law found the yellow box truck backed into the rightmost garage bay. Its engine was still ticking as it cooled down. It had been parked within the garage just minutes before she had first peered over the boundary wall. There were only five inches between the back bumper and the rear wall. Someone was confident in their parking skills. The truck was impossible to unload in its current position. Was everything still inside it?

She took out her flashlight and lifted the back gate up enough to peek into the cargo hold. The truck was empty.

She crouched down in the dark, thinking hard. The murder house was proof that something vital had been on the truck—important enough to kill all the pack bearers and take the truck. Widget had tracked the truck all through town. Law and Bare Snow had watched the pack bearers load it up with food and supplies. None of those supplies had been unloaded at the murder house. The truck had come here, was unloaded first and then had been backed into the garage. Everything on it probably had been moved into one of the nearby buildings.

She still didn't know how the *nactka* were being transported. In several small packages or one large case? There was an entire three-hundred-acre cemetery to search.

Her gut was telling her that now was the time to call in reinforcements. Was her gut feeling strong enough reason to get more people involved? She had no control who Alton would call; he might recruit Yumiko and other *yamabushi*. At that point, there could be a cascade of disasters.

Bare Snow's entire family had a death warrant out on them for the assassination of Howling, Windwolf's grandfather. They had been tricked into it. Bare Snow hadn't even been born at the time. It didn't matter—if the Wind Clan *sekasha* discovered her true identity, they would hunt her down and execute her, just like they did to the rest of her family.

Law had been careful to keep Bare Snow hidden. There were very few people who knew about her. The Bunnies and Ellen McMicking knew a sanitized version of Bare Snow's history. Pat Hershel might remember Bare Snow. Law had filled up at Hershel's Exxon a few hours prior to the June Shutdown and bought some clothes for Bare Snow. Pat could have forgotten by now; it was in the middle of normal Shutdown chaos. Law had been careful not to introduce the young elf to anyone else. If Widget had told her the truth, then not even the Kryskills knew about Bare Snow.

The *yamabushi* had a direct pipeline to the Wind Clan *sekasha* via Tinker *domi*. If they found out about Bare Snow, the tengu might feel honor-bound to tell the elves. It was a risk that Law didn't want to take.

Oktoberfest, though, would have been a blood bath if she hadn't called Alton. Everything Yumiko told Law made the *nactka* sound a hundred times more dangerous than a train full of oni warriors. The smart thing to do might be to get more people involved and then ghost out—let the *yamabushi* deal with the mess alone. She and Bare Snow could go back and raid the food warehouses. That would be safe and profitable.

She pulled out her phone to call Alton.

She didn't have a signal.

"Shit, shit, shit," Law whispered as she waved her phone around, trying to connect to a tower. She had full bar reception at the murder house just a few blocks away. She had considered calling Widget but decided to limit the number of times Duff would know what Law was doing.

While the graveyard didn't have streetlights, there were some on the other side of its boundary wall. She realized for the first time that they had never turned on as dusk deepened into night. She'd been so distracted looking for the enemy that she hadn't noticed earlier that the power was out in the city. The oni must have taken down the cell phone towers and the power grid at the same time. The war had kicked into full swing.

She and Bare Snow were on their own and time was running out.

There was a rustling noise that grew louder and louder. She slipped out the garage bay to scan the surrounding area. The floodgates had opened somewhere. Oni were starting to pour into the cemetery through the main gate. They were coming quietly; she had heard them only because of the sheer numbers involved.

Law swore softly. The oni were going to cut her off from Bare Snow. She better search the maintenance compound as quickly as she could. If she needed to, she could slip over the boundary wall and circle back to her truck.

In the leftmost garage bay was a giant pile of cubed ice, slowly melting in the Indian summer heat, and a hoverbike, its engine still warm. Judging by the small puddle of icy water under the bike's parking studs and the lack of water on its fenders, someone had emptied a large ice chest after the hoverbike had been parked. She was guessing the container was one of the huge YETI hard coolers from the third warehouse.

The next building over was the salt shed. At first she thought it was empty except for a shallow layer of salt covering the floor. On second glance, she noticed that one of the ice chests was sitting against the back wall. It was only visible because of the elfshines gleaming dimly in the tall roofed space. As she stared at it, she noticed that it was actually floating several inches off the floor.

"What the hell?" she whispered.

The oni had a spell running on the all-plastic container. It had rope tie-downs keeping it anchored in place.

She could see someone keeping a hundred pounds of fish in a big cooler. Certainly that's what she did with hers. Making it float? That screamed that the chest contained something much more exotic than dead trout.

A distant muttering of oni from the oncoming troops reminded her that she was running out of time.

She crept into the salt shed. The coarse salt crunched loudly under foot.

She just had to undo the anchors on the ice chest. The magical spell on it, keeping it floating, meant she would be able to float it right over the boundary wall. In. Out. Gone before anyone noticed that the cooler was gone.

There was a flash of light and suddenly she was on the ground, unable to move. It felt like a giant elephant was pressing her to the floor of the salt shed. The gleam, she realized, was a spell activating.

She'd walked into a magical trap.

"Well, that's disappointing," a woman said behind her. "Set up a trap for a ghost and catch a housecat. Pfft. I suppose there's still hope for the ghost—she's here someplace. I'd be careful on how you struggle—the gravity of the situation will only crush you faster."

The woman walked away.

Law lay helpless on the floor, panting. It was hard to breathe, the force pressing down on her was so strong. She might be able to call out but that would only lure Bare Snow into the trap faster.

Could she free herself?

She struggled to stay calm and survey the salt shed.

It was only then that she noticed the puffball sitting in the corner, armed and ready to go off.

9: FLYING THE NEST

"Oh! Oh! They're doing it again!" Jillian yelped as she leapt out of the casting circle.

"Jilly!" Louise cried in surprise and fear as her twin left the invisible protection of their shield spell.

Waves of tengu adults had been leaving Haven all day, responding to mounting emergencies in Pittsburgh. The first had left before dawn to search for Dufae's spell-locked box. After that, the crow-winged warriors flew out to fight black willows. Toward the end of the day, it seemed like the sky was constantly filled with black wings as adult after adult headed into battle.

It meant that the twins had been able to work unquestioned, even as they pulled in more and more of the teenage tengu children for help. In the end, she and Jillian had gathered all the tengu children of Haven within the protective circle, unsure what exactly the oni magic might do or who it would be aimed at.

Louise couldn't normally see or feel magic as it was invisible to the naked eye but when it built up to a dangerous level, it glowed purple. Thus, she hadn't felt the oni attack spell hit but she had seen it crawl across the domed surface of their protective shield like enraged lightning. Judging by the whimpers of fear from the younger kids, the tengu had also seen it.

The oni had eleven *nactka*. They could use a second one at any time.

"Wait. Just wait," Jillian murmured as she snatched up her tablet and started to scribble something.

"Are we safe?" Crow Boy asked.

Louise closed her eyes tightly and considered the question. Could she sense if there was going to be a second attack? Nothing came to her. In other attempts to see the future—successful ones—she had reformed the question while considering implications. It was as if she needed to enter search words to lock in on a vision.

Dufae feared for his family, so it was logical that the first attack would be aimed at *domana*. Had the babies found Tinker and Oilcan and gotten them the spell? Were she and Jillian the only ones left able to cast spells? What happened to Windwolf and all the elves off fighting the oni deep in the forest?

"The great Stone has been shattered and lies in ruin!" The words came to her fast and powerful. "The torch that is the true flame gutters on the ground. The wolf stumbles but does not fall! It stands ready, teeth bared! The light of Brilliance shines alone in the darkness! Stand! Fight! Or all will be lost!"

"That doesn't sound good," someone murmured.

"What do we do?" one of the teenage tengu asked.

"We do what we were told to do," Keiko Shoji said bitterly. As part of the tengu Chosen bloodline, Keiko was basically a princess and semi-in-charge while the rest of the royal family was scattered throughout Pittsburgh or still recovering from laying four massive eggs the day before. "Stay hidden. Protect the young. Be ready to flee."

"Ohhhh, farts!" Chuck suddenly exclaimed, her robot mouse body stirring to life. They had protected the babies' eggs with their shield but, because of the metal inner workings of the tiny robots, the mice had been left outside the casting circle. All four mice were getting to their feet.

"Language!" Jillian said out of reflex.

"What's wrong?" Louise asked.

"The oni cut the phones!" Chuck grumbled. "We got bounced back to the tengu network. We were halfway to the graveyard with the Mark Two."

"The graveyard?" Louise echoed in surprise. "Why were you going there? And what's the Mark Two?"

The babies all started to speak at once. It was nearly impossible to tell who was talking as they sounded alike when they were all squeaking loudly. "We told you that we found a big printer that no one was using..." "Alexander had these cool plans on her computer with everything all figured out and ready to go..." "The DJ said we should go to Oakland but we ran into this little old elf woman..." "Female! If she was a woman then she would be human!" *"Ixnay onyay ethay anktay."*

"Tank?" Louise latched onto the last word in pig Latin.

The babies paused to look at each other.

"It's not really a tank," Chuck Norris said. "Just a naming convention. It's like Tesla the robotic dog, only...only...only..."

"Only better!" Red Jawbreaker finished the sentence for her sister. "She said she was our grandmother and that we needed to go to the Allegheny Cemetery to save the baby dragons..."

"Also Sir Galahad and the White Goat!" Green added.

"Who?" Louise said.

"They're just some people with cool names," Green said.

"Everyone in Pittsburgh has cool names!" Chuck waved her tiny fists. "I'm staying Chuck Norris!"

"I'm Scarlet Overkill!" Red jumped up and down.

"I want a cool name too!" Green whined.

"I still don't think their names are Sir Galahad and White Goat," Nikola said. "I think they're just code words for people— like the ones that the Resistance is using."

"Vive la résistance!" his sisters squeaked in chorus.

"Who told you to go to the cemetery?" Louise asked loudly.

"Grandma elf!" the babies all shouted.

"Try and keep up!" Red muttered darkly.

"Oh! Oh! I found a way back to the Mark Two via the military communication network," Nikola said.

"Go! Go! Go!" Chuck cried even as Louise shouted, "No! Wait!"

But all the mice went still and silent.

"Shit," Louise whispered.

"Language," Jillian repeated as she scribbled on her tablet.

"We need to teach them stranger danger," Louise said. "They shouldn't be doing dangerous stuff just because someone told them that they were our grandmother. We don't have a grandmother! They're all dead!"

"Unless we have a great-grandmother who is an elf," Jillian said with amazing calm for the situation. "The tengu say that we have an elf grandfather in town. We could have an elf grandmother too."

"If she knew that the babies were her grandchildren, why would she send them to the graveyard?"

"Because there's no real way that they can be hurt?" Jillian said, pointing up toward the nest far overhead. "They're really here in the village. It's just some electronic ghosts or something that they're projecting—into some kind of tank apparently."

"They're babies!" Louise hadn't understood—back when they went to Perlman—why their teacher refused to let them help with giving first aid to the bombing victims. They were right there and certified first responders. After watching Jillian slowly lose it—after killing someone herself—Louise understood the danger. "They'll be scarred for life if they go around killing things. They'll be born with PTSD or something."

"They might not remember anything from before they were born. We didn't."

"We didn't have a tank! How can you be so calm?"

"Because I'm afraid of breaking!" Jillian snapped. "I have to believe that everything will work out. We can handle anything. We're amazing. We saved Alexander and Orville—Tinker and Oilcan. They both got the spell off. They're fine. We're fine. Everything is fine."

"How do you know that they are okay?"

"Because I can feel people when they tap the Spell Stones. Tinker and Oilcan are bouncing messages off them in Morse code," Jillian flipped her tablet to show that she was translating the code into English. "Tinker is going someplace—I think Oakland. They're using personal code words. She's told Oilcan to stay where he is—which doesn't seem to be Oakland."

"Anyone else get the spell up?" Louise asked.

Jillian shook her head. "There were only three shields, counting ours. Tinker and Oilcan aren't together and no one seems to be with them—casting spells at least—so it's just us four. We're going to have to go to Pittsburgh."

"Us?"

"There were eleven baby dragons just like Joy in Dufae's box—they might even be other parts of Joy. The oni just killed one of them to cast that spell. We need to save the rest—and stop our baby sisters and brother before they emotionally scar themselves."

Louise pulled up the Pittsburgh map on her tablet, wondering how they would get to the cemetery quickly. The whole thing about Haven being "a village hidden deep in the forest" meant that it wasn't on any map nor were there any roads or even dirt paths leading to it. The tengu had flown everything in just so there would be no trace of their passage. She knew that Haven was roughly northwest of Pittsburgh—so they would need to go southeast an unknown number of miles through dense virgin forest full of man-eating creatures and plants. And cross a three- to four-hundred-foot-wide river. At dusk. With a storm rumbling off in the distance.

She found the cemetery. It was uncomfortably close to Oakland, which was being invaded by an oni army. How were they going to get there? Airship? "Our monster call worked on the gossamer. Could we use it to get to Pittsburgh?"

Jillian narrowed her eyes as she considered the idea. "Doubt it. Gracie had 'seen' that something earthshaking was going to happen with Windwolf's gossamer. She had her *yamabushi* grab a pilot before they gave chase. Besides, what do we do with the gossamer once we get there? An airship isn't like a car that you can park anywhere. It needed all those people on mooring ropes to make sure it wouldn't drift away with the wind. I don't think the kids here could manhandle the tethers—and I don't want to be responsible for their safety."

And the tengu adults wouldn't let the twins go charging off into trouble.

"We could just drop out of the gondola with a shield up," Louise said.

Jillian thought a moment and shook her head. "Nah, we're going to need a way to get back out of whatever mess we drop into. I don't want to try and outrun an army while corralling the babies."

"Yeeeaaahh." That would be bad.

"Oh!" Jillian said. "I've got an idea but it's a little crazy."

"In comparison to what?"

Jillian pointed right as if indicating an event on the "crazy" bar. "Crazier than blowing up our playhouse." She pointed left. "But not as crazy as storming Laurel Caverns."

Louise flinched at the memory of the cavern. The falling rock. The knowledge that Yves had been snuffed out—erased from existence; a dark empty space like her parents. *I killed a man. I can't let the babies kill. I can't let them feel this way.* "What's your idea?"

"While you were recovering at the caverns, I found this one spell in the Codex. It can apply acceleration to an object. I played with it—just writing it out because I didn't know we could tap the Spell Stones. By itself—using just ambient magic—it's fairly powerful. If we used the Spell Stones, then the sky's the limit. There was notation for the fingering. It seemed easy—kind of like throwing a ball."

"But we're the ball?"

"We're the ball." Jillian repeated. "Happy fun ball. We can bounce over to Pittsburgh, grab Dufae's box, and bounce out."

Crow Boy didn't like "Plan: Bounce." He didn't say anything but you could tell it by the way he was trying to keep his face neutral. He didn't quite have control of his eyebrows, which kept flexing between "surprised" and "worried."

"Oh, God," Keiko murmured. "You're just like Tinker *domi*. This is something she would come up with."

Louise wasn't sure if she was pleased or annoyed by this statement. Maybe both.

"I would say they're all just like Esme," one of the new tengu kids murmured. "She had the babies of a dead man that she'd never met, jumped through time to rescue Jin Wong in orbit, and then delivered him to her daughter so that *domi* could protect all of our people."

"Esme is one powerful dream crow," another tengu teenager murmured.

Listed together, the events made Esme sound God-level amazing.

"I'm coming with you," Crow Boy finally said.

Jillian glanced at Louise as if she expected Louise to make the call.

How did it become her decision? Was it because she said, "Stand! Fight!"? She wasn't even sure what that meant—not in any specific detail. The twins had already worked out one backpack full of useful things that they could take with them. Did she want Crow Boy—or anyone else for that matter—to come with them?

Crow Boy was taller and stronger than them, which had come in handy in the past when brute force was needed in lifting and carrying. He had actual weapons supplied to him by the other *yamabushi* when they arrived at Haven. He had learned to let the twins lead. What might be more important, Jillian would probably be braver with him backing them up. Having backup felt good—but was that "feeling" just sheer logic or something more?

"Yeah, sure," Louise said, trying not to feel guilty. If he was hurt, it would be her fault. She focused on the fact that Crow Boy would be dead at the mansion if they hadn't freed him from the cage that Yves had locked him in. What's more, he'd probably try to follow them if they didn't take him along.

Jillian didn't seem happy but she did look relieved.

"Okay! Jumping!" Jillian clapped her hands together to signal the start of their casting protocol. Since the acceleration spell was complex—and they were complete noobs at using the Spell Stones—they decided that Jillian would control their movement while Louise maintained a shield around them.

"Grab hold," Louise told Crow Boy as she wrapped her right arm tight around Jillian. "Hold tight."

"We're leaving now?" he said in surprise even as he wrapped an arm about each of their shoulders.

Louise nodded as she focused on tapping the Spell Stones. She cocked her fingers and brought them to her lips and spoke the key word. She might not be able to see magic or feel someone else cast a spell but she could feel the power suddenly surge into her. It felt like she put her hand down on a massive machine, rumbling with potential. Her heart was pounding with excitement and fear. She was a *domana* elf who could do the most powerful of spells—and they were about to risk all three of their lives on the possibly wrong hope that she could maintain a shield as they fell out of the sky.

She changed her fingers, spoke the key word, and felt the world get muffled by the powerful shield. "Shield up!"

"Jumping!" Jillian warned, wrapping her left arm around Louise. She clenched tight as she brought her fingers to her mouth. Jillian tapped the Spell Stones and then stepped through the gestures that defined the acceleration spell's parameters of direction, angle, and speed of the thrown object.

They were jerked straight up in the air as if fired from a cannon, bursting through the forest canopy. Louise yelped in surprise and dropped her shield. The smell of bruised green flooded in. They kept rising, the world beneath their feet becoming an unending patchwork quilt of autumn leaves. The setting sun was a menacing red gleam on the horizon. Dark clouds blanketed the sky. Lightning flickered a few miles away and several seconds later thunder rumbled over them.

"Lou!" Jillian shouted.

Louise snapped through tapping the Spell Stones and reestablished her shield just as they started to fall toward Earth. "Got it!"

Jillian nodded for a full minute, swallowing hard. "I'm still trying to get our bearings."

"We need to head south," Crow Boy said. "The setting sun to the west is straight ahead, so we need to go left. Go straight south until we hit the Allegheny River. A landmark like that will make it easier to keep our bearings at dusk."

Jillian cast the acceleration spell a second time, aiming in an upward slant toward the south. They shot off to their left. Somehow the change of direction was more frightening than just falling. Louise whimpered in fear but held her shield tight. The lateral speed seemed slower than their rocket upward had been, but it could have been the lack of reference points against the sea of leaves.

"The edge of that storm is five miles out," Crow Boy said. "We need to outrace it. You can't fly in cumulonimbus clouds. They have insanely powerful updrafts and downdrafts. The turbulence can be strong enough to tear an airplane into pieces. If we were over plains, we could just simply fly under the storm but with the hilly forest, there's very little room to maneuver safely."

"Understood," Jillian said in a carefully monotone voice. She cast the spell again and they shot upward and forward, noticeably faster.

Lightning flickered again, lighting up the world. This time Louise counted it out. *One one thousand. Two one thousand. Three one thousand.* She'd gotten to *"Twenty-five one thousand"* when the thunder rumbled over them.

Crow Boy had been correct; the storm was five miles and closing quickly. The stormfront was moving west to east as they headed straight south. The only way they could "outrun" it was to reach Pittsburgh before the storm swept over the city.

Jillian cast the acceleration spell again and again, flinging them southward in giant arcs. It felt like they were on an invisible roller coaster, soaring upward on lift hills and then plunging down runs. It reminded Louise of riding the Jersey Devil Coaster at Six Flags. She and Jillian had worn thick-soled shoes last summer so they would meet the four-foot-tall height requirements. The Jersey Devil had been built to be scary with sudden twists and turns. It hadn't scared her because she knew that the carts were firmly attached to a sturdy steel frame.

This was so much more terrifying. It took all her willpower not to whimper and yelp in fear with each jerk upward and plummet downward. Her stomach flipped and flopped to the point she was starting to feel queasy.

Forest stretched as far as Louise could see in patches of autumn yellows, oranges, and reds. The ironwoods were mostly shades of gold but dotting the canopy were the blazing orange-reds of Elfhome maples and the darker rust of Wind Oaks. The treetops tossed in the wind and little whirlwinds of dead leaves swirled up. She kept her eyes on the southwest horizon, willing for Pittsburgh to appear in the distance.

The lightning moved closer. The thunder grew louder.

"There's the Allegheny River," Crow Boy said.

"Where?" Jillian and Louise both said, as they could see nothing but dark forest.

Lightning lit up the sky. Where there been only darkness below, there was a bright ribbon snaking through the trees as the river mirrored the sudden light.

"Oh, there it is," Jillian and Louise both said.

"We need to go west," Louise added. "To what is left of the Fortieth Street Bridge."

Jillian turned them downriver. "*Washington's Crossing to Nowhere?*"

"Uh-huh," Louise murmured as she scanned the darkness ahead of them. It was one of the first animations that they'd done as Lemon-Lime JEl-Lo. The bridge's official name was Washington Crossing; it had been named after the fact that George Washington had nearly died crossing the river at that point during the French and Indian War. He'd been dispatched to tell the French that they needed to give up the lands around Pittsburgh or prepare for a military strike. The bridge hadn't survived the first Startup: the Rim took out the piers on one side and several deck sections had collapsed. The American officer dispatched to deliver a similar "give up your land or fight" to Windwolf had driven off the end of the bridge, suffering the same fate as Washington. It seemed too perfect not to make fun of it.

It was difficult not to see it as karma that they would enter the city for the first time via the site of their first animations. Had she known? Was her gift quietly guiding her back then or was it just stupid luck? It would be nice to think that they had an ace in the hole, that she could see disaster looming and avoid it. The problem was she had a growing sense of dread that could be just common sense and logic.

"There it is!" Crow Boy's night sight was better than hers. It was another minute before the dark arches of the bridge came into view. Three massive stone piers supported the two surviving decks seventy-two feet above the water. The fourth pier had been razed out of existence by the Rim. The deck ended abruptly at the third pier in the middle of the river.

"Okay, I see it," Jillian said. "I'm taking us in."

"Wait, wait, wait!" Louise cried. "If we hit the bridge at this speed, we'll punch right through the deck."

"I got it covered," Jillian said even as they plummeted toward the deck. She cast another spell, one that Louise didn't recognize. They checked in midair and then started to float downward.

"Oh, wow, that's cool!" Louise said.

"I think the translation of the key word is 'soft,'" Jillian said. "Oh God, look at the Thirty-first Street Bridge!"

The next bridge downriver seethed with oni. The headlights of large trucks shone on hundreds of warriors moving across the deck.

"That column just keeps going," Jillian whispered. "There's thousands of them."

"Do you think they see us?" Louise asked.

"I doubt it," Crow Boy said. "The light from the trucks will diminish their night vision."

They drifted down to land on the second span of the Fortieth Street Bridge, a safe distance from the jagged end of the deck.

Lightning struck the western bank of the river, lighting up the world with a deafening crack and immediate boom. Rain came sheeting down, sweeping across the river and washing over them. It smeared down over Louise's shield.

"We're behind enemy lines," Crow Boy whispered. "We must stay hidden. We can't take a whole army by ourselves."

"The cemetery is away from that mess." Louise pointed upriver. "It's about a dozen blocks that way."

10: LOST YOUR MITTENS, YOU NAUGHTY KITTENS! THEN YOU SHALL HAVE NO PIE.

The black tom barn cat had feral kittens.

Olivia hadn't realized that Tommy Chang was the patriarch of a large sprawling family but all the clues had been there. Unlike the Undefended, who hid behind fake identities, the prostitutes of Tommy's stable used their real names. Not all were named Chang but a goodly number were: from small witty Mokoto Chang to big quiet Babe Chang to sharp-tongued Lauren Chang. Everyone in Pittsburgh knew that if they messed with a Chang, they would face Tommy's wrath. Having seen him walk into the heavily guarded shipyard without fear, she understood now why no one wanted to mess with him.

Two of Tommy's feral kittens climbed into the truck cab with Olivia. Zippo looked like he could be Babe's younger brother. He had that same big-teddy-bear vibe going on with a massive build and a warm grin. Zippo shyly flashed his smile as he got in but said nothing the entire trip. He watched every move Olivia made as if ready to bolt. The small, fierce Alita climbed up to perch on her cousin's lap. It was hard to judge the kittens' ages. Zippo seemed to be around sixteen but Alita could be as young as thirteen or as old as nineteen. She was tiny and flat chested, but her Goth makeup was applied with a practiced hand.

Olivia fumbled through making sure she was in neutral gear,

starting up the engine, turning on the headlights, and setting the windshield wipers at their highest speed. The heavy rain reduced her line of sight to a hundred feet or so even with the wipers whipping back and forth. She double-checked their fuel level, knowing that big trucks were gas hogs. The gauge had been at full when she appropriated the big truck. They had driven close to twenty miles all told during the day. The needle had barely moved, suggesting a massive gas tank. There was no danger of them running out of fuel. She did the complicated foot dance of brake pedal—clutch—gas—clutch—gas to get the big truck rolling through the empty city streets in third gear.

As Olivia drove, Alita talked at machine-gun speeds about why she couldn't warn Duff via her radio. Olivia was surprised by Alita's candor: she'd expected more growling and hissing. Alita seemed to think that Olivia had won Tommy's trust. Olivia doubted that she had won over the tom barn cat completely but she was glad for the information.

"The Resistance got started up shortly after the July Shutdown when Tinker got kidnapped. Everyone knew about the oni then . . . well, knew *something* about the oni." Alita used the fingers of her left hand to tick off what Pittsburghers had learned since that Shutdown. "They knew that the oni had tried to kill Wind-wolf, were responsible for the shoot-out on Veterans Bridge, had kidnapped Tinker and set loose the giant electric catfishes—but that was it."

That matched with what Olivia knew until she tracked down Forest Moss and became entrenched in the elf society. Every day she learned something new about the enemy, either from the royal marines or the Wyverns or Forest Moss.

Alita pointed to the right. "Turn at the next intersection. Until Tommy teamed up with Oilcan, we couldn't say boo about the oni. Anyhoo, the Resistance felt like they were fighting ghosts, so they figured that they needed to be ghosts too. Now take this upcoming right. Not that right! Sharp right! Watch the fire hydrant!"

It had been a Pittsburgh intersection with five possible directions, none of them being straight. There had been a small forest of DO NOT ENTER signs barring most of them. The sharp right took them onto a street paralleling the river until they got to the Smithfield Street Bridge.

There were ROAD CLOSED and BRIDGE OUT signs at the intersection.

"Oh, crap," Alita cursed. "Bridge out? What the hell? Did the train derailment take out part of the bridge?"

Olivia hadn't noticed any obvious damage to the Smithfield Bridge earlier in the day, but she'd been distracted. She'd gotten to Aoife's place via the light rail train that crossed upriver on a different bridge. She'd followed Linda Gaddy to the North Side via the West End—maybe because of the closed road. Still, she should have noticed if large parts of the bridge were missing as she traveled through the area.

The thing was, she couldn't think of any other bridge that connected to the South Side. Since she didn't own a car, her knowledge of the city was limited to its mass-transit lines. The next bridge downriver was Fort Pitt Bridge and it funneled into the Fort Pitt Tunnel that went . . . somewhere . . . She tried to remember if there were bridges upriver that went to the South Side. Surely there were but she couldn't recall any except the Liberty Bridge that similarly channeled traffic through the Liberty Tunnel.

"They might have closed Smithfield until they could inspect the bridge for possible structural damage," Olivia said slowly as she hated the plan that was forming in her mind. "We could see if we can get across."

"Nah! We'll cross Fort Pitt Bridge." Alita indicated that they'd continue straight instead of plowing through the signs. "We can take the West End exit and do a U-turn onto Carson Street. Technically it's not legal but we look like we're the EIA and they do anything they want."

"Okay!" Relief flooded through Olivia. She hated the idea of risking the lives of everyone in the truck by attempting to cross a possibly damaged bridge. She was glad she had someone with her who knew the way.

"The rest of our cell are too young and stupid to be real spies," Alita continued her rapid-fire explanation of the Resistance. Olivia wasn't sure how it related to the reason that Alita couldn't radio Duff and warn him. "They were hanging out at Eides at the end of July, looking at videos to rent and talking about setting up a cell because they couldn't get into Hot Metal. Part of me was like 'Do you really want to trust these people to have your back?' The other part was like 'No one else is going to let you join a *secret* organization without asking dangerous questions.' So I gave them fake names, wore a disguise, and pretended that I was just going overboard on the whole spy thing."

Olivia nodded along. She was just as guilty about pretending to be someone she wasn't. More so. If Alita had joined the Resistance prior to Tommy rescuing Windwolf, then she had been protecting her entire family by using a fake identity.

Theirs had been the only vehicle moving on the streets as they worked their way across the Monongahela River to the South Side neighborhood. There they found evidence that there had been fighting in the streets; some of the buildings looked like they had taken mortar hits.

Alita pointed right. "Take this upcoming right onto South Eighteenth Street. It snakes its way up the hill, so you'll probably want to slow down a little. This place is a maze and I think some of the little narrow side streets turn into stairs."

"Stairs?"

"So I've been told. I've only been up to the top of Mount Oliver a couple times." Alita changed subject without taking a breath. "The thing is, my cell isn't one of the power hitters. Our youngest member is twelve and the oldest is seventeen. We're just a band of little wannabes, close enough to the action to know what is what, but far enough out that we didn't even have a name for a long time. We had two guys quit because we didn't have an official name before our leader put out the word that we're the Palm Garden Trestle. Talk about a total W.T.F. Where the hell is Palm Garden? What the hell is a trestle?"

"Palm Garden is a big apartment complex near where I used to live on Mount Washington," Olivia said, surprised that she knew something about the city that Alita didn't. "It has its own station on the T. When I took the light rail out of town, Palm Garden was the next stop after mine. Trestle means it's a bridge that only a train uses."

"It's real? I thought Steve made the name up to make us feel better."

"Steve?"

"Our cell leader. Steve. The seventeen-year-old. A complete idiot. His older brother Ricky is in Hot Metal with Dog Bow-Wow but wouldn't give Steve the commends to be part of it. How fucked up do you need to be that your own brother doesn't trust you? And his brother is right not to: I shouldn't know that Dog Bow-Wow is the leader of Hot Metal. But that's beside the point. Any way you slice it, Duff isn't going to believe me if I start blasting over the radio that *maybe* the oni are on their way to the bakery. He probably doesn't even remember me, I was just a girl who handed him chili hot dogs at the racetrack. Chili, cheddar cheese, jalapeños, diced onions, and sour cream. If Duff knows anything about Palm Garden Trestle, he knows Steve is the leader and a complete idiot and we're not supposed to have a radio. I'm not going to explain over the open air who I am and how I got my headset. It would put both our families at risk if I try to convince him that he can trust me."

"That's fair," Olivia said.

A tall ridge ran along the Monongahela River opposite the Downtown triangle. Olivia had been told that at one time there were a dozen small distinct communities dotting the top of the steep hills. Once Pittsburgh had been shifted to Elfhome, though, the population of the suburbs started to shrink drastically. Mount Washington stayed popular because of the inclines and the light rail line. The other neighborhoods suffered from the fact that many of the side streets became bobsled runs during the wintertime. Their population shrank. The Elfhome wilderness pressed in. Communities were merged together until there were only two distinct ones.

Olivia had found a home at the edge of Mount Washington. It was a ten-minute walk to the incline but also the same distance to a little grocery store and the bakery in Mount Oliver. Alita had been right to call the place a maze, as the steep slopes of the hillside dictated placement of the roads.

South Eighteenth Street was terrifying in the dark and rain as she navigated the big truck up the narrow winding road. Kansas, where she'd learned to drive, didn't have hills and turns like this! The farm roads were all flat and in perfectly square grids to give access to the thousand-acre cornfields. Each time she had to downshift on the steep grade, she whispered a prayer that she wouldn't stall. When she reached the top of the hill, her hands hurt from gripping the steering wheel so hard.

Alita had said that she didn't know her way around Mount Oliver. Olivia had been concerned that they wouldn't be able to find the bakery. As they reached the top of the hill, however, she realized that South Eighteenth Street turned into Brownsville Road as it crossed into the Mount Oliver neighborhood. It meant that they were a block from the bakery. She made the sharp right onto Arlington Avenue.

The bakery was an old Dollar Tree store in a small deserted-looking strip mall. The sign of the variety discount store had been taken down but the letters remained visible as ghost outlines on the faded white paint. The glass doors and big windows had been boarded over as protection against Elfhome's larger predators. Olivia had been told that the other business in the strip mall had been a medical clinic but all evidence of it had been scrubbed away when it was abandoned. Even the clinic's doors had been bricked over as the bakery expanded into the space.

The mall's big parking lot was empty, cracked, and weed choked. The Dollar Tree looked as abandoned as the stores and homes flanking it. The bakery's owners liked it that way, since half of its workers had been illegal immigrants like Olivia. They had no choice—finding someone in Pittsburgh who would get up at two in the morning to bake bread for minimum wage was otherwise impossible.

Most of the employees worked between midnight and sunrise. Many lived within walking distance. Those who drove to work ignored the parking lot that faced Arlington Avenue. They parked behind the bakery, continuing the illusion that the building was abandoned. Oliva turned down John Street, heading for the back of the bakery.

Duff's pickup was tucked in the far corner of the rear parking lot. It was the only car they'd seen since they crossed the Fort Pitt Bridge. The floodlight over the bakery's loading dock was on, evidence that the building had power. Olivia swung wide to the right and then backed the big cargo truck up to the dock. If the oni showed up, she wanted to be able to take off running.

"We're stopping?" Alita peered up and down the obvious back alley. Only a block long, the cobbled lane gave access to a handful of backyards and garages. "This is it? When you said 'bakery,' I imagined, you know, cookies and cakes in a big window like at Market Square."

"This is it." Olivia snapped off the truck's headlights. Rain drummed on the roof of the cab. The Dollar Tree blocked most of Olivia's view of the main road. She could only see the mouth of the alley where it met Arlington Avenue. The power lines that wove a net over the main road gleamed brighter and brighter, indicating that a car—screened by the surrounding buildings—was approaching the intersection.

The cargo truck's windows were manual crank to open. Olivia lowered her window, letting in the rain and cold. She called back to the marines. "Shhhh, everyone just hold tight for a minute!"

She heard Aoife repeating the order in Elvish. Olivia winced as she realized that she'd slipped back to English after talking with Alita.

Olivia half-climbed out of the truck so she could lean over the hood to see more of Arlington. The sound of engines grew louder. There was more than one vehicle coming. It sounded like a convoy of big trucks. She pressed close to the window frame to lessen her profile.

A big yellow box truck rumbled past—slowly—as if stalking something. It felt so predatory that it put a shiver down her back. At least the lead truck didn't stop. There were more vehicles behind it. Olivia slid the rest of the way out of the driver's window and down to the ground.

Alita whispered, "Where are you going?"

"I'm checking the area." Olivia wasn't sure how else to quickly explain.

Alita and Zippo scrambled out as Olivia hurried to the back of the truck.

Her nerves were jangling with fear, urging her to run. She struggled to stay calm. Panic was her enemy.

The royal marines were all at the tailgate like a pack of eager puppies. Olivia put up her hand to keep them in place.

"Dagger, come with me," Olivia commanded. The tall, willowy female acted as the informal leader of the platoon. Olivia could explain their situation to Dagger and know that the appropriate orders would be given. She pointed firmly at the others as Dagger jumped out. "If we need to move, it must be fast and quiet. No loud noises. Take guard points on the—"

What was the word for truck? She glanced at Aoife for help. The anthology grad student knew a lot more Elvish than Olivia did.

"Wagon." Aoife supplied a suitable word. "Keep close to the wagon."

That worked.

"Keep out of sight," Olivia continued. "Don't fire unless fired upon. We're probably outnumbered. Stealth is vital. Be aware that we might have to leave in a hurry—be prepared to quickly get back into the wagon."

"Yes, *domi!*" they whispered as one.

Olivia hurried to the corner of the cinder-block building and peered around it. Dagger, Alita, and Zippo crouched at her feet, huddled together so they could watch Arlington Avenue with her. Olivia felt like a mother hen with a litter of kittens trying to huddle under her wings. Rain beat down on them, quickly soaking through Olivia's sundress. At least the others had on coats to protect them.

A second and then a third yellow box truck rumbled past the strip mall. All three trucks were heading up the winding, steep Arlington Avenue.

"I was really hoping that Texas Holdem was wrong," Alita whispered. "I didn't know where Duff was broadcasting from other than Mount Oliver. I figured that out from a lot of random clues that I put together. I could only guess it was Duff broadcasting because I recognized his voice. And I only know what he sounds like because he hung out with his cousins at the racetrack. That and the fact that the Resistance's 'boonies' are definitely the hats that Andy ordered by mistake for Team Tinker. Roach was pissed as hell—you could hear him all the way to the concession stand. Someone must have ratted Duff out."

Olivia shook her head. "The oni probably are triangulating on Duff's radio signal."

"You can do that?" Alita whispered.

"Yes." The joy of being raised in a religious cult which routinely broke a dozen state and federal laws was that she'd been trained in all methods of urban warfare.

Luckily triangulation was a slow game of "hot and cold." The trucks continued up the hill, past the strip mall, following Arlington Avenue as it snaked through a nearly empty residential area. There was nothing in that direction that would warrant three big trucks. The business district of Mount Oliver, tiny as it was, was all down Brownsville Road. The trucks would probably make several left turns as they spiraled inward on the bakery.

The trucks continued on, slowly, until the sound of their engines was washed out by the heavy rain.

"Dagger, those wagons are using a type of human scry magic," Olivia said. "They're going to circle around, trying to find this spot. Keep watch for them."

Dagger nodded.

"Come on," Olivia said to Alita. "We only have a few minutes before they find us. Go stop Duff from broadcasting."

Alita's eyes went wide. "What? Me? No, no, no, Duff isn't going to trust me. That's the whole point of driving over here. Weren't you listening?"

Olivia had listened to someone who seemed smart, bold, and daring, talking her way into a Resistance to milk it for information. Had Alita only been brave because the kids in her cell didn't know the real her? Certainly Olivia couldn't have walked Liberty Avenue as a hooker if anyone from the bakery was watching. The other bakers had all treated her like a baby sister.

Olivia had wanted to stay close to the truck, as it was their only means of escape and no one else could drive it. Trying to talk Alita past her fear, though, would chew up too much time. "Come on."

She led Alita up the back steps.

The back door was unlocked, which was normal—at least when she worked at the bakery. Only one of the overhead lights was on but it was enough to dimly illuminate the cavernous loading bay. There was no sign of forced entry—it seemed as if they had just beat the oni to the area.

Olivia cautiously stepped into the loading bay. The original Dollar Tree receiving area had been expanded into the abandoned medical clinic, as the bakery needed to quickly take delivery of an entire month's worth of supplies from Earth in a single day. Walk-in coolers had been added to take pallets of butter, cream, milk, and lard. When she'd started two days after Shutdown, the area had been stuffed with paper goods and baking ingredients. Bread bags. Cupcake cups. Donut boxes. A dozen different types of flour from plain white to rye. Cane sugar. Brown sugar. Powdered sugar. Yeast. Seeds. Nuts. Spices. It was a carefully calculated supply to keep a half dozen storefronts stocked with bread, cakes, cupcakes, donuts, and pastries until the next Shutdown.

Then Tinker *domi* had destroyed the orbital gate. Without another Shutdown in the foreseeable future, there was no way to restock the bakery. All of the new hires were let go.

The loading bay had been half-empty on Olivia's last day. She expected to find it bare, but there were hundred-pound grain sacks piled up high over her head. They looked Elvish in design, elegant despite the rough weave of the sackcloth. Wheat was scattered on the ground—although the individual grains were smaller than she was used to seeing at the Ranch. A big commercial grain-milling machine sat to one side, dusted with white flour. Somehow the bakery was getting Elvish wheat that they were milling into flour. It explained why the various storefronts were still open, although no longer selling cakes and cookies.

The loading bay had been set up as an airlock so the dirt and weather couldn't spill into the kitchen areas. When she worked at the bakery, coming in after the first shift of dough makers, both doors were always unlocked. Considering what Duff had been doing in his spare time, it was not surprising that the inner door was bolted. An old fashioned voice-only intercom station had been installed since she was let go.

She rang the button on the intercom and then pounded on the door.

"H-h-h-hello?" a female said over the intercom. The woman sounded familiar but Oliva couldn't put a name or face to the voice. "Who's there?"

"It's Red!"

"What's red? Who are you? What are you doing here?"

Olivia had invented "Red" when she started to walk Liberty Avenue as a hooker. What name had she used with the bakery? Oh, yes, she'd been too naïve to use anything but her real name. "It's Olivia! I used to work here. Duff trained me. He was my manager. Oni are coming here to kill him."

"What's the password?"

"There's three trucks of oni warriors on Arlington Avenue looking for Duff! How's that for a password?"

"What?" the girl—because she sounded younger as she reacted to the news—cried. "The oni are coming here? How do you know that?"

"There's no time…" Olivia said.

Alita stepped up and leaned close to the intercom. "We are Team Tinker. Priority Code: Take the trolley to the Neighborhood of Make-Believe."

The door jerked open. The mystery speaker was Widget,

the computer guru who would come to the bakery with Hazel Bunny. The African American girl was only a year or so older than Olivia, brilliant in terms of computers and things but stupidly naïve in the way of the world. She'd run away from a safe and normal life to chase after a dream of sexy elves and magic. Olivia had been a bit jealous of her. Widget had landed on her feet in Pittsburgh despite a string of utter stupidities. Olivia had continued to stumble and fall.

All things considered, it wasn't entirely surprising that Widget was risking everything again by being part of the Resistance.

"Blast it all!" Widget pointed at the two Chang cousins. "Who's this?" And then past the feral kittens to Dagger, who was leaning through the back door with a worried look. "Is that really a royal marine or just an oni disguised as one?"

Fear spiked through Olivia at the look on Dagger's face: something had gone wrong already.

"A real royal marine. Widget, this is Alita." Olivia pushed Alita through the door. "She's part of the Resistance. Alita, this is Widget. Make it work."

"What?" "Huh?" "Olivia?" the two girls cried in dismay.

"Get moving!" Olivia said. "With three trucks full of warriors, the oni are going to be able to search door to door quickly."

She hurried back to Dagger.

"What is it?" Olivia asked quietly.

"Listen." Dagger cupped her pointed ears and turned toward the south. "The enemy wagons are returning."

Olivia listened carefully. Over the white noise of falling rain, she heard the rumble of big engines growing closer. "Fudge," she whispered. The oni wouldn't be able to track the signal if Duff stopped broadcasting, but they might still stumble over the bakery by accident.

11: STORM FURY SIX

The Rim was weirdly quiet as Jane Kryskill parked her SUV in an empty lot beside Sacred Heart. All the enclaves seemed to be in lockdown with their front gates shut and windows shuttered. Rain had started to fall. It shimmered oddly as it interacted with the enclaves' protective shields. It seemed like a giant bubble rose over the walled compounds, causing the rain to bounce off in a visible haze.

Jane wished there had been time to pull Bertha out of hiding. Her family's cannon was hidden out at Hyeholde; Marc would have needed an hour to drive there, mount the gun to his Hummer, and drive back. Getting the radio station back on air was more important. Nor would Marc be able to operate Bertha alone. Jane or Geoffrey or possibly both of them would need to load and fire the gun as Marc drove. She wasn't sure she wanted to use the cannon in an area as densely populated as Oakland. Bertha could turn a normal building—and all the buildings behind it—into Swiss cheese in a matter of seconds.

But if the oni army was massive, they might need that kind of power regardless of possible collateral damage.

She'd put on her body armor at her brother Marc's house on Mount Washington. When she stopped at WQED to drop her team off, it had started to rain. She pulled their rain gear out of the cargo space, along with her weapons. Her poncho sat folded beside her with her double rifle case in the passenger foot

111

well. She pulled the cape over her head, put on her bucket hat, grabbed her guns, and stepped out of her SUV.

She scanned the area as she opened the SUV's lift gate, letting out her elfhound, Chesty. The big dog bounded out of the cargo hold, ready to work. He knew that when she had rifle case in hand, it was time to be serious.

The city landscape of Pittsburgh abruptly ended where the Rim cut through the area in a northwest-to-southeast swath. Following the curve of the Rim was a strip of no-man's-land that had once been typical urban sprawl. Buildings, sidewalk, and side streets had been cut in half by the Rim; important structural pieces had been left on Earth when Pittsburgh shifted to Elfhome. The crumbling remains had been cleared away, creating a long, narrow, graveled parking lot. The elf-owned enclaves stood a few feet beyond the gravel, each half a block wide and a mile deep, surrounded by tall stone walls. Dirt side alleys ran between the enclaves, strategically wider than a man or elf could leap.

On the left side was what was now called Oakland. It was a "human city." Two lanes of paved streets. Sidewalk. Businesses with big glass window storefronts. Town houses. Apartment buildings. An abandoned high school.

Or at least, there had been until August. Some idiot with a camera and telephoto lens had taken Peeping Tom pictures of Tinker *domi* in her nightgown, and Windwolf had not been amused. A short time later, an oni fired a rocket from one of the town houses, killing a gossamer airship moored in the airfield beside the last enclave. The Viceroy decided he wasn't comfortable with human buildings overlooking his people. Jane couldn't blame him; a sniper with a scope could hit anything that a camera could see. Windwolf ordered the entire human side of the street demolished. Before the work could be finished, though, Oilcan laid claim to Sacred Heart High School.

The building sat alone on the ruined left side of the street, opposite the elegant beauty of the enclaves. The rubble of its demolished neighbors hadn't been totally cleared away, leaving a raw sense to the landscape.

Jane hadn't seen Sacred Heart since the day that the gossamer airship had been killed. (Hal and Nigel insisted that they must seize the opportunity to examine the massive dead body.) It was an imposing century-old redbrick building with lovely stone accents. A twelve-foot wall of tan limestone had been built around it, giving it a true enclave vibe. The ironwood gate that her brother Geoffrey had made had been installed just that morning. The invisible bubble of protection hazed the rain just like its elfin neighbors.

She'd parked beside Geoffrey's pickup—painted Harry Potter scarlet and gold with "Gryffin Doors" written on the tailgate. Her little brother had spent the last few days crafting ironwood lumber into a large, sturdy front door and a massive back gate for Oilcan's enclave. Roach had said he'd called Team Tinker to help move the heavy things. The team's presence was evident by the number of hoverbikes next to Geoffrey's truck. There was also Moser's rusty passenger van held together by posters for his band, Naekanain. The van's hood was up and a piece of cardboard slid under it, littered with tools, suggested that the van had barely made it to Sacred Heart and might not be able to leave. Guy's vintage Ford was nowhere to be seen. Roach had said that his little brother Andy and Guy had gone someplace with Oilcan, to help move something heavy. It would explain Guy's missing truck.

Several pickup trucks pulled in beside her SUV. Men and women spilled out of them, ranging between eighteen to thirty years old. Some were dressed in hunting camo. Others wore dark rain jackets. A few had on black garbage bags as ponchos. They carried rifles and shotguns and handguns and machetes. They were all wearing the blue boonie hats of Hal's Heroes. It made for a sorry-looking, ragtag group. Jane recognized various cell leaders as they climbed out of their trucks. Each cell in the militia had taken the name of a local bridge to identify themselves. Smithfield Street. Veterans. Homestead. West End. McKees Rocks. Fort Pitt. Fort Duquesne. Hot Metal. Mon-Fayette Expressway. Pittsburgh had a lot of bridges and they were all named. They tried to keep the militia membership secret but every cell leader was well known to her. Her brothers. Old classmates. Neighborhood kids. Members of her church. Off-duty cops and firefighters.

Every death was going to cut deep.

Alton came up the street with his squad, darting shadow to shadow. Jane had hated getting her brothers involved in the militia but she needed their network of trusted friends to leapfrog the membership forward. As oldest of her brothers and the one with the lowest public profile, Alton was her second-in-command for the militia. He'd gathered together the foragers who supplied the enclaves with wild game, the members of his old high school rifle club, and some of the tengu elite for a ranger-style group.

"We've been sweeping to the east and north of the enclaves since the first black willow got reported," Alton said. "The enemy seems to be concentrated entirely to the west. The tengu says that they're advancing in a single column up Liberty Avenue. There's no sign of them spreading out into the city or setting up any fortified positions. Their commander seems to be focused on taking the enclaves."

That made things easier than if the oni were merely trying to establish a toehold within the city. The militia would have to simply block the oni from reaching the enclaves.

Jane nodded her understanding as the militia gathered around her. Chesty grumbled annoyance at so many strangers with guns closing on Jane. She patted him on the head to reassure him that the situation was fine.

The cell leaders greeted her with murmurs of "Colonel" as their squads eyed her with surprise and interest. Up to this point, only the cell leaders knew who was leading the militia.

"What's the plan?" Mon-Fayette asked. His family ran a small butcher shop deep in the South Hills.

"The oni are coming up Liberty Avenue from Herrs Island!" Jane pointed northwest. "It means they have to cross the busway to get to here. The gorge isn't as deep here in Oakland as it is down by the Strip District but it's filled with Jersey barriers and chain-link fences, making it difficult terrain. The oni will probably head for the bridge at the most shallow point, which would be the one at South Aiken. We'll stop them at that choke point."

The militia nodded their understanding. In the last two months, Taggart had drilled the cell leaders in the basics of urban warfare. The irony being that he'd become a nature documentary photographer to escape being a war correspondent.

"Homestead and Hot Metal, you'll be point." Jane indicated the leaders of the two largest groups. Jane had intended for the cells to stay small; she told her leaders to recruit only people they trusted with their lives. She discovered, however, that the more charismatic cell leaders quickly gathered large numbers of followers who were deeply loyal only to them. It seemed wiser to keep the larger cells together than to try and splinter them into smaller groups with leaders not entirely trusted by the members. Some of the "cells" were large platoons not small squads. Hot Metal was the members of the oldest elf fusion-rock band in Pittsburgh named Bow-Wow *Mau* and its rabid followers. Homestead were a bunch of off-the-grid sheep farmers in the South Hills. Rachel Carson Bridge was a single large family, headed up by the small, spunky blonde Martha Champagne, who had been in Geoffrey's woodshop club in high school and a fellow fan of Harry Potter. Smithfield Street was Alton's squad.

Jane pointed at the piles of material from the demolished buildings. "Use this rubble to build barricades. Pull out anything large but still easily moved and get it to the South Aiken Avenue Bridge. Smithfield, move to Baum and Centre in case they try to outflank us. Set up barricades in the intersection but take sniper positions in the four-story building at the corner. Play Whac-A-Mole. Carson, support Smithfield at Baum and Centre."

Both Smithfield and Carson were small units but with different skill sets. Martha's family were builders, understanding how to erect barriers quickly. Alton's group was easily the best marksmen of the entire militia. By taking position in the four-story building, they should be able to provide support for much of Oakland.

"Mon-Fayette, we need a fallback position," Jane said. "Scout the buildings at this location and pick one for us to fall back to. You want something tall, concrete or brick, with multiple exit points. Remember to stick to blackout protocols—light will make you a target as it gets darker."

Ragtag as they were, they scattered to their assignments in an orderly fashion.

Sometime during the short briefing, Geoffrey had slipped out of Sacred Heart and joined the back of the crowd. As the militia melted away, he moved forward.

"Good boy." Geoffrey let Chesty sniff the back of his hand. Over his elf-styled clothes, he wore his camo rain poncho and Hal's Heroes bucket hat. He had his hunting rifle and scope covered against the drumming rain. "I'm glad you have him with you, Jane. This is going to be hairy."

Geoffrey had Snapdragon and Moser with him. The young male elf was a drummer in Moser's band but had trained as a *laedin* warrior before coming to Pittsburgh. Jane barely recognized Snapdragon. He had his long black hair twisted up into a messy manbun and wore the leather chest armor that marked his caste. He carried the normal *laedin* weapons of a bow, a quiver full of spell arrows, and a short sword of ironwood. He and Moser both had the woven straw capes that elves used as rain protection.

"Where's Guy and Andy?" Jane asked the question closest to her heart. "Roach said they went somewhere with Oilcan."

"They're at my workshop," Geoffrey said. "Guy called me before the phones went down. I didn't really follow what he was saying—something about cotton candy ice cream, a baby dragon . . . and talking mice? They're at my place because Oilcan needed to use my casting circle."

Roach had mentioned that the kids were going for ice cream. "Baby dragon" could be the creature Nigel saw with the twins. Jane drew a blank on what "talking mice" might mean. Was it a new code word for the militia? At least it meant that Guy and Andy were out of harm's way.

"What about Forge and Jewel Tear?" Jane had mobilized the militia on a guess that the oni would take out the heavy hitters first. She hoped that she was wrong. "Can we count on them for backup?"

Geoffrey and Moser shook their heads, making water sheet from the brims of their hat.

"A spell took them both out before yinz arrived." Snapdragon used the Pittsburgh slang for plural "you," since Moser had been the one who taught him English. "The *sekasha* have the *domana* on the second floor. They are not letting anyone near them."

"The *domana* are alive?" Jane asked since elves usually burned bodies as soon as possible. She would hate for Forge's people to burn Sacred Heart down while the militia was trying to defend it.

"I believe so," Snapdragon said. "If the *domana* were dead, his *sekasha* would have stormed out for revenge. It is what the holy ones do."

"They were polite but scary firm," Geoffrey added. "No 'outsiders' are to step foot on the stairs. I'm human and Moser's people are Wind Clan."

That sounded like more than just Snapdragon was with Moser. "Who do you have here in Oakland?"

Moser blew out his breath. "My whole commune. We got the report saying that the oni were on Herrs Island. That's only a few blocks from my place. I didn't want to risk my people by staying put. We're fortified against wargs and steel spinners, not full-out armies. Our van wasn't able to make it more than a mile or two. I thought Oilcan would be here."

Jane nodded to this. Moser had become Geoffrey's best friend shortly after they learned to walk, as Moser's family lived two houses down from their mother. The two boys teamed up with Roach when all three started high school and, sometime after that, Oilcan came into the mix. Their lives had been tightly interwoven since then.

"Will we be able to use the enclave at all?" Jane said. "In case we need someplace to fall back to that's more fortified?"

"We control both the front door and the back gate," Moser said. "But Briar Rose isn't going to let just anyone in, though; she's scared shitless. We came up with passwords."

Moser told Jane the passwords; it was a nonsense string of Elvish words. It was a phrase that most humans had some difficulty pronouncing correctly if they hadn't learned the language very young—like the locals had. Somehow Briar Rose had been able to confirm that the oni mangled the words worse than humans.

"There is the rest of West End Bridge." Snapdragon waved to some incoming pickups. Their cell was made up of Geoff's friends and fans of Moser's band, Naekanain.

"Moser, find Mon-Fayette and let him know the passwords." Jane pointed in the direction that the squad had gone. "Snapdragon, can you tell the enclaves not to freak out over all the armed humans showing up?"

The two nodded and took off.

"Geoff, you and Snapdragon are probably the best known to the enclaves. I want your cell to act as go-betweens. With the *sekasha* in Sacred Heart, we can't be certain Briar Rose will stay in command of the gates. We might need to fall back to one of the other places if the fighting goes badly. Also some royal marines or Wyverns might show up. I don't want them attacking our people out of confusion. Intercept any incoming elves. Explain. Be careful."

"Me?" Geoffrey laughed. "You're the one who's getting married in two weeks. Mom will have a fit if you screw up her plans."

Jane growled in frustration. Her wedding was the least of her problems. "Moser is the one that should be worried. Why did he pull his band?"

"We got that cleared up." Geoffrey waved to the passenger van sitting with its hood up. "He meant his van wasn't going to make it out to Hyeholde. He's trying to track down a replacement but I'll drive him there if I have to. I want Floss Flower and Snapdragon at the wedding."

Geoffrey was dating both of the elves. He was never going to find a better time to break the news to their mother—as long as the wedding was going well.

Jane nodded to this. "I thought Snapdragon was living at Moser's so he wouldn't have to fight."

"He didn't want fighting to be his entire life," Geoffrey said. "As a *laedin* living at an enclave, he would have had to spend every day training, patrolling, and maintaining his weapons. It wouldn't have left any time for music. Worse, no one was willing to teach him drumming."

Someone from the West End called to Geoffrey as the *Chased by Monsters* production truck drove up. For some reason Juergen Affenzeller was driving it. Since it came out that Chloe Polanski had been an oni mole, Jane had been suspicious of her coworkers. Juergen was the mechanic at WQED—he never left the station.

"Got to go!" Geoffrey gave Chesty one last pat. "Keep her safe, boy! Jane, be careful! You're getting married in two weeks!"

Jane was looking forward to *being* married. The upcoming battle seemed less stressful than her wedding—but she had always seen killing dangerous wildlife as a good way to relieve stress.

Speaking of which . . .

"Whoa, whoa, whoa!" Juergen cried, backing away, hands raised. "Don't kill the driver!"

"Why are you driving the *Chased by Monsters* truck?" Jane said coldly. "I wanted the *PB&G* truck."

Chesty growled as he picked up on Jane's annoyance.

"I'm in the militia!" Juergen cried. "I'm Greenfield Bridge!"

"That doesn't answer my question," Jane snapped.

"Dmitri made us take the newer equipment," Hal said, coming around from the passenger side. "The *CBM* truck has cameras with night vision and the like. He also wanted someone to stay with the truck in case it needed to be moved. For some reason, he thought we would need someone to babysit it."

She wanted the *Pittsburgh Backyard and Garden* truck because it was ancient and thus more expendable in the grand scheme of things. It wasn't compatible, though, with the cutting-edge equipment that came with the *CBM*.

Jane had also wanted Nigel and Hal to stay with the truck. She didn't want to go into battle with the two naturalists in tow. Much as she loved Hal and Nigel, they had the survival instincts of toddlers. (With six younger siblings, she had seen toddlers try to pull off impossibly dangerous stunts. It amazed her daily that her brothers had lived through all of their misadventures.) But her grandfather had told her once that war was as much about the next century as it was about the next second. Her team might be the only people out in the field, recording the battle. It would be important to show the oni attacking civilian targets—not only to audiences on Earth, who hopefully one day would be able to send reinforcements, but more importantly to the humans of Pittsburgh who might believe that they could stay on the sidelines of this conflict.

"Fine." Jane pointed toward the line of pickups heading toward the South Aiken Bridge, loaded down with rubble to build a barricade. "Try to find a parking spot that puts some buildings between the truck and the busway."

Taggart and Nigel were gearing up in the back of the production truck. Jane climbed in with Chesty and signaled Hal that she was set. Nigel was doing vocal warmups while checking levels on the soundboard. Taggart had been tucking away memory cards where ammo clips normally went. He glanced up as the truck started to move. A warm smile spread across his face that sent giddy warmth all through Jane. It amazed her that she still felt that school-girl-crush feeling. She loved everything about him. It went beyond his wild-man good looks—his dark eyes, his thick eyebrows, his long black hair pulled back into a loose ponytail. It was the fact that every day he proved himself to be intelligent, artistic, compassionate, and brave. It was the fact that when he saw her, he smiled like he was looking at the most amazing thing he'd seen in his life.

"Hey," he said.

"I love you," she said because there was a chance that if she didn't say it now, she would never have the chance to say it again.

His smile saddened a bit as he acknowledged the truth of the moment. "I love you."

Unlike Geoffrey, he felt no need to tell her to be careful. He trusted her.

And she trusted him. Taggart had been a war correspondent for years, so he had the most combat duty experience in Pittsburgh. He even had his own combat vest that he had brought with him from Earth.

"I threw this in our truck at the last minute." He made sure his vest covered his chest without blocking his neck movement. "Everything—the information blackout, the trouble with the visa, the news that Windwolf had been attacked and possibly dead—gave me chicken skin."

It was the Hawaiian way of saying "goose bumps."

"I promise to keep my head down low," Nigel said to them. "I would stay in the truck but I think that I need to be the one that Earth needs to see on the front line. They'll trust me to tell the truth. Also, I think I'll be needed to keep Hal reined in so you can focus on the fighting."

"Thank you," Jane said.

The truck stopped moving.

South Aiken Avenue was a mix of big stately brick homes built a hundred years ago and ugly mid-century brick boxes. A huge, six-story brick, turn-of-the-century flour mill had been built on the hillside beside the bridge. Shortly before the first Startup, it had been converted into an office building with sleek modern windows. Its lowest floor sat far below the bridge, level with the busway. The fourth floor was at street level and accessed via a rear parking lot.

Juergen had parked in the rear lot. The rain started to thicken and lightning flashed on the western horizon. Jane, Taggart and Nigel ducked under a portico connecting the main building to a tiered parking lot on the hillside beside it.

Jane used her family call sign over her militia headset. "Beater One to Keeper."

"Keeper here," Duff answered, sounding tense. Her little brother was working as the militia's communication hub. It was a lot of responsibility and danger to put on an eighteen-year-old but she wanted family that she could trust in the position. Too much rode on it.

"Any word on our target?" Jane said as thunder rumbled over them. The lightning storm was still far off, pushing rain ahead of it. It was roughly three miles from the Thirty-first Street Bridge to where Jane was standing now—all uphill. It would take a human an hour to stroll it. It had taken her ten minutes to drive from Marc's house to Oakland. (Granted she broke the speed limit and ignored the possibility of collision at intersections due to lack of working traffic lights.)

"The city power is still out." Duff couldn't say that the traffic camera system was offline without endangering their use of that resource. "BW is scouting."

BW, or black wing, was code for tengu. Most likely it was Yumiko, as the female had been blowing up black willows a few blocks away earlier in the afternoon. Yumiko could vanish in broad daylight, which made her a perfect scout.

"Copy that," Jane said.

Hal and Juergen got out of the front of the production truck and dashed through the rain to join her under the portico.

Hal was beaming with excitement. He'd taken off his "Hal's Heroes" hat, leaving his blond hair sticking up in short spikes. He had his boonie in his right hand and his antique pith helmet in his left. "Which hat would be better? The pith is more dashing."

Jane covered her mic. "Don't stand out. Wear what everyone else is wearing or snipers will target you. Get ready to go live."

Hal's smile dimmed slightly—probably at the prospect of blending in. His ego liked standing out to the point that it over-whelmed both the great intelligence and little wisdom that he had. "WQED has backup power but most of our viewers don't. No one is going to be watching the evening news."

"We're going to jury-rig a connection to WESA via the walkie-talkies and broadcast over the radio."

"Really?" Hal said. "We can do that?"

"Yes," Jane said without explaining more. She and her broth-ers had kept Hal in the dark about many aspects of the militia since he was such a loose cannon. They decided that he might be less dangerous if he didn't know everything.

Duff had reported a successful test last week. Jane hadn't thought of the radio station needing an emergency generator at the time. She shook her head at her stupid mistake. *Should have, could have, would have.* Roach promised to get the radio station quickly back on the air. If anyone in Pittsburgh could track down a generator and get it installed in minutes, he could. At the moment, though, her portable radio was transmitting static instead of WESA.

"Roach is hooking up a generator so the radio station will be back on air shortly. Taggart, film Nigel's intro now. We'll do fill-in if there's a lull."

Hal pulled on his blue bucket hat and started his vocal warm-ups, trilling up and down.

Jane turned to Juergen. The parking garage had a heavy steel beam barring vehicles over six feet seven inches from entering. The *Chased by Monsters* truck was a whopping nine feet tall. "This is a dead end for the truck. If the oni push through the barricade, the truck will be pinned down here. Move it back up the street."

Juergen nodded and headed back to the truck.

Nigel, Taggart, and Hal set up a shielded light on Nigel and started filming. "We've received word that a large oni force is heading toward the elf enclaves in Oakland. When we arrived, we were informed that the *domana* are unconscious, seemingly struck down within their walls by an oni spell..."

"Beater One, this is Keeper," Duff said over Jane's headset.

"Beater One here," she responded quietly after moving out of earshot.

"BW has sighted oni on Liberty Avenue—two thousand feet and closing."

Two thousand feet was less than a half mile, which would put the oni near Morrow Park.

"Copy that," Jane said. "Going to command."

"Copy that," Duff said.

She switched channels on her radio. "This is Storm Six."

She'd been thinking of an odd conversation with Tooloo when she picked out the call sign for the command unit. The old female elf had cautioned Jane to keep her cards close to her chest. It was the reason Jane later set up the militia in spy cells. The old elf had called Jane "my little storm fury" as she walked away with her pet rooster. The entire conversation had proved to be an earworm as Jane couldn't stop replaying the exchange over and over in her head. "Fury" was too easy to garble but "storm" worked as a call sign.

"I'm in position," Jane said over the headset. "Smithfield, Carson, what's your twenty?"

"Storm Six, this is Smithfield," Alton said. "We're in the eagle's nest."

"Storm Six, this is Carson," Martha Champagne said. "We're establishing fortifications at current position."

"Target is approaching Liberty and Baum," Jane said. Smithfield would be able to see which direction the oni headed once they hit Baum Boulevard.

"Copy that!" Smithfield said.

"This is Hot Metal! Copy target position!" Hot Metal's excited baritone chimed in. He was a good man but he liked being in the spotlight.

"This is Homestead," Kate Emerson calmly added as the Homestead Bridge cell leader. She was legendary as an unshakeable hunter. "No sign yet at front line."

Jane waved to Taggart to indicate that she was leaving. She headed around the corner with Chesty on her heels.

The bridge on South Aiken Avenue was two hundred feet long and wide enough for three lanes of traffic and sidewalks on both sides. Jersey barriers separated the vehicle traffic from the pedestrian walkways. A tall chain-link fence kept people from stepping off the bridge's deck.

Far below were two sets of train tracks protected on both sides by high cement walls, topped with a chain-link fence to keep people and animals off the rails. The rail line continued past the Rim, laid down by the elves two decades ago, heading northeast to meet up with the main train line out of Station Square. Slightly higher were two lanes of bus roadway that stopped abruptly at the rim. Beyond the road, there was another fence, to keep people from trespassing on the limited access busway. While the oni could muscle their way across all barriers, it was unlikely that they would try.

Her side of the bridge was controlled chaos. Hot Metal and Homestead were using pickup trucks to ferry rubble from beside Sacred Heart to South Aiken Avenue. The front vehicle shone its headlights onto a wall of bricks and cinder block and steel girders at the end of the bridge, just shy of where the Jersey barriers stopped. The wall was already four feet tall and growing taller. The section on the left was higher to create a safe escape route to the driveway. Beyond the barricade, concertina wire created a web of sharp metal shards.

Doug Bowser was the leader of Hot Metal, although most

people knew him as Dog Bow-Wow. He stopped what he was doing when he spotted her—they had beaten saluting out of him early on because it told enemy snipers who was in command. Doug was sporting his signature dog collar but managed to score true military camo rain gear. "Sir, should we wait until we see the whites of their eyes or what?"

"Shoot as soon as you have a target." Jane suspected that the oni were going to come in a wave, hoping to overrun them with sheer numbers. Normally she would have ordered the militia to conserve ammo but the point of creating a choke point was to make it like shooting fish in a bucket. "Remember that the tengu are our allies. Don't shoot at them!"

"Yes, sir." Doug moved off to spread the word through the ranks.

Almost as if summoned, Yumiko ghosted out of the darkness. She was panting from flying. She'd dismissed her wings as if she was afraid of being shot. "There's thousands of them. They have wargs on leashes and something in cages. They've got tarps over the cages, so I could only get a quick look at one of them. I didn't recognize the creature but it had spell runes written all over it. I think the greater bloods plan to enlarge the beast like they did the foo dogs."

Jane's stomach gave a sickening lurch. Hot Metal and Homestead were less than a hundred people combined. They weren't going to be able to stop the flood of oni. The bridge, though, created the only possible stopping point. If they let the oni get past it, they could spread out. It would turn fighting into a deadly game of hide and seek with the enemy having scent-tracking wargs.

Yumiko jerked around to stare toward Downtown. "Jin Wong calls!" She stood silent, listening to a voice that only the tengu could hear. "He's ordering the Flock to Oakland! Tinker *domi* is awake and angry."

That was the first good news of the day. The tengu admitted to having twenty thousand of their people on Elfhome.

"How many?" Jane asked.

Yumiko shook her head with dismay. "Everyone who is fit to fight. If Tinker falls today, we will lose our protection. More *domana* will come from the Easternlands to battle the oni but they will judge us as one of the enemy. Tinker must survive this battle."

Jane winced. She hadn't been entirely happy with the fact that the tengu *yamabushi* had been watching over her family, especially since the oni hadn't moved against them after they rescued Boo. Today, though, she had found the knowledge comforting, especially in Duff's case. She could understand why Jin Wong was committing everything to stopping the oni before they overwhelmed Tinker *domi* and the enclaves. At least it meant that the militia only needed to hold the bridge until reinforcements arrived.

Chesty growled softly, staring across the bridge.

"They're coming!" Jane called out, taking hard cover. "Turn out those headlights! Take cover! Get ready to fire!"

She motioned to Chesty to lie down, as close to the wall as he could get. She crouched down beside him. "Stay down, boy."

Quiet fell as the headlights turned off and plunged them into rainy darkness. In the silence, they could hear horns blowing. Jane couldn't identify the type, it wasn't as metallic as a truck or train horn. It was mellow like a trumpet playing a slow growling fanfare, but deeper. Chesty grumbled with annoyance at the strange noise.

"What is that?" someone asked fearfully in the darkness. "Are those kusei?"

"No, not kusei." Kate had a herd of the shaggy Elfhome elephants. She would know. "Not saurus either. Maybe some kind of new monster."

"War horns," Yumiko said quietly. Apparently the tengu female thought it was up to Jane to decide if the information should be readily spread. "They're made from the tusks of animals like kusei hollowed out into large wind instruments."

"It's just horns!" Jane shouted. "They're like the horns that people play at football games! The oni are trying to psych us! Just ignore them!"

"*Three worlds bridged by a single span,*" Dog Bow-Wow sang in the darkness. "*Steel that climbs from earth to sky. Freedom to create, freedom to fly—one world, one people, one kind. We are Pittsburgh.*"

"We are Pittsburgh!" His people chanted to drown out the horns. "We are Pittsburgh! We are Pittsburgh! We are Pittsburgh!"

For a few minutes, it worked. Then the oni advanced and the horns grew louder.

"Pipe down!" Jane shouted. The horns and chanting were going to drown out orders. The rain grew heavier, beating down on her shoulders and the pavement around her. The gutters were starting to overflow. If the sun was still up, it was lost behind the thick clouds. The other end of the bridge vanished in the dark and rain. They were going to be shooting blindly.

Lightning grew closer, the thunder coming faster after the sky flashed to white.

Taggart, Hal, and Nigel came scuttling up to her, running low to keep behind the protection of the stone wall. Hal shook his head to indicate that WESA wasn't up and broadcasting yet. Nigel was monologuing. Taggart panned over the militia. He had the *Chased by Monsters'* night vision camera out that they used to film nocturnal animals, wrapped against the rain.

"Keep low," Jane cautioned her crew. "What can you see on the other side of the bridge? How close are they?"

Taggart rose up slightly to film over the wall. "The front line is about three hundred meters from the end of the bridge. They're spread from sidewalk to sidewalk."

With the length of the bridge added onto that number, the oni were currently beyond the effective range of the hunting rifles and shotguns that most of the militia had. The bullets might hit them but they would have no penetrating power—not at that distance. They needed every bullet to count.

"How fast are they moving?" Jane asked.

"It looks like normal walking speed."

Which meant the oni would be at the end of the bridge within a minute or two. The problem was that the militia couldn't see what they were shooting at. Even if they turned the truck's high beams on, it would illuminate the full bridge. It would make the militia's thin ranks visible. Was it worth the risk?

"Strike a blow!" Hal suddenly exclaimed loudly, standing up. "For Freedom!"

"Hal!" Jane shouted.

Hal held a tube above his head. Jane realized it was a rocket flare as he pulled the cord, launching the flare. The rocket whooshed away. A heartbeat later, it exploded over the far side of the bridge—a sudden white nova of light. The parachute illumination flare started to drift downward, lighting up the street beyond the far side of the bridge.

The enemy troops surged forward, breaking into a run. They formed a massive wall of creatures, from pony-sized wargs to eight-foot-tall hulking oni. They carried a bizarre assortment of weapons. She caught glimpses of assault rifles, spears, shields, scimitarlike swords, and massive axes.

"Shit!" Jane reached up, grabbed the back of Hal's collar, and yanked him down as both sides opened fire.

Guns boomed all around her in a deafening unending staccato. Bullets whined overhead and ricocheted off the pavement behind them.

Jane growled a few more curses as she gave Hal a shake to let him know how angry she was with him.

"We can see now!" Hal shouted, somehow projecting even over the deafening loud noise. "Look!"

Yes, they could see the enemy. They were terrifying. The oni could also now see that they vastly outnumbered the militia. They came charging forward, roaring.

The militia wasn't going to hold.

"Go!" Jane pushed Hal toward the driveway. She tapped Taggart and pointed. He nodded grimly and took off in a crouching run. Nigel gave her a look of utter despair but followed Taggart.

The concertina wire slowed the oni down. The first rank stumbled to a screaming halt as they were entangled with the sharpened spikes. The second rank shoved them forward, ignoring their screams.

Jane fired as fast as she could pick a target, killing the nearest oni even as she scanned the ranks for their leaders. If she could take down the commanders, she might be able to sow enough chaos that the tide of enemies would check. The front warriors seemed to be all cannon folder. Boo had said that the true bloods were the most intelligent and they needed to wear masks to appear more fearsome to the animalistic lesser bloods. She spotted two that had stopped at the edge of the bridge, urging the others forward. She took them out with head shots through their fearsome masks.

The wave of oni hit the wall of rubble.

The rocket flare guttered and died, plunging them back into darkness.

"Pull back!" Jane shouted, shooting blindly. "Pull back!"

Two machine guns opened up, strobing the darkness with

muzzle flare. The bullets crisscrossed in amazing precision, punching back the oni.

Who the hell on her side had machine guns?

Jane backpedaled from the wall, keeping low, as dead oni tumbled forward off it. Corg Durrack and Hannah Briggs crouched behind the very end of the Jersey walls that flanked the bridge sidewalks, using the concrete barricades to rest the tripod of light machine guns. They fired on full auto, unloading a massive number of bullets into the oni.

Jane paused to fumble her whistle to her mouth and blew it just in case the people around her hadn't heard her shouted commands. If they didn't move now, they would be overrun the moment that Durrack and Briggs ran out of ammo.

Lightning struck a block away to the west, whitening the sky. The thunder was almost instantaneous, momentarily drowning out everything.

In that moment of brightness, she saw an oni with a rocket launcher pointed directly at her.

She jerked her gun to the right to take aim. Her line of sight was eclipsed by a massive brute of an oni bearing down on her with an eight-foot sword. Cursing, she shouldered her rifle, caught the oni by the wrist, and used his own momentum to throw him. Chesty leapt forward, growling like a bear. Even as she threw the brute, she saw the rocket flashing toward her.

She swore and tried to leap away. The rocket exploded just inches from them. Jane saw it blossom into flame. Heard the oddly muffled boom.

She felt no pain. The flames stopped inches from her, spreading sideways instead of forward.

The oni brute was suddenly without a head.

Despite the fact it was still pouring down rain, it wasn't falling on her anymore.

"Oookay," someone said in the muffled quiet, sounding at once relieved and extremely stressed out at the same time.

Jane turned.

Oilcan stood in the center of the road, his left hand up and cocked in an odd position. He was panting slightly. The Pittsburgh Salvage flatbed sat a dozen feet back, doors open, windshield wipers going, headlights flooding the night with light. Oilcan looked like he did the few times that their paths had crossed over the years. Summer field parties. Pig roasts. Building Geoffrey's casting circle. Places where Roach and Geoffrey had invited both friends and family. He still wore a T-shirt, blue jeans, and biker boots. The only difference was Oilcan's ears were now definitely longer and pointed.

Flanking Oilcan were two *sekasha*, one male and one female, both with Stone Clan Black tattoos on their arms. The female, though, wore a Wind Clan Blue wyvern-scale vest. This must be the infamous Thorne Scratch on Stone who had killed Earth Son.

Who was the male, flicking blood from his sword after beheading the brute?

"You're Geoffrey's big sister, right?" Oilcan said. "Jane?"

"Yeah," Jane said as she glanced around. The oni seemed to have realized that a *domana* with *sekasha* had joined the fray. They were falling back. It might be in fear, or it might be to change battle tactics.

12: BURNING BRIDGES

Oilcan could barely believe that this was his Pittsburgh. A wall of rubble blocked South Aiken Avenue at the bridge over the busway. Dead oni littered the payment. Humans—friends and neighbors he'd known half his life—in camo rain gear and plastic trash bags, gathered tight within his shield. They gripped rifles, splattered with blood. Oni blood. Their own blood.

The rain did little to wash away the smell of gun smoke.

He thought he'd been racing to Oakland to save Tinker. He'd managed to beat her there. He hoped it meant that she was slowed down by organizing a larger force than what he had to bring to fight.

What he found made him glad that he'd come as quickly as he had. These were his people. He was the only one that could protect them until Tinker showed up.

Geoffrey Kryskill and Snapdragon had flagged Oilcan down near Sacred Heart.

"Oh, dude, so glad to see you! Everyone here is fine for now." Geoffrey had pointed toward South Aiken. "But the militia needs *domana* backup at the bridge over the busway!"

Anyone else, Oilcan would have ignored and checked on Forge. Geoffrey was careful and precise. Measure twice, thrice even. Oilcan trusted Geoffrey to have weighed the situation as carefully as he worked with wood.

Snapdragon had handed a quiver of spell arrows through the

131

driver's window to Moon Dog. "Take these, holy one. I will get more from the enclaves."

"*Waya!*" Moon Dog said. "I was low! Thank you!"

Oilcan didn't expect to find Geoffrey's older sister leading the militia. Jane had been grappling with a male nearly two feet taller than her, shouting out curses, even as death was blasting toward her. Oilcan barely got his shield up in time to stop the rocket from taking out Jane and the rest of the militia crouched behind the wall.

The Kryskills always had that Norse god vibe going on. Jane Kryskill turned—tall, blond, and regal as a Valkyrie. Her hair had come out of its ponytail when she'd grappled with the oni brute. It fell down over her shoulders in a golden mane. She wore the same neutral warrior mask of the *sekasha*: rage burned in her blue eyes but otherwise didn't show. Lightning flickered across the dark sky behind her. Her big elfhound, Chesty, stood in guard position, rumbling threats.

"We should move," Jane said in clumsy high school Elvish. She obviously wanted the *sekasha* to understand her tactics upfront. "If we were fighting humans, this is when the enemy would call in an airstrike to soften up the target."

"I agree with this assessment," Thorne Scratch said.

"Pull back!" Jane shouted, waving to the militia. "Follow me!"

Jane crouched as she ran, keeping behind the wall of rubble as if Oilcan wasn't holding an impenetrable shield. He couldn't blame her—he hadn't been able to see the magical protection until he was made an elf. Her elfhound and the militia followed her.

Oilcan held his position, keeping the shield up as the militia retreated. The people he knew waved and smiled. One or two laughed, being as it was the first time they'd seen him since he became an elf.

"Nice ear job!" Dog Bow-Wow shouted as he followed Jane in a crouching run.

"Can I have one too?" Scary Mary asked, probably in all seriousness, as she kept glancing back with longing on her face.

Jane thought that the oni were pulling back to do an air strike. Certainly the enemy seemed to be retreating. Oilcan wasn't sure, though, what to prepare for. More rocket grenades—or a dragon?

"What would the oni use to do an air strike with?" he asked Thorne.

Thorne Scratch clicked her tongue in an elvish shrug. She followed with guesses. "There is a chance that they will use human weapons—more of those that you just stopped. They know you are here, holding a shield, so that is unlikely. I believe it will be some kind of monster. Jewel Tear warned that they had horrors at the camps."

Oilcan had been at the top of the Cathedral of Learning during Windwolf's fight with Malice. It had given him a bird's-eye view of the massive dragon trouncing the elf lord. The idea of fighting something that big and intelligent scared Oilcan. He backed up, following the militia as he maintained his shield.

Jane crouched at the corner of the driveway at the end of the bridge. The rest of the militia was retreating to the parking lot behind her. A fifteen-foot-tall redbrick wall lined the left side of the two-lane driveway. Ivy-covered steel girders spanned the lane overhead, spaced a dozen feet apart, seemingly acting as structural support to the century-old building. While the two-hundred-foot passage was safe from gunfire from the bridge, it seemed like a solidly narrow box to get trapped in.

"Is that safe?" Oilcan waved his right hand down South Aiken Avenue. "Shouldn't we head to the enclaves?"

"We need to hold them here at the busway," Jane said. "There's no other choke point. If they spread through Oakland, they'll just roll over us."

Oilcan nodded even though he had no idea how to hold an army. He could barely see in the rainy dark, and his night vision had improved since being made an elf. Jane probably couldn't see anything.

Amazingly, Nigel Reid was halfway down the driveway, being filmed by a cameraman. What was the Earth-based naturalist doing on Elfhome? When had he come to Elfhome? Oilcan doubted his eyes but there was no mistaking the Scottish burr as the man said, "We had to skedaddle off as the situation got a bit radge. I think we're alright. That was a barry display of *domana* spell-casting, it was!"

Nigel must have come to Elfhome during the last Shutdown. Oilcan's and Tinker's lives had imploded after saving Windwolf in June. They changed species. They moved to new homes. They abandoned their business. They fell out of contact with many of their old friends.

Oilcan had even stopped listening to the radio. Thanks to Chloe Polanski, the media was full of outright lies, half truths, and pure speculation that were all emotionally painful. It reminded him too much of the days immediately after his mother's murder. Oilcan used his ancient iPod to listen to music instead of the radio.

Lightning flickered, striking nearby. Thunder boomed, making Oilcan flinch. On the oni side of the bridge there were weird flashes of magic, like firecrackers going off against his new senses. He wasn't sure what it meant—he didn't have the experience to translate the input. The snap and crackle went on and on. What was that?

He backed up more, following the retreating militia so his shield would continue to protect them.

Jane moved down the driveway, giving orders over her headset radio. "This is Storm Six. Hot Metal, find an escape route from the parking lot. We can't get bottled in here. Homestead, move into the building. Use windows for sniper position but stay back from the sills..."

"Oh, geez! Not again!" Corg Durrack yelled from somewhere behind Nigel. "Incoming! Freaking huge bees!" There was a burst of machine-gun fire. "How do you kill these things?"

A swarm of the giant hornets came flying out of the dark rain—too many to count, and each the size of a wolf. The massive insects were too widespread; Oilcan couldn't block them from attacking the scattered militia. He had no idea how to expand the diameter of this shield.

"We just need to kill one," Moon Dog said. "The swarm will focus its attack on those nearest to the death scent."

Oilcan remembered that Moon Dog had them burn Rebecca's clothes to get rid of the attack pheromones soaked into them. He concentrated on keeping his left hand cocked, holding the shield spell, as he summoned a force strike. He aimed toward the bridge instead of the driveway, hoping to lure the swarm away from the militia.

The force strike took out a half dozen hornets, reducing the massive wolf-sized bodies down to rat-sized smears on broken pavement. Instantly the swarm turned and dove at him. They landed on his shield, closing off what little light was left in the night. It plunged them into utter darkness, surrounded by the deafening noise of hundreds of giant insect wings sounding like a thousand angry violinists.

Thorne Scratch took out a spell light and activated the shining orb with a word.

It was not an improvement.

The hornets' alien amber faces, close enough to reach out and touch, gazed in at them—each as large as a dinner plate. Antenna quivering. Wedged shaped jaws working. Butcher-knife-sized stingers jabbing against his shield.

Normally, Oilcan wouldn't have said he was afraid of bugs; this day was testing that belief. Even knowing that the hornets were magical constructs, that the real insects hidden inside the fake puppet shells were less than a foot long, didn't help.

Lightning flashed, barely visible through the thick layer of massive angry hornets. Thunder boomed loudly. Even as it faded, something trumpeted nearby.

"War horns," Thorne Scratch identified the sound.

"They are releasing a horror," Moon Dog added. "That is the command to clear the area as a horror will readily attack the oni army if given a chance. The creatures kill anything in front of them. The oni are to swing southwest."

Thorne Scratch glanced hard at Moon Dog.

Moon Dog took the look as a question. "I was on a gossamer with veterans of the Oni War for a week. I made good use of my time. You know what Tempered Steel says..."

"'The true battle starts before the first weapon is drawn,'" Thorne Scratch and Moon Dog said together. They'd both studied under one of the most famous *sekasha* at Cold Mountain Temple. While they had just met this morning for the first time, they had known of each other for years due to the common connection.

Oilcan hadn't wanted another person following him around, but he was glad now that Thorne Scratch had backup. He tried to shut out thoughts of how it could all end badly. What should he do now?

Southwest would take the oni to the Centre Avenue Bridge across the busway, over three blocks away.

"The oni are heading to Centre Avenue!" Oilcan called to Jane. "I'll deal with whatever they're throwing this way. You should move to Centre."

"Roger that!" Jane shouted.

It meant that Oilcan would have to handle the horror solo while the militia dealt with the main oni force.

If he could handle the horror...

First he needed to kill the hornets.

Holding his shield stable with his left hand, he flashed through force strike after force strike. He was beating the hornets to a pulp when he felt a huge flare of magic on the other side of the bridge. It felt the same as the firecracker motes that had preceded the hornets but on a larger scale.

"Here it comes!" He moved away from the driveway's mouth, hoping to lure the mystery beast away from the militia. "Whatever it is!"

A creature came bounding over the bridge, jumping from point to point, ignoring the concertina wire, the dead bodies, the rubble wall. It was like nothing Oilcan had ever seen before. It had the general build of a warg—if said warg was as big as a house. It had a thick armored hide that reminded Oilcan of an ankylosaurus. Random spikes and tusks and horns protruding all over its head and body.

"*Kau!*" Moon Dog said in his thick Stone Clan accent. "It is a *baenae!*"

"A what?" Oilcan asked.

"You should know the shield that you are currently holding has limits," Thorne said quickly. "It is very strong against sudden impact like a force strike or human guns. It allows, however, certain elements like sound, light, and air to pass. It must or we would be deaf and blind on the battlefield and would slowly suffocate. Unfortunately, to allow these elements in, others can follow. We need to kill this horror quickly."

In other words, the beast did something that would penetrate his shield over time. Oilcan could feel the chill of the night. The wet of the air. While the thunder was muffled as it rumbled over them, it was still shockingly loud. Any number of things could breach his protection.

The creature slammed into the invisible edge of his shield, snarling. A pungent smell like an angry skunk seeped in over the smell of rain, mud, oily pavement, and wet dog. Moments later, his eyes started to burn.

"Is it poisonous?" Oilcan guessed.

"Among other things," Thorne said.

Oilcan hit it with a force strike, trying to knock it back. The thing hunched its massive shoulders, digging into the pavement with claws the size of pickaxes. Mist blasted out of its nostrils, freezing the rain puddles around it. A thin frost formed on the outer edge of Oilcan's shield. The stench intensified. Tears started to well up in his eyes.

He needed to get some breathing space! If he couldn't knock it back, could he move them?

"We're moving!" he warned the two warriors. "Grab hold of me!"

A childhood full of experimenting with the written spells within the Dufae Codex was all he had to pull from. He hadn't had time to properly learn the Stone Clan *esva* as it was meant to be used.

Holding his shield tight, he cast the spell that he and Tinker called "catapult."

"Wh-wh-what?" Thorne Scratch cried as they soared up in the air. "This is not how you use that spell!"

"*Waya!*" Moon Dog shouted joyfully as if he were on a roller coaster.

As they soared upward, Oilcan aimed force strikes at the utility poles that lined either side of South Aiken. The tall creosote-soaked poles shattered at their base, tangling the beast in electrical lines, streetlights, and transformers. One of the barrel transformers struck the *baenae*, making it flicker, revealing the animal within controlling the puppet shell.

Moon Dog shot a spell arrow in that instant. It flashed forward, transforming into a beam of light. It struck the inner beast but missed a killing shot as it flinched its head to the side at the last moment. Its ear was clipped and its shoulder grazed by the laser-intense beam. The puppet shell went back to solid. The creature roared with pain.

"Ah, I got greedy," Moon Dog said sadly. "I should not have gone for a head shot."

The *baenae* drew back its head and then lunged forward to breathe out a blizzard of cold.

The world went white around them. The rain smearing down Oilcan's shield turned to thick ice. His breath misted in the sudden cold within his protective circle. The cold seemed to suck away all his heat, leaving him shivering. He could barely see as his eyes burned like hot cinders, and tears poured down his cheeks to freeze.

He cast catapult again. The momentum shattered the ice encasing them. They shifted only a dozen feet before starting to descend again. He cast the spell again to boost them high up in the air. He felt two more large spikes of magic on the other side of the bridge. The oni had created two more horrors. "We have two more incoming!"

"We cannot stand against three of these," Thorne stated calmly, as if they weren't fighting for their lives. "The poison will overwhelm us."

"Okay," Oilcan said while thinking fast. "We can hurt it if I hit it with a big hunk of metal and you two shoot spell arrows." The only thing he could see that qualified as "a big hunk" was a red fire hydrant, just beside the driveway that the militia had vanished down. A childhood with Tinker made him very familiar with how they worked. He'd have to hit it so that the water pressure within turned the pieces into projectiles. "Ready?"

Oilcan landed them with the edge of his shield nearly touching the hip-high pipe. He hit it with a force strike. The metal sheared off at the weak point, the massive water pressure within the pipe shooting the pieces out to slam into the oncoming monster. The solid illusion of the horror flickered, revealing the beast within. Instantly two shafts of light leapt the distance as the *sekasha* released their spell arrows. They both had gone for the heart, choosing the sure kill. The massive beast staggered and went down.

Even as it collapsed, Oilcan's eyes teared up until he was blind. He staggered backward, blinking and wiping at his face with the hem of his T-shirt. Two more horrors were coming at them and there were no other handy pieces of metal lying around.

Flaaammbooom!

Blind as he was, Oilcan couldn't see what had just caught fire. Whatever it was—it was huge. The light and heat and smell of burning asphalt washed over him even with his shield up. As he blinked his vision clear, a second column of flame bloomed mid-bridge. Massive. Hot. Loud. The horrors were on fire. Even as they thrashed about, howling in pain, a third and fourth and fifth column of flames beat down on them.

"Thank the gods," Thorne murmured. "Tinker *domi* has arrived."

13: ENTER THE GODDESS OF WAR

Setting an entire section of Oakland on fire did not make Tinker feel any better.

She had the comfort of seeing Oilcan safe and sound. Well... mostly safe. He smelled worse than a roadkill skunk and his eyes were watering.

She smacked him with her right hand since she was maintaining a shield spell with her left. Rain smeared down the invisible dome around them. "I told you to stay at McKees Rocks!"

"I couldn't run and hide when everyone was in danger," he said. "And literally *everyone* we know seems to be out here fighting."

"Stupid people," she muttered because there were none of them in sight, helping Oilcan. Not that there was much that they could do against the massive creatures. Despite the stench, she hugged him hard.

He laughed. "You're going to smell as bad as me if we keep this up."

"I don't care," she said fiercely.

"Oh, you'll care in an hour or so."

He was probably right. Her eyes were starting to water.

"This is why 'deodorize' was probably invented. Datapad!" She dropped her shield. Cold rain poured down on her. She snapped her fingers to get her datapad carried over to her by one of the tengu that had come with Riki. The male made faces at the smell as she looked up the spell. She could draw it from memory:

139

smashed skunks were a common problem at the salvage yard. She had never memorized the *domana* finger positions since she hadn't recognized the notation as something more than random squiggles. The fingering was fairly simple. She handed the tablet back to the male and waved him away so the metal wouldn't interfere with her spell-casting.

The spell felt like a thousand tiny fingers scrubbing over her skin and through her hair. A little creepy but not painful. She wondered how it worked. Combining electrons? Now was not the time to be distracted.

The stench vanished from everyone and everything in a wide radius around her. She recast her shield, keeping out the rain.

"You were probably too busy to notice," she said, "but those little twerps just bounced their way from Haven to somewhere near Washington Crossing Bridge."

Oilcan tilted his head in confusion. "Which little twerps?"

"My little sisters!" Tinker smacked him again. "They're tapping the Spell Stones and using catapult."

"They're coming to Oakland?" Oilcan asked. "Why?"

"Who knows! The mind boggles. The tengu from Haven are like 'they were playing nicely with the other children when we left.' Gods knows what insanity they could wreak with a horde of tengu children at their beck and call. You know that I'm at my worst when I have a construction crew!"

"That's true," Oilcan said.

She was tempted to smack him again. "The twerps stopped short of Oakland. They might be lost. They're somewhere behind the oni army."

Oilcan pointed west toward the burning bridge and the smoking oni dead, raising one eyebrow.

"Yes. Over there," Tinker said. "I can feel them holding a Stone Clan shield over there—nearly to the river."

Oilcan looked down as he focused on his new ability to feel magic. He nodded. "Yeah, I can feel it too."

"I was going to send tengu to scout for them but if the girls have Little Miss Pocket Dragon with them—and a plan—I don't think the tengu will be able to fetch them."

"Joy is with the mice," Oilcan said. "They're the ones that gave me the spell at the ice cream shop on the South Side. They said something about a print job being done and took off."

Tinker pressed her palm to her forehead. Unborn babies running about Pittsburgh with a dragon. Nine-year-olds bouncing into the city like giant rubber balls. All up to gods knew what. If it were her, she'd shanghai any adult sent to fetch her. Sending tengu after them might have been throwing manpower into a black hole.

"I'll go after them," Oilcan said.

She looked up in surprise.

"If anyone can talk them into an alternate plan, it's me," he said. "I have the most experience with this kind of thing."

She didn't like the idea but he was completely right. He had always been able to talk her into alternate routes when her original plan was too insanely dangerous.

Even if she gave him a score of tengu, it felt like she was sending him out shorthanded to deal with two of her sisters. He'd be outnumbered even if he never encountered oni.

It was then she noticed that he'd picked up another *sekasha*: a young male in Stone Clan black who was all wide-eyed and amazed about something. That made her feel a little better. The summer had been one long accidental lesson on how effective just one of the warriors could be.

"Who is this?" she asked in Elvish, unsure of the protocol. There was some weird custom between the *domana* involving rank but she wasn't sure if it applied to another caste. There was so much she didn't know about elves.

The male warrior sketched a bow and gave an impressively long name made of words that she didn't know. Her confusion must have shown on her face.

"His name is Moon Dog," Oilcan added in a mix of Elvish and English. This triggered a quiet explanation from Throne Scratch to Moon Dog that humans liked to give nicknames to everyone, ignoring whatever name a person got cursed with at birth.

Cursed with?

The warriors in her Hand nodded at Thorne's explanation. Did they all dislike their names as much as she hated "Alexander Graham Bell"? She felt weird for not knowing that they didn't like their given names. It would explain why they all used nicknames when referring to each other.

"They can do that?" Moon Dog whispered in surprise.

"They do it for almost everyone," Thorne Scratch murmured.

"*Waya!* I like that," Moon Dog said. "I am Moon Dawg."

A thunder of guns to the west reminded Tinker that she didn't have time to stand and talk.

"*Domi,*" Riki said quietly. "The militia is holding the bridges at Centre Avenue and Baum Boulevard. They're vastly outnumbered even with us backing them up. They need you."

Militia? Pittsburgh had a militia? Since when? Why hadn't anyone told her? Or had they told her and she misunderstood what they were saying? That was how she ended up an elf and married to Windwolf.

"Okay," she said. "Let them know I'm here."

"Oh, everyone in Oakland knows you're here," Oilcan said.

She considered sticking her tongue out at him but decided that she shouldn't be immature in front of people she was about to lead into battle. She hugged him instead. "Be careful."

"I always am," he said. "It's how I survived your tween years."

She let go of Oilcan to smack him again. Lightly.

The militia had taken the most direct route from South Aiken Bridge to Morewood Avenue. They had run through the parking garage, gone over a six-foot garden wall, across a backyard, and down multiple back alleys. Tinker had a small army with her: the EIA troops, royal marines, a random Hand of Wyverns, and tengu coming out of her ears. Some were on foot but a majority of them were in trucks. The most direct route was out. She headed in the general direction of the Centre Avenue Bridge while giving out orders.

Oilcan had the right of it; almost everyone they knew was in Oakland fighting the oni. She tripped over one person after another. Moser. Snapdragon. Geoffrey. Bo Pederson. Scary Mary. Durrack and Briggs. Babs Bunny. Even Ellen McMicking was there with her tiny house diner, dishing out free food. With every step, Tinker felt like the weight of the city was pressing down on her more and more.

All these lives were dependent on her.

She might be a *domana,* but she knew only a handful of attack and defense spells. Worse, the oni most likely had another *intanyai seyosa* like Chloe Polanski directing the attack. Tinker needed to be clever and unexpected.

At least she had a large construction crew to pull from. She grabbed Geoffrey as the person who most understood magic and human technology.

"You remember my pipe experiments?" she asked him as she pointed to the twenty-foot-long, eight-inch-wide PVC pipes strapped to the roof of the EIA cargo truck. The soldiers had ignored all the writing on the outside of the white tubes, so they were haphazardly stacked. Granted, some of it was random graffiti that Team Tinker had scribbled on them years ago. The team had found her initial operating icons too cryptic and had added clarifications to her pictograms. As usual with a group project, it quickly got out of hand. Andy's name was the most noticeable from where they stood, done in his then ten-year-old's wobbly print. The "N" was backward, which was typical Andy.

"Oh, geez, that was ages ago!" Geoffrey said. "But yeah, my aunt is still mad about her lilac bush."

The pipes needed a crew to position them so she had tested them out at the Roach landfill. Mistakes were made—hence the need for clarifications to the operating icons.

"Yeah, well...Captain Josephson!" she called out to the EIA commander. "Assign a five-man work crew to Geoffrey here!"

Josephson looked surprised but nodded, calling out names of men.

"Oh, here." She found the sketch of the converters that she made on the way out to Oakland. It was as much as she dared with an enemy *intanyai seyosa* possibly watching her every move and trying to guess what she planned to do next. "There's a portable generator on the truck. These things convert electric into magic. Set them up beside the pipes before you get started—but use the extension cord to keep them away from the generator!"

"Wait, wait, wait!" Geoffrey cried as Tinker headed toward the battle. "Is there only the pipes?"

"Nah, everything you need should be on the truck! Sawhorses. Mallets. Metronome. Golf balls." She was glad that she'd stored all the things together so that the EIA troops could just snap them up. "If anything is missing—improvise. I believe in you! Make it work!"

Somewhere along the way she'd picked up one of Forge's Hands. It was troubling that they were with her, not Forge. The good news was it was only one of his Hands. The bad news was that it was his First Hand, led by Dark Scythe.

She wanted to ask "Is Forge still alive?" but guilt made the words stick in her throat. She managed to ask, "How is Forge?"

"We have cast a healing spell on him to speed his recovery," Dark Scythe said. "He should wake soon but we have little hope that he will be able to fight. A genetic scan has shown that the attack damaged his genetic key to the Spell Stones. Jewel Tear is similarly wounded. The others are seeing to her."

Tinker nodded her understanding while trying not to wince. She'd forgotten about the female elf who had been through hell and back. Tinker was really letting things slip through the cracks. To be fair, there were currently a lot of cracks.

"Does Forge know how to fix this?" She didn't have time to scour through the original Dufae Codex to see if anything that her grandfather edited out could be helpful.

Dark Scythe growled. What was that supposed to mean?

"No?" she guessed.

"It is a guess," Dark Scythe said, "but I think he will know a spell that could reverse the damage but its range would not be that of the enemy's. It is a matter of cohesion. All spells cast by *domana* uses the caster as the foci. From the caster, none of our spells are effective beyond *matimo*."

Matimo was roughly twelve and a half miles. The *domana* in Pittsburgh weren't a problem; she could gather them together in one place. The problem was the counter spell wouldn't reach Windwolf or the East Coast holdings. Windwolf's brothers and sisters had gathered to his defense over the last few weeks by moving into his scattered "holdings." (Tinker wasn't sure what they were beyond Aum Renau and the port of Brotherly Love. She should find out what-all she needed to protect.) The important fact was that all of Windwolf's responsibilities were within one *mei* of Pittsburgh. It meant all of her in-laws were probably now helpless. It was a sure bet that the oni planned to attack the East Coast. Maybe once Pittsburgh was subdued; maybe before then.

Dark Scythe continued. "Since the attack knocked Forge and Jewel Tear unconscious, even if Forge can 'fix' the others, his spell would render them comatose for a second time. It would be too dangerous to cast in mid-battle. We would need to be sure that Wolf Who Rules' siblings were in a safe place. Two such spells, back to back, might also be too much for any person to survive."

She nodded her understanding even as she considered all the

implications. She couldn't safely flip Forge and Jewel Tear back with a localized version of the spell. She'd need to wait for the survivors of the forest expedition to return or at least find a safe place to hole up. Jin Wong had said that the oni transformed his people using the dead body of Providence. He warned that if oni used one of the egg-shaped magical traps that held baby dragons to cast a spell, the results would be far reaching. It seemed as if she wouldn't be able to reverse the spell at the same scale without one of the traps.

And she had no idea where the oni had them hidden.

She was almost to Morewood Avenue when someone called out from the deep shadows, "Tinker! Tinker! I've got something important to tell you! Life and death!"

She knew that the voice was familiar but she couldn't put a name to it. She veered toward the shadows, still maintaining her shield just in case. "What is it?"

A large man stood tucked in an apartment building's side entrance. Like many of the people she'd seen so far that evening, he wore a black trash bag as rain protection. Unlike everyone else, he'd simply pulled it over his head and torn out eyeholes.

"What the hell?" Tinker said. "Who are you? Take that off."

"It's me," the man started to pull off the bag. "Bingo."

"Oh! Shit!" Tinker glanced at her Hand. They all had swords in hand. Things weren't going to get better when the trash bag came all the way off. "It's okay! He's one of Oilcan's Beholden! Stand down."

Bingo was one of the Chang boys who worked security at the racetrack. All her past interactions with him revolved around drunken race fans, potential stalkers, and attempted thefts from Team Tinker's storage locker. Tinker had known him too long to think of him as "not human," but he was one of the half-oni. He was built like a mastiff dog—large and powerful. He had nothing as obvious as Tommy's cat ears, so he could pass as full human. But once you knew that his father was a lesser blood oni, it was impossible not to see the evidence of the Skin Clan's genetic tampering. His big square head. His odd puglike nose. His drooping jowls. His oversized ears that had a slight tendency to flop.

Bingo looked brutish but he wasn't cruel. He could be painfully

honest and stupidly blunt but he never said anything unkind unless
provoked. He was surprisingly polite for his size and looks. He
said "please" and "thank you" as if they had been ground into
him by a loving but relentless mother.

"He's one of Oilcan's Beholden!" Tinker repeated loudly so that
any random trigger-happy elf behind her wouldn't kill the male.

She was glad that she had because when he pulled off the
trash bag, it revealed that he was half-naked and covered in oni
warpaint.

"What the hell?" Tinker said. "Why—why—why—?" There
were so many questions that she wanted to ask but couldn't
decide where to start. "Why are you painted?"

Bingo was too dumb to cut to the point. "I was looking for a
new warren for us. Tommy doesn't like where we are now—but
he's the only one. Anyhow, I started in the Strip District and got
all the way out to the Rim when the area flooded with lesser
bloods. I had this big-brain moment: If I disguised myself, I might
be able to use all the confusion and find out what their battle
plan was. So I stripped down, helped myself to some war paint,
and blended in. I grew up with them all around us; I knew how
to walk the walk."

"Get to the point, Bingo!" Tinker growled. She didn't want
the militia to be completely overrun before she got to Centre
Avenue Bridge.

"The lesser bloods aren't all stupid. They knew some stuff
and were flapping their mouths a lot, partially showing off but
mostly bitching. 'The plan' up to a little while ago was to have
Okami Shiroikage—the Unmaker—in Pittsburgh when the invasion
started but something happened to him. The lesser bloods think
he got stuck on Earth when you pulled the gate down. It meant,
though, that the leaders got scrambled to fill the gap. Kajo was
supposed to lead the troops into Oakland because Lord Tomtom
kept killing prisoners by mistake. The lesser bloods figure that
Kajo didn't want the battles to turn into a bloodbath. They were
told over and over again to only kill humans that shoot at them:
EIA, cops, and whoever else shows up to help the elves. That's it.
No killing and eating college students and whatnot. Kajo doesn't
want to fight the humans—yet."

"Bingo!" Tinker shouted. "The point!"

Bingo pulled out a phone and tapped on it until he found a

photo. "Mokoto showed me how to take pictures with my phone. This is the greater blood who's leading the troops in Oakland."

It was a blurry picture of a person in a scary-looking wooden mask, painted white with red accents. Big red horns on the head. Little red horns on the jowl. Red eyes inset in a black band across the nose.

"So we really don't know what he looks like?" Tinker said.

"Trust me, he won't be taking this off as long as he's surrounded by lesser bloods. Greater bloods aren't much different from humans—they're just prettier. Some of the lesser bloods are really dangerous stupid. They'd eat their own littermates if they thought they could get away with it. The greater bloods stay in command because of these scary masks—and the biggest bodyguards that they can trust."

Bingo obviously thought that the mask was super important. Everything from the look on his doggy face to the way he gave little "take it" pushes with his phone made that clear. If he were a full dog, he'd be wagging his tail. Was it something about the oni that Tinker didn't understand, or was Bingo just stupid?

"So the commander is wearing this mask...?" Tinker prompted.

Bingo frowned a moment, apparently picking up—finally—her confusion. "There isn't a subcommander with them. That's what the lesser bloods were all bitching about. With this last-minute shuffling, they've been shortchanged on leaders. Lord Tomtom was supposed to be out in the forest with the *domana* fodder. Kajo was supposed to be here in Oakland with his little posse of mask-wearing greater bloods—but he took off days ago with all but two of them. Those two got into a big yelling fight just before I showed up and the girl took off."

"Girl?"

"The 'greater blood'"—Bingo did air quotes with his fingers—"who took off was a human female. A girl. Well, a woman. She's not young but not as old as my ma."

"Wait. What? How do you know?"

Bingo tapped his wide nose. "A mask doesn't cover up her scent. I didn't even have to get close; her smell lingered long after she left the area. My nose says that she's not an oni or elf but a human—one who's fussy about how she looks under that mask. The thing is, most lesser bloods haven't been around enough human women to know what it is that they're smelling.

Fancy soap. Expensive perfume. Makeup. Hairspray. Some of her clothes had even been dry-cleaned."

That would describe Chloe to a T. Was this a sister to Chloe? How many sisters did Chloe have? *How many aunts am I going to have to kill?*

"Is she still on the other side of the bridge?" Tinker asked uneasily. Chloe had been able to guess all her moves but the last one. Tinker had less time to prepare—she had fewer aces up her sleeve.

Bingo shook his head. "No. Like I said, she took off. The girl seemed sure that taking the enclaves was going to be easy as taking candy from a baby. Mori didn't think so."

"Mori?"

"Moriyajuto. All the greater bloods have stupid-long names that sound scary. Mori and the girl were fighting because both of them seemed to think that they were in charge. The girl knew somehow that Oilcan wasn't going to be caught up in whatever they did to cripple the *domana*. The girl told Mori that he was to throw the *baenae* at Oilcan because, as Stone Clan, he would have a hard time killing them before their poison got him. The girl wasn't sure if you would show up but if you did, Mori was to use horrors that are immune to fire. She seemed sure that they would just roll right over you. She took about half of the lesser bloods and left."

"Oh joy." Tinker knew the finger positions for much of the Stone Clan *esva*, but in the last few weeks, she'd learned that knowing and doing were two different things. Tinker had never done anything that required her to rapidly bend her fingers into exact patterns. Even her typing was hunt and peck. Oilcan had the advantage that he had played guitar for years. She had practiced holding various shields and doing the flame strike but little else.

At least it sounded as if she wasn't going up against someone who could see the future.

"Domi, it would be useful to circulate the photo," Stormsong murmured quietly.

Tinker called over her datapad and got Bingo's phone to transfer the photo on to it. "See that Captain Josephson gets a copy of this."

The tengu holding her datapad nodded and faded back to make it so.

"Do you know where the woman went with the other half of the lesser bloods?" Tinker asked one last question.

Bingo waved vaguely toward the west. "No, not really. She said she had more important things to see to. The lesser bloods didn't know where she went but it sounded like she headed off to the big cemetery near the Rim."

The Allegheny Cemetery? It was dangerously close to where the twins had landed. Where Oilcan was headed.

Tinker had an army in motion: she couldn't abandon all these people to go running around blind in the dark. Much as she hated the idea, she would have to trust that Oilcan could get the twins to safety without her.

14: CRY "HAVOC!" AND LET SLIP THE GODDESS OF WAR

It had been a mad dash through the parking garage, over a backyard wall, and down rain-dark unlit streets to get to the Centre Avenue Bridge. It was a thousand feet of running down back alleys beside the wide curve of the bus way. Tall chain-link fencing, Jersey barriers, a rail line, and a steep hillside on the opposite side of the limited access road reduced the risk of being overrun by the oni.

Chesty kept to Jane's side. He gave no warning of hidden danger. Still she chanted "keep down, keep moving" to the people around her.

Yumiko raced with her, explaining that the first wave of monsters had been some weird magical puppet construct. "You need to hit the creature inside the outer shell to do any real damage! It can be anywhere within the puppet's skin: maybe in the head or the center of the chest. Any bullet you fire at it will be slowed down and deflected, so it's going to be difficult to kill the horror."

That explained why Jane's carefully aimed headshots had done nothing to the dog-sized hornets. Even Durack's machine-gun fire seemed to be ineffective.

"Understood." Jane glanced back in time to see something the size of a house charge across the South Aiken Bridge. It was a monstrous thing, looking like someone had smashed together a triceratops with a warg. It felt wrong to leave Oilcan alone with that thing.

Oilcan did something that knocked the monster back with a force that shook the ground.

Okay, clearing the area was the best idea. Her people couldn't handle the creature. Jane was glad that she'd had Juergen move the *Chased by Monsters* truck out of range.

"Storm Six, this is Storm One," Duff suddenly said over the radio. "Bullhorn is a go! I repeat, Bullhorn is a go!"

Her portable radio stopped broadcasting static. The afternoon deejay, Marti Wulfow, was doing a speedy intro, followed quickly by a news bulletin about the oni attack on Oakland.

"This is Storm Six, copy that! Hal!" Jane shouted as she realized that both naturalists had stopped to stare back at the monster at the bridge through *CBM*'s night vision binoculars. Taggart was ducked down beside them, filming the creature.

"We're trying to determine its species!" Hal pointed at the beast without lowering his binoculars. "It seems to have an additional magical attack beyond the normal warg's frost breath."

She grabbed hold of Hal, trusting that Nigel and Taggart would follow. "Hal! You're live! Talk to Pittsburgh! Make them care!"

"Oh!" Hal put a hand to his ear. "This is Hal Rogers, the voice of freedom! Oakland is under attack! I'm calling out to you, the people of Pittsburgh! If you value all that is good, grab your rifle and get to Oakland! We need every hero that we can muster to stop them. We need your fighting spirit at the Centre Avenue Bridge!"

"Run!" Jane grabbed him by the shoulder. "Hal! Run and talk!"

She dragged him round the curve to the Centre Avenue Bridge. The Smithfield cell had taken up position in the five-story redbrick office building between Centre Avenue and Baum Boulevard. It gave them command of the two bridges that crossed the busway. Jane could see the dark wave of oni warriors pouring down Centre Avenue toward the bridge. It seemed like an unending flood. Thousands of them. How were they going to stop them? They only had a hundred people!

"Homestead! Hot Metal! Get inside with Smithfield!" Jane ordered. "Stay back from the windows. Stay low!"

There was a massive explosion of flame from the South Aiken Bridge. Jane skittered to a halt to look back. Flames erupted again and again.

"What the hell is that?" Jane said.

Yumiko stopped beside her. "It's Tinker *domi!*"

Yumiko had said earlier that Tinker was angry. Judging by the multiple columns of flame erupting on the South Aiken Bridge, Tinker was hell-bent on reducing the dinosaur warg to ash.

In a thunder of wings, tengu came flying down to alight all around them. There were hundreds of them. The numbers started to tilt in their favor.

"Tinker *domi* is here and she is glorious!" Hal reported. "Our little goddess is here and she's raining fire on our enemy!"

15: WOLF WHO RULES WIND

The storm was upon Wolf. It whipped up the red-hot cinders of the forest that True Flame had burned. It made the trees still standing thrash and creak. Here and there damaged trees gave up the fight and came crashing down with a long cracking sound. They struck the ground with loud booms. The sewage smell of the camp and the stench of blood and burnt meat came and went in the shifting winds. Lightning struck all around them, hitting the tops of the towering ironwood trees. Thunder clapped deafeningly loud and rumbled into the distance.

Their path decided, Wolf stood on the stone outcrop overlooking the nearby marsh with those who would fight beside him. Everyone else rushed to carry out his plan.

Wolf cast a scry, wishing he had access to one from the Stone Clan. The Stone *esva* was weak in attack spells but made up for it in superior shields and better information gathering spells. He picked up Darkness's gossamer hovering over the nearby marsh as it dropped mooring ropes. Once moored, it would ferry away the wounded. All around Wolf, the updraft of the burning forest stirred the air. To the immediate south, he sensed a small number of troops—what he could only assume to be Sunder's people—nearing the outer edge of the defense perimeter set up by the royal marines. Far off but moving toward him, was the massive oni army.

Most importantly he could feel the potential for lightning all around him. He had never cast call-lightning during a storm before.

Normally he'd have to prime the wind and ready the ground. Tonight, he would need only to establish link points to create lightning. Control was going to be difficult, as any connection he made between sky and earth could propagate much farther than he intended. He wouldn't be able to shield his people since the spell used both hands. While the oni were at range, he could use the storm, but once they closed, he would be forced to change attacks.

Red Knife had sent all but True Flame's First and Second Hands to get the wounded up to the gossamer and lead the royal marines out of the forest on foot. This included the still unconscious True Flame. It surprised Wolf that Red Knife decided to stay behind with him rather than to go with his *domou*. Wolf was not sure if this was a show of trust or belief that the Wind Clan could not hold.

He took a deep breath. With the Stone Clan in camp, the battlefield was clear of allies. He could start his attack.

Wolf suddenly felt Tinker tap the Fire Spell Stones again and again. It surprised him with the speed she cast the spell that she'd never been formally taught. The teachers that he'd sent for were responding with the normal speed of people who had lived for thousands of years. Glaciers moved faster. It was, however, the only spell she was casting of the Fire and Wind *esva*.

Wraith Arrow noticed his focus to the west. "What is it?"

"My *domi* is fighting something. She is doing flame strike as fast as she can call the spell. The oni must have unleashed horrors in the city."

Wraith Arrow grunted and shook his head. He'd questioned the wisdom of transforming Tinker. If it had not been for the presence of the oni in Pittsburgh, he would have forbidden it. Still, he didn't fully approve of her transformation. Tinker, however, wouldn't have survived the summer without being *domana*.

"I do not feel her holding a shield," Wolf spoke his fear. "I am afraid she has forgotten to be careful in her anger."

"Wood sprites are deadly when cornered." Sunder came limping out of the darkness. "They are as cautious as they are clever. She would not forget such a simple thing. I suspect she is holding a Stone Clan shield but I cannot be sure. I have lost all connection to the Spell Stones."

Despite the rain and ash and soot, there was still something oddly ethereal about the warlord who was neither female nor male. It could be the white face paint with the narrow strip of black across hir eyes, or the spell orb that orbited hir or the cloak that drifted about hir like a living thing.

"Sunder," Wolf acknowledged hir arrival as senior *domana*. Wolf scanned the warriors behind Sunder. Wolf's *laedin* were in hir ranks, returning safely. That was good news. Ruin with all of Darkness's Hands were also present. That might be bad news. Sunder might attempt to take command from Wolf. The Stone Clan had seniority and hir forces outnumbered his but by hir own admission, Sunder could no longer protect their people. The royal marines would be fodder to the horrors if Sunder failed to stop them. It was Wolf's city that would suffer if the oni army reached it.

"Your beloved is what we all could have been if we had not been so afraid of each other." Sunder plucked the spell orb out of its orbit about hir. "We learned the wrong lessons from the Rebellion. We have always been stronger when we stand together. We should have learned that hard truth on the Blood Plains but we let our petty fears divide us first into caste and then into clans. 'You are not like me, so I will fear you.' It is a shameful thing we have become. And the worst of it, we cannot move past it. As we grow old, we grow fixed in place. We cling to the vain illusion that we are the superior to the others. We teach it to the young, refusing to allow them to break free of our shackles."

Wolf realized that hir was not speaking to him but of the Stone Clan *sekasha* about hir.

"I am upright but only just," Sunder said. "I do not have the strength to swing a sword. I would be only a hinderance. I will loan you what strength I can and lend my wisdom to the retreat of the royal marines."

The Stone Clan *sekasha* were staying behind with him? As he glanced toward Ruin and Sunder's First, both males nodded. Yes, he would stay in command with the Stone Clan acting as support.

Sunder held out hir spell orb. "This will cast a shield if needed. It charges up while it is in orbit about you. The area will be quite large but the duration is short—ten minutes at most. It is a last resort."

Jewel Tear had such devices and he always thought them annoyances. Hers had cooled the air around her and scented it with perfume. Since his strongest attack took both hands, though, an orb that could cast a shield could be a lifesaver.

"Thank you," Wolf said, giving a bow.

Sunder explained how to activate the orb. Wolf set it whiz-zing above his head.

"May the gods bless you." Sunder bowed and headed north to guide the royal marines to safety.

Wolf set up his link to the Wind Clan Spell Stones. He felt the magic gathering to him in a wash of heat. The wind shifted from the west, bringing the smell of wood smoke and the rich earthy scent of wet forest floor. The clouds were already primed—he only needed to seize hold of them with his right hand. The hairs on his arms lifted as he took control of the ground with his left hand. The critical point already existed. He brought his hands together, aiming the channel at the heart of the oni army. The faint leader flashed downward, out of the dark sky, barely visible. The brilliant return stroke leapt from within the oncoming warriors, meeting the leader with a deafening clap of thunder. The channel open, the lightning struck again and again, dancing between cloud and ground. It flashed the night to a white haze, illuminating the entire battlefield.

The oni army was marching through the forest leveled by True Flame. Shoulder to shoulder. Thousands of them. Hundreds of wargs mixed into their ranks. In the back, large cages on wheeled carts. The horrors.

He could not let them get past him and attack the retreating royal marines. He couldn't leave them alive to go on and attack Pittsburgh.

Wolf brought his hands together again and again, connecting sky to ground, creating channels that the lightning could follow. The night flashed white again and again as the lightning flickered down, blasting everything it touched. He focused on the cages in the back, hitting them with every strike. The oni, even with their great numbers, were a nuisance compared to the horrors if they were enlarged.

"They are charging," Wraith Arrow said calmly as the *sekasha* picked off the wargs with spell arrows. The shields of the *sekasha* could deal with the crude weapons that the oni carried en masse. Their protective spell, however, could not block powerful magic effects like frost, fire, and lightning.

"They have been told enough about their enemy to know that call-lightning cannot be used at short range," Ruin said.

It couldn't be used for short range because Wolf wasn't able to cast a shield to protect himself nor the *sekasha* while doing the spell. The call-lightning had the widest area of effect. It was his strongest attack—which made it most dangerous to his own people. He had Sunder's spell orb whizzing around his head but its protection was short lived.

The flickering lightning made the image of the advancing oni jerk as if still pictures were being used to show the enemies' charge. Each picture they shuttered closer and closer. The holy warriors activated their shields, slid their bows into their back scabbards, and pulled their *ejae*. The oni collided with the wall of *sekasha* with shouts, roars, and growls. The smell of blood became mixed with the heavy wood smoke.

Wolf channeled the lightning over and over, until the sky stayed static white with the falling rain and brilliance of the lightning. The clap and rumble of thunder merged into one continuous tumult. He wanted to do a scry, to see if the things within the cages were surviving his attack, but he didn't dare let up the onslaught.

One of the cages suddenly shattered as something big and glowing expanded up out of it. It took form as a gleaming stag that blazed white hot in the rainy dark. It was bigger than even the phoenix scorpion had been. It stood at least sixty feet tall from dark hooves to a majestic set of shining antlers. Despite its deerlike appearance, it had sharp tusks on either side of its boarlike snout.

"What is that?" someone called out.

Wolf was glad that someone else had no idea what the creature was. He didn't recognize the voice, so it was not one of his three Hands.

"It is a storm hart!" Ruin—the oldest and most experienced of the *sekasha*—shouted. "Wolf, put up a shield! Quick!"

Wolf dropped the call-lightning and put up the largest shield that he could cast to protect all the *sekasha* standing with him.

There was a moment of muffled peace as his shield blocked the attack of the oni warriors and the dying rumble of thunder. The night was suddenly dark except for the lone gleaming figure at the back of the battlefield. The oni army fell back, at first leery of Wolf's attack. Then, as they glanced behind them and realized that the horror had gotten loose, panic swept through them and they started to scatter.

"I thought storm harts were mythical," Wolf said into the sudden quiet.

"They are." Ruin was the only one old enough to maybe know the truth. The world's early history had been erased by the Skin Clan as they subjugated the original nomadic tribes that predated the Clans. "All horrors are creatures that never naturally existed. They were pieced together by the Skin Clan to resemble legendary monsters. They wanted to use our own myths against us. Luckily this made them too unnatural to procreate. The phoenix scorpion you fought today was a pale shadow of those we faced during the Rebellion."

Wraith Arrow nodded to this.

"This creature is more of the same." Ruin pointed at the storm hart. "It's some piecemeal monster put into the fake skin of a beast that never existed beyond the spell runes on a puppet's skin."

"Oh, I see." Wolf understood what Ruin was saying. The outer shell of the horrors that they were fighting was a solid illusion, projected by a spell written on the smaller true animal. "There is no reason for the illusion to look identical to the creature within."

Ruin nodded. "All that matters is the creature has some instinct to use the abilities that the Skin Clan bred into it."

"You've seen these puppet things before?" Wraith Arrow asked Ruin.

Ruin waved his hand, indicating that the truth was too gray for him to comfortably speak. "The wood sprites created the concept as part of their escape from the Skin Clan. They were just small children; they needed strong allies to succeed. They had a handful of small pets that they gifted with powerful abilities by writing spells directly onto them. We did not like the practice—it felt too much like lying. We asked the wood sprites to not use it to make things be what they were not. The concept, however, was the precursor to the *sekasha* shields."

"Someone perfected it after the wood sprites abandoned the concept," Wolf guessed.

"Yes," Ruin said. "We thought we sterilized that rat's nest after the Rebellion but apparently one of the rats skittered away to Onihida to perfect the concept."

"Any guess what this can do?" Wolf figured that Ruin had some idea if he had Wolf put up his shield.

"It reasons that our enemy tailor-made the horrors within the camp against you and Prince True Flame," Ruin said, "as the oni could not be sure if the Stone Clan would cooperate with the Wind Clan in this battle."

Lightning flickered—naturally generated out of the storm—and hit the storm hart. The horror glowed brighter, electricity arcing up its massive antlers. There was a pulse of magic, like what the phoenix scorpion had cast to pinpoint Wolf. It washed over him like a static-filled fire scry.

"It just targeted me," Wolf said. "Does it throw lightning?"

"That is my guess," Ruin said.

Wolf felt the faint trace of a leader arcing toward him and, moments later, a massive bolt of lightning followed. His shield flared to blinding white. The sound of the clap and boom of the thunder was instantaneous and deafening loud.

The *sekasha* switched back to bow and a swarm of spell arrows streaked through the darkness.

The storm hart, though, had vanished even as the arrows left the bow.

"Stack!" Wraith Arrow shouted.

All the *sekasha* leapt toward Wolf, surrounding him tightly, *ejae* drawn.

The storm hart suddenly appeared within Wolf's shield. It towered over them—sixty feet tall—gleaming brightly. It swiped its massive tusks at Wolf, flinging aside the *sekasha* who were protecting him. Their personal shields took the worst of the impact but flickered and failed even as the warriors were tossed aside with their wyvern chest armor sliced to shreds.

Wolf punched the hart backward with a force strike, knocking it beyond his shield.

All the warriors who had protected Wolf were battered and bleeding. Their weapons had done no damage to the beast. Worse, their chest armor would not protect them from a second hit.

"If it's like the phoenix scorpion," Wolf said, "we will not be able to harm it without killing the beast within that is guiding it!"

Wolf hit it with a flame strike, hoping to burn it to nothing. It didn't absorb the power like the phoenix scorpion had but it seemed unharmed. He did a scry to probe further. "It has a shield as well as the illusion protecting the true beast."

If the inner beast was small, it would be like coring an apple while it was hidden within a very mobile house.

"Spell arrows will bypass its shield," Wraith Arrow said as the hart teleported across the battlefield. "But it needs to stay in one place for us to hit it!"

"Hold your arrows ready," Wolf said. "The storm hart will teleport back inside my shield once it realizes that it can't damage us from a distance. The conditions are right for a fog wall."

Wraith Arrow understood Wolf's plan. "If it cannot see us, it will not realize that we are lying in wait for its return."

Red Knife agreed to the plan with a nod. "It is much taller than us. We can loose our arrows without fear of hitting each other."

The Stone Clan nodded their agreement.

Holding his shield with his right hand, Wolf cast a fog wall with his left. Red Knife had insisted he learn the spell as a child. Wolf had thought at the time—wrongly—that with the Clan Wars over, there would be no need for him to fight in a battle like this. The spell rapidly chilled the air close to the ground where the moisture content was high. The night closed in as the fog thickened until the storm hart was just a gleaming smudge in the dark. The horror shifted place to place, randomly teleporting in a circle around them. It struck Wolf's shield again and again with lightning. The earth shook beneath their feet with the strength of the blows. Even muffled by his shield, the sound was stunningly loud. Wolf's Hands gathered close to him, acting as Shields. The rest of the *sekasha* stood ready, spell arrows nocked, tips pointed skyward.

The lightning stopped.

"It comes," Wraith Arrow said softly.

Wolf activated Sunder's spell orb. A second shield went up around him and his Hands.

Suddenly the storm hart was among them, towering overhead, already swinging its tusks toward the *sekasha* protecting Wolf. The massive tusks struck Sunder's loaned shield again and again.

Spell arrows whistled skyward, turning into shafts of light. They riddled the storm hart. One hit the hidden beast within the puppet skin. It shrieked and stumbled. The *sekasha* fired again, releasing another gleaming swarm. Another true strike and the deer fell to the ground, panting hoarsely. The illusionary skin was accurate enough to show the animal's panic in its eyes. The *sekasha* pressed their attack, shooting volley after volley of arrows into the massive body, hoping to hit the hidden beast.

The storm hart shuddered as a third arrow found its true heart, and went limp.

They stood a moment in the silence, gazing down at its still gleaming form.

"It is done," Wraith Arrow said.

Wolf scanned the battlefield. The oni who survived the lightning had fled in all directions. They might regroup now that the horror was dead. "We will commence an orderly retreat, killing anything that follows us."

"Yes, *domou*," Wraith Arrow said.

16: A BIRD IN THE HAND

It started to rain as Tristan walked away from the incline station.

The observation platform beside the incline gave a commanding view of Pittsburgh. The city stood dark in the falling twilight. The lines of the skyscrapers blurred as the rain swept forward block by block. He heard the rain coming, the leading front sounding like an oncoming train. Lightning flickered in the dark clouds. He took the rain jacket from his backpack, put it on, and pulled up the hood moments before the front washed over him.

The WESA radio tower was a red skeleton frame surrounded by a tall iron fence. The gate stood open. A pickup truck was backing a trailer-mounted generator through the opening. The generator had WOLLERTON HARDWARE printed across its side.

An old UPS delivery truck sat in the parking lot. It had been painted with a flock of colorful cartoon sheep. All up and down the street was a small fleet of vehicles parked haphazardly, suggesting that their drivers had rushed to the scene.

Tristan walked past the parking lot and stopped under the marquee of a small ice cream shop, which gave him the excuse that he'd paused merely for its shelter. The rain drummed loudly on the pink-striped canvas. He took out his phone and pretended that it didn't have a signal to buy himself time to think of what little he did know about his brother's plans to take the city. Even as their father cast the spell to render the *domana* helpless, Lucien's people had shut down the city's power grid and telecommunication systems. His brother wanted to be able to take out the enclaves in Oakland without the humans rallying to save the elves. The randomly scattered acts of sabotage would keep Director Maynard and his EIA forces busy elsewhere. With the power off, there was no need to worry about the television stations reporting their attack on the enclaves. Lucien had moles at the big three radio stations—KDKA, WQED, and WTAE—who would keep a lid on news reports.

Chloe hadn't told Lucien about WESA. It was a hole in their blackout plans. Obviously the power outage had damaged WESA's ability to broadcast but that was about to be solved. Tengu were working with the humans to get the generator connected to the tower. Their black wings were unmistakable, even in the downpour. The tengu belonged to the changeling. If they were here, then WESA was of more tactical importance than Chloe had believed.

Tristan needed to sabotage this effort somehow. It shouldn't be too hard. Electricity and rain did not mix.

He put away his phone.

"Ah, there you are!" a female said directly behind him. "My little flying monkey."

Tristan jerked around, half-expecting Esme since that was her old nickname for him. It wasn't his sister but a tall stranger: a female elf with long white hair, faded gown of fairy silk, and high-top tennis shoes. He had no idea who this was but felt a weird sense of sudden familiarity as if this person was deeply important to him. "What?"

"Here, take this," the female said and pressed something warm and fluffy into his right hand. She caught his left hand and guided it up to cup whatever she had handed him as it started to squirm. It was something small and living.

"What in the world?" He would have dropped the creature if he could but she still had hold of his hands, forcing him to hold it. It was some kind of baby bird, all yellow fluff and light bones and tiny sharp talons. It cheeped at him, a small piercing sound. He wasn't sure but it seemed like it was a baby chicken. "What? No. I don't want this."

"What does that matter?" the female elf said. "You've taken on harder responsibilities that you didn't want from your father and brother. Find this person. Find that person. What does it matter that finding them leads to blood?"

He stared at her in horror. How did she know that? How did she get so close to him without him realizing that someone was nearby? "Who are you? What do you want?"

"I want you to be responsible for this fragile life and the others that you hold within your hands. Your sister's children are so young and brilliant—and headstrong. They are in terrible danger and only you can save them."

Did she mean the twins? "They're with their grandmother."

"Your mother is dead."

"What? No. That's not possible."

She gave him a look of pity, shaking her head. "Your mother could have lived forever. She had the blood of dragons and elves flowing through her. It would have been simple for your father to bring her here and give her back her immortality. He was too afraid to—just as he's afraid to give it to your baby sisters. To your big brother. To you. He lost everything because our bloodline lived long enough to spit in his face—he will never make any of you immortal again. None of you will live to see the end of his unholy war."

"My mother is not dead. I saw her just a few weeks ago."

"She is gone. Cold and unclaimed and will go a pauper's grave because there's no one there to claim her body."

"My father's people will—"

"They fled into the night as your sister's children burned the house down as they escaped. No one is on Earth to mourn your mother. All her bloodline is trapped on this world with you."

"No. That's not possible. The twins can't be here."

"They are. Charging into danger even as we speak. Whoever came up with the phrase 'more fun than a barrel full of monkeys' had never dealt with the phenomenon. The noise that they make alone is deafening."

Tristian paused, confused. Was she literally talking about a barrel filled with pissed-off primates somewhere in the city? "What monkeys?"

"Your sister's children. I have no idea what Esme was thinking when she loosed that chaos on the world. One was all that was required. Why did she feel the need for more?"

The old woman meant the changeling and the twins. "I don't think Esme intended there to be more than one."

"It is neither here nor there; what is done is done," the old elf female said. "They're flitting around the city, getting into trouble."

Tristan shook his head. This couldn't be true. The twins were on Earth with his mother and Yves...

Adele said that Yves was dead. Buried under a ton of rock. Father must have known about some secret cavern pathway—too small and dangerous to use often. Was Yves bringing the twins to Elfhome when it collapsed, killing him?

"Your father will not let them live," the female said. "He will kill your sister's children. All of your sisters. Your brother too—no matter how faithful his service has been. Your father is too afraid of our potential to allow any of us to live. He's already killed the sister you loved the best. She saw what was coming and tried to escape."

Did she mean Bethany? No one would talk about his favorite baby sister. He'd been afraid that something horrible had happened to her but he didn't want to believe that his father would actually kill one of the Eyes. His entire childhood, he'd been told that all the secrets they kept from his mother had been for a good reason. A just reason. That not telling her the truth would protect her from their terrible enemies.

No. He couldn't believe it. He wouldn't believe it. This random stranger had to be lying. "*Our* potential? Shouldn't it have been 'your family's' potential?"

"Where do you think your family's ability to see the future comes from? He made me from bits and pieces thousands of years ago with no idea how dangerous a dragon can be—even one torn down and rebuilt into another race. Dragons' minds are not like elves'; our souls can be separated from our bodies and rejoined to another. I remember everything that he has done to me. For thousands of years, I've worked to undo that damage."

Was this female claiming to be his ancestor somehow? He laughed, shaking his head. "My mother isn't a half-elf. Neither was my grandmother."

"These pointy ears were an afterthought to mark one's slaves. They vanish after two or three generations—just in case you want to elevate some ill-begotten bastard to legitimate status. Had you not noticed that, for a family of wealthy bankers for generations, there were no photographs of them?"

He had. They had photos of houses and dogs and horses for his maternal line but few photographs of the actual people.

The chick squirmed in his hands and cheeped loudly.

"Why are you telling me this?" he said. "Why the chicken?"

"You're to give this to your niece when you see her. Tell her to remember her chess moves. It will be important."

"I don't understand."

"It's better that you don't."

The female picked up an umbrella that was leaning against the doors of the ice cream shop. The outside was black but when she opened it up, it had a family of chickens printed on the lining: a rooster, a hen, and four baby yellow chicks that could be siblings to the one he held. She stepped out from under the marquee, the pounding rain making a misty halo above her as it bounced off her umbrella.

"Wait!" he said as she turned the corner. He ran after her but she had vanished as mysteriously as she had appeared. The alley was blocked by a dark tall picket fence.

He stood in the pouring rain, staring in confusion at the empty alley. Who was that? Where did she go? Was what she told him true? Were his mother and Bethany dead? He could believe the latter easily—everyone had dodged his questions about her for over a year. He didn't want to believe his mother was dead. He couldn't ignore the cold fear that he had when he tried to see her last. There, in the magic-rich grounds of the mansion, he'd been sure that he would never get the chance to say goodbye. He'd been equally sure that with the twins in the house, his father's punishment for him not leaving quietly would have been swift, sure, and painful.

His mother was dead. She'd died alone, just as he feared.

He stumbled back under the marquee, suddenly blinded by tears. His hands were full of baby chick, so he scrubbed at his face with the wet cuff of his rain jacket.

I don't have time for this, he forced himself to think despite the fact his heart felt like a black sucking hole within his chest. *If I don't shut down this radio station, we might lose. Father will be angry . . .*

The thought of his father's rage was like opening a box and seeing plain truth within it.

Father killed Bethany.

Tristan was suddenly as sure of it as if he witnessed it him-self. Bethany was sweet and gentle but unbending. Her sweetness came from the knowledge of her own strength; she was above the petty jealousy and fears of her sisters. She did not fight; any hostility, she would step aside and let it pass. If trouble broke out, Bethany could not be found.

If she realized that their father planned to kill them all if they somehow survived the war, she would have run.

What do I do?

He knew that he needed to do something. Run. Plan. Fight. He'd been taught how to survive since he was very young. But he'd been equally taught from birth to be loyal his father, to take extraordinary risks merely to be sure that his father wouldn't be unhappy with him. The two powerful forces were nothing compared to the black hole of grief that was swallowing him up.

He could only slide down into a ball and weep.

17: GATHERING FORCES

With all the bridges in Oakland blocked by the fighting, Oilcan wouldn't be able to drive the flatbed to find Tinker's twin sisters. Going by foot would be too slow and dangerous; he had miles of oni-infested city to cover. He drove back to Sacred Heart to get his hoverbike.

Every legal parking space had been taken up by a massive collection of pickup trucks with empty gun racks. It seemed that after the fighting started, people just abandoned their vehicles any random place. Some of them were blocking the way for ambulances that were coming and going. Linda Gaddy was running from one pickup to another, checking to see if the keys were in them. Those without, she put into neutral and drifted downhill. The others, she started up and moved so the emergency equipment could get through.

Oilcan recognized the vehicles clustered around his newly installed gate: Geoffrey's pickup, Moser's van, Blue Sky's hoverbike, and a dozen more belonging to Team Tinker. He pulled up onto the sidewalk, blocking in the van. Judging by the hood up on the van and the engine parts scattered around, Moser wasn't going to be driving anywhere.

"We'll get the weapons crate," Thorne Scratch said.

Oilcan nodded. He hadn't thought that they would need her backup weapons on the shopping trip, but he was glad now that Thorne Scratch had insisted on bringing the crate along. She was also right that they couldn't just abandon it in the middle of a warzone.

One hoverbike isn't going to be enough, Oilcan realized. He needed to bring two people back. Hoverbikes required some balancing. One untrained passenger made going through a turn difficult but two novice passengers could easily tip the hoverbike over. And the twins were probably not alone. Yes, Tinker could bully people into crazy things but he couldn't believe that the entire tengu race would let two nine-year-olds go into a combat zone alone. He had to assume that there were more than just the twins behind enemy lines. Tinker wouldn't leave a friend behind, so Oilcan would also need to rescue anyone traveling with the girls. Thorne Scratch wouldn't let him go alone and the day had proven that she needed the backup that Moon Dog provided. It added up to four or more passengers.

Oilcan scanned the area. Was there anyone around that he knew and trusted? The person he needed most was Roach, who was the master of coordinating large groups of people.

He spotted a familiar figure. "Hey, TC! Is Roach around?"

TC was one of Roach's cousins on his dad's side of the family. He'd been a part of Team Tinker since the beginning. He glided his wheelchair over to Oilcan. Pittsburgh was not a very wheelchair-friendly city as it had shifted to Elfhome prior to the federal accessibility laws kicking in. Tinker had custom-built TC a chair that hovered to compensate. TC had a camouflage poncho over his chair and hunting rifle to protect them from the rain.

"Roach took off shortly after you left with Andy and Guy," TC said. "He had to deliver something to Jane. Andy left his phone in the dumpster hauler that Roach was driving. Geoffrey told everyone that if Andy and Guy showed back up with you, I was to take them home."

"I sent them someplace safe with my kids," Oilcan said, mind racing. He would have to grab people without Roach's help. It was best that he pick people that he'd known half his life and could trust completely. "I need some help."

"What's up?" TC asked. "What do you need?"

"I need to go rescue someone trapped behind enemy lines," Oilcan said without going into detail. "I need a couple of people on hoverbikes. Three at minimum. Five would be better."

"Sounds fun," TC said. "Count me in!"

Oilcan considered the offer. TC had two custom-built vehicles: the hoverchair for indoors and sidewalks and quiet side streets; and an oversized green hoverbike nicknamed "Hover Hulk" because of its beefy square shape. Most of the team didn't realize that Hover Hulk was a prototype for an actual hovertank that Tinker wanted to build when she was younger. (There was a reason Oilcan wouldn't have been surprised if Tinker ended up riding around Pittsburgh on the shoulder of a giant robot. Her Hand might be deadly but they were much better for her and the city at large.)

All of the team members had an odd mix of keen intelligence, reckless abandon, steely courage, and yet a decent amount of self-preservation. They needed to keep up with Tinker yet survive her insanity. Andy was the only exception to the rule. TC had pulled his weight through all the insane stuff Tinker came up with in the past. The Hover Hulk could carry TC, a passenger, and a small amount of cargo while keeping up with the racing bikes that the rest of the team used. With TC along, they could take the weapons crate.

"Thanks," Oilcan said and then waved over Thorne Scratch and Moon Dog. "This is a friend of mine. He's to be trusted. His name is TC."

"I am Moon Dawg," Moon Dog mangled the English word. "Tee Cee has no meaning?"

"No, it doesn't," Oilcan said before TC could go into the story behind his nickname. It was short for Talmadge Carl Carr the Second. TC was named after his father and a "Second" because his father didn't want to stick "Junior" onto his son. Beyond that, Oilcan didn't have a clue what "Talmadge" might mean. It sounded vaguely French.

"I want TC here to take the weapons crate on his vehicle." Oilcan pointed at the big green Hover Hulk.

Oilcan spotted Linda Gaddy moving toward him, once again on foot. "Gaddy! Do you have your hoverbike handy?"

Linda Gaddy wasn't a member of Team Tinker but he knew her well through her work with the Pittsburgh police. On Shutdown and Startup days, she'd help him clear wrecked cars off the road so traffic could keep moving.

"Yeah, it's just up the street." She pointed away from the fighting.

"I need to go behind enemy lines to rescue some people stuck there," he explained. "And some extra bikes to pick them up."

"I'm in," Gaddy said.

They managed to snag five more members of Team Tinker: Gin Blossom, Tate Holland, Brandon Hendricks, Abbey Rhode, and Axe Man. Oilcan paired Moon Dog with Gin Blossom; as a *laedin*-caste elf, Gin was the one best able to deal with the Stone Clan *sekasha*. Axe Man had a sidecar on his hoverbike. Altogether, it meant that they could ferry nine adult passengers. Thorne Scratch and Moon Dog took up two of those slots but it still left seven spaces for the twins and anyone traveling with them. Hopefully, it was overkill.

They took one of the alleys that ran between the enclaves to their back border wall. There they turned west and headed through the forest as fast as Oilcan dared. The woods in this area were fairly safe, as the elves gleaned firewood from them year-round. The only real danger was running into the oni. Judging by what they found, though, the oni had kept to the city streets.

He could sense Tinker holding a Stone Clan spell steady in Oakland. It was a comforting feeling. To the west, someone was calling a shield and a variety of other spells from the Stone Clan Spell Stones. It had to be the twins.

Finding the twins, therefore, shouldn't be difficult.

Getting them to come with him to someplace safe... that might be impossible.

18: TEARS IN THE RAIN

Tommy hated rain. Nothing made him put his ears back more than a cold heavy downpour. Nor did he like crowds, and the Rim in Oakland was a madhouse. It seemed like half of Pittsburgh had spilled into the area in pickups. Judging by the homemade flak jackets and number of visible weapons, the crowd was Alita's "Resistance." Tommy wove through the rainy darkness, clouding the mind of anyone who swung a flashlight in his direction.

It was a day that Tommy had known was coming since he was a child but it was still unsettling to see. Most of his life, he had assumed that the oni would win. After Tinker killed his father he'd started to hope that the elves had a fighting chance.

It wasn't clear how the war effort was going. There were walking wounded, leaking out enough blood to taint the night air. There were people loading stretchers of critically injured into makeshift ambulances. Men trotted past, shouting out the names of bridges like "Fort Pitt!" or "Fern Hollow!" and getting answered with "Here!" One idiot was wandering up and down the street, yelling "Schenley!" over and over again. Work crews were frantically building barricades out of rubble at strategic spots—obviously bracing for the oni to wash through the area. By the sound of the gunfire, the front line was only a few blocks off. Something pulsed rhythmically brilliant in the direction of Centre Avenue, although Tommy couldn't guess what it was or which side it belonged to.

The oni had taken out the phones and the power to the city. They probably did it to keep the EIA busy elsewhere. So far it seemed to be working, as there was no sign of the UN forces. Nor were there any elves in sight. Lord Tomtom had anticipated that the elves would hide in their enclaves. Each compound housed twenty to thirty *laedin* warriors. While the buildings along the Rim were protected by a magical defensive shield, the rest of the half-mile-long enclosures were unprotected beyond their high stone walls. It meant that the *laedin* were stretched thin guarding three sets of gates and patrolling a hundred acres of farmland.

Alita said that the oni had used some kind of genetic spell bomb to take out the *domana*. Was Oilcan still alive to protect the half-oni? Was Jewel Tear okay?

Sacred Heart's new ironwood front gate was closed and barred. The stone walls were completed and rain sheeted down the nearly invisible magical shield over the building. There was no getting in beyond knocking on the gate and hoping someone heard him. He didn't know who was on door duty. It meant he couldn't cloud their minds so that they saw someone they trusted. He rang the front gate's bell, hoping for the best.

For some odd reason, the female singer from Naekanain answered the door, sliding open the small spy hole. He'd crossed paths with the elf fusion band during raves but always interacted with only the human leader, Carl Moser. Tommy hadn't dared to speak face-to-face with any of the elves in the band, even though they were probably young enough not to know what an oni looked like.

"I cannot let you in," the female said in Elvish.

Tommy locked down on a frustrated growl. Scaring the female wasn't going to get him in the door. What was her name again? Some kind of prickly flower. Thorn? No, that was Oilcan's First. Thistle? Briar? Briar Rose! "I'm Oilcan's Beholden, Briar Rose."

"I know who you are and what you are but I cannot let you in," she repeated.

"Is Oilcan even here?"

"No." Briar Rose glanced behind her and then switched to English to elaborate. "Just Forge and he was unconscious until a few minutes ago. He is up and doing crazy wood sprite stuff just like Tinker *domi*. His holy ones are jumpy as shit and that is why I cannot let you in. They are giving us stink eyes and that is just because we are Wind Clan. I do not know what they would do to you."

Oh, she thought she was protecting Tommy. How...strange.

Did "Just Forge" mean that Jewel Tear wasn't there either? Tommy had worked hard the last few days to make it seem like he had no interest in the female *domana*. Asking about her first would probably be a mistake.

"Where's Oilcan?" Tommy asked instead.

"*Domi* told him to fetch someone. He was here a little while ago, collecting Team Tinker members to go with him. He took Abbey, Gin, TC, and some others. Oilcan did not tell them where they were going. It seemed like he did not know himself. So... who knows where he is?"

It meant that both Tinker and Oilcan were awake and fighting—which was good news. "Unconscious" suggested that the spell had taken out Forge. It was surprising that Forge was already awake—Oilcan had been a bitch to wake up hours after he was made into an elf. What about Jewel Tear? He saw her at Sacred Heart in the morning but she might have left later on. Would her armed escort know how to get her back to the enclave? Who would she have left with? Most of the Wyverns left the city with Prince True Flame. He couldn't stand here and pump Briar Rose for information when every question exposed his interest in Jewel Tear.

"I need to fetch my cousin, Spot. I left him here." Tommy figured Spot could give him a full accounting of what was going on without the fear of exposing Tommy's relationship with Jewel Tear.

"The kids are not here. Oilcan sent them off with Geoffrey's little brother to someplace safe. Spot is with them."

Another Kryskill in the middle of things. No wonder Alita figured out that Duff was running communications for the Resistance.

"Jewel Tear?" he risked asking.

Briar Rose peered out past Tommy before whispering, "I think the crazy bitch snapped. She started to scream and wail and throw around furniture after she woke up. She tore out of here in her nightgown."

The news did weird shit to his heart.

He struggled to keep it out of his voice as he asked, "Alone? She didn't have Wyverns or royal marines with her?"

"There was no one here to go with her," Briar Rose whispered. "Oilcan has no *laedin* yet. Snapdragon and the others from our place are out fighting. The few that Jewel Tear had either died with her Hand or fled back to the Easternlands. Forge's *laedin* have not arrived yet—those who came with the gossamer were all masons. One of Forge's Hands left to support Tinker *domi*. The rest of the holy ones will not leave their *domou* while he's vulnerable to attack."

Somewhere out in the darkness, the sound of battle died off, as if either the humans had been overrun or the oni had run away. Tommy wasn't sure which. Neither was good. Lesser bloods would flee in every direction, crawling into the smallest hole that they could find, making it hard to hunt down and kill them in large numbers. The Resistance was too few and too far between to keep handfuls of oni from roaming Oakland.

"Which way did Jewel Tear head?" He managed to sound only curious.

"I thought she was going to Poppymeadows. I followed her out to the curb to see if she got there safely but she headed toward Pitt."

Why would Jewel Tear head that way? She'd only been in the city for a little while; maybe she didn't realize how big it was.

"It's an enclave's duty to keep its guests safe," Briar Rose said. "As Oilcan's Beholden, she is your responsibility. You should go after her."

He planned on it. He turned away from the gate to go.

"Be safe!" Briar Rose called after him.

That felt weird. He would have never thought an elf would say that to him and mean it.

His nose wasn't as keen as Spot's or Bingo's. The rain was quickly washing away any hope of tracking Jewel Tear, but he could pick up hints of her passing.

She had gone in a straight shot toward the Cathedral of Learning. At the massive lawn, though, she had meandered in a circle. She had stopped several times long enough to lay down a strong scent trail. Had she literally "snapped" or was she looking for something? He couldn't imagine what. Oilcan? Prince True Flame's camp? Tommy? He felt a little stab of guilt that he had not given her any idea how to find him. At the corner closest to the museum, she had crossed into Schenley Plaza. He dashed across Forbes Avenue in the rain, hoping that she didn't cross the bridge to Schenley Park. The place was dangerous even in the daylight.

He found her at the merry-go-round, sitting in the bright colored saddle of the Pitt Panther, weeping. She wore a human-made nightgown of yellow cotton that was soaking wet and clung to her like a second skin. It showed off all her fading bruises. A freaking huge black sword leaned against her mount. It was so long that he couldn't even imagine her wielding the sword. It seemed to be made of some kind of wet black stone but had magical runes etched onto the entire length of it.

It started to rain harder, so he stepped up onto the deck of the ride.

"Hey," he said quietly so as not to startle her. It was his experience that when women snapped under the pressure of their life, anyone and everything became a target. He didn't want Jewel Tear to be swinging her big-ass sword at him.

She jerked her head up, blinking back tears. When she saw it was him, she started to wail. "I am lost! I am so lost! I do not even know who I am anymore."

Did that mean she didn't know who he was?

"You're Jewel Tear," Tommy said.

She laughed bitterly. "Oh gods, yes, I'm certainly Jewel Tear on Stone. How damned I was—even at birth. The priestess took one look at me and said, 'You will never be happy.' Is it my lot in life to only suffer? Was it not enough every 'safe investment' I made suffered some impossible disaster? That I lost what little backing my clan fronted me? That my thrice-cursed clan leader with her misbegotten traitorous child forced me to swallow my pride and come to this wilderness that terrified me? To 'help' the male that I had spurned on their urgings? Offered me a great reward if I killed another *domana*—in the middle of a war zone? That I lost all of my Beholden while I slept in a house that that cursed spawn told me was secure? Gods, I was so naïve. And when I thought the worst that the oni could do to me is rape and torture, they found a way to utterly break me. I thought I was safe—and they unmade me. What am I if I am not a *domana*? What will become of me now? What am I to do? My clan only supports me because I can tap the Spell Stones! Wolf Who Rules will not pay for my housing if I cannot fight. I cannot crawl back to the Easternlands on the pittance that I have to my name. Even if I could, where would I go? I do not know if my parents would take me in. I have no skill beyond being a *domana*. I would be no use to them."

"My mom always said that as long as you have breath in your body, you can change the world." Tommy's mother said it every time his father beat him. "You're stronger than you think. You got up every time you were beaten down: you had to be powerful to do that. A weaker person would have failed long ago."

"I am so tired of being strong," Jewel Tear said.

"I know." Tommy was well familiar with the feeling. He cautiously moved closer to her and put out a hand to her. She slid down off the panther to collapse into his embrace.

"If you need a place," he said, "you can stay with me."

He knew it wasn't a smart idea but he wanted her safe. He could protect her best if she was with all the others who needed him. Besides, he couldn't very well drag her kicking and screaming back to Sacred Heart. Forge's people wouldn't like him manhandling her and Oilcan had limited space. Sacred Heart couldn't really afford a nonpaying customer taking up one of Oilcan's biggest bedrooms.

Jewel Tear pressed her face into Tommy's shoulder, clinging to him. They stood in silence for a minute before she murmured, "Will they let me go and do as I please if I can no longer call the Spell Stones? I could disappear in the confusion of this night, but I could not stay hidden forever. What would they do when they found me?"

She had warned him that they had to keep their relationship hidden from the *sekasha*. It was the warrior's holy duty to keep the *domana* bloodlines pure. If she just vanished, then things would look bad for Tommy—but what if she merely "moved"?

"We've taken over a ..." He paused as he realized that he didn't know the Elvish word for "hotel" other than "enclave." Could not the William Penn be considered an enclave? "We started an enclave for the humans stranded in the city. It's quite large—much bigger than Sacred Heart. We have ... several ... men already paying to stay at our enclave." He couldn't remember how many Trixie had checked in. "We are giving them a place to store their stuff and sleep. We're cooking for them. It's an enclave only for humans—at the moment. We could take in elves ..."

She shook her head. "I do not think they will let me join your household. Such things are not done. A *domana* leads, not follows.

Nor could I ask you to break your alliance to Oilcan. Such bonds are sacred."

Did she misunderstand and think that he just proposed to her? Should he be happy with her reason for saying "no" to him?

He tried a different phrasing. "Would they be upset if you changed to another enclave?"

She blinked at him for another minute of silence before finally stuttering out, "I-I-I cannot pay."

"We're stretched thin. You could help out as a way to pay for it."

"What would I do? What could I do?"

He wasn't sure, so he named the things even the tweens could do. "We've got more children than adults. You could play with the little ones. See that they're clean and fed." He skipped over diapering. No one liked that duty. Was there anything that she alone could do? "Teach them how to read and write and do math?"

He'd picked up Elvish from a lifetime of living on Elfhome. He still couldn't read their language. His mother and aunts had homeschooled Tommy, Bingo, and Mokoto but as the number of children mounted, the less time there was for teaching.

"Oh! I could try that." Jewel Tear pressed closer to him, shivering from the wet and cold. "It would be good for me to learn how to deal with children. I never even saw a child until I came to the Westernlands."

She was going to get sick if she stood around soaked to the skin.

"Come," he said to get her to start toward his hoverbike.

She took a step away from him to grab her massive black sword. Despite its length, she shifted it as if it weighed nothing. The magic spells on it must negate its weight. "I was looking for Forest Moss's *domi*."

She had been trying to get to the Phipps Conservatory? No wonder she got lost.

"His domi is out with her royal marines," Tommy said without going in details. "She's not home."

"Oh." Jewel Tear seemed to shrink with disappointment.

"My cousins are with her, so she should return to my place." It was a guess based on the fact that Olivia was cautious with other people's lives. She wasn't the type to drop Alita some random place in the city. "You can wait there for her to return my people."

"Once again, you save me," Jewel Tear whispered.

He took that as a "yes" and led her to his hoverbike.

19: HIDE AND SEEK

It was a deadly game of hide-and-seek. Arlington Avenue lay to the north. John Street was a narrow, one-way alley that ended a hundred feet to the south of the bakery. It collided with two other streets to make one of Pittsburgh's weird five-way intersections. If the oni obeyed traffic laws, they would have to come from the north. Given the sound of their engines and the nature of their search, though, they would most likely be coming from the south.

The floodlight on the loading dock was shining as testament that the building had power in the middle of a citywide blackout. She didn't want to waste time tracking down the light switch. Olivia pointed up at the bulb. "Dagger, break that glass."

Dagger reached up with her knife and smacked the floodlight with its hilt. Glass rained down onto the dock.

"I believe the oni will come from that direction." Olivia pointed toward the five-way intersection as she let her eyes adjust to the rainy darkness. "Tell everyone—quietly—to hide behind cover. Do not fire your weapons unless fired upon. Use blades to defend yourself if a stray oni stumbles upon us. Be quiet. Stealth is vital for success. Also be prepared to board the wagon as we might be fleeing."

"We're not going to fight them?" Dagger asked in a disappointed tone.

"Our priority is to keep our communication device safe," Olivia said. "It is the human's distant voices."

"Ah! I understand." The female hurried off to repeat Olivia orders via sign language and pointing. There was a duplex beside the bakery's employee parking lot. Its front doors opened directly onto the sidewalk, leaving no space for anything that could be called a front yard. The backyard, though, was a large grass lot with a detached garage. The royal marines spread along the side wall and spilled into the backyard.

The sound of the oncoming trucks grew louder. As Olivia feared, the oni were approaching from the south. The overhead power lines started to silver, reflecting the headlights of the oni's vehicles. As she watched, the truck appeared on Amanda Street, rumbling up to the five-way intersection. The lead truck stopped at the stop sign, flooding the road with light. The other two trucks pulled up behind it, making the first vehicle gleam brightly in the falling rain. John Street joined the intersection at an odd dog-leg angle—their headlights didn't reach the bakery. Straight would take the oni on up Amanda and safely past them.

"Keep going," she whispered to the enemy convoy. "Move on."

She wanted to look back at the bakery's door to see what was taking Duff and the others so long. She couldn't pry her eyes away from the unmoving convoy. Her heart was hammering in her chest.

She'd been worried when she plowed through the shipyard's gate but not overly so. She was just a distraction while Tommy found and freed the kidnapped prostitutes. She had been fairly sure that the humans would be confused and slow to react. Things had gone as she expected until the oni arrived. The oni hadn't hesitated—they opened fire as soon as they arrived.

It meant that the oni on the trucks would attack the moment that her people were spotted. The trucks could easily hold three times their number.

The Lord will pass over the door, and will not suffer the destroyer to come in unto your houses to smite you.

"God in heaven," Olivia whispered, "please, let them go straight and pass us by. Protect all of those with me from this harm."

The trucks sat in place, headlights bright in the rainy darkness. Her fear spiked as oni started to pour out of the vehicles. Dozens of the tall, fierce-looking males. All carrying rifles.

"Oh, dear God." Olivia tore her eyes away to look back again at the back door to the bakery. Duff and the others had finally appeared, carrying equipment wrapped in plastic. She realized the loading dock ramp had a steep drop between it and the employee parking lot beside it. A chain-link fence kept people from falling but it also kept Duff from getting to his pickup without going out into the street. If the oni were like the elves, they would be able to see someone moving in the darkness.

"No, no!" Olivia spread her arms, blocking their way. "The oni are here. Don't go out into the street."

Zippo hopped over the fence near the foot of the ramp and used his height to reach up for the equipment. "Pass it here."

Alita cautiously peered down the street and whispered out a horrified, *"Cào nǐ zǔzōng shíbā dài!"*

Someone had gotten out of the passenger side of the lead yellow box truck. Olivia couldn't tell if they were oni or elf or human. They were shorter and slimmer than the beefy male oni warriors. They were dressed in unisex one-piece hooded camo coveralls. The curves of their hips, as they stood in front of the headlights, suggested a human female. The woman held out some kind of small electronic device about the size of five smart phones stacked on top of each other. Olivia guessed it was a tracking device as she waved it toward each direction of the five-way intersection.

The female shouted something that made Alita grunt.

"Did you understand that?" Olivia whispered.

"She said that she lost the signal," Alita whispered. She paused, listening, as the female continued to speak in what Olivia guessed to be oni. "She's going to 'use the old-fashioned method.'"

"What is that?" Olivia whispered.

Alita shook her head. "I don't know what that means."

Duff, Widget, and Zippo came scurrying over, having secured Duff's radio equipment in his pickup.

"What shitty bad timing!" Duff whispered fiercely. "I just got word from the tengu out in the forest with Windwolf. The elves walked into a huge ambush and need extraction. Someone needs to get a train out to them."

Olivia stomach churned queasily at the news. If Alita was right about the spell rendering the *domana* helpless, then an ambush would be deadly.

"We'll work on that once we get away safely," Olivia vowed. "Are you ready to go?"

"We're loaded and ready," Duff whispered. "What's the plan for getting out of here?"

Hunting dogs usually went after the rabbit that bolted, missing the one that stayed still and quiet in thick cover. With as empty as the Mount Oliver area was, the oni were going to go after the first thing that moved. "Duff, put your truck into neutral and coast into the backyard beside the parking lot. Be careful not to flash your brake lights. I'll go first. Let them chase me. I'll draw them away from you."

Duff frowned but nodded. He didn't like the idea but wasn't going to argue with her. "I need to get someplace with power to set back up."

Like she would know of such a place! In that moment, she remembered that Duff was only two years older than her. Everyone, even the marines, were technically children.

"Go to the William Penn," Alita whispered. "Mokoto should have the power back on by now. We'll meet you there."

"We?" Olivia whispered. She had thought that Alita and Zippo would go with Duff, since it was safer.

"You don't know your way around," Alita whispered. "I'm your native guide."

Olivia couldn't argue with that, not with the lives of the royal marines depending on her.

"Get ready to move," Olivia said as Dagger joined her to confirm all the marines were on the truck.

The woman down the street had taken a red ribbon out of her pocket. She threw back her hood, revealing pure white hair, cut boy short. There was something familiar about her face, as if Olivia had seen her somewhere before.

"I thought she was dead," Alita whispered in shock.

"Who is she?" Olivia whispered.

"I think that's Chloe Polanski—but Tinker killed her!" Alita said.

"Chloe Polaski danced rings around me until I figured out what she was doing," Tinker *domi* had said. *"She could see the future."*

"Oh, this is bad," Olivia whispered. "Move! Move! Move!"

The feral kittens scrambled into the truck.

The female tied the red ribbon over her eyes as a blindfold. As Olivia climbed up into the driver's seat, she could see the female languidly moving her hands as if she was doing a hula.

The woman paused and cried out in English, "Oh, damn it all, those mice again! Shit! Shit! Shit!"

Olivia wasn't sure what it meant, but it confirmed her guess that the female was a human.

The woman started to hula again, muttering angrily.

Olivia sat, tense and ready, her fingers on the key and her feet poised on the clutch and brake pedals.

The female finished her dance and pointed up John Street, straight at Olivia. She barked a command and the warriors around her clambered back into the three yellow box trucks.

Please God. Please God. Please God. Olivia turned the key, whispering a prayer that she would get the complicated dance of clutch and gas right.

The big truck lurched forward like an ungainly beast. She wrestled with the steering wheel to make the tight turn. Zippo reached over and helped her wrench it hard to the right. They jumped the curb and took out part of a wooden fence beyond it.

She could hear the female shouting in oni but she couldn't take her attention off driving.

"Straight!" Olivia cried so that Zippo would do the turning as she needed one hand to shift. She danced across the clutch and gas to shift into second. The big truck roared as she pushed it up to speed with the gas pedal to the floor between gear shifts. As they hit third at the top of the hill, she risked glancing behind her. The oni warriors had reloaded into their vehicles and all three trucks seemed to be charging after her.

"Alita, watch where they go!" Olivia ordered as she refocused on driving. "Make sure they all follow. Right turn!"

Her choice of turning east onto Arlington was dictated by the knowledge that the oni trucks were newer and smaller and thus probably faster. They would be sure to catch her on the steep winding uphill climb to the west. Better to go downhill, back to the areas that the feral kitten knew better.

"They're all coming after us!" Alita shouted. "Oh, shit! Polanski has a hoverbike!"

Four targets, Olivia thought grimly.

There was a thunder of guns immediately behind her. The marines had opened fire on their pursuers. They must have decided that her earlier instructions about not shooting were no longer valid.

"Woo-hoo!" Alita shouted. "They took out the driver of the lead truck!"

The lead truck careened out of control, veering off to smash into an abandoned apartment building.

Three targets, but she was about to take the snaking South Eighteenth Street at full speed. It was a bobsled run downhill but it was less likely that the remaining oni could cut her off. "Brace yourselves!"

She cut through a gas station's parking lot to make the sharp turn onto South Eighteenth Street without slowing down. The marines must have heard her and took it as an order as the shooting stopped.

If she thought coming up hill on South Eighteenth Street had been frightening in the dark and rain, it was terrifying down-hill at high speed in the big, ungainly truck. The first bend was a swing to the left. She fought the steering wheel to make the turn. Her headlights swept across high stone columns marking the entrance into a cemetery. Half of the stone gate was missing, as if someone hadn't made the turn.

The next turn came seconds later at a near forty-five-degree angle to the right with a warning sign suggesting that she should slow to fifteen miles per hour to make it safely. She dropped down through the gears so she could power through it. The left side was a twenty-foot-tall retaining wall painted with a mural. Zippo reached over and helped her turn the steering wheel. She whimpered as they mounted the curb, took out a reflective cau-tion sign, and came within inches of glancing off the wall. The painted faces of a nun and bishop stared at her with concern.

She shifted back to sixth gear and kept to the middle of the road as it snaked back and forth down the hill. She glanced in her side mirrors. The trucks were strung out behind her as two sets of headlights.

"Where's the hoverbike?" Olivia focused back on the upcom-ing bend. Did hoverbikes have headlights?

"I don't know," Alita said. "The bitch took off on it."

Had the woman gone after Duff?

No, probably not. With three trucks to command, the woman could have split her forces more evenly. If she was after Duff, she would have taken at least one truck with her. The woman might be able to see the future but she had been as easy to distract as a bird dog. She'd spotted the fleeing rabbit and given chase, sure that it was what she was after. Her focus now probably was on how she could stop Olivia. She would have seen that Olivia would choose to run downhill. Did the female know where this chase would lead?

Olivia had no clue. She was merely running blind. Was that wise? Should she know where she was trying to get to? Not the hotel where Tommy's family lived—she couldn't risk leading the oni back to it.

Maybe not choosing a destination would be the best way to outmaneuver a woman who could see where they planned to go. She'd focus on scraping off the two remaining box trucks. How could she stop them? Olivia was sure hers was the more durable vehicle as it was built for actual combat duty. She couldn't play demolition derby with the enemy, though, without serious risk to her passengers.

The oni apparently didn't share her concern. The lead truck surged forward, jockeying to close on her on the left.

Yellow hazard signs warned of another sharp, forty-five-degree curve to the right ahead. To the left, a narrow sidewalk was all that separated the street from houses and apartment buildings. On the right, there was only darkness beyond the sidewalk as if the land dropped off to a cliff. The dark and the rain kept her from seeing how big the drop was. Considering the steepness of the hill, it could be anywhere from a ten-foot drop to a fifty-foot one. At one time there was railing to protect pedestrians but it was gone. Going off the road on either side was deadly even without the added danger that the oni represented.

Olivia whimpered as she downshifted to power through the turn; she needed to worry about staying on the road over what the oni were doing. It slowed her speed, allowing the lead oni to close the gap until it was almost even with her.

"He's coming! He's coming!" Alita warned as Olivia started to crank the steering wheel hard to the right around the next steep curve.

In her sideview mirror, Olivia saw the lead truck swerve toward her, attempting to ram her back end.

"Help me!" she cried to Zippo as she stomped on the gas pedal. They had to dodge right to evade the oni.

"I don't actually know how to drive," Zippo said as he pulled hard on the wheel.

Too hard.

They veered off the road.

Everyone yelped in fear as the truck mounted the sidewalk.

"Back! Back!" Olivia cried as they crossed the sidewalk. "Good Lord, save us!"

A miracle happened—there was a parking lot beyond the sidewalk. Their headlights swept over the small store painted all black as she and Zippo wheeled to the left. The building had "350" written in big numbers.

The oni had swerved with them, still trying to ram as they went off the road. It skidded on the wet pavement and smashed through a wooden fence at the far edge of the parking lot. It disappeared into the darkness beyond with a loud crash.

"I think they're out of the running," Alita said staring back.

"Still one left," Olivia said.

"Two," Alita said. "There's the hoverbike—someplace."

Assuming that the woman was even giving chase. There was a possibility that her sudden outcry about mice meant that she realized that she was needed elsewhere.

The road was steep and straight ahead. The houses lining the street stopped. Trees pressed in close on the little-used road, branches forming a tight, dark tunnel. The remaining oni truck followed close on her tail, weaving back and forth, trying to find a way to pull even with her. It forced her to weave, trying to keep it blocked.

Her headlights picked out arrows indicating that the road curved to the left ahead. SLIPPERY WHEN WET signs joined the warning arrows pointing left. The road curved and curved until she was sure that they were going to do a full 180-degree turn.

The remaining oni truck suddenly sped up and rammed her from behind. She struggled to keep on the wet slippery curving road while speeding up, out of the oni's reach.

"Fine," she whispered. "Demolition derby it is."

"What?" Alita shouted.

"Brace yourselves!" Olivia gave everyone a few seconds to prepare.

The oni surged forward, trying to ram her again. She jerked to the left to hug the inside curve and slammed on her brakes. Immediately she needed to downshift to keep from stalling as the truck slid forward on the wet pavement.

The oni had been speeding up to ram her again. It missed her by inches. It took off her side mirror as it passed. She stomped on the gas and wretched the wheel to the right, aiming for a solid glancing blow to its butt. With the big engine and cavernous box back, the pivot of the oni truck would be in the front. At high speed on the sharp turn, the nudge was enough. The driver-side back wheels lifted from the road and the whole truck started to tip.

Olivia was too busy fighting to keep control of her vehicle to watch the resulting crash. The glancing blow ricocheted her hard to the left. It careened her into a narrow side street.

"Oh, he's down!" Alita proclaimed, hanging out the passenger window to watch the crash. "Where are we going?"

"I have no idea," Olivia admitted.

"I told you this place is a maze once you get off South Eighteenth Street," Alita said. "There's a lot of dead ends."

The one-way street was straight, narrow, and level as if built on a shelf in the hillside. There were empty lots here and there, giving a view to the river valley below. As lightning lit up the night, they caught glimpses of South Side still far below them. There seemed to be a ravine or something between the street that they were on and the river bottom.

Olivia drove a long way, three or four blocks at least, without seeing a way off the narrow lane. The first side street was even more narrow. Olivia drove past it, fearing that it might lead to a dead end. A few hundred feet after it, the road branched into a steep uphill climb and the slalom run downhill.

"Downhill. I think," Alita said as Olivia slowed down to give herself time to consider the choices.

A hundred feet or more and the road branched again. To the right was a bridge over the ravine while to the left-hand branch was an extremely narrow and weedy road heading uphill.

Olivia chose to go downhill again, over the bridge. A few minutes later they reached the flat city-grid of South Side—someplace.

"This is South Twelfth Street!" Alita said at one corner. "I know where we are. Where should we go?"

Duff had said that the elves in the forest needed a train. Until he got his radio set back up, he couldn't coordinate with the Resistance. If Olivia had failed to distract the oni from Duff and his equipment, then maybe no one would ever know that the *domana* needed help.

"We're going to Penn Station," Olivia said.

20: BETWEEN A STONE
AND A HARD PLACE

The scrape of a boot on cement warned Tristan that he had another visitor.

Tristan blinked away tears to look up.

It was one of Boo's older brothers. Which one was it? Duff? Alton? No, it was the brother named Marc, the twenty-year-old police officer.

Lucien's notes had said that the man's nickname was Stone. He lived up to the name by kneeling down in front of Tristan to study him in complete silence.

Tristan had no idea what to say. He hadn't expected any of Boo's family to be at the radio station. He had a cover identity but no ready reason why a supposed fifteen-year-old boy would be sitting on Mount Washington, weeping. The one thing he did know was that liars often revealed themselves by giving too much information, trying to disguise their lie with a barrage of random truths. Of all Boo's brothers, the police officer would be the one who recognized a fake story buried in extraneous facts.

Tristan's best bet was looking like a lost child, holding off on an explanation for his presence until he was directly asked a question. He focused on calming himself. He had let the old female rattle him. Clearly that was what she set out to do. She knew who he was and what he was doing here. She'd told him the one truth that would slide through all his defenses and hit hard enough to count. She might have wanted him to go looking for the twins in order to protect them—but even more likely she simply didn't want him to sabotage the radio station. She obviously wanted him to flip sides and fight against his father.

Marc reached out and patted Tristan on the shoulder. The man stood up and motioned for Tristan to stand. "You'll be safer with us."

That was debatable. The old female was most likely the hidden enemy *intanyai seyosa* that his sisters had been fighting against. She would not have left unless she was sure that the situation had been swayed in the direction that she wanted it to go.

Was he flipped? He didn't know himself. Maybe she just wanted to delay him until some crucial moment had passed. The humans might have already gotten some vital message out so that whatever Tristan did—flee or stay—didn't matter. No, there were other ways to delay him without giving out such vital information. The Eyes worked best in secrecy. Maybe there was something else, something more important than the radio station that she just derailed him from. Finding Boo?

And what of the baby chicken still cupped in his hands? What was he supposed to do with that? Give it to his niece? Which one? He had three but he didn't know where any of them were at the moment. The changeling had managed to fall off the Eyes' radar for a second time. She could be anywhere in the city, doing weird, impossible things. If Yves died while escorting the twins through a cavern system, then they could be trapped underground somewhere—but that didn't match up with "charging into danger." What classified as "danger" depended heavily on where they were. Earth? Elfhome? Pittsburgh? Easternlands? The mind boggled as to where in the multiverse the two might have ended up from his father's mansion.

He followed Marc Kryskill through the pouring rain with "flee or stay" looping through his head. He could flee easily. Marc seemed to have bought the "little lost boy" façade. He could come up with some innocent reason that he was bawling his eyes out in the rain and then say that he lived nearby and needed to go home to his parents. Most people didn't want to be responsible for a stray child. Should he flee?

If he stayed, he might learn if Boo had made contact with her family after disappearing from Sandcastle. Adele stranding him on Mount Washington meant that he'd missed his chance to target Boo's mother. Marc had approached him, so the man would be less cautious of Tristan than if Tristan had sought him out. It was a golden opportunity to observe and perhaps gain trust.

The old female had rattled Tristan hard. Maybe she wanted him to flee. People were more vulnerable when they were running scared. Or maybe she was trying to keep him from following through with Adele's directive of checking out WESA. Chloe and the others had overlooked the pirate radio station. The flurry of activity around it, though, suggested that "the cool kids" had joined sides with the changeling and her tengu followers. He should stay long enough to know if the work party was success-ful at getting WESA back on the air.

There was a web of wires running from the cinder-block build-ing to the old UPS delivery truck. Up close, the hand-painted sheep on its side seemed to eye Tristan with suspicion. While the back gate was up, there were strips of thick black fabric hanging over the opening. Marc indicated that Tristan was to get out of the cold rain by climbing up into the back of the truck. No one else seemed to be paying attention to Tristan. If he got them used to his presence, he would have free run of the situation. He stepped up into the truck, ducking through the fabric panels.

At first glance, the interior matched that of a wool delivery truck. Bags of raw wool and skeins of dyed yarn festooned the ceiling and sides. There were wood storage bins marked CARD-ING BRUSHES, DYES, AND BAGS. The cabinets, though, stood open, revealing electronics.

A woman with headphones was fiddling with a large micro-phone and laptop computer and something that looked like a soundboard lifted out of a recording studio. Every few seconds, she would pause and do a sound check on a large microphone. The truck was obviously a covert mobile radio station. The wool served as soundproofing. The heavy rain had been muffled to silence.

"WESA had an emergency backup generator at one time," the woman was saying as she changed settings on her laptop. "You can see that all the wire connections are all there. Just sometime between NPR pulling out and us taking over, someone walked off with the generator. Not surprising, considering that Pittsburgh normally spends the first few hours after Shutdown and Startup without power. It happened to the other station that shared office space with WESA back in the day."

Tristan studied the other person in the truck. It was Boo's cousin, William Roach, who went just by his last name. He was the business manager for Team Tinker, which might mean that the tengu presence was because of his connection to the change-ling. Tinker would trust her old friends over anyone new. Did the changeling send Roach to oversee...?

Tristan's brain froze as he realized that there was a third person in the van: Boo.

She had been curled into the driver's seat. She leaned out to look back at the deejay. Her white hair spilled down over her shoulders in loose curls. Tengu warpaint streaked her cheeks in a blue that complemented her stunningly blue eyes. She wore an oversized jacket over a black tank top and cutoff blue jean shorts. Her skin was so white, even in the warpaint and borrowed coat, she seemed ethereal and untouchable. So fierce. So vulnerable.

"Storm One says that Storm Six is in position," Boo told the woman.

Oh, shit, Tristan thought. Boo had rejoined her large extended family. Most likely, she'd been with them since she disappeared from Sandcastle in July. The Kryskills were a perfect storm of bootleggers crossed with career military. Of course they could and would create a covert human fighting group, armed with detailed knowledge of Lucien's organization. Worse, they had teamed up with the tengu.

No wonder the Eyes told Lucien to get rid of Boo.

The most important question was, how large a force had her family built? Boo's older brother and cousin were here at the radio station. One had to assume the other siblings and cousins were involved. Was it just their extended family? Or were they just the tip of the iceberg?

The deejay nodded but added, "We're dead in the water until we get power to the tower."

There was a sudden deep rumble of big equipment from the trailer-mounted generator. A few seconds later, an answering hum from inside the cinder-block building.

A tengu male pulled aside the fabric hanging to say, "We're up and running!"

"Quick, close the back!" the deejay said, hitting buttons and pulling her microphone close.

The male reached up, grabbed the bottom of the gate, and pulled it down.

Tristan forgot how to breathe. He was locked in a truck with Boo and her cousin. If Boo recognized him, he would have to fight his way out. The only other exit was in the front, beside her, but so far she hadn't even looked at him. Her focus seemed to be on the earbud in her right ear. He turned away from her, pulling the hood of his rain jacket lower.

"Storm One, this is Bullhorn," Boo said quietly to whoever was on the other side of the link. "We're going live."

"This is WESA!" the deejay said. "I'm Marti Wulfow! This is an important emergency news bulletin! The oni army has attacked the city. I repeat: the oni army has attacked the city. They have taken out the city's power and telecommunication grid. A large heavily armed force has been spotted on Liberty Avenue heading to Oakland. Hal Rogers is live in Oakland reporting on the situation. Hal, are you there?"

Wulfow moved sliders on her sound console, muting her microphone while unmuting the feed from the field reporter.

"...is Hal Rogers, the voice of freedom! Oakland is under attack! I'm calling out to you, the people of Pittsburgh! If you value all that is good, grab your rifle and get to Oakland! We need every hero that we can muster to stop them. We need your fighting spirit at the Centre Avenue Bridge!"

Was this the reason the female elf had waylaid Tristan? Was it so he couldn't stop this broadcast? Or was something even more important than that rally call to the humans going to happen shortly? He wasn't sure that a random reporter calling for help would have much effect.

"Run!" a female barked orders somewhere close to the reporter. "Hal! Run and talk!"

"Jane," Boo whispered, sounding like she was about to start crying.

"Hey!" Roach moved to Boo, pulling her close. "She'll be fine. They've been planning for this for weeks."

Tristan pressed his lips tight, keeping his eyes locked on his feet so that his hood shadowed his face. He hadn't recognized the name at first but Hal Rogers was the host for the show that Jane Kryskill produced. Chloe had been dismissive of the possible dangers that Jane's show represented. How wrong had she been?

"Homestead! Hot Metal!" Jane continued to shout in the background. "Get inside with Smithfield! Stay back from the windows. Stay low!"

The Kryskills had squads of people out on the front line, operating with code names.

Oh, this is bad. Lucien had hoped that they could keep the humans from joining the elves. It was why they triggered a communication blackout while keeping the EIA forces busy. Earth could be convinced to ignore the war as a local political conflict that had nothing to do with humans—as long as humans weren't killed in the fighting. Of course, this wouldn't be a problem if they couldn't get a gate up and working, reconnecting the worlds. The knowledge of how to build a gate was out there and such things were dangerously hard to kill.

There was the noise of an explosion through the radio connection.

"What the hell is that?" Jane shouted.

"It's Tinker *domi!*" someone answered.

"Tinker *domi* is in here and she is glorious!" Hal reported. "Our little goddess is here and she's raining fire on our enemy!"

That was the worst piece of news of all: the changeling was using magic to fight. All the *domana* should have been unconscious. Her connection to the Spell Stones was intact. It meant all the *domana* could be unaffected. Had Lucien gotten something wrong with the spell? Their father would be furious. Dangerously furious.

Surely their father wouldn't punish Lucien too harshly. The changeling had been doing all sorts of impossible things all summer. Lucien had scribed the spell but Yves had been the one who originated it. Their father had checked Lucien's work. Said that it was good. Cast the spell himself.

"He's already killed the sister you loved the best—she saw what was coming and tried to escape... Your mother is gone. Cold and unclaimed and will go to a pauper's grave because there's no one there to claim her body."

Bethany is dead, Tristan thought. *My mother is dead. Chloe too. Danni is on the front lines against a fully powered changeling. Father might kill Lucien in a rage before the night is out. I have done horrible terrible things only to be left utterly alone.*

Grief suddenly flooded through him, washing away all reasoning. He folded into a ball, struggling not to cry. The tears burned in his eyes.

I want my mother.

That it was utterly impossible only made his eyes burn more. He was lost in utter despair.

21: WHIZBANGS AND WHATNOTS

Baum Boulevard and Centre Avenue bracketed a big five-story, redbrick building that had been a Ford plant and showroom in the early 1900s. The University of Pittsburgh had bought the site prior to the first Startup, planning to turn it into research labs. The plan was delayed for decades as the university adapted to life on Elfhome. Construction had started just that spring, gutting the interior and decorating the outside with warning signs. One proclaimed EVERYONE GOES HOME SAFE AT THE END OF THE DAY!

Tinker truly hoped that the slogan boded well for the battle.

The busway ran under the parallel bridges in what used to be a deep river channel. The far side of the ravine had a sheer fifty-foot-tall retaining wall. At the bottom, there were two sets of railroad tracks and two lanes of limited-access highway, both closed in by tall fences, creating an obstacle course that the oni probably would avoid at all costs.

Centre Avenue was the shorter bridge but the one closer to the enclaves. While both bridges had been barricaded and strung with concertina wire, the human militia seemed to be concentrated at the end of Centre Avenue.

What do you know—Pittsburgh has a militia, Tinker thought. They were a sorry-looking, ragtag lot but it was a militia. At least half of their number wore garbage bags as rain ponchos. The rest were in hunting gear. Some had cooking pots on their heads as helmets, but most wore blue bucket hats like the ones that Roach had wanted to order for Team Tinker.

Jane Kryskill seemed to be the one in charge. It was at once surprising and yet not. The Kryskills had a military air around everything that they did. Roach and his family were leaders by nature and happiest in a crowd. Roach managed Team Tinker. His older brother Sean was one of the most popular deejays in Pittsburgh. His father Bill was the president of the Pittsburgh chapter of the Rotary club. The Roach men could gather and organize large crowds with ease. The Kryskills were more reclusive than their cousins. They marched to the beat of a different drummer, often alone, and perfectly happy that way.

There was nothing ragtag about Jane Kryskill as she stalked toward Tinker, snapping orders over a radio. All her equipment was military-grade, from her rain gear to her boots. Chesty, her big black elfhound, followed on her heel, eyeing up the newcomers with suspicion.

"This is Storm Six." Jane issued commands over her headset as she handed off her rifle to her cameraman. Judging by her glance toward Pony and the other *sekasha*, Jane didn't want to look like a threat to the elves. "Homestead. Hot Metal. Shift to target two."

"Long time, no see," Tinker wasn't sure what to say. Jane wasn't like other authority figures that Tinker had plowed through in the past—she was practically family. Certainly every time that they had crossed paths before, Jane had operated as everyone's older sister. She punished everyone who ran with her younger brothers and cousins when she caught them doing something that they shouldn't be doing. She also would protect the entire pack of younger children if someone picked a fight with one of them.

"Is Oilcan okay?" Jane said. Because of Geoffrey, Jane knew that metal and magic didn't mix. She shrugged off her chest armor before closing on Tinker, handing it off to another one of her film crew members who looked weirdly like Nigel Reid. Jane obviously wanted a private conversation, not a shouted discussion at twenty paces. "I hated leaving him but we needed to reinforce these bridges."

"He's good." Tinker dropped her shield and then recast it to include Jane. "Thanks for holding the oni until I could get here."

"We only managed to hold here because of the barricades our people set up earlier," Jane reported. "That and the tengu reinforcements at the last minute. I don't know if it's because

Oilcan was at the other bridge, or the added guns, but they didn't try to wade through the concertina wire like before. They hit our barricades and pulled back. They're dug in on the other side—building something."

Between the darkness and the rain smearing down her shield, Tinker couldn't see anything beyond dark shadows moving about.

Jane continued her report. "The tengu say that they think that it's bonfires but they're not sure. The scouts report that the oni are muscling cages with horrors down Centre Avenue. The tengu couldn't get close enough to tell what type of horror; the cages are covered up. They think the covering is to keep the horrors somewhat docile until the oni can get them into position and use the enlarging spell on them."

The EIA arrived in trucks. Tinker waved Captain Josephson over to her, dropping and raising her shield so he could join the discussion.

"This is Jane Kryskill," Tinker handled the introductions. Most locals didn't like the EIA, as they were off-worlders who created huge legal difficulties for Pittsburghers while they dealt with life isolated on Elfhome. What they could import. What they could export. What they could gather from the forest around them. It created a lot of hostilities that could boil over on the battlefield if the EIA assumed that it was in command. "I've known her for years. I trust her completely. She's in charge of the militia. You're to work with her. Understand?"

He nodded. Hopefully he understood that he wasn't to go around stepping on Jane's toes. Tinker wasn't totally sure Jane wouldn't shoot him if he did. Kryskills were usually the type to punch first, ask questions later.

"Jane, this is Captain Josephson. He's in command of a special operations unit. They backed me up at the whelping pens earlier this summer. They're good but they're new to Elfhome, so they don't know the area well and they're not totally familiar with some of the more dangerous things like black willows."

Jane nodded. The two shook hands.

"It looks like the oni are focusing on Centre Avenue. You two cover Baum Boulevard," Tinker told them. "If they send more horrors this direction, I'll hold them off."

Captain Josephson nodded again.

"Don't throw yourself into a no-win fight," Jane said. "If you have to retreat, pull back. We'll hightail it and regroup someplace else. Remember: he who runs away, lives to fight another day."

This sounded like a speech Jane gave proto-Team Tinker when Tinker was twelve. She and Oilcan had gone to a street fair with a horde of Roach's cousins and friends. Some older kids picked a fight with them for reasons that Tinker could no longer remember. What she did remember was that Jane—after breaking up the fight and chewing out her family and their friends—promptly ignored her own advice when the tallest of the idiots who started the fight threw a punch at Jane. It was an impressive and quick beatdown.

"We will retreat if we have to," Tinker promised. "We" because she suspected that none of the *sekasha* would leave her, no matter what she told them. The knowledge made her a little queasy in the stomach. What were the oni going to throw at her?

Jane suddenly turned and pointed an angry finger at a short man who had been creeping toward them. "Hal! Behind the building!"

Hal Rogers was shorter in person than Tinker imagined him to be. Why did she think he was taller? He wavered in place, apparently well aware that Jane could and would hurt him if he disobeyed her without reason. "I should interview Tinker *domi* for the listeners!"

"Oh, dear gods, no!" Tinker said. The last thing she wanted Pittsburghers to hear was how she didn't have a clue what she was doing.

"Go." Jane put a hand to her ear, listening intently while looking toward the darkness that held the oni. "They're moving. Brace yourself. Hal! Back! I mean it!"

"I'm moving! I'm moving!" Hal scurried back to his hiding place behind the nearest building.

The smell of gasoline flooded through the night. The oni must have poured out hundreds of gallons of the stuff for it to smell so strongly.

"What are they doing?" Tinker asked.

Flames shot up from stacks of gasoline-soaked piles of wood. The fire brightly illuminated the far side of the bridge. The oni were retreating back up Centre Avenue, leaving behind a wagon carrying something square, covered with a black tarp. It must be one of the cages that Jane mentioned.

Dark Scythe growled softly as he realized what the oni were doing. "This was a common tactic for phoenix scorpions."

"A what?" Tinker said.

The roaring fire suddenly snuffed out. The creature within the cage started to glow brightly. There was a flare of magic as a powerful spell went off. The monster suddenly expanded in size, shattering the cage until it was the stuff of nightmares. Giant pincers. Big glistening mandibles. Stinger tail the size of a backhoe curled over its back. Translucent wings that unfurled.

"Shit!" Tinker whispered. "It can fly?"

"Yes, it can fly," Dark Scythe said, talking quickly. "Fire attacks will only make it stronger. A nulling shield will cancel its sound attack but you cannot cast it and hold a Stone Clan shield at the same time."

Tinker dropped the shield she'd been holding with her left hand. She set up a link to the Wind Clan Spell Stones and cast a shield with her right. "Nulling? Grandpa erased that spell out of the codex. How do you do—"

The scorpion started to make a noise like a Godzilla-sized cicada. The sound felt like a nail being driven straight into her skull. Everyone around her cringed, bowing before the sound.

There was a quick exchange of blade talk between Pony and Dark Scythe. Pony stepped aside. Dark Scythe caught hold of Tinker's left hand, molded her fingers into the correct position, pressed them to his lips, and spoke the key word to link her to the Stone Clan Spell Stones. He changed her fingers and spoke a second key word.

The silence was blessed.

"That sound you heard," Hal Rogers said quietly in the background, "is a monster that the oni have unleashed on Oakland. It's massive—nearly the size of a wyvern. It looks like a scorpion forged in the heart of the sun! If we had any questions about what the oni plan for the humans, I think we just got our answers. Tinker *domi* will kill this beast but she needs us to mop up the rest."

Yeah. Sure she will, Tinker thought. The problem was she only had two hands and she was already holding two spells active. Worse, there were more cages farther up the hill, probably holding more phoenix scorpions. At least the militia was making it hard for the oni to release the other monsters.

"The beast will locate you via your shield," Dark Scythe warned as he let go of her hand and stepped away. "You will feel it. It will attack you once it has located you."

Bullets from the militia and the EIA troops pinged off the glowing chitin, not doing any damage. The *sekasha* fired spell arrows, hoping to luck into hitting the hidden creature within. Judging by the lack of response, they missed.

She'd used an electromagnet on the foo dogs that attacked Windwolf in her salvage yard. Metal also disrupted the spell. The area was scattered with possibilities but she had both hands engaged.

"How do I hurt it?" Tinker said nervously.

"That falls to us," Pony said.

Magic pulsed from the scorpion. It washed over Tinker like white static.

"It's targeted me," Tinker said. "Here it comes!"

It lifted off and flew toward her. Seemingly large in the distance, it became impossibly huge as it rushed toward them. It filled her vision, blotting out the night, with a glow so bright that she found herself squinting against the light. It slammed into her shield and rebounded, then hung for a moment, its translucent wings blurring as they beat the air. Its huge alien-looking head worked its mandibles only yards from her face. It had eight legs like a spider, each ending with sharp hooks that were bigger than her torso. Its chitin was golden yellow, glowing as if it was made of molten metal. The only black on it were two dark spots on its head that she assumed were its eyes, staring at her intently. Spikes covered its body like massive individual strands of hair. She could only guess that they were to sense vibrations. It was too alien for her to understand what hovered before her.

"Goddamn son of a bitch," she whispered as she held her shields tight. Stone Clan with her left hand. Wind Clan with right hand. Everything about the giant monster was sending fear shivering down her back and that made her angry. This thing didn't really exist. There was some little creature inside, running the monster like a puppeteer. The creature within shouldn't even exist—wouldn't exist except for the Skin Clan being assholes with god complexes.

The scorpion landed at the edge of her shield. Rain hazed as it turned to steam on contact with the glowing shell. The nulling shield was keeping out its magical sound attack but she could feel the vibration from it under her feet.

Her shields kept the monster on the bridge but she couldn't do any damage nor could her people. If it decided to attack someone else, she couldn't stop it. Behind it, on the hill leading up Centre Avenue, four more bonfires flared into being. The oni were making more horrors!

Tinker frantically looked around, squinting against the brilliance of the fiery scorpion. There was nothing useful to her right, just the bare asphalt of a parking lot. To her left was the construction site. There might be something they could use among the building materials. She spotted a pile of galvanized steel fence posts.

Stormsong had told Tinker once that she needed to trust her Hand to do their jobs. Tinker knew what needed to be done. She hated it even as she shouted, "Pony, to my left, those poles!"

"Yes, *domi!*" Pony dashed to the pile and picked up one of the poles. Holding the length of galvanized steel like a spear, he rushed at the scorpion. Dark Scythe and his people moved forward to join Pony, activating their personal shields as they left the protection of Tinker's shields.

"Ready arrows," Stormsong ordered, taking charge of Tinker's remaining *sekasha*.

It took all Tinker's will power to simply hold her shields and trust her people to do their job.

The horror grabbed at Pony with both its pincers as he closed. Dark Scythe and his Second sprang forward and parried the massive claws with their *ejae*. The force of the strike pushed them back even as they strained to control the massive limbs. The huge barbed tail slashed forward. The others of Forge's First Hand stacked themselves in front of it, stepping aside as their shields failed before the blow.

Pony rammed the post into the gleaming chitin with his full weight behind the blow. The illusion flickered, going transparent to reveal a dog-sized glowing insect inside. In that moment, Stormsong, Cloudwalker, and Rainlily released their spell arrows.

The giant scorpion crumbled to the bridge's deck. The illusion continued even though the creature inside was dead. The horror took up much of the bridge, motionless as a puppet with its strings cut. The fiery glow, though, slowly waned.

Up the hill, the bonfires snuffed out. The cages holding the proto-horrors shattered as the creatures within them enlarged into giant fiery forms. It was like the sun had suddenly risen in the heart of Oakland. In the sudden brilliance, Tinker could see that all the oni were retreating at a full run, fleeing in terror of their own creations. There was nothing orderly about the withdrawal; it looked like sheer hysteria.

Tinker cursed. "I count four more incoming." She dropped her shield so Pony and the others could rejoin her. She recast it when they were safe beside her.

"We will not be able to repeat that maneuver with four at the same time," Pony said.

Dark Scythe nodded in agreement.

The woman who might be Chloe's sister thought that these horrors would roll right over Tinker. The possibility was real. Chloe, though, hadn't been able to see the trap that Tinker created with the mix of science and magic. Tinker had proven that given time to prepare, she could outfox her aunt's ability to see the future. It was only a question of time: did she have enough of it?

Bong! A loud oddly musical sound rang out and a thick shaft of light flashed overhead. It pierced through the lead horror, instantly killing it.

"Yes!" Tinker cried.

Geoffrey had gotten the coherent light pipe up and running!

When Tinker was little, she had plans to create a tank that could fire spell arrows. She no longer remembered why. Back then such projects often didn't need a "why" beyond "because I want to!" The proto-cannons were her first experiments toward a tank. She inscribed spells on the inside of PVC pipes that would accelerate an inert material—golf balls worked best—while converting them into a powerful beam attack. The tubes were wildly successful in terms of damage output but were far too long. She later drastically changed the design, printing the spell onto the ammo instead allowed for a shorter barrel.

Bong! Bong! The light strobed the night, again and again. Geoffrey's team was doing a great job of reloading the pipe. Aiming could be improved; the cannon was punching holes to the right and left of the three remaining horrors. This section of Oakland was going to look like Swiss cheese by the end of the fight.

Unlike the trial run of the pipes, years ago, she could feel the magic within the pipes activating as the mallets provided the sound that the spells were keyed to. It was an odd thrumming sensation, like someone plucking a guitar string while she pressed her arm against it.

There was a second, different ping against her senses. Short and piercing, more like a needle stab than a vibrating string.

"What was that?" Tinker said even though she knew no one else probably sensed it.

One of the remaining scorpions turned and headed away from the fight.

"Where's it going?" Tinker said.

"They are not trained beasts like elfhounds," Dark Scythe ventured after a long silence around her. "They act purely on instinct encoded into their genetics. They will kill anything before them, even their own creators. That is why the oni pulled back their troops when they released the horrors."

The white static of the scorpions' targeting magic washed over Tinker again and again.

"The other two just targeted me!" Tinker warned. "Here they come!"

The nearest horror took wing, heading toward her. Tinker braced for the attack. A beam of light punched through the monster, missing the main puppeteer body hidden inside but taking out its right wing. It veered drunkenly in a half circle.

The second gleaming scorpion came in a scuttling run, burning through the concertina wire on the bridge like it was cobwebs.

Ba-Boong! The second pipe sounded off. It had a weird deepening reverb, meaning it was probably the gravity pipe. It had been a bitch to aim when they were kids, hence the loss of the prized room-sized lilac bush in the Roaches' backyard. In the flashing brilliance of the coherent light attack, one dark orb arched high up in the sky to fall down toward the bridge. Seconds before the shot hit the deck, everything around it was sucked inward. The oncoming horror vanished as if it had been turned to dust and vacuumed up. Chunks of asphalt ripped free, flying upward before vaporizing. The structural beams cracked loudly, never meant to take an upward pressure. The dead horror at the edge of the bridge was dragged backward and then it too vanished into nothing.

There was loud cheering from the militia from their position within the research building.

The wounded horror gave up trying to fly. It charged forward across the bridge.

There was a loud cracking noise and the bridge collapsed in giant slabs of concrete. The giant gleaming insect skittered on the falling deck, its one remaining wing beat as it tried to fly to safety.

Ba-Boong! The gravity pipe sounded from behind Tinker. The dark orb followed the same trajectory, landing square on the horror that was scrabbling to free itself from the collapsing bridge.

The horror and parts of the bridge vanished, compacted down as gravity in their immediate area momentarily increased a hundredfold.

"Wood sprites and their dangerous toys," Dark Scythe murmured, shaking his head.

22: THE MONSTER MASH

With one last jump, the twins arrived at the graveyard.

It was hard to navigate in the pouring rain. The power was out in the city. They jumped high up into the sky, arcing to the east, and floated down to land within the wooded grounds of the graveyard. Lightning flickered. There were towering obelisks, gravestones large and small, playhouse-sized crypts, and statues all around them.

"Hide!" Jillian whispered fiercely as she ducked between two large crypts.

"Why are we hiding?" Louise whispered as she and Crow Boy hurried after Jillian. Thunder rumbled. Louise couldn't see anything in the rainy dark but the sense of danger pressed in on her like solid black dread.

"Because we're behind enemy lines in a war zone!" Jillian whispered. "And this place is scary."

Louise hadn't expected the graveyard to be scary. Calvary Cemetery had been near their home in Queens—you could see it from the Long Island Expressway. It had been open and orderly compared to the Allegheny Cemetery. Calvary had straighter roads, far fewer trees, fewer hills—resulting in gravestones that had been in rows a bare ten feet apart. It looked more like a parking lot or a department store showroom than someplace scary. She always thought Calvary would be an interesting place to have a picnic and sightsee the many statues.

Allegheny Cemetery—especially on a dark rainy night—looked like something out of a horror movie. It was easy to imagine monsters lurking behind every tree and stone. Worse, she couldn't even wave the possibility away, saying it was her imagination. This world had monsters.

Lightning flickered again and Jillian jerked her hand up to her mouth, shouting the word that linked her to the Spell Stones. Louise yelped in surprise and scrambled to cast her shield.

Crow Boy pulled out the pistol that he wore low on his leg like a gunslinger cowboy.

Louise trembled as she held her shield. "What? What?"

"Oh, geez!" Jillian shook her hand, breaking the link. "I thought that statue was someone standing there. I almost hit it with a force strike."

Said marble statue was a robed woman holding what looked like a flower blossom in her hand that she was about to drop onto the grave before her. It was very lifelike and probably historic.

"That would be bad," Louise whispered and jumped as the thunder rumbled loudly. She was still holding her shield spell.

Crow Boy holstered his pistol. "The dark is to our advantage. Don't let it spook you."

Easier said than done.

Louise took a deep breath to calm herself. "Let's find the babies first and then go after the *nactka* to free Joy's brothers and sisters."

Jillian looked around, peering hard into the darkness. "Where do you think the babies are?"

"They said that they had a tank," Louise said, trying to remember everything Chuck Norris and the others told them. The babies had talked to an elf who claimed to be their grandmother—which seemed impossible but could be true, considering they had a grandfather elf in Oakland. They also said something about Sir Galahad and a goat that didn't make any sense. "A tank shouldn't be too hard to spot."

"That's what I thought but this place is a lot bigger—and scarier—than I thought." Jillian turned suddenly to peer into the darkness. "What are they doing over there?"

Louise followed her gaze but couldn't see anything. "Who? What do you see?"

"I don't see—I feel," Jillian said. "Someone is using magic over . . . there?"

Jillian waved toward the rolling hills covered with gravestones and trees. They stared hard into the darkness, at first seeing nothing. Then far in the distance, the underbellies of the cloud lit up gold and red with sudden flame.

"Oh, wow!" Jillian breathed as a noise like cannon fire rolled in from the direction of the massive explosions. "That's a flame strike! We're seeing a flame strike in person! We can see it all the way from here? That is so awesome! Who is that? Windwolf? Prince True Flame?"

"No," Louise said without thinking. Was that right? Was it a guess or her power kicking in?

"Windwolf and the prince were deep in the forest this afternoon," Crow Boy said. "I doubt it is either of them. It must be Tinker *domi*; she can use Fire Clan *esva*."

"Can we?" Louise asked as Jillian brought her hand up to mouth again, this time to try and call the Fire Clan Spell Stones.

Crow Boy shook his head. "Tinker *domi* is able only because Windwolf gave her access to both Wind Clan and Fire Clan Spell Stones when he transformed her into a full-blooded elf."

"Shoot," Jillian muttered with disappointment. "How are we going to find the babies? We didn't give them a plan—not that they would actually follow a plan."

Their parents always had an "if we get separated" plan of action. She and Jillian thought it was silly as they always believed that they were far too smart to get lost. Six Flags Great Adventure—the second largest theme park in the world, filled with loud, fast-moving, colorful distractions—had proved them wrong. One minute they had been obediently following after their parents and the next they were lost in a sea of people. It had taken them an hour to admit defeat and follow the plan of asking a staff member to escort them to the "lost parent" counter.

The cemetery was nearly as big as Six Flags. There was no lost parent counter. No helpful employees. No parents to claim them at the end of the night.

My parents are dead and buried in a place like this, Louise thought, and tears welled up in her eyes. It was like a black hole had bloomed in her chest with the gravity of thousand suns. The weight of the grief nearly took her to her knees.

Jillian turned in a circle. "We don't even know if the babies got here yet—they could have gotten distracted by something shiny or yet another complete stranger handing out Arthurian quests. Find Sir Galahad and the White Goat!"

Louise blinked away her tears as she forced herself to focus. She couldn't afford to be lost to grief. Not here. Not now. How would they find four tiny dream-walking souls inside some sort of highjacked robotic tank? "Joy is with them. If we do a scry, we should be able to get a ping off of her."

"Oh, yes, that's right." Jillian took off her backpack to dig through it. "I printed a bunch when we were stuck out at Laurel Caverns. I thought we might have to hike to Haven."

Louise realized that she had let her shield spell drop during her explosion of grief. Her left hand was stiff and sore from maintaining the shield the entire way from Haven. She massaged her fingers and palm, trying to ease away the pain. "A scry would work best with a strong source of magic. Are we near a ley line?"

"We're standing on one." Jillian took out the spells printed out on their printer loaded with metallic ink. "That's why I picked this spot. More oomph to anything we tried. Here. Take these. I can hold the shield to give you a break."

"Thanks," Louise said.

They'd printed out copies of spells for the nestlings rescue mission. They stored them in plastic sandwich bags to protect and isolate them so they couldn't be accidently triggered. The names of the spells were written on the outside in big letters to make it quick and easy to find the ones that they needed. Shields. Healing. Scry. Traps. They had taken anything that might be useful. They could probably now cast everything using the Spell Stones but they only had the fingering for a handful of spells memorized.

Louise found the papers printed with the scry spell, took out one, and laid it on the stone footing of the crypt. She spoke the key word. With the extra power of the ley line, a massive dome gleamed to life over the paper. The cemetery took form in ghostly outlines, stretching in all directions around them. All the gravestones, statues, obelisks, crypts, and the decaying caskets under the dirt were shown in wispy details. She, Jillian, and Crow Boy were three small dots in the middle of the landscape of death.

The outer edge of the cemetery was marked with a tall stone wall. There was a cluster of buildings in one corner with a massive number of glowing dots of different intensities moving around them. One building had an active spell running that took up almost its entire footprint. The tracings were too small and blurred for Louise to recognize it.

"Oh, shoot." Jillian stared off into the darkness in the direction of the buildings. Her ability to feel magic meant that she could sense more from the scry than what could be seen within the gleaming display. Louise could only wonder what it felt like. "That has 'Villain Hideout' written all over it."

Crow Boy crouched to study the distant signatures within the glowing dome of the scry spell. "They're definitely oni." He pointed out various signatures. "These are probably wargs. Those are most likely lesser bloods. I think there are true bloods scattered in. They're not spell-worked, so they're less magical than the lesser bloods. They might even be humans. There doesn't seem to be any of the fake ones that were on Earth with Okami Shiroikage. I wonder what spell they have running in that one building."

He meant the elves pretending to be human who worked under Yves. Of the people that they fought at Laurel Caverns, only one or two had worked at the mansion. It meant most of the staff was still unaccounted for. There was no way of knowing if they had been with Yves or had stayed behind on Earth.

"Joy really stood out when we did this during the rescue," Jillian said. "I don't sense her now."

Louise ignored the confusion of bodies moving around the buildings to scan the rest of the glowing dome. It didn't seem possible that the babies hadn't arrived yet. They could have gotten lost, though, within the mazelike cemetery grounds.

Jillian frowned as she continued to stare into the darkness, considering what only she could sense. "I can feel a bunch of little weird things. Are those the *nactka*?"

Louise spotted a lone glowing dot as something darted unseen through the cemetery, bearing down on them. It was only thirty feet away and closing fast.

"Incoming!" Louise jerked out one of the spells labeled "trap" and slapped it down. The twins had combined "gravity" with "tethers." It could hold down and then tie anything in its area of effect. She shouted the key word.

There was a startled yelp as the trap went off.

"You got them!" Jillian shouted with fear.

Crow Boy had pulled his kusarigama. He held the chained

sickle ready as he stared into the darkness. "They must have some way of being invisible. I can't see them."

"Sh-sh-should I hit them with a force strike?" Jillian said.

"Please do not!" a female voice called out of the darkness in English. It switched to Elvish. "I am not sure who you are but the tengu are aligned with Tinker *domi* and would not betray her, so I think we are allies."

"How can we trust you when we can't even see you?" Louise called out in Elvish.

The female whispered something—most likely the key word to the invisibility spell—and appeared at the center of the trap. The female elf was young, black haired, and very, very naked.

Louise and Jillian both yipped in surprise.

"Where are your clothes?" Jillian shouted as Louise asked, "Why are you running around naked in the middle of a thunderstorm?"

"I'm looking for Law," the female said slowly in English as if she wasn't completely fluent in it yet.

Louise winced, realizing that in their surprise, she and Jillian had switched back to English.

"Law?" Jillian echoed in confusion.

Unless it was short for Lawrence, it didn't seem like a human name. It sounded like a nickname for an elf whose full name might be the "Protection of Law and Order in Wind" or "Justice Striking with Fire" or possibly "Lawfully Farts a Lot in Wind." Some elf names could be downright cruel—what were their parents thinking? It was possible, though, that the female was looking for the police.

"You're looking for a person named Law?" Louise said in Elvish.

"Yes!" the female cried. "Law is brave and noble! A protector of those who are weaker."

"Sir Galahad, I presume," Jillian murmured.

Did that make this female the White Goat?

"What is your name?" Louise said.

"Law calls me Bare Snow!" the female answered in her slow fumbling English.

Which probably meant Law was human, using a nickname for the female. Maybe Law *was* short for Lawrence. Snow was white but there was nothing goatlike about the elf. Then again, she might be using the English nickname because her real Elvish name was something like Screaming Goat on Bare Snow.

"Law is here—someplace?" Jillian asked.

"Someplace. We...we..." Bare Snow stumbled in English and then switched to a mix of the two languages. "We were following a yellow truck around the city. We thought it came to this very odd garden of stones but we were not sure. This place is so big and odd. To cover the area faster, we split up. We were to meet at the little stone house with the reclining monster cat women but Law did not return."

Reclining monster cat women? Louise glanced at Jillian. Her twin shrugged.

The graveyard was filled with death symbology that the elves were unfamiliar with. Bare Snow might mean one of the many angel statues or there might be something more exotic—maybe something Egyptian themed.

"Save Sir Galahad?" Jillian murmured.

"If we don't, the babies will try to do it," Louise said.

Jillian sighed. "That's so true. Okay, I've got a plan: Death from Above."

Louise could guess the plan solely on the name. It was a rehash of an abandoned idea from their museum heist. "We're going to bounce into the middle of that compound?"

"I hate this plan already," Crow Boy said.

Jillian glared at Crow Boy. "Dropping into the middle means we don't have to push through all that nastiness and we'll have the element of surprise."

"We might be only surprising ourselves," Crow Boy muttered unhappily.

Jillian pointed out the big active spell on the scry. "I think this is the *nactka* and that is a gravity-and-tethers spell functioning as a trap; it's almost the same as the one that we just used. To me, it looks like the *nactka* were out in the open like bait, and I'm guessing this dot here in the middle of the trap is our missing Sir Galahad. We drop in, grab the *nactka*, free Galahad, bounce out. Even if I'm wrong, we can just bounce out before they figure out what's going on."

Uneasiness washed over Louise. It felt like they were racing a clock; if they waited, the situation would get worse. "Let's do it."

The reason for Louise's uneasiness became clear as they vaulted several hundred feet straight up into the rainy sky—this time with invisible Bare Snow added into the mix. Once above the cemetery stone walls, the canopy of trees, and the steep hillside that led up to Oakland, they could hear the endless gunfire of the front line. The oni were pushing toward the enclaves where most of the elves in Pittsburgh lived. Any powers-that-be on the elves' side were going to be focused on that fight. Their small foursome were the only ones who were free to save the baby dragons within the *nactka*. One had already been murdered, rendering most of the *domana* helpless. Louise had the growing sense that a second might be killed at any minute.

Jillian cast "soft" at the peak of their climb, cancelling their acceleration. "They must have generators at the maintenance compound—there's some lights on." She turned suddenly to look behind her. "What the hey is that? It just popped up out of nowhere."

"That" was a giant glowing insect only a mile or so away from them. It seemed to be a scorpion with two massive front pincers and a curled stinger tail—except house-sized and flaming.

"A phoenix scorpion," Bare Snow said. "The oni are unleashing their horrors."

Louise assumed that both names were self-explanatory. "Fire makes it stronger?"

"Yes," Bare Snow said.

"It's going for Orville or Alexander!" Jillian said. "They were both fighting a few minutes ago but one pulled out of the fight."

"Tinder *domi* was hurt?" Crow Boy asked in an alarmed tone.

"I can't tell who is fighting the horror," Jillian said. "I don't know why one of them stopped fighting."

The scorpion made a horrific noise—painfully loud despite the mile or two distance between them. The sound rose and fell like a siren but somehow not as mechanical—almost like the call of some bird or animal.

"Sounds like a cicada," Jillian said. "A freaking huge one."

The scorpion flew forward, a blur of motion. It was breathtakingly fast.

"We need to get in, get the *nactka*, and get out," Louise said. "Now."

"Okay, let's do this!" Jillian said.

Crow Boy activated his black wings and let go of the twins.

Louise knew that the plan was for the older kids to move out of her protective shield and search for the *nactka*. Still, her heart dropped as he left the safety of her side.

"Ready!" Crow Boy winged close, hand out.

Louise felt Bare Snow let go and leap, invisible, to Crow Boy. It spoke of impossible courage and naïve trust. Bare Snow seemed to believe that since the twins were using *domana* magic, they were totally trustworthy. Crow Boy knew how badly their plans could fail.

The tengu boy dipped down as he caught Bare Snow. A moment later, Crow Boy vanished out of the sky, using his *yamabushi* ability.

The scry had pinpointed where both the *nactka* and someone who might be Sir Galahad were located but the area swarmed with oni. The twins were to serve as a distraction as the two invisible people found the *nactka* and freed the trapped human.

"Going in hot!" Jillian announced.

They'd been drifting down toward a tight cluster of buildings in the corner of the cemetery. The maintenance compound matched up to the map that Louise had studied before they left Haven. A new long building of rough-hewn ironwood had been erected beside them, screened from the outside by the stone boundary wall and a tall line of evergreen hedges.

With Louise holding the shield strong, Jillian used the acceleration spell to slam them down toward the wood-shingled roof like a cannonball. They smashed through it, shattering rafters and support beams, to crash hard into the stone floor. Shingles rained down around them. The whole building groaned and shifted alarmingly.

The interior of the long, rough-hewn building reminded Louise of an Amish barn. They had landed in the northern bay. The space was dim, lit by floating elf shines and the purple haze of magic was so dense that even Louise could see it. The floor was made of white marble, its surface polished to a gleaming finish. In the corners of the room were gasoline generators connected to a dozen magic generators—the source of the purple haze. They had always suspected the disappearance of the generator's inventor had been Ming's doing. This was proof of it.

A massive spell was marked out on the marble. It reminded Louise of the spell under the cage that they had found Crow Boy locked in. Looking at it made her skin crawl. At the very center, there was a blank circle the same size as the *nactka*'s shell with black lines acting like jumper cables on a circuit board. Obviously the *nactka* was the missing core to the spell.

There were curtains of fabric hung from the framing timbers, obscuring the rest of the barn.

"Oops! That might be a problem later," Jillian murmured, gazing up at the hole they had punched through the roof. It was shifting out of alignment for their takeoff as the entire building canted. "Think they haven't noticed?"

"They noticed." Louise sensed danger drawing near. She quickly scanned around them. There was no doorway near them, only solid ironwood walls. "We should get out of here before—"

Shadows loomed behind the gauzy fabric of the curtains. Wargs and ogre-sized lesser blood oni shifted forward, a chorus of growling and dangerous muttering. There was no sign of the *nactka* or Sir Galahad or either of the invisible searchers—but that was kind of the point of their landing choice. The twins were to draw the oni troops away from the real prize.

"Oh, crap," Jillian whispered.

"Language," Louise murmured, making sure that she was holding her shield firm.

A woman ghosted through a part in the curtain. There was something oddly familiar about her. She wore a white dress and held a red ribbon in her hand.

"Oh, Esme, you didn't stop at one, did you?" the woman breathed. "How many more little monsters are you going to pull of your hat?"

The woman looked like Anna Desmarais. Tristan had asked about his sisters. What had been their names? Adele. Bethany. Chloe. Danni... Yes, that felt right.

"Danni," Louise said.

Danni frowned and then smoothed away the evidence that she was surprised and annoyed by Louise knowing exactly who she was.

Jillian shot Louise a side glance. *Who?*

Had she told Jillian the names of Tristan's sisters? Had she even mentioned that part of the conversation? The odd reaction of the staff to Tristan's question?

"No matter," Danni said as she tied the red ribbon across her eyes as a blindfold. "You. Your changeling sister. Your annoying knight errant. I expected one or all to show up."

By "knight errant" did she mean Sir Galahad or Crow Boy? One was already trapped. Had she expected the other? What was Crow Boy walking into?

Wargs pushed through the curtain, a dozen in all, snarling. The building groaned and the storm wind gusted the fabric about, showing flashes of true blood oni with heavy machine guns and the ogre-sized warriors with spell-engraved spears. Lightning flickered as rain drummed down through the broken roof.

Why wasn't Danni ordering an attack? Was she trying to scare the twins into surrendering? Or was she worried any collateral damage could bring the roof down onto the casting circle before she could finish her work? Or had she foreseen the building collapsing? She was drifting from right to left, maybe heading for the nearest door.

If Danni had prepped expecting Tinker, then she would have chosen effective weapons. Louise was fairly sure that, given time, the wargs' magically cold breath could penetrate a *domana* shield. The shields allowed light to pass freely and leaked in air, heat, cold, and moisture. The twin's cold damp clothes were proof of how even the rain could seep through the powerful barrier. Then there were the spell-marked spears. Louise could only guess that they were tailored to fight *domana*.

Of course, the moment that the battle started, it would be an endurance race of Louise's shield versus the staggering number of oni that could come into play. Danni seemed unprotected but she was drifting toward an exit door. She might be worried that she could take collateral damage if she unleashed her troops immediately.

Jillian caught Louise's right hand with her left. For a moment, Louise thought it was just her sister seeking emotional support, but then Jillian tapped her fingers quickly through Morse code.

DC. FB. Five. L.

Divide and conquer, fade to black, on five at Louise's signal.

They were familiar tactics out of their playbook of how to get around any adult. They had worked countless times in the past but never with stakes this high. *Divide and conquer* meant that one twin took point and created a distraction to allow her sister to do something unobserved. Jillian normally took point as she was better at lying while Louise was better at not getting caught while trying to be sneaky. *Fade to black* meant that the person who wasn't point created a means for them to escape. Louise would start the countdown once she set up a means to escape.

Louise tapped back "okay" even as her heart went into overdrive. Jillian was counting on her to figure a way out of this mess—probably because Louise could see the future. Louise stuck her hand into her backpack, searching blindly. What could she do with what little she had within her bag?

"You cannot hope to stand against me," Danni said. "I am an *intanyai seyosa*. I can see what you're planning before you can even act."

Jillian started her part, keeping Danni's attention on her by making dramatic gestures with her hands. "Adults have been saying that to us since we were born! Your father probably has said it to you more than once. You do remember your father? Edmond Desmarais? Heaven's Blessing? Emperor of Elfhome?"

Jillian had figured out who Danni was.

Danni laughed. "Oh, child, he'll be dead in a few minutes along with his snobby-nosed cohorts."

Louise gasped as she realized the significance of the spell etched onto the floor before them.

"You're killing them all?" Jillian said in surprise.

"It will be a clean sweep." Danni smiled widely. "We're getting rid of all the elves in the Westernlands. The Skin Clan. The Imperial forces of the Fire Clan. All the thousands of Wind Clan. Even the pockets of the Stone Clan. Empty out the entire continent. Dismantle the Spell Stones while there is no one to protect them. At that point, Pure Radiance can rage all she wants in the Easternlands. Any *domana* she sends over the ocean will be like any other elf up against troops with machine guns and cannons."

Danni was talking too much. She was obviously trying to distract them while buying time to either trigger a trap or escape or maybe both. It was painfully obvious. She had something up her sleeve that she thought trumped their plan.

Was she right? Whatever they did, they better go big.

Louise's fingers found what she needed. She hadn't known what she was looking for exactly but brushing across runes printed on slick plastic clarified a plan in her mind. She tapped out *"On Five"* and braced herself for action.

Okay, Jillian tapped back and then let go of her hand. Louise felt like she'd been set adrift without Jillian anchoring her. Who was the brave one now?

"What about the sixty thousand humans here in Pittsburgh?" Jillian said. "They have guns and they outnumber you."

Five.

Danni snorted. "You don't know your history. Humans have always been fine with subjugating natives to plunder their resources. Christopher Columbus helped to wipe out entire tribes of Caribbean Indians and the United States still honors him hundreds of years later."

Four.

"Besides," Danni continued, "the transients outnumber the locals by tens of thousands," Danni continued. "They thought they were here just for a month or two. They're desperate to return to Earth. All they care about is what goes into their pocket before they go back home."

Three.

"What about Tristan and Lucien?" Jillian said. "They might not survive a spell aimed at elves."

Danni gave a breathless laugh. "It's not like any of us are going to survive my father. His children are disposable tools. Used until they're broken and then discarded without a care."

Two.

"So you're just going to kill Tristan?" Jillian said. "A little boy who loves his mother?"

"He, at least, had a mother," Danni growled. She glanced slightly to the right. It made Louise aware of an incoming motorcycle or hoverbike, oncoming at incredibly fast speed. Danni had been delaying for reinforcements. One of her sisters was coming to even the numbers.

One.

Jillian put her hand to her mouth and cast a massive force strike at the nearest support timber. It cracked loudly and the building started to lean at an impossible angle.

Louise pulled the monster call whistle from her backpack and blew the "come here" command. In the distance came a roar of an answer. An incoming horror should distract the oni long enough for the twins to escape.

Danni shouted something. The wargs breathed out. The world whited-out. Louise's invisible shield became a solid dome of bitterly cold ice. The twins both yelped in surprise and dismay. Jillian cast force strike after force strike. Shards of ice broke and fell to the ground only to be replaced by another breath attack from the wargs.

"We can't stay here!" Louise shouted and hit the support

timber again. It gave a long creaking noise and the building started to fall.

"Okay, okay, I've got this..." Jillian said.

"Duck!" Louise jerked Jillian down and a moment later a gleaming shaft of light flashed through the air where Jillian had been a moment before. It had gone through her shield as if it wasn't there.

"Spell spears?" Jillian shouted because she was scared. "Is that a thing?"

"Apparently." Louise fought to keep her voice calm.

"I can't see the hits coming!" Jillian shouted as Louise threw them out of the path of another spear of light.

"Jump us!" Louise said. "I haven't had a chance to practice the spell."

"Jumping!" Jillian clapped her hands together to signal the start of their casting protocol.

"Shield up!" Louise wrapped her right arm tight around Jillian as she was already holding the shield.

"Jumping!" Jillian warned wrapping her left arm around Louise. She cast "jump" but they collided with the falling timbers and dropped back down to the floor. "No, no, no."

Louise yelped as Jillian tried to jump again and they ping-ponged through the collapsing building. "Stay calm! This is not the time to panic!"

"This is a perfect time!" Jillian shouted. She finally managed to leap them out of the hole that they had made in the roof. They broke out into the dark night. Rain smeared over their shield. Lightning flickered in the distance. High in the sky, the lightning was a thousand times more frightening than when they were safe in a house.

There was no sign of Danni but Louise felt weirdly sure that the woman had escaped the collapsing building. Danni was still a threat. A massive number of oni had gathered around the building's exit. They pointed upward at the twins, and then a wave of awareness went through them of a bigger threat. They turned and looked eastward and then started to run.

Louise turned to look. A scorpion was rushing toward them like a flaming comet. "We've got trouble incoming."

"That was your distraction plan?" Jillian shouted, pointing at the horror.

"It's distracting them!" Louise pointed down at the scattering oni.

Jillian jumped them westward to get them out of the path of the horror. The massive glowing insect veered to follow them.

"It's locked onto us! Why? How?" Jillian cried and then answered her own question. "It must be the shield! It's a magic unique to *domana*. It identifies us as the enemy. Well...might as well use it to our advantage! Hold on!"

Jillian dropped them down into the compound proper. There were a half dozen buildings flanking the large L-shaped driveway of crumbling asphalt. All the structures looked like they were a hundred years old, made out of a faded saffron-colored brick with slate roofs. They landed in front of a low-slung garage with seven bays. A large yellow box truck sat within the right-most bay.

There were a hundred oni or more in the area. They turned toward the twins, reacting first with surprise and then, as the horror came roaring after them, with panic.

"What do we know about this thing beyond its name?" Jillian shouted as she flung them toward the end of the driveway, plowing through the oni a few feet off the ground.

"Nothing!" Louise shouted.

Louise spotted an ice chest floating inside a building that looked like a salt shed. A woman was lying on the ground in front of the ice chest, pinned in place with a faintly glowing spell. She shouted something like "Puffball!" as the twins zoomed past the building. If she was Law, then Bare Snow and Crow Boy were someplace close by.

"We need to get this thing away from the others!" Louise shouted.

Jillian nodded and took them down the compound's drive and out into the city street beyond. "What do you think it's vulnerable to?"

Louise looked behind them. The scorpion plowed through the oni troops as it charged. Random items were catching on fire: cardboard boxes, litter on the ground, and all the oni troops with fur. "Not fire! Rain doesn't seem to bother it. Or bullets."

This was because some of the oni had shot at it. The bullets had seemingly caused no damage to it.

Lightning flickered in the sky.

"Maybe electricity?" Jillian guessed.

"Power is off in the city," Louise said. "We don't have access to Wind Clan Spell Stones. Maybe if we dropped a building on it or something."

Jillian landed them in front of a redbrick duplex. The entire building seemed abandoned with the front picture windows boarded over with plywood. Jillian tried both doors and found them locked. "Oh, come on!" She hit the left doorjamb with a controlled low-power force strike, splintering it at the deadbolt. "We're hiding in here! It won't be able to fit through the door."

The interior of the building had been cleared of everything that made it a home: curtains, rugs, wall art, but someone had moved in recently and started to remodel. The front room had been turned into a makeshift kitchen. It smelled faintly of toast and bacon. A refrigerator stood in the far corner, purring softly, meaning that the building somehow had power. A battered wooden table served as counterspace, holding a toaster and electric can opener. Beside it was a big freestanding commercial sink cluttered with dirty dishes. A large new industrial stove stood under the boarded over front window, hooked up to a large propane tank just inside the front door. Boxes of supplies sat open and partially unloaded. The back of the house was under construction with walls partially removed to make the duplex into one big home.

Something about it felt like Danni, even though there was nothing with her name on it. The house seemed like it might be Danni's secret campsite—close enough to the cemetery to be convenient without making it obvious that the graveyard was Danni's main focus in the area. Louise was sure that if they went upstairs, they would find a bedroom fit for a princess complete with canopy bed and spare clothing all in Danni's size.

It was all very rustic and homey—if one ignored the army of oni in the area, all wanting to kill them.

Louise tried not to think of the swarms of oni. *Stay focused!* They had come to the cemetery to get the babies and save the *nactka*. Until they killed the horror, they couldn't do either.

"I don't know how to hurt that thing." Louise tried to shut the door but the force strike had torn the entire frame loose. "The refrigerator is running on a one-ten line. The breaker will trip if we try to just use that outlet. If we could find the breaker box, we could bypass it and maybe jury-rig something."

"Too complicated!" Jillian caught Louise's hand and pulled her out of the kitchen, into the dark hallway beyond. "We don't have any tools or ten-gauge wire or even know if electricity can hurt it. I like the idea of dropping a building on it. With these holes already knocked into the walls, it probably is structurally weakened."

"I'd rather not be in the building when we drop it," Louise said.

"I'll try to keep that in mind," Jillian said. "It's going to keep chasing us unless you drop our shield."

"I'm not dropping the shield!" Louise had already been shot once this summer. She was not going to go through that again. There were too many armed oni in the area to move around without protection.

The scorpion landed with a heavy thud, the light from its glowing skin flaring through the open door. Its massive pincer probed the doorway, catching the jamb on fire.

"It's going to set that propane tank off!" Louise cried as she felt the oncoming danger. "This building is going up!"

The horror made a loud hissing noise like steam engine letting off pressure.

"It's going to sing!" Louise warned.

The scorpion made the loudest noise that Louise ever heard. Louder than any train horn or car alarm. It felt like the sound became a physical object to be shoved into her ears and pierce her brain from both sides. She clapped her hands to her ears, forgetting to maintain her shield for a moment. Her palms did little to mute the painful sound. Louise gave up trying to block the noise and recast her shield.

She glanced back as Jillian pulled her through the dark house. The flames had spread from the broken doorjamb to the walls. In a matter of seconds, they would reach the propane tank. Jillian jerked open the back door. Damp night air washed over her. The piercing call of the scorpion was even louder. They stumbled out into the rowhouse's cement driveway just as the propane tank exploded in a wash of flames that blossomed out of the open back door. Rain poured down over her shield. The scorpion gleamed like a rising sun behind the house.

Louise expected Jillian to jump but her twin pointed toward the alley that ran behind the rowhouses. *Right. The scorpion might be able to quickly triangulate our position if we leap straight up.*

By staying at street level, Jillian probably hoped that the horror would think that they were still somewhere within the house. With luck, maybe the building would collapse on it.

How clever was the monster?

Louise glanced back to see that the scorpion was plowing through the building, setting the wreckage aflame even as it rushed toward the twins.

Clever enough! The collapsing house wasn't even slowing it down. It came roaring forward, rain hissing and steaming off its glowing shell.

She braced herself, hand locked in a shield.

The scorpion slammed into her, skidding her back on the wet pavement. The heat of its glowing shell washed over her even through her shield, suffocatingly hot. The blare of its call was unbearable, taking her to her knees.

We can't fight this!

Jillian cast force strike. The power of the spell washed over the creature but didn't seem to damage it in any way. Jillian was shouting something but Louise couldn't make out her words over the scorpion's call.

The horror beat on her shield with its massive pincers and stinger tail.

What should she do? Even if they jumped, the winged scorpion could chase after them. It was possibly faster than them in the air. They didn't have any attack spell memorized except force strike, which was mysteriously ineffective against the beast. They had the spells written out on paper but they depended on local magic level. They simply wouldn't have the power to work on such a large monster. The trap spell might be able to pin down a person but it wouldn't be able to stop a speeding car. There was just too much momentum to cancel out. The scorpion was bigger than a car. The sound made it difficult to even think.

The horror shoved them across the driveway and up against something metal. It gave a hollow *bong* as her shield hit it. Louise realized in terror that it was a five-hundred-gallon gasoline storage tank.

"Why does Danni have so many things that explode?" Louise cried. "Did she know we were going to be running through her house with this thing chasing us?"

Jillian pointed to her ear to indicate that she couldn't hear Louise over the din of the scorpion's call.

If the tank exploded, they would be trapped in the heart

of the fire. Her shield wouldn't protect them against prolonged exposure to heat and smoke.

"We need to jump!" Louise pointed upward.

Jillian clapped her hands together to signal a jump and then caught hold tightly to Louise.

Louise nodded and focused on keeping her shield up.

Jillian cast the spell. They started upward, only for the scorpion to bat them back down to the ground with its tail.

"Stupid scorpion!" Louise did a force strike, trying to push it back.

Jillian tried again to launch them but the scorpion had them pinned.

The air within her shield was stiflingly hot. She was starting to feel lightheaded. The gasoline tank hadn't exploded yet. When it did, the heat would overwhelm them even if the shield protected them from the blast.

She had to do something. But what? They hadn't had time to prepare. They'd rushed to the cemetery to save the baby dragons. Baby dragons? Wait. There *was* something she could do. They'd discovered earlier that Joy could teleport and seemed to be monitoring their conversation with something akin to telepathy.

"Joy! Help!" she shouted. "Joy? I'll get you candy!"

The world was suddenly quiet and cool.

"Stinky bug!" Joy muttered from Louise's shoulder. The little dragon's mane flowed as if she was standing in a strong wind despite the fact that the air within the shield was perfectly still.

"Joy, can you call Impatience like you did before?" Louise said.

"Pfft, don't need hurry-hurry boy," Joy said.

A massive column of light punched a giant hole through the scorpion.

Louise watched in confusion as the horror suddenly shrank in scale from larger than a house to something only the size of a Saint Bernard. The insect had spell runes etched onto its carapace, although some sections of the spell were now missing, along with various body parts.

"What the hell just happened?" Jillian asked in the sudden silence.

The massive laserlike attack had come from a big square machine. It looked vaguely like a tank with a rotating cannon turret on top but it had no track or wheels of any kind. It just floated in the impossible way that a brick might float. The hover-tank came floating over to the twins.

"Tu-tu-doo!" Red did a trumpet impression over a speaker.

"Tesla Mark Two to the rescue!" Chuck shouted. "Hooyah!"

"Tu-tu-doo!" Green copied Red's impression.

Louise had thought one time that the babies in Tesla were like a crew of a tank. Had that thought been foresight?

"What are you guys doing here?" Nikola asked.

Getting in over our heads, Louise thought. "Crow Boy was securing the *nactka*. Something went wrong."

She spoke without thinking. *Why do I think that?* She remembered the odd shout of "puffball." She was suddenly sure that the trapped woman was calling out a warning to her rescuers.

"Lots of things went wrong," Jillian muttered as she hugged Louise tightly. She was shaking.

"Where is Crow Boy?" Nikola asked as the tank's turret swung right and left as if looking around.

"There's an enemy *intanyai seyosa* here someplace," Louise said. "I think she 'saw' that someone was going to try and rescue Sir Galahad and set a trap for them."

"We can take her!" Chuck said.

"No, you will not take her." Jillian headed down the alley to cut around the burning house. "You can't go around killing people even before you're born. That's bad."

"Woof-woof-woof!" Chuck pretended to bark. "That's my other dog imitation."

That felt like a movie quote but Louise wasn't sure from where. It was odd to think that the babies might know something that she didn't. It made her feel even less in control. To be truthful, they were rarely in control of the babies. Oilcan was right to be worried.

23: IT WAS A GRAVEYARD SMASH

Oilcan could feel the Stone Clan shield that Tinker's little sisters were holding far to the west of Oakland. He followed the feeling through the forest to almost the shore of the Allegheny River. At the last bit, he veered south, coming back into the city at Butler Street. Something huge and glowing was plowing through a house, setting it on fire.

"A phoenix scorpion!" Thorne Scratch nestled close behind him on his hoverbike. "We will not be able to easily fight it. Your shield will attract it, so we will have to face it."

Before they reached the scorpion, though, a massive spell arrow killed the monster.

A hovertank came flying out of a side street. It turned and then did an odd hop up as if it was visibly startled at their presence.

"It's Oilcan!" Nikola's little boy voice came out of the tank's speaker.

"Oilcan! Oilcan! Hey, Oilcan!" the three little girl voices joined in.

Dear gods, where did my baby cousins get Tinker's hovertank when she never found a big enough printer to actually make a final version? Are they actually inside the tank or is this some other kind of dream walking?

Oilcan dismounted from his hoverbike and waved the others to stay back. Thorne Scratch had already met the babies at the ice cream shop, both as mice and a large dog, so she seemed

229

unsurprised by the new twist to their appearance. Nevertheless, she and Moon Dog started to raid the weapons crate for supplies.

The tank glided over to him in a way that would have been intimidating if it wasn't for the babble of tiny little voices all talking at once.

"We found a back door to Tinker's computer system..." "We met our grandma elf out on Neville Island..." "Marti says you're Orphan! Well...she didn't actually say it to us..." "...we didn't hack Tinker's system or anything—someone else did that..." "We've joined the Resistance!" "...we hacked Marti's email looking for information on the Resistance..." "...and we found the plans for this tank!" "...but that is so cool! We listen to your songs all the time!" "...grandma elf said we need to save..." "...Team Mischief reporting for duty! Vive la Résistance!" "...Sir Galahad, the White Goat, and the baby dragons inside the *nactka* before it's too late!"

"Whoa, whoa, whoa!" Oilcan waved at the tank. "Not all at once! What grandma elf?"

"That doesn't matter!" A mini Tinker ducked around the tank. Joy sat on her shoulder, eyeing all Oilcan's rescue and retrieval crew with suspicion. The mini Tinker looked exactly like Tinker had when she was nine, down to the bad haircut. More importantly, she looked just like Tinker did when she was shaken and scared but trying not to let it show.

"At least, right now it doesn't matter," she clarified. "One of Esme's evil half sisters—Danni—is trying to use a *nactka* to kill all the elves in the Westernlands! We stopped her for now but she might have a backup casting circle."

One of her half sisters? Did Lain have a horde of evil siblings that she never mentioned? It didn't really manner who this mystery woman Danni was related to, he couldn't let her kill all the elves.

A second mini Tinker joined the first. She looked as scared as Twin One but was trying to put on a brave front. It was possible that someone who didn't know Tinker well would be fooled, but Oilcan saw all the little tells. It went straight to his heart. When Tinker told him about the twins, he hadn't considered that just looking at them would trigger all the protective feelings he had for his cousin.

"The *nactka* are in there," Twin Two said as she pointed toward the Allegheny Cemetery. "With a lot of scary things—besides the graves and dead people and possible ghosts. The oni have some kind of magical spear that can go through our shield."

"It's okay, I'm here—" Oilcan stopped as he realized that he couldn't keep thinking of them as Twin One and Twin Two. "I wasn't told your names."

"I'm Louise," Twin One said.

"I'm Jillian," Twin Two said.

They weren't identical twins but close enough that most people would have trouble keeping them straight. Louise looked a little more like Esme while Jillian more resembled their grandfather, Tim Bell.

Gaddy and Team Tinker were staring in amazement at the twins. He hadn't told them yet who they were going to rescue.

TC shook his head and muttered softly, "Tinker's really outdone herself this time—she's cloned herself twice."

"Is this"—Oilcan motioned to indicate the twins and the tank and Joy riding on Louise's shoulder—"everyone in your group?"

Louise shook her head. "No. Crow Boy was going to get the *nactka* while we created a diversion but something went wrong. He's a tengu who came with us from Earth. Jin told Tinker about Crow Boy. His real name is Haruki Sansei, but I guess Tinker never told you about him."

"There's also a human named Law and a female elf named Bare Snow," Jillian added.

Oilcan didn't recognize either name. Tinker had told him that the twins had arrived at Haven with a horde of tengu children that they had saved on Earth. If this Crow Boy was among the rescued, then he was also a child.

"Sir Galahad and the White Goat!" the tank said in a chorus of four tiny voices.

Gaddy gave a surprised laugh.

Oilcan looked at her in confusion.

"I went to school with Law," she explained. "Lawrie Earie Monroe is her full name. Monroe as in Monroeville. Extremely local. Sir Galahad is a good nickname for her; she's a bit of a white knight. She likes to ride out and save girls in trouble, carrying things made of wood. Baseball bats. Hockey sticks. Big sticks. Rumor is that she's picked up an elf still in her doubles but no one has actually laid eyes on the female. That might be Bare Snow."

A fourth child needing to be saved in the middle of this mess.

"Okay, we'll get the *nactka*." Oilcan indicated himself and the *sekasha*. Tinker wouldn't abandon her friends, so he would have to assume that the twins wouldn't leave without Crow Boy no matter what reassurances Oilcan gave them.

"Hooyah! We'll find Crow Boy!" Chuck announced suddenly and the hovertank raced away.

"Can they get hurt?" Oilcan asked the twins.

"Physically, no," the twins answered together.

"Mentally?" Louise continued. "Maybe. If they remember this at all...afterward...?"

After they were born...

Right.

"I'm sorry," Louise added.

Oilcan understood. He always felt responsible when Tinker went out of control. He also knew how hard it was as a child to deal with one's own mess without having the responsibility of taking on another person's chaos too. "It's okay, it's not your fault. We'll work together to deal with this."

Louise suddenly hugged him hard like she was worried that a flood would carry her away.

A moment later, Jillian joined her sister and the twins were perilously close to crying.

"It's going to be okay," he repeated, patting them on the back, glad that they were miraculously trusting him on sight. He understood better than anyone in either universe what they were going through. Loss of parents. New world. Mind-boggling, out-of-control younger child to take care of while still a grieving child in their own right. He'd been suspicious of his grandfather and Tinker at first but they proved themselves trustworthy quickly. Of course, they weren't in the middle of a war at the time...

"I'm going to move ahead and protect the *sekasha*," Oilcan said.

The twins went stiff, probably bracing for a fight against what he would suggest next. Certainly that was what it meant when Tinker squared her shoulders that way. He needed to give the twins something useful to do.

"If something went wrong with Crow Boy, then chances are good that either he or one of the others are wounded. The three need to be found and gotten to medical help." He indicated Gaddy and the others. "The rest of these people are Team Tinker, who

I have known for years and years. They're good friends. Keep a shield on them and once you get Crow Boy and the others, pull out and go to Oakland with them."

The night lit up with another monster-sized spell arrow from the hovertank.

"And see if you can talk your sisters and brother into leaving too," Oilcan said.

The twins nodded.

There was a brief shuffle to get the twins—and Joy—onto the hoverbikes. He was afraid that they might want to drive because Tinker would. Joy insisted on Hover Hulk because TC kept a stash of homemade cookies in his saddlebags. She started to raid them by phasing the cookies out of the compartment even as the twins got settled into the sidecar.

Oilcan mounted up and they all chased after the hovertank.

The driveway led to an L-shaped courtyard faced with a half dozen garages and warehouse buildings. The broken pavement was littered with dead bodies. Some of them were burnt beyond recognition by the phoenix scorpion. Others were slashed by a blade. A few he couldn't tell what had killed them.

"We found him!" the hovertank called at the far end of the courtyard.

Oilcan raced forward.

A tengu boy, no more than fourteen years old, leaned against the hovertank, panting. He bled from a dozen wounds on his arms and legs, but none of them seemed serious once you calmly analyzed the streaming blood.

The twins, however, weren't taking it calmly. "You're bleeding! You're hurt! We need to stop your bleeding! We forgot a first aid kit! We could use our shirts!"

"Wait! I have supplies!" Gaddy cried to keep the twins from disrobing. She pulled out gauze and tape and handed them to Louise. "I brought lots."

"I'm ... I'm fine," the boy panted. "Yes, yes, I'm hurt, but I will not die of these wounds. I had some cover when the puffball went off. The bitch swarmed us with her warriors and took the *nactka* while we fought for our lives. We only survived because the horror frightened all but the most valiant away. Bare Snow went after Danni. See to Law. I promised Bare Snow that I would keep her safe."

Law's wounds were more serious. She had managed to kill some of their attackers before collapsing on the ground.

Gaddy knelt beside Law to treat her wounds. "Ever the white knight."

"Jump?" Jillian asked her twin.

Louise shook her head. "It would be too hard to keep everyone linked together. We might drop someone."

Team Tinker had lived through enough mad-scientist experiments to look alarmed.

"The hoverbikes will only take a few minutes," Abbey said to counter the suggestion.

Tate and Abbey would take the twins. Brandon would take the wounded tengu boy. They bundled Law into Axe Man's sidecar. Gaddy was the only one who knew the area well, so she would lead them out.

"We need to go!" The babies were upset by the delay due to organizing the rescue. "The bad guys are getting away!"

"No, they aren't!" Jillian took out a piece of paper with a spell drawn on it. She slapped it onto the wet concrete and spoke the key word. A gleaming dome appeared but she ignored it, instead looking out into the cemetery. "There! Can you feel magic? If you can, you can sense the *nactka*! They're there! Moving away from us!"

Oilcan could feel the *nactka* clustered together behind the lift drive and spell chain of a hoverbike following the tall stone wall alongside the cemetery's northern boundary. Normally even an unskilled rider would be able to pop a bike up and over a ten-foot barrier but it seemed as if Danni was towing the *nactka* behind her somehow. The redistribution of weight would mess up the lift drive's ability to "pop" up. She was speeding along the wall, probably looking for a low spot or the end of the boundary line. If he remembered correctly, it changed to a chain-link fence that stopped abruptly a few blocks east.

Someone with an active spell running was chasing Dani on foot, lagging farther and farther behind the speeding hoverbike. Was that Bare Snow? The spell on her didn't feel like a shield. He was too inexperienced to tell for sure what type of magic she was using.

"I sense the *nactka*." Oilcan climbed onto his hoverbike. Thorne Scratch slipped quickly on behind him. "Gin and Moon Dog follow—"

"Tu-tu-lo!" the tank cried and roared off.

"No!" the twins both shouted but the tank had vanished into the night.

"It's okay," Oilcan said so that they wouldn't feel responsible for whatever chaos the babies were about to create. "Just focus on getting the wounded to Oakland. Law needs treatment quickly."

The twins nodded solemnly. They had the look Tinker would get that meant she would plow through the heart of a mountain if she had to.

Oilcan took off after the hovertank. He sped up, trying to overtake it. Gin Blossom and TC followed close behind.

The hovertank fired its cannon, lighting up the night. In the moment of brilliance, Oilcan spotted Danni on a hoverbike with a floating box tethered to its back. It wasn't a spell-locked ironwood box as he expected, but one of the massive plastic ice chests that the foragers like Alton used, big enough to store a human body in. It certainly was big enough for ten *nactka*.

He could throw all power into the spell chain and catch Danni but it would put himself between her and the cannon. He wasn't sure if the babies knew not to shoot him by mistake.

The hovertank fired again, lighting up the night. Danni dodged to the right. The much heavier tank didn't corner as well. Its turret whipped right even as the hovertank struggled to turn. The cannon fired a second time; this time, Danni dodged straight into the path by mistake. The beam clipped her lift drive and the rope tethering the floating ice chest. The drive engine was instantly reduced to a pile of slag and machine parts. The hoverbike dropped like the lead weight that it was.

The ice chest started to drift upward.

"I'll get the box!" TC called as he surged forward. The Hover Hulk had a bigger engine, which allowed it to pop up to higher elevations.

"Watch out for friendly fire!" Oilcan called warning.

"I'm watching!" TC shouted.

The hovertank continued to fire at Danni, who was scrambling up through a massive oak tree in an attempt to catch the ice chest before it floated away. The woman dodged the brilliance. The dead oak leaves flashed into flame despite the heavy downpour of rain.

TC popped up to catch the dangling end of the tether, trying to pull the ice chest downward to the ground. For a moment he hung there, impossibly static in the night sky. Then the Hover Hulk reached its height limit and started to drift downward. TC struggled to keep hold of the unwieldy floating chest and the oversized hoverbike.

"Stop shooting!" Oilcan shouted again at the hovertank, unable to close on Danni because of the friendly fire.

Oilcan could hear the tiny mice voices arguing even as they shot the cannon again and again, chasing Danni down out of the tree and through the graveyard. The massive beam of light disintegrated everything it hit, vaporizing trees, gravestones, and crypts.

"Lou and Jilly said no! We really should stop!" "That was an innocent stone angel, not her! Don't fire until you see the whites of her eyes!" "She's going to go right, left, left, up, down, sword swipe!" "Sword? What sword?"

The mice all screamed as Danni swiped a massive black sword at them.

"That sword!" either Red or Green shouted.

The blade took out a six-inch-thick gravestone of solid granite.

"She has a rune sword," Thorne Scratch murmured into Oilcan's ear. "*Domana* used those during the Rebellion until the wood sprites invented the Spell Stones. Their length gives them a slower attack speed than an *ejae* but they can cut through almost anything—even *sekasha* shields."

The blade was at least six feet long and a foot wide. It seemed to be made of obsidian, polished to a black-mirror finish and etched with runes. The spells shimmered faintly, showing that they were active. Judging by the way that Danni swung the massive blade, one of the spells was some type of antigravity, making it lighter to lift. It seemed that none of the spells cancelled the momentum that the sword's great mass created. It meant once the blade was in motion, it was difficult to stop. It would be like controlling a wrecking ball with a joystick. A flick of the wrist set it swinging. Stopping it was another matter.

"Watch, watch, watch!" either Red or Green shouted and a moment later the hovertank's cannon took out a tree dangerously close to Oilcan.

He dodged the falling tree as it thundered to the ground. "Stop shooting!"

There was deep boom and then a crack almost like lightning

striking even as one of the Jawbreakers shouted, "Incoming!" In a streak of flame, a rocket came out of the darkness from behind him. It struck the hovertank and exploded. The tank crashed barrel-first into the ground.

"Oh heck!" "What the frigging hell was that?" "Language!" "Take cover, Oilcan! The gunner's got a machine gun too!"

Oilcan ducked his hoverbike behind a marble crypt for hard cover seconds before tracer bullets sprayed out of the darkness. The loud swarm of white-hot metal chewed at the stone over his head. He ducked down, cursing. He'd lost track of the others. Where were TC, Gin Blossom, and Moon Dog?

Oilcan slid off his hoverbike so he could cast a scry. The spell picked out the lift drives of the missing hoverbikes. They were behind two different mausoleums about three hundred feet west of him. TC was still struggling to control the floating ice chest filled with *nactka*. With the machine gun focused on Oilcan, the others were safe from the bullets.

The gunner was hundreds of feet to the north, perched on the roof of a building outside the graveyard. He or she had to be using night vision goggles even to see Oilcan in the rain-cloaked night. The person with the active spell—Bare Snow, he assumed—had given up on catching Danni and was closing on the gunner fast.

Danni was using the cover fire, though, to head toward TC.

"She's heading for TC!" Oilcan shouted in Elvish. He dropped his scry, put up his shield, and took off running toward the mausoleums. Thorne Scratch kept pace with him as bullets rained down on them, pinging off his shield.

The machine gun suddenly went silent. Bare Snow must have reached the gunner.

Moon Dog was closing on TC from the opposite direction.

TC had hold of the large ice chest via its tether. The spell had been set to lift a much heavier weight. The plastic box was trying to float skyward, threatening to take TC with it. The cut tether was too short to attach the chest to anything. Preoccupied, TC didn't see Danni and Moon Dog racing toward him.

"TC!" Oilcan shouted.

Moon Dog reached TC first, yanking him backward off the Hover Hulk even as Danni swung her massive black sword at him. Missing its mark, the blade cut through the mausoleum's marble.

"Give that to me!" Danni shouted.

"No way!" TC growled, clinging tight to the chest.

Moon Dog flung TC toward Gin Blossom. TC sailed through the air, yelping in surprise. Gin Blossom caught TC and headed back toward her hoverbike. Moon Dog continued to spin, kicking Danni mid-body, sending her in the opposite direction.

Oilcan shifted round to block Danni from chasing after Gin Blossom even as Thorne Scratch and Moon Dog squared off against the woman, *ejae* drawn. Rain poured down them, bouncing off the *sekasha*'s personal shields.

Tinker had said that none of her Hand could land a blow on Chloe, not even Stormsong. Danni, Thorne Scratch, and Moon Dog launched into an elaborate dance with not one swing connecting with the intended target. The two *sekasha* ducked and dodged, not attempting to parry the massive black sword with their wooden *ejae*. Despite the cumbersome size of her weapon, Danni was evading all strikes at her.

Oilcan held his shield, protecting TC and Gin Blossom. The *sekasha* were too close to Danni for Oilcan to hit her with a force strike. But there was another possible target: the boundary wall. If he took it out, Gin could easily flee the rough terrain of the graveyard. On the city streets, Gin could go at top speed away from the fight.

Oilcan aimed a force strike at the boundary wall. He hit it hard, blasting the large fieldstones into pieces. "Gin, if you can, take TC and go."

"I am trying," Gin Blossom growled with TC tucked under one arm and digging through her bike's leather saddlebag with the other hand. "It is like juggling wyvern eggs!"

"Just put me down and get this box out of here!" TC grumbled, still holding onto the floating ice chest.

Oilcan realized that TC was telling Gin to abandon him to protect the elves of the city but Gin was much too loyal to Team Tinker to do that. He would have to help Gin accomplish both before she would flee. Oilcan backed up, keeping his shield up, eyes on the *sekasha*.

Moon Dog barked something in Elvish that Oilcan didn't know.

Danni, Thorne Scratch, and Moon Dog suddenly froze in place.

"Damn you," Danni growled, sword upraised. "What are you up to?"

"You cannot defend against attacks without forethought," Thorne Scratch said.

Danni laughed. "You can't attack without thinking."

"You do not know our ways," Moon Dog said. "The outcome of this battle was decided the moment you hesitated."

Oilcan wasn't sure what was about to happen but it seemed like the tide just turned. He reached Gin Blossom and TC. "I'll take him. You secure the box."

Easier said than done, as Gin Blossom was nearly a foot taller than Oilcan. She'd been holding TC like a giant ragdoll. Oilcan struggled to keep the man upright while holding his shield. Gin pulled tie-down straps from her saddlebag.

There was a rumble of a hoverbike and a rider came bouncing across the rooftops of the houses that lined Stanton Street. It hit the building directly opposite the hole that he had blasted and came floating down with a roar of the lift engine at maximum power.

"Oh, you think you can take me?" Danni said. "How about times two?"

One of Esme's half sisters, the twins said. It meant there was more than one. It explained the insane rooftop stunt with the hoverbike.

The incoming sister had her pale blond hair buzz-cut short and was wearing camo coveralls. She roared toward the unmoving sword-wielders, obviously intent on breaking the stalemate.

"Adele!" Danni shouted. "Get the box!"

Adele slowed as she glanced toward Oilcan. "I don't have anything that can deal with a *domana* shield."

Danni growled in frustration and swung at Thorne Scratch. Instantly, the *sekasha* struck. Danni jerked back, barely avoiding the tip of their blades. Thorne's *ejae* sliced open Danni's right cheek, cut off a lock of her long pale hair, and amputated the tip of her right ear. Moon Dog's blade slashed open her left arm just above her elbow.

The three froze in place again, swords upraised.

The *sekasha* had no forethoughts about attacking. They merely were waiting with the impossible patience of someone over a hundred years old. Once Danni swung, the size of her sword committed her to a full swing. Moon Dog was right—Danni had lost the fight the moment she paused her attacks.

Danni whimpered, her left arm sagging down as she lost some muscle control. Wounded as she was, she couldn't wait forever but *sekasha* could.

"Danni!" Adele dropped her hoverbike to the ground and pulled a machine gun from a saddle holster. It had a belt of ammo feeding out of her backpack.

Oilcan shouted a warning. He couldn't hit Adele with a force strike as the power of his spell would continue in a straight line and hit the *sekasha*. Their shields, though, could not take the rapid fire of a machine gun. He couldn't protect both the *sekasha* and Team Tinker.

Adele suddenly went tumbling away from her hoverbike. She came up running, still holding the machine gun. "Goddamn elves! We told them that the Death Wind was too dangerous to use!"

"You don't need to see her to hit her!" Danni shouted.

"That may be true for you!" Adele shouted back and opened fire with the machine gun, spraying the night with brightly burning bullets. They pinged off Oilcan's shield. She was firing wildly, chewing through her ammo in a mad attempt to hit whatever was attacking her. She wasn't aiming at the *sekasha*—but if she continued to spray the area, she was going to hit Thorne Scratch and Moon Dog.

"I got it!" Gin cried, having secured the ice chest to her hoverbike via a tie-down. "Give TC to me!"

Oilcan handed the man to Gin Blossom.

Whoever was chasing Adele—Oilcan couldn't see who or what she was targeting—herded her around the battlefield. The arc intersected with the hole that Oilcan had blasted through the boundary wall.

"Watch out!" Danni cried as Oilcan did a force strike.

He hit Adele, sending her flying across the narrow road and through the front window of a brick duplex. He slammed a second strike into the house, bringing it down.

"Adele!" Danni cried. She swung at Moon Dog.

Thorne Scratch struck hard and quick. This time Danni didn't dodge in time. Her head tumbled to the ground and a moment later her body crumpled.

There was a moment of stunned silence and stillness as the battle was suddenly over.

Moon Dog sheathed his *ejae* and held out his hand to the

dark rainy night. "Do not be afraid. We were allies in this fight. Will you not show yourself?"

In all the confusion, Oilcan had nearly forgotten about the last child. "Bare Snow? My people took Law and the children to a safe place. We need to leave. This place is not safe. Can you come with us?"

Thorne Scratch whipped the blood from her blade and cleaned it on Danni's fallen body. She stood, sheathing her *ejae*. "Child, you have our word: you will not be harmed. We are leaving. If you do not show yourself, you will be left alone in this place."

A young female elf suddenly appeared before them. Her black hair was tied up in twin ponytails. She held two daggers that looked like small *ejae* in her hands. Other than that, she was completely naked. She dropped to her knees and then bowed forward until her forehead nearly touched the ground. "I put myself into your care. Please protect me."

24: FLYING THE COOP

Tristan was trapped, listening to his family fall into ruin.

All he could do was huddle in a ball on the floor, a baby chicken inexplicably cradled in his hands, as Hal Rogers reported one death blow after another. The changeling was on the front line with all the powers of a *domana* with three *esva*. She had *sekasha* from three different clans fighting beside her. She'd called in *all* the tengu—thousands of them pouring in to answer her summons. She'd unearthed dangerous toys that Roach called "xylophones of doom" and killed the horrors that were meant to plow through the elves unchecked. There were EIA troops on the scene and more expected to arrive. There was a well-organized militia of an unknown number of humans backing her up.

Worse was the information flowing in from other quarters.

Boo squeaked and waved her hands to attract her cousin's attention while covering the headset's microphone. "Duff says Sean is on the family channel. He wants to talk to someone here."

Sean was the oldest of the Roach brothers. He'd left Elfhome to live in Alaska for several years before moving back to Pittsburgh.

"Someone?" Roach looked confused for a moment and then understanding dawned on his face. "Jane didn't tell him about... the big news... yet?"

Boo shook her head. She disconnected the headset so she could hand the base to Roach.

Jane hadn't told Sean that Boo had rejoined the family? No

243

wonder Lucien's spies hadn't been able to find Boo if she was being kept hidden even from close family.

Roach clicked transmit and spoke into the radio. "What's up, Kodiak?"

"We were totally right about the cockroach," Sean said. "What chaos! I've never had so much trouble squashing a bug before but he's flat on his back, legs in the air. The thing is, he did manage to take out our production trucks. Instead of rewording the news coming from the front, I'm going to rebroadcast Bullhorn's signal. I thought it common curtesy to let Bullhorn know."

Sean was a deejay for KDKA, the largest of radio stations in Pittsburgh. Lucien had foreseen that once they cut the power, Pittsburghers would be turning to the radio for news. He'd planted trusted moles at the three official radio stations, counting on anything small and indie like WESA not having a generator. Apparently said mole at KDKA hadn't realized who he was dealing with in Sean Roach. Lucien might not have warned their mole because the Eyes already doubted the wisdom of keeping Boo alive. The less said about Boo's extended family, the better.

Roach handed the radio to Marty.

"Bullhorn here," Marty said. "Permission granted. Bullhorn out."

"Roger that!" Sean said. "Kodiak out."

Roach handed the radio back to Boo, who reconnected the base to her headset.

Father was going to be furious and yet it was his fault. He'd taken the reins of power from Lucien, stripping away Lucien's ability to keep a close eye on the Kryskills just as they awakened to the knowledge of his father's plans. If Lucien had been able to keep his careful watch on them, he would have seen them gathering up people and resources to fight back.

Tristan needed to warn his brother. If things continued to unravel, their father's anger would come crashing down on the nearest person he could punish. Lucien needed to shift to a safe distance.

Boo hissed a curse word.

"What's wrong?" Roach asked.

"The oni are closing on Duff's location. He's gone dark. Our communication hub is down until he's moved to someplace safe. I think he's got that one bunny with him, but there's no one else with him on Mount Oliver."

"I've got to go pick up some troops," Adele had told Tristan. *"And search out a nest of troublemakers on Mount Oliver."*

Adele had gone to find the militia's communication hub. She was going to kill Boo's brother if she found him.

"I'll tell Marc." Roach brushed past Tristan to reach the back door.

Roach hauled up the van's back door. The rumble of the generator and rolling thunder flooded in with the smell of rain and diesel exhaust. Roach stepped out of the van, heading toward the knot of people on the other side of the big generator and the pickup truck that had towed it to the station. "Marc!"

Tristan slid out into the rain and dark behind Roach. If he was asked, he planned to say that he was going to find a bathroom. No one seemed to notice or at least care that he left. He ducked to the left, putting the van between him and the people working on the generator.

Tristan walked quickly away from the van, taking the first turn that took him off the main street and into a back alley. Once he was out of sight, he searched out a hiding space. He tucked under a set of stairs that led up to a second-story apartment and struggled not to hyperventilate in pure panic.

The baby chicken in his hand peeped, oblivious to his fear. Perhaps it was also caught up in its own trauma of losing its entire family. Maybe that was why it kept peeping.

Tristan pulled out his phone. He had to juggle the baby chick into his left hand so he could thumb through the address book. Adele didn't answer Tristan's desperate warning call. The phone rang three times and dropped into voice mail. A computer voice instructed him to leave a message. He left a terse warning of incoming tengu and hung up. Thinking maybe that he'd guessed wrong who was who, he tried the number assigned to "Sissy." The same response. He repeated the warning.

He called Lucien. Tristan expected it to just ring three times but the phone rang and rang. It made sense that Lucien didn't have his phone set up the same way as the Eyes. His brother would need time to get out of their father's hearing to answer his phone.

Just as Tristan started to think that Lucien wouldn't answer, his brother's voice said, "What is it?"

"Everything has gone south," Tristan said. "The changeling

wasn't affected by the spell. She's killing the horrors right and left. There's at least two radio stations broadcasting the fighting. All the tengu are fighting—"

"What about Boo?"

You've got to get away from Father, Tristan wanted to shout but he answered the question as calmly as he could. "She's back with her family and they organized an entire frigging militia—"

"Is she safe?"

Tristan nearly screamed. He stopped. Counted to three.

"Is she?" Lucien asked again. "Is she safe?"

"Yes, she's safe." He forced himself to be calm. "She's with her older brother Marc and their cousin William Roach and a bunch of tengu. She's obviously told them everything she knows about you and the Eyes and our plan."

"I kept her innocent of our plans." Lucien's voice went soft and gentle. "Nothing she can tell them can harm us."

She told them enough!

Tristan dropped the chick into his lap so that he could rub at his forehead. The chick viewed this as being abandoned and started to peep louder and faster.

What should I do? How do I save my family?

Tristan comforted himself with the knowledge that, since their father avoided technology, Heaven's Blessing wouldn't be receiving any panicked phone calls from the battlefront, updating him on their failures. Still, Tristan needed Lucien to leave the camp as soon as possible.

"You need to distance yourself from Father." Tristan was direct as possible. "It's too dangerous to stay near him now."

"He plans to head to Aum Renau to take out the Spell Stones."

That made sense when there would be no *domana* able to protect the stones. He would still have to mow through *laedin* and whatever *sekasha* the Viceroy's siblings held, but machine guns and rocket launchers would make that fairly simple. Once all the elves were dead, Heaven's Blessing could deactivate the powerful shield that protected the Spell Stones and blow them to pieces.

The plan was pure suicide if any of the *domana* at Aum Renau still had their powers.

"The changeling is throwing *domana* magic around," Tristan said. "It's possible that all of the *domana* were unaffected by the spell. Father will be furious at our failure."

"Yves is—was—not a radical thinker. His spell had flaws that I did not have permission to fix. It was generalized to take out single *esva* using *domana*. I had doubts about the changeling, what with her cousin able to use the Stone Clan *esva* before he was changed, and the fact that it was the wolf child's genetics that were used to shift her back to full elf. She's been fiddled with so much I doubted that Yves's spell would take her out. It's why I told Chloe to kill the changeling despite her value as a gate builder. I'm sure the Harbingers and the other Stone Clan are dead in the water. Prince True Flame too."

Lucien hadn't included the Viceroy.

"What of the wolf child?" Tristan asked.

"He might still be a problem," Lucien said. "Yves's spell should have had a secondary function to deal with special cases like the wolf child and the changeling. Maybe now that Yves is dead and his spell has failed, Father will let me improve on the design."

How could Lucien be so calm?

"So we're dealing with both the changeling and the wolf child?" Tristan said.

"He's out in the forest with dozens of horrors and thousands of our cannon fodder to wear him down. He's quite alone with so many to defend."

Alone and outnumbered was not the same as powerless when talking about a *domana*. They were walking cannons.

Except Lucien wasn't focusing on the Viceroy or the upcoming attempt to destroy the Spell Stones.

"You saw her?" Lucien looped back to Boo. "Healthy and safe? With your own two eyes?"

Tristan took a deep breath. Counted. "Yes, with my own two eyes."

"Can you capture her safely?"

Tristan wondered if Lucien meant "without harming her" or "without getting yourself killed." Probably the first, since both boys had spent their entire childhood learning the art of assassination. There was even a time that Tristan had believed the lie that he was being taught self-defense. He had never actually killed anyone. Once he explained the setup to Lucien, he was fairly sure that Lucien would suggest the obvious tactic.

Marc had assumed that Tristan was a harmless lost child and Tristan hadn't done anything to dissuade him of that belief. It would be easy for Tristan to regain entrance to the van. He could simply say that he'd needed to go to bathroom and slipped out to do it out of sight. Lucien knew that theoretically, Tristan would only need his little Swiss Army knife to take out everyone but Boo. While he probably could, Tristan didn't want to.

"No," Tristan said, struggling to keep his voice level and detached. "I'm not going to be able to slip her away from her family. Not by myself. There's too many people protecting her."

The chick climbed up Tristan's chest, peeping.

"What is that noise?" Lucien asked as the chick got close enough to be picked up by Tristan's phone.

Tristan shook his head. "It's a chicken. A little one."

Lost and afraid as I am, he didn't add.

There was a pause as Lucien dealt with the non sequitur. He decided to ignore the information. "Where are you?"

Lucien was twenty minutes out by hoverbike. Longer by truck. Could Tristan get Boo's family to abandon the radio tower before Lucien arrived? Doubtful. With the militia's communication hub unable to transmit, the tower was the only means of communicating with the city's population and the militia's scattered units.

"Little brother?" Lucien murmured.

It was a warning from their childhood, a not-too-subtle reminder that Lucien was older and taller and stronger. It required an immediate answer.

"Adele dropped me on Mount Washington," Tristan said.

"Mount Washington?" Lucien murmured. "Oh, that janky pirate radio station that Adele likes so much. I thought yanking the generator out would be enough to keep it from broadcasting during our Oakland push. I would have pulled down the tower but Adele had indoctrinated Boo in the music that they played. Boo would have been sad."

Lucien's fixation on Boo was worse than Tristan thought. No wonder their sisters wanted to get rid of her.

"I think Adele might be back soon," Tristan lied. "I might have to leave to keep her away from Boo."

"Yes, that would be for the best," Lucien said. "Keep an eye on Boo for as long as you can. I'm coming to get her."

That worked to get Lucien out of Father's reach. Now to get Boo out of the area.

✧　　✧　　✧

Tristan headed back toward the van, wondering how he was going to juggle this. The militia needed the radio tower but surely with the generator in place and their little brother in danger, Boo's family would leave its defense to others.

When he got back to the main street, he noticed all the tengu were gone along with all of the pickup trucks. Had everyone charged off to save Duff? That was good news regarding Lucien but bad for Adele.

"What do you think you're doing, Tristan?" a familiar female voice said behind him.

It was the one person he never thought he'd see again. She'd gotten on a spaceship nearly nineteen years earlier and disappeared out of his life.

"Esme," he breathed.

She didn't look a day older. Same purple-dyed hair. Same big-sister superior smirk as she caught him doing something he wasn't supposed to. He wilted with guilt before the look. He'd done so many evil things since he last saw her.

"Tristan!" She used that "you've been a bad boy and I'm disappointed in you but now I get to gleefully punish you" voice that went with the smirk. She could always come up with the most embarrassing punishments.

Tristan attempted to hold onto his eighteen years of maturity since he last saw her. "What are you doing here?"

"Discovering that my baby brother didn't come see me after I'd finally managed to make my way back to solid ground." She crossed her arms and looked vaguely cross but the smirk lingered.

"I didn't know until earlier today," he could say truthfully enough. "No one told me until Lucien showed me..."

He shouldn't have mentioned Lucien. He *really* shouldn't have mentioned Lucien!

"Lucien is here too?" someone said behind him.

For a moment he thought it was his mother. Lain had gotten old since he last saw her. She'd aged into the mother he remembered as a baby.

"Oh!" The word of hurt pushed its way out. "Oh! Oh, no!"

Lucien was coming. Tristan had fond memories of his older sisters but he wasn't so sure about Lucien. His older brother had borne the brunt of their father's expectations. Worse, he was coming to kidnap and possibly murder people. Lain and Esme would never forgive such actions—it's why their father hadn't tried to use them as tools. And Tristan suspected that Lucien wasn't completely sane after years of being a tool.

"I-I-I'm lost." Tristan defaulted to his earlier script. "I've only recently come to Elfhome and I took the wrong subway car."

He waved in the general direction of the transit stop and then remembered that he was carrying the baby chicken in one hand. He held it out to Lain. "I'm supposed to give this to Tinker. I don't know why. Some crazy old female elf gave it to me. She said that she was part of our family."

"Yes, Tinker is my daughter," Esme said, coming forward to rescue the chick.

"No, the crazy old female elf. She claimed to be our mother's great-grandmother or something like that. That Anna is part elf. Was. She said that mother is dead."

He didn't even have to act. It was like he'd regressed back to being a baby. The tears came and he couldn't control them. "Could...could you take me to your place? I've been squatting here and there. I really don't have any place to call home."

"Oh, baby boy!" Lain gathered him into a hug. "You can come live with me."

Esme made a noise that indicated she thought Lain was being a pushover.

"Hush, you." Lain guided Tristan toward a big SUV. "He just found out his mother died. We can worry about the fine details after we grieve."

25: THIS TRAIN IS BOUND FOR GLORY

Liberty Avenue—for the whores who worked it—started at Market Square and ended at Penn Station. In reality, it stretched all the way out to Oakland, but the streetwalkers didn't work beyond the train station. Near Market Square they could attract the off-world businessmen, diplomats, and EIA staff members on short-term assignment. It was high traffic, high profit, so the Chang stable claimed the best parts at that end. The Undefended, made up of illegal immigrants, drifted across the rest of the half-mile stretch.

The Undefended rarely complained of this because most of them, like Peanut Butter Pie, had a kink for male elves. It was the sole reason that many of them were on Elfhome. They could quote the Lord of the Rings movies and something called Lemon-Lime JEl-Lo. They shared candid pictures and fan artwork of Windwolf and his *sekasha* on their phones—some of the drawings were highly pornographic in nature. (Olivia was glad that Forest Moss had arrived in Pittsburgh after they lost contact with Earth as it greatly reduced the chances of her ever having to see artwork featuring him with random partners.)

The train station had been the only outpost of elves in the Downtown area before the war broke out. From what Olivia could piece together, the elves knew that humans never did anything for more than one or two centuries. Even the great civilizations like the Egyptians and Romans had shifted power bases, beliefs, and practices every hundred years or so. Sooner or later, the gate between the worlds would fail and everything stranded on Elfhome would become the elves' responsibility to maintain. Because of that, the Wind Clan elves had been learning how to run and maintain the trains to the East Coast.

The Undefended would hang out near the train station, soliciting men until the elves came off duty. Once the royal marines started to arrive in Pittsburgh, it became a holy mecca for the women.

Penn Station was a beautiful century-old brick building with tons of tall arched windows. There was a massive rotunda in front of the entrance that the wagons would park under while waiting for incoming marines. Normally, the rotunda would be all lit up with warm yellow lamps so that it glowed golden at night, but the entire city was currently dark, shrouded in rain.

Olivia pulled under the dome, truck headlights gleaming off the entrance into the station proper.

Normally, the doors to the station stood open, allowing passengers to freely come and go. Tonight they were shut tight. Olivia recognized an auto-locking solid metal security door when she saw it. The Ranch had installed them on all the houses in case of police raids. Even a door ram would have trouble with them.

With the doors shut, there was no telling if there were any employees or trains at the station. Hopefully there were.

"What's that smell?" Alita whispered.

Olivia sniffed. Now that they were stopped, she could smell diesel strongly. "Oh, shoot!" She looked at the fuel gauge. It showed that they had less than a quarter tank. "We must have a leak!"

She snapped off the truck's headlights, dropping them into darkness. As she climbed out of the cab, Alita and Zippo got out on the other side. In the quiet of the night, she could hear a dripping coming from under the truck. The leak must be fairly big for her to hear it.

Alita shone a light under the truck. Olivia knelt down to look. Luckily, she'd parked so the truck straddled a storm drain so the leaking fuel wouldn't be underfoot, but judging by the speed of the dripping, she'd be out of diesel soon.

The back gate of the truck was riddled with bullet holes, instantly taking her mind off the fuel.

"Is everyone okay?" she asked as she scanned the eager faces of the royal marines. They didn't look worse for wear.

"That was fun, *domi!*" Rage said. "Like a sled ride down a mountain!"

"We are fine, *domi!*" Dagger said. "Are we getting out here?"

"I'm not sure," Olivia said. She had grown up in South Boston, which was linked to the rest of Massachusetts via passenger trains. Those trains would stay at a remote rail yard until needed at a station. She wasn't sure how the Elfhome trains worked. "What we need might not be here."

The marines took that as a "yes" and tumbled out of the back but kept close in case it was actually a "no."

Olivia assumed Penn Station and its trains were much the same as those of South Boston. She liked to peer into the driver's cab to study the controls. It always surprised her how simple they seemed. Some of the older ones had been little more than a big lever that the driver worked back and forth to speed up and slow the train.

The Pittsburgh trains might be as simple. She would rather not be the person driving the train. She doubted that anyone else in the truck—Aiofe, Alita, Zippo, and the twenty royal marines—could do any better than she could. She was going to need an engineer. There was only one place that she could think of to get one.

"Aiofe." Olivia turned her attention to the EIA translator. "Can you call Director Maynard?"

"The phones were down earlier." Aiofe took out the clunky odd phone that Maynard had given them earlier in the day. She turned it on and gave a slight sound of surprise. "The EIA must have some kind of backup network for their phones. Maynard's phone has a signal."

"Good." Olivia had hoped that the United Nations security force was using a separate system that would be harder to take out. "Ask him for an engineer to drive the train."

Aiofe nodded as she dialed Maynard's number. "Okay, engineer to drive the...what? Oh!" She noticed where they were. "We're stealing a train?"

"Commandeering," Olivia said firmly.

The royal marines crowded around her, happy and eager despite the day's insanity.

"Oh, the train!" Ox recognized the location. "Are we going on the train now? We liked the train!"

Several of them attempted to make the sound of train horns. Seriously, it was like having a bunch of five-year-olds. Were they all really eighty years older than she was?

"There should be two platoons of royal marines here," Dagger said, looking around. "Patches said that both her platoon and Tar's had pulled night duty here. They were annoyed that they got boring guard duty instead of going on the forest hunt. Patches was pretending to pity me for us having the more tedious watch."

"Being with *domi* is not tedious!" Ox defended Olivia loudly.

A noise like the clatter of a security door opening made Olivia sidestep so she could see around the truck. For a moment, she thought it was an elf coming out of the building, but then realized it was a tall, willowy man in an EIA uniform. By luck, the chaos of the royal marines was hidden from him.

Olivia pointed firmly at the ground, whispered, "Stay," to the marines, and moved to intercept the man. He probably had keys to get through the door. She needed to get his cooperation or she was going to have to ram the doors open with the truck.

The man marched toward her, calling loudly, "You can't park that truck there! Where did you get it? That's an official EIA vehicle!"

He was speaking English, so Olivia felt free to lie a little. "Director Maynard left it at Station Square for me to use. Who are you?"

She wanted a name so she could have Maynard deal with the man instead of having to verbally spar with him.

"I'm Lieutenant MacFarland of the Elfhome Interdimensional Agency," the man said as if Olivia should be impressed by the low rank. "I doubt very much that the director gave a cargo truck to a civilian. Have you been joyriding around the city in an EIA vehicle? On a night like tonight? Shame on you! You should be shot."

She'd been on shaky ground since she had no real proof that it was Maynard that left the keys in the truck or that he meant for her to take it. She had nearly been cowed until MacFarland spoke the word "shame." No, she'd been shamed enough in her life—all without any reason other than someone wanted to control her. She was saving lives. She'd saved the Undefended, Duff, and Widget. This man had no right to condemn her without facts.

"I am Olive Branch over Stone," she said. "I was within my rights to commandeer any vehicle that I want. This city—this world, Elfhome, belongs to the elves. By the *dau* mark on my forehead, I have the right to do whatever it takes to win this war. No lowly lieutenant of a foreign power—from Earth—has the right to shame me for my actions."

The man snorted in contempt. "You're just a streetwalker with aspirations. That smudge on your forehead just says that you've sold yourself to the insane male who was ancient before even your grandfather was born. You have no right to this truck, those warriors, or anything in this city. Go home."

"I need a train—" Olivia started.

He laughed. "A million-dollar piece of equipment vital for the city's well-being? No! They aren't toys for you to play with. They're Wind Clan property. Even if you flaunt your smudge mark around, you have no right to it."

"Chi-chi-chi," Dagger said in Elvish coming to join Olivia. "What is this human barking about? I don't like his tone. He cannot talk to our *domi* that way!"

I told you to stay, Olivia thought strongly at the marines' informal leader. Or had Dagger picked up something that she missed? Aoife, still hidden behind the truck, motioned to Olivia. Oh, Dagger was a distraction move by Aoife!

The lieutenant frowned even as he realized that Dagger wasn't alone. The other marines were taking positions around the rotunda. MacFarland switched to Elvish to say, "The trains belong to the Wind Clan. The Stone Clan *domi* has no right to them."

"Who are you to determine what we elves will or will not allow?" Dagger drifted to the left, drawing the man's attention. The elf seemed more dangerous than Olivia; Dagger had more than a foot in height and had three more weapons. "You know nothing of us! You have been peering through the spyhole, seeing only the Wind Clan for a few short years! What do you know about how we think and act in war? Pfft, Wind Clan will allow the royal marines to take a train."

"I won't let you bully the Wind Clan into this." MacFarland started to slowly back up. Probably a tactical retreat through the locked doors—counting on the politeness of elves to allow him to flee.

Olivia hurried to Aoife.

"I got through to Maynard," Aoife whispered. "I don't know what to say to him."

Olivia took the phone. "You said you wouldn't stop me because you don't know Sunder's heart. I need to take a train and Lieutenant MacFarland won't let us pass."

"MacFarland?" Maynard said. "What is he doing there? That's not where he's supposed to be."

Olivia hadn't considered that the EIA was filled with moles. The oni had lured the elves out into the forest, leaving the city almost defenseless. Almost all the *domana* and thousands of royal marines were trapped miles from Pittsburgh. The only way to quickly transport them back was by train. Had MacFarland misdirected the royal marines guarding the building? Killed them? Killed the Wind Clan elves who knew the inner workings of the train system?

Olivia handed the phone back to Aiofe, unslung the rifle from her shoulder, and shot MacFarland in the leg. She'd aimed for his knee. She was a little high but it still took him down.

"You shot me!" MacFarland shouted in surprise.

Why are men always so surprised at being shot after pissing off an armed woman?

"He has keys on him. Find them," Olivia told Dagger. She took the phone from Aiofe. "Director Maynard, I'm sorry but I've winged your man. I'm assuming he's an oni mole but I could be wrong. You should send an ambulance. Windwolf has called for a retreat and needs transportation. I'm taking the train out to pick up Forest Moss and the others. I need an engineer."

"Ah," Maynard said and fell silent a moment as he processed that. "Okay. The elves there should be able to provide an engineer. I'll see if I can send you some humans just in case something has happened with the elves, but if you can move out without my people, just go. Godspeed."

This being a *domi* rocked.

MacFarland hadn't killed all of the elves at Penn Station. It turned out that Tinker *domi* had taken away the royal marines in trucks before MacFarland showed up. His actions had alarmed one of the noncombatants—one of the older males who had spent the most time working with humans. MacFarland had managed to slip him off to the side and quietly kill him. The rest he convinced that the oni army had overrun the enclaves and would arrive shortly. He told them that their best course of action was to barricade themselves in a storage closet.

It made them prisoners of their own fear. MacFarland had

also added a travel door lock to the outside, effectively making them real prisoners.

It took the marines a while to talk the elves out of their bolt-hole. In the meantime, Alita and Zippo confirmed that there was a diesel engine with twenty passenger cars sitting at the station. "The plan" had always been that the train would pick up the *domana* after the battle. Penn Station had been waiting for an order to be relayed that MacFarland obviously hoped to intercept.

Dagger finally got the Wind Clan out of their self-made prison by shouting, "Oi! You Wind Clan are a bunch of cowards! Your *domou* needs you, and you cannot think past yourself and your piss-filled pants!"

The female added a bunch of other words that Olivia didn't know. Neither did Aiofe, judging by the fact that the anthropology grad student took out her tablet and made notes on them.

The door unlocked and the sheepish Wind Clan elves came out.

Aiofe handled explaining about Windwolf calling to be picked up because the explanation required a mix of English and Elvish words that neither Olivia nor the newly arrived Fire Clan knew.

"Duff is back on the air," Alita reported. "Since these tracks go through Oakland, I let him know how things stand here. He says that the rails are possibly blocked—Tinker compacted a bridge or something like that. I'm not sure I understood that completely—it could have been a code that I'm not cleared to know. He's asking the militia to make sure a train can get through that area. He'll let us know if the tracks are clear."

Olivia nodded as she only had a vague notion where the rails led to. She'd ignored the train the entire two months that she'd been in the city. She'd run as far from the Ranch as she wanted.

Aiofe turned to Olivia. "The damn gobshite MacFarland killed the engineer. This here is Nuthatch. He's fully trained to drive the engine but he's never driven one beyond the rail yard."

Nuthatch wore the blue denim bib overalls and pinstripe cap of an engineer but somehow looked like he was a tall human cosplaying an anime mash-up character. The male was painfully skinny and his hands nervously flitted about as if he had no real control over them. He bowed in greeting, spilling his long braid of black hair over his shoulder. His hands gathered it up, fingered the braid nervously, and then fed the end of it into his mouth, chewing on it without seeming to be aware of what he was doing.

Aiofe dropped to a whisper to add, "Frankly, he's scared shitless, but he's willing to give it a go as long as the marines come along."

None of this filled Olivia with confidence. It was what it was.

Aiofe waved toward the platform. "The engine is fueled and ready to go. The mechanics will ride along to deal with emergencies—again—if the marines come with us."

Alita held her hand to her ear, listening to something that Duff was telling her over the radio. "We've got an all clear for the tracks through Oakland, though Duff says we should be aware of possible snipers."

Olivia expected the Wind Clan elves to give some signal that they were boarding the train and then realized that everyone was waiting on her to say something. "Let's go!"

"You're going on the train with them?" Alita whispered.

Was she? Olivia hadn't even considered not going, but there was no real reason that she had to go. Or was there? The royal marines wouldn't go without her—their orders were to protect her. The elves who knew how to run the train, though, were frightened and unarmed. They wouldn't be able to deal with anything unexpected down the road.

"Yes," she said. "I'm going."

"We want to go with you!" Alita whispered. Zippo nodded behind his tiny cousin.

She hadn't expected Tommy's fierce kittens to go with her. They were just blocks from the William Penn Hotel. "It's going to be dangerous."

"We're probably never going to have another chance to ride the train," Alita whispered. "It's an elf-only kind of thing. The passenger trains used to go past our old place out in Oakland. When we were little, we used to hang out the windows to watch them go by. We'd hear the rumble of the engine and rails ringing and such even when we weren't looking. There was always something about it—like it was a promise that the elves wouldn't lose the war and we'd be free of the oni. We've always wanted to ride the train! Leave Pittsburgh. See something of the world beyond Oakland."

"See the ocean," Zippo added.

Olivia understood then. She used to watch the trail of dust kicked up by cars driving past the Ranch on a distant country road. She imagined hiking out and trying to convince the drivers to take her back to Boston. Back to her grandmother's house where she could see the ocean from her bedroom window. "Okay. You can come. Stay close. Oh—we should make sure that MacFarland is tied up or something before we leave."

"Oh, he's dead," Alita said in the polite tone usually used in telling someone that it was a bank holiday and their restaurant was closed for the day.

"What?" Olivia gasped. She was sure she hadn't hit an artery. He hadn't been bleeding that badly.

Alita winced. "Yeaaah, the marines seemed to think that you meant to kill him. His throat was cut—sometime after we found the elves locked in the closet."

How was Olivia going to explain that to Maynard? She'd have to deal with it later.

While the passenger cars looked like those on a typical Amtrak train, the engine didn't resemble the ones on Earth. It had a massive hatchet nose instead of the standard low cowcatcher. The windshield peered over the wedge of metal, allowing the driver to see the tracks.

Aiofe noticed her gazing at it. "The entire rail system is a fascinating adaption of technology. The elves set up wards that keep most animals off the tracks. The nose will plow through any larger creature that gets past the shielding. The wards also drain off magic in the area near the rails so it can't pool and interact with the metal bits of the train. All the engines were built for Elfhome. Their electronics are especially insulated and they have fewer computerized fussy bits than the more modern ones of Earth have."

"Tell the mechanics that we want the lights off in the cars while we go through Oakland," Olivia said and then explained, "That way snipers won't be able to see any possible targets on the train."

Aiofe squeaked with alarm and went off to find the mechanics.

Olivia motioned for the royal marines to enter the passenger car directly behind the engine. "We don't have enough people to guard the entire train. There's four side doors and the passageway to the next car. Split into teams of five, one team on each side door in this car."

"Yes, *domi!*" they said but then bounded from car to car like golden retrievers in a pickup bed. She assumed that once the train got moving the marines would actually do what she told them.

Olivia found Nuthatch inside the engine cab. The controls on the front panel, below the windshield, looked fairly simple but Olivia was glad that she wasn't the one responsible for driving. She paid close attention, though, just in case she ended up having to.

Nuthatch engaged a knife switch straight out of an old Frankenstein movie. "We weren't sure when *domou* would send word for the trains, so we didn't have them idling. It's a waste of fuel."

From there, Nuthatch flipped about a hundred switches on a circuit-breaker panel. Some were simply labeled LIGHTS and FUEL PUMP while others were more obscure like DPC and LRMS POWER. From there he turned and held a switch labeled FUEL PRIME—ENGINE START.

That part she understood as it wasn't much different from the older tractors on the Ranch. On deep winter mornings, the diesel engines needed to be primed with fuel before they could be started.

Once the engine was primed, Nuthatch flipped the switch to START and the massive engine rumbled to life.

"We're ready to move?" Olivia asked.

"Almost." Nuthatch fluttered his hands about and then chewed on his braid, apparently thinking. Not reassuring. Then almost singing the order of operations, he punched various buttons, flipped switches, and turned knobs. "There!"

She was never going to remember that.

Nuthatch tooted the train horn as a warning that the engine was about to start moving. As Olivia suspected, moving forward was simply taking off brakes and moving the one big acceleration lever on the control panel. They started slow, pulling out of the station.

Alita and Zippo came into the engine from the passenger cars.

"Did the marines stop running around?" Olivia asked.

Alita was grinning ear to ear inside her black hoodie. "Yeah, they did. I can't blame them; we were exploring too. These things are nicer than the light rail! And they have bathrooms too!"

Alita ducked her head as if embarrassed by her childlike glee.

They passed under the three main bridges of Oakland. The area was complete chaos. Parts of the city were on fire. One of the bridges had been completely blown away, its broken decks just narrowly missing the railroad tracks. Something was flashing brilliant white with a loud *bong* noise. Rifles cracked overhead and occasional bullets whined through the train.

And then they were out in virgin forest, surrounded by darkness, chasing the light thrown by their lone headlight.

"So cool," Alita whispered in a mantra. "So cool. So cool."

"How far is it to where the *domana* are?" Olivia asked Nuthatch.

"It is less than an hour at this speed—at least that is what the daylight engineers who shuttled out the royal marines told me. I do know for sure that it took two hours to go out, unload, and come back for the next load. They were using one of the old work camps that we used while laying the tracks. I think I'll be able to spot it despite the dark and rain. All the camps are well marked and maintained in case of breakdowns."

Olivia was glad that they had a little time before arriving at the camp: she needed to pee. She made her way to the bathroom of the first car, glad to discover that the mechanics had turned the lights back on. On the way back from the cramped toilet, she discovered that the mechanics had also brought baskets full of food on board. She hadn't eaten since morning and started to feel queasy. She accepted a sandwich made of a rye bun stuffed with smoked ham, thin sliced raw onions, a goudalike cheese, sweet pickles, and a coarse ground mustard. It wasn't like any sandwich that she'd had before but she knew that if she didn't eat something soon, she'd throw up what little she had in her stomach.

She took three of the sandwiches to the engine for Nuthatch, Alita, and Zippo. The trio were staring out the windshield as they roared through the dark rainy night. Alita updated her on what the militia knew, based on how the fighting was going in Oakland. Forge and Jewel Tear were without their *domana* powers and had been unconscious until Forge's *sekasha* woke them up using some kind of healing spell. Tinker and Oilcan had dodged the oni spell—the militia wasn't sure how—and were out fighting.

"Forest Moss has not made you *domana* yet...because of the child?" Nuthatch suddenly asked.

Alita had been speaking English. Olivia didn't think that Nuthatch knew the language but apparently he knew enough to follow the discussion.

"No," Olivia said. "Nor do I want to be changed."

"I would not want to be made human and left on Earth to fend for myself," Nuthatch said with hands fluttering. "Nor would I want to be made *domana*. I think if I did not like my basic self, maybe I would be quick to change but I like the way that the gods have made me." He held up his sandwich that he'd denuded of pickles. "There is no good reason that I like onions and not pickles—but I do and that is me, and I am fine with that. It might be uncomfortable at times to be of nervous nature—but that is how I am and I do not know if I would like being otherwise. It makes me cautious around the big engines and pay close attention to details. The one I love thinks my timid nature is endearing. Would I actually like the type of person who wants a bold partner? My beloved is gentle with me and that is what I love about them."

"They will not let Forest Moss and me stay together if I'm not *domana*," Olivia said.

"Pfft!" Nuthatch said. "That is Clan War talk. 'Be afraid of the other' is not the same as living cautiously. I—of all people—should know. We have been at peace for longer than most of the elves in Pittsburgh have been alive but our society has not changed since the Rebellion. I do envy the ones who have started households with humans. They have so much more freedom to explore what they want to be. I had to leave everything behind to come to Pittsburgh and learn the trains. I was only allowed because I was a jeweler and had apprenticed on clockworks brought from Earth. If I had been *laedin*, I would have been barred from anything but standing guard on them."

"Yeah, screw them," Alita said. "The only reason people are so nuts about elves are because they're pretty. It's like they're movie stars or rock idols. Really—all common sense goes out the window when they see elves. It was always frustrating as hell to know my family got the wrong end of that stick."

"Oh! Oh!" Nuthatch waved out the windshield. They were crossing a bridge made of massive ironwood timbers. "We are coming up on the camp! We cross this bridge and it is another few minutes. Should we start slowing down? I think we should—it is not as imperative as if we were pulling a heavily loaded freight, but it will take some effort to come to a full stop safely."

"Slow down," Olivia said.

Nuthatch eased back on the lever that controlled speed. "I will start applying brakes once we bleed off some speed."

They rounded a wide gentle bend and the camp appeared on the left side of the tracks, lit by elfshines in massive numbers. There was something huge and gleaming standing on the rails. It was some kind of giant glowing scorpion. There were royal marines dashing in and out of the light thrown by the monster, shooting gleaming spell arrows at it. The marines' attacks seemed to be having no effect on the insectoid creature.

"Oh, shit!" Alita whispered.

Nuthatch grabbed another lever and started to apply it. The train shuddered and brakes squealed.

"No, no, no!" Olivia shouted. "Hit it!"

She jerked off the brakes and pushed the acceleration to full. She reached over and grabbed the train horn. She blared it long and loud to let the world know that they were coming.

She let up on the horn to shout, "Brace for impact!"

She heard Aiofe repeat it to the royal marines.

She laid on the horn, bracing against the strike. Zippo suddenly enveloped her in strong arms and lifted her away from the panel. He sat down, still holding her, and braced his legs. She had a moment of confusion and then realized that he was protecting her baby. She clung to him, whispering a quick prayer that she hadn't just done something incredibly stupid.

The gleam of the monster became a dawning sun in the cab and then they hit. There was a violent slam forward as they struck the immovable object and then a shudder as pure momentum plowed the massive iron hatchet nose of the engine through the monster. The train shuddered and then leapt forward.

"Slow us down!" Olivia tried to reach the accelerator. "Ease off!"

Nuthatch grabbed hold of the lever and slowed them. Muttering, he eased on the brakes and slowly brought them to a halt.

"Wow! We really nailed it!" Alita said, leaning out the side door to look behind them. "I'm fairly sure it's dead. It's laying there like a smashed cockroach—legs up and not twitching."

"Oh, thank God," Olivia whispered.

Because the elves might be hair trigger around anyone who wasn't an elf, Olivia attempted to keep the first passenger car for her people and the Wind Clan. (Since the half-oni were Oilcan's

Beholden, they were technically Wind Clan. Olivia was hoping that was enough to keep the two Changs safe, especially big shy Zippo.) Ox volunteered to go out and find Forest Moss in the flood of elves retreating out of the forest. The rest of her escort guarded the doors, directing Stone Clan and Fire Clan to the other cars.

It was an orderly retreat. The royal marines—with their complete trust of their officers—sorted themselves into waves and gave priority to the *sekasha* and *domana* among them.

"They're not going to all fit," Olivia murmured to Alita as she watched the clearing fill up with warriors.

"Duff was working on getting a second train up and running," Alita said. "They were running three trains to get everyone out here so the other two are someplace."

Hopefully not on their way to Brotherly Love. There was nothing Olivia could do now, so she sat in one of the front chairs and fretted.

Glaive Smites the Sun and the other four Wyverns who made up her normal escort carried Forest Moss to the first door, with Ox going, "This way holy ones, this way please!"

She knew that she loved Forest Moss just by how horrible the sight of his still body made her feel.

"Is he hurt?" she asked as they settled him into the first window seat at the front of the train.

"The oni have stripped him of his connection to your Spell Stones," Glaive said. "Nothing more. They did the same to Prince True Flame and the Harbingers. Wolf Who Rules Wind is the only one who is unaffected. We are going to entrust Forest Moss on Stone to you, his *domi*, and return to supervise the retreat."

He is useless to them now so they abandon him to his madness, Olivia thought. She brushed the thought aside. They had carried him to safety and entrusted him to someone who loved him. They could have left him lying in the woods.

"We have put a spell on him to wake him up," Glaive said, indicating Forest Moss's torn left sleeve and the runes inked on his skin. "But he has not roused yet. The Harbingers say he will rouse shortly."

The Wyverns bowed to her and left.

A horrible feeling welled up inside her. They'd left her alone with Forest Moss when he was completely helpless. How was she to care for him? Was he really unharmed? If he didn't wake, how could she get him back to their place? Was their place even safe? Oakland had been filled with chaos when they rode past it.

"Do not worry, *domi*," Dagger said. "You have us! We will keep you safe!"

She gave a breathless laugh because it had been so hard to see the royal marines as anything more than a class of five-year-olds, needing to be *kept* safe. Yes, they were fearless in battle but they didn't know anything about Pittsburgh. The truck had been leaking fuel since Mount Oliver. In the hour since they parked at Penn Station, it could have emptied out completely. If the truck was out of diesel, she didn't even know how to get them back to Oakland short of walking half the night. "I don't even know where to go after we get back to the city. I don't know where we'll sleep."

"You can stay with us!" Zippo said from the window seat behind Forest Moss.

"Yeah, you could!" Alita leaned forward from the aisle seat. "We're running the William Penn as an enclave! We've got plenty of beds and bathrooms. You can stay the night and figure it out tomorrow."

Run to the Changs if you're scared, the Undefended used to tell her.

She was scared. She glanced at Forest Moss. Did his pulse always leap so visibly at the base of his neck? She took his limp hand and was alarmed to find it cold and wet. She rubbed it between her own as she realized that he was completely soaked to the bone. They needed to get him into something dry and warmed up.

Still, it felt wrong to throw herself onto the good will of Tommy's baby cousins. His family had to be in dire straits if so many of them were out walking Liberty Avenue.

"I—We can pay," Olivia said. She had an entire purse of elf gold ingots hidden back at Phipps. "We're going to need a lot of rooms."

"If you can pay," Alita said, "then you stay as long as you want. That's what a hotel is for!"

"That sounds fun," Aiofe said from the floor in front of Olivia with Rage and Ox. "It'll be like a sleepover party."

Aiofe had spent the entire day—between gun battles—grilling

the royal marines about their culture and language. She saw it
as her duty (and pleasure) as a graduate anthropology student to
gather as much information as possible on the Fire Clan while it
was in Pittsburgh. Since Maynard had reassigned her to Olivia,
she didn't even need an excuse to tag along. Olivia couldn't send
her away to protect her.

Nor did she really want to. The older girl at least understood
the complexities of the human world. Olivia suddenly desperately
didn't want to be alone in the big empty hotel with just the royal
marines and the unconscious Forest Moss.

There was a stir among the elves within the car and Wolf
Who Rules Wind boarded, followed by fifteen of his *sekasha*.
They were muddy and worn but seemed unharmed. One could
almost feel the love and awe that his people radiated toward him.

It seemed so unfair that it had been denied Forest Moss.

With a distressing whine, Forest Moss stirred. He struggled
to open his one good eye, stark fear on his face. When he saw
her, the fear slipped into confusion.

"It's okay," she murmured. "You're safe. I'm here."

"Oh, my *domi*," he whispered, gripping her hand. "As long
as I have you, I do not care what else I have."

26: ONE SHOT TO RULE THEM ALL

-→⊶═◯⇌-→⊶-

Where was the rest of Pittsburgh?

Jane crouched behind a stack of bricks in the upper story of a building under construction, wondering at the pitiful number of fighters on the allied side. There were sixty thousand humans in the city. There were only a thousand or so militia who were trusted locals—family, soulmates, and close friends, all stitched together by confidentiality. Jane and the others that helped her organize the militia had hoped that once the fighting started, all of Pittsburgh would rally to their cause.

Monsters in Our Midst had been created to build awareness of the oni lurking in the shadows. Yes, it was to gather together militia members but it also was supposed to bring the common masses to their feet when the hammer dropped.

Of the sixty thousand humans on Elfhome, close to eighty percent were off-worlders. They were EIA soldiers, diplomats, embassy staff, businessmen, college professors, and students. Almost all of them were armed—rifles were standard-issue for almost all non-students who "visited" Elfhome. Even the college students who were studying xenobiology and interdimensional geography would eventually arm themselves. The likelihood of colliding with something deadly in your backyard or nearby side alley was too high to go unarmed.

Hal's call to arms had generated maybe a few hundred more fighters to their side, but there were tens of thousands unaccounted for.

Thank God that Oilcan and Tinker had been still up and fighting. Without them—and the tengu that Tinker commanded—the oni would have plowed right over the militia.

"What are those... things that Geoffrey is firing?" Nigel said as Tinker's pipes *bong*ed loudly and blasted out a massive ray of destructive light. Taggart was swapping memory cards so it was safe to talk.

Jane motioned to Hal to cover his mic. He was still broadcasting live to WESA. KDKA had picked up the feed and was rebroadcasting it.

She covered her own mic so she wouldn't be spamming the command channel. "I don't know what their proper name is but my family calls them 'the xylophones of doom.' Tinker invented them the summer that my cousins first met Oilcan and Tinker. I think she was ten at the time. They would go to my aunt's place and hang out, doing insanely inventive things like catapulting a car engine through the roof of one of my uncle's equipment sheds."

Geoffrey had talked endlessly about his newfound friends who were teaching him magic. For some reason, Jane had thought that Tinker was Oilcan's little brother, not his female cousin.

"The xylophones were turned backward the first time the kids fired them," Jane said. "It almost took out my aunt's house. She had this huge prize lilac bush beside the back porch. The xylophones left nothing but a crater where the lilac used to be. The bush never grew back. The xylophones got packed up and nearly forgotten except as a family legend. Every spring my aunt bitches about it on Easter Sunday—which is around the time that lilac would have been blooming."

"How do the xylophones work?" Nigel said.

"They're like spell arrows." Hal's tone indicated that he was smugly happy to be able to answer the question. "Geoffrey explained them to me once—the best he understood. I've never seen them, but like Jane said, it's a family story that gets repeated a lot."

Hal got invited to all her family events simply because he would otherwise be dangerously alone on holidays. Unfortunately, her family events always included vast amounts of food, booze, cameras, and guns. It meant Hal was never suicidal but still dangerous. There was a reason why her family viewed Hal like an unruly child. Jane sincerely hoped that he wasn't going to go on a rampage at her wedding. Maybe she should ban all guns?

"We should probably explain the xylophones to the radio listeners." Taggart shifted his camera back to his shoulder. "They're very visible. People might think they're oni weapons. We can get footage of them shooting for future viewers."

Jane nodded agreement to this. "Stay as general as you can, we don't want people trying to re-create them after the war. They're dangerous as hell."

"No worries," Hal said as he straightened his shirt and brushed dirt off his knees. "I don't understand them well enough for someone to copy them from my explanation. I can handle the technical end. Nigel can do color."

"Go." Jane waved them off as Captain Josephson was making his way toward her. They moved off to get a better view of the pipes.

"Storm Six, this is Storm One," Duff suddenly reported after being silent for several minutes. "My position has been made. I'm going dark. I'll contact you once I find safe shelter."

The channel went dead.

"Shit!" Jane swore as she felt like she'd been hit in the heart. The oni were after her little brother! They'd put the communication hub on Mount Oliver because it was one of the highest points in the city, allowing them to transmit down into Downtown, Oakland, and the other possible areas of conflict. The bakery and several of the neighboring houses were owned by her mother's first cousin, who had married into the aptly named Baker family. The building was outfitted with a generator in case of power outages. Anyone witnessing activity at the bakery would think it was related to making bread. The only true drawback to it was the fact that it was extremely isolated. His location had been one of their most protected secrets. Duff's cell was purposely the smallest of the militia—he'd recruited only two or three tech-savvy young people. He'd talked about sending some of them to the museum to scour any computers left behind by the oni. There was a good possibility that Duff was all alone.

Jane glanced around and spotted Alton. "Alton!" She waved him over. "Do the tengu have eyes on Duff?"

Alton shook his head. "There's some *yamabushi* on Mount Washington guarding Boo, since she's part of the Chosen bloodline now. Jin Wong called all the other tengu into Oakland under Tinker's orders."

Jane swore softly. She had been hoping that Duff's guard was still on Mount Oliver with him.

"I'll send one of my tengu to Jin Wong," Alton said. "He might be able to use his 'Chosen One' powers to quickly shift some of the *yamabushi* on Mount Washington to Mount Oliver."

Alton left in a crouching run.

Captain Josephson took the space vacated by Alton. "Are your people still on the bridge at South Aiken?"

Jane shook her head. "Wyverns took command there. I have no authority to move them."

Josephson nodded his understanding and added, "We've been warned to keep a wide berth of them."

The *sekasha* had lately started to lop the heads off people right and left. Lots of oni disguised as humans. Sparrow. Earth Son. Nathan Czernowski. The holy warriors had hair triggers on their sense of justice.

It was her experience that "make-shift" equaled "untrustworthy" in most people's eyes. The militia had jury-rigged equipment and a haphazard sense of style. She was worried about letting them anywhere near the *sekasha*. She herself had tiptoed around Tinker's Hand.

"At this point in time, I'm not willing to expose my troops to the Wyverns," Jane said. "They have some royal marines with them and seem to be focused on doing mop-up, so I asked the tengu to keep eyes on them. Where are all the EIA troops?"

"Scattered from one end of Pittsburgh to the other," Josephson said. "The oni started acts of sabotage early this morning. Plowing cars into substations and the like."

That explained the power outage that morning at WQED.

Josephson continued, "Troops were spotted in the South Side, apparently chasing after Oilcan. There was an outbreak of fighting on Neville Island. We had enemy movement as far south as Southeast Rim near Wheeling. We're spread too thin to be effective."

"Can we expect any reinforcements?"

"Maynard is sending three squads from the South Side but they'll be another ten minutes."

That was something. At the moment, they had a choke hold on three access points merely because the oni weren't using their superior numbers to swarm down into the busway and into Oakland.

Considering that the humans had machine guns, it wasn't a completely stupid tactic. The oni were probably being conservative because they weren't expecting human resistance and didn't know the size of the allied forces. That could change if the oni command realized how few humans were standing against them.

It was the first time in her life that Jane was happy for a dark, stormy night. The only illumination came from the lightning, the xylophones of doom, and the fiery horrors on the other side of Centre Avenue Bridge. The storm was moving fast, whipping the treetops on the other side of the busway. If the earlier weather report was correct, the bulk of the storm had already passed over them.

"I think we should hold our position," Captain Josephson said, "at least while Tinker *domi* is dealing with the horrors. Those pipes aren't very portable and crossing that busway would be suicide. Once we're sure that the horrors are dead, we can reevaluate the situation. By then the EIA troops should have arrived."

"I agree."

"Tinker *domi* gave me this intel." Josephson pulled out a phone, unlocked it and found a photo. "This is the enemy commander. His name is Moriyajuto. He's a greater blood under Kajo. Tinker *domi* says that the oni command structure is stretched as thin as we are."

Jane studied the photo. It was blurry. In a nightscope, everything would be shades of gray but the white and red of the mask would make the pattern unmistakable. "So, if we can take him out, there's no other officers to pick up the reins?"

"From the intel she got, Moriyajuto is the only commander," Josephson said.

That could explain the caution that the oni were taking in using their superior numbers. A surge down and across the jumbled mess of the busway and then uphill against humans who were under heavy cover would have needed high morale among the oni troops and strong commanders to carry it off.

Allied troops continued to trickle in. More tengu arrived from Haven—out of breath but able to hold a rifle. The EIA troops arrived. Teenagers and twentysomething locals and handfuls of graduate students. The average humans, though, stayed away.

She couldn't understand it. They were trapped on Elfhome.

Over the last few months, the evidence mounted that the oni were willing to do anything to win. If the elves were wiped out, the oni would turn their attention on the humans.

It was sheer stupidity to ignore the war on their doorstep.

She'd known that the oni had powerful connections on Earth. They'd blocked Nigel's and Taggart's visa requests for years. They'd kept a news blackout going across the board—so much so that even the top-rated TV show *Pittsburgh Backyard and Garden* couldn't be syndicated on Earth. If the humans from stateside continued to stand back and do nothing, then the oni might lose this battle but win the war. Sooner or later, Pittsburgh would be reconnected to Earth. If the oni had managed to hold the elves and their allies at a stalemate, their network on Earth could kick in. The elves might not like it but anyone who came to their defense today could end up facing charges in a human court in the future. She knew it was a possibility going in but she thought that the chances were low. Now, as she watched it all play out, the odds were racking up against the militia.

They had to win. After winning, her team would need to focus on damage control.

Alton returned. "Jin Wong managed to reach the team at Bullhorn on Mount Washington. There was a running fight down off of Mount Oliver that ended well for our side—but Duff wasn't part of it. The oni were chasing the Dove."

"Who the hell is that?" Jane said.

Alton shrugged, blowing out his breath. "Some little redheaded girl that Forest Moss marked as his *domi*. No one knows much about her. She's not a local—possibly illegal. The elves gave her the name of Olive Branch. Noah's ark. The bird that brings back the olive branch. Code name: the Dove."

Random dots connected for Jane. There had been a post that morning on the militia's message boards. A bunch of illegal immigrants had gone missing, most of them known Liberty Avenue streetwalkers. The post asked for any information that could confirm their safety if they had simply taken shelter someplace. Duff had mentioned, during one of Jane's many phone calls during the day, that he was worried about a redheaded girl the bakery let go. That would explain how the Dove ended up in the otherwise abandoned part of town.

Alton continued to explain: "The Dove has been spotted all

over town with an honor guard of royal marines and a possibly stolen EIA cargo truck. Rumor is that she shot Jonnie Be Good for some reason—although that man needed to be shot. I'd been tempted to do it myself in the past. The tengu aren't sure what the Dove is doing but they're fairly sure that she lured the oni away from Duff."

Jane let out her breath. Duff hadn't been alone when he went dark. A platoon of royal marines would have given him enough covering fire to slip away. Duff had studied that area of the city until he knew it inside and out, just in case he needed to rabbit. Jane had to trust that her little brother had been smart, kept his cool, and gotten away safely.

"The EIA says that the oni are stretched as thin as they are." Jane updated Alton on what Captain Josephson had told her. "There's been strikes all over the city. The bulk of the oni troops in the city are the ones we're fighting, but there's just one commander: a greater blood named Moriyajuto."

"So, if we take him out, their chain of command here will be broken?" Alton asked.

We. Alton recognized it was a job for a sniper. The question was only who would pull the trigger.

Her younger brothers had put too much on the line already.

"See what the tengu know about the oni command," Jane said.

She had her father's rifle and his night scope. She didn't like what she had to do. Somehow picking one person out of a crowd was so much harder than aiming at an entire mob of people shooting at her. There's the knowledge that at the moment, they're not actively trying to kill her specifically.

It had been an innocent game her father taught her. Read the patterns of the troops' movement. Runners would lead you like ants to the nest. Leaders tend to stand still—in the back—so that followers could find them in the confusion of the fight. They would have bodyguards, also standing still, keeping watch. The guards paid attention to who came and went, verifying that no mole reached the leader. Once you found the central point where the runners kept returning, then watch for an indication of who listened and who spoke. Who pointed. Who nodded.

It meant a long study of the enemy, carefully filtering through the chaos of a battlefield to find the leader. The age of radios had changed the game slightly but not completely. A beginner sniper needed to learn the basics—thus the version that her father had been taught and passed on to her.

The white mask with red horns made it easier to verify that she'd found the right rat's nest. The idiot had made a tent to hold off the rain. They'd lured in elfshines to light the place and then tried to shield it from snipers with flaps that only occasionally were drawn to protect those within from sight. She forced herself not to think of this person whose name was Moriyajuto, or that Boo probably knew him. Had known him for years. All that mattered was her distant target: the bull's-eye in the shape of a horned mask.

Jane focused on the foot-wide break in the tent flaps, controlling her breathing, trigger finger loose, waiting for that flash of white.

When it came, she took the shot.

She didn't even get to see the bullet hit. The flap was dropped even as the bullet leapt the distance.

Did she hit?

There was a new small hole in the canvas. She sat waiting, eye to scope, watching.

Then—unexpectedly—the bodyguards fled in all directions. One of them tripped over the tent guidelines and brought it down. The nearby troops noticed the collapse and the desertion. Panic started to spread, slowly, as the allied forces held most of the oni's attention. Little by little, the front line noticed the sudden exodus.

As the oni front line turned and fled, a confused and tentative cheer went up from the militia. They didn't understand what had happened. They didn't know why the oni were fleeing. Last time the oni had retreated, it had been just to clear the field for the horrors. The giant gleaming bodies littered the battlefield, killed by the xylophones of doom. Was it over? Had they actually won?

"We've won the battle but not the war. Not yet," Jane whispered. The question was: at what cost? Who had they lost? How many friends and neighbors of the militia had been killed? Had Duff found someplace safe?

Almost as an answer, Duff came back on air.

"Storm Six, this is Storm One," Duff said.

"Storm Six here!" Jane said.

"The dog needs his basket," Duff said. "The dove is taking the basket to the dog. Is the way clear?"

She didn't expect Duff's first transmission to be so on point but that was fine. If he felt safe enough to transmit, then she was okay with that. Overjoyed even.

She focused on the coded message. The dog was Windwolf. Basket was the train, as in "don't put all your eggs in one basket." Dove was taking the train to Windwolf? Really? Why her?

"We're talking Echo One?" Jane asked, using the code for Penn Station. The passenger trains and freight trains used two separate rails in and out of Pittsburgh proper. The freight trains ran alongside the Mon River, through South Side, to the freight yards near McKees Rocks. The passenger trains diverted deep in the forest to cut through Oakland and end up Downtown.

"Yes, Echo One."

It meant that Dove would send the train straight through the battlefield. Of all the insanity!

Jane waved Alton to her. "We need to know if the tracks are clear from Penn Station to the Rim."

"On it." He turned to call the tengu to him.

She wanted to ask Duff where he was. How safe he was? Did he need support? How did he get teamed up with the Dove? Jane didn't ask. One wrong word could put him back into danger.

27: FORMERLY KNOWN AS
THE WILLIAM PENN HOTEL
◂✛▭◗ ◖▭✛▸

"This is Tommy's enclave?" Jewel Tear asked Tommy as she slid off his hoverbike.

He started to nod and then realized that all the elf enclaves were named after the head of the household. "We humans use family names. It's the Chang enclave."

"Chang," Jewel Tear said. "Does it have a meaning or is it like Tommy?"

"If it has a meaning, my mother never told it to me," Tommy said as he eyed a pickup parked in front of the William Penn Hotel. It had "local" written all over it, from the "classic" age of the truck to the WESA bumper sticker to the gun rack in the cab. There was a teenaged black girl standing, talking with Quinn. She seemed to be the pickup's owner—she was holding keys in her hand—only Tommy didn't recognize her. Between the dance raves and racetrack, he knew most of the local young people.

He motioned to Jewel Tear to stay back, under the awning over the front door, and stalked over to the truck.

"What's going on?" he asked Quinn.

"Neither one of us knows how to drive," Quinn said.

"How did it get here then?" Tommy asked.

"Duff Kryskill showed up in it shortly after you left," Quinn said. "Alita sent him."

"He told me to move his pickup to someplace...better?" the girl said. "He forgot I don't know how to drive."

Tommy glanced at Quinn.

"She's one of the bunnies," Quinn murmured. "Widget."

The bunnies were all illegals. Duff was a regular at the racetrack, hanging out with his cousins on Team Tinker. If they weren't running from the oni, they were perfectly safe to interact with his family. But if Duff was hiding from the oni—they needed to get the truck out of sight.

"Where's Alita?" Tommy asked.

Widget looked puzzled. "Who?"

"Short, dark, and scary," Quinn said, holding up his hand to indicate Alita's size.

"Oh, she went with the royal marines." Widget waved in what might have been a random direction or out toward Liberty Avenue.

Since most of his family couldn't leave the restaurant, most hadn't learned to drive. If he remembered correctly, Trixie had learned to drive after running away from home to hide from his father's warriors.

"Get Trixie to move it," he told Quinn.

He pulled Jewel Tear into the lobby of the hotel.

The huge room with crystal chandeliers and groupings of beautiful seats was filled with little half-oni—some able to pass as human and some who couldn't—running loose. It was the three- through six-year-olds. They were old enough to walk without fear of them falling face-first but still too young to be without constant supervision.

"Hey! Hey!" He called to get their attention. "What are you doing?"

"Tommy!" the children all shouted and swarmed him.

"What are you doing down here?" he repeated sternly. "Why aren't you in your rooms?"

"We're hungry!" "When's dinner?" "The lights went off and the elevator stopped working, so when the lights came back on, we played with it!" "We want to go swimming too!"

"They are so little," Jewel Tear whispered in Elvish, looking down at the children clinging to his legs. All of them were under four feet tall, with some as short as three feet. "They are even smaller than Spot."

"They're not supposed to be down here," Tommy growled. They hadn't been in the hotel long enough to set up routines of how to efficiently get food to the little kids. It didn't help that not all of them were his aunts' offspring, so he couldn't just send them to their mothers.

"Where's Motoko?" he called out in Chinese.

"He's putting out fires," Trixie said while heading toward the front door to move Duff's pickup.

"Literal fires or just emergencies?" Tommy called after her.

"Emergencies!" Trixie shouted back before disappearing outside.

"Quinn, get the kids back upstairs and then tell the tweens to find something for them to eat," Tommy ordered.

"Me?" Quinn said in surprise. "I'm supposed to be guarding the front door and holding down the front desk."

"You said you needed help with the children," Jewel Tear whispered in Elvish. "Did you mean these children?"

"Yes, but you need to get warmed up and dried off or you'll get sick," Tommy said, pulling her toward the elevators. "You can help after that."

His room was one temptation after another. The big bed. The hot, steamy shower. The knowledge that she was on the other side of the bathroom door and would probably welcome him showering with her. He focused on going through his clothes to find something for her to wear. He had plenty of black T-shirts. Normally he had at least one pair of panties mixed in with his boxers when they came back from the laundry. His family did not disappoint. He had no idea which cousin was missing her underwear but they looked like they would fit Jewel Tear. He also found her a pair of sweatpants with an elastic waist, clean socks, and a pair of house slippers.

He hesitated when she called out to him but then pushed the bathroom door open. She was sitting on the edge of the tub, a big towel wrapped around her.

"I cut my feet," she said tearfully.

She had left Sacred Heart in only a housedress. She must have cut her bare feet on broken glass lying in the street. He hadn't noticed because all the wounded in Oakland masked the scent of blood on her.

"It's okay," he said. "I have some medicine."

The question was where. He dug around in the drawers until he found where his family had put his first aid supplies.

He cleaned her wounds, making sure that there was no glass

embedded in them, sprayed the cuts with disinfectant, and put bandages on them.

"As *domana*, I was taught how to do healing spells but not how to clean and bandage wounds. It is as if such touching other people was beneath me. I always hated being a *domana*. I was told that I should always be separate from those beneath me. I wonder, though, if all I was taught was wrong. I see how Wolf's new *domi* is with their people and how fiercely loyal they are to her. If I had lowered myself...maybe my *laedin* would have attempted to save me themselves? Or at least stayed in Pittsburgh long enough to see if I would be rescued?"

"That was my father's way," Tommy said. "To be separate and above. He saw people as things to be used and abused however he wished. He was more careful with his weapons than he was with any of us."

She leaned forward to rest her cheek against his head. "I used to hate my parents. I thought they were evil." She gave a breathless laugh. "I did not know true evil. I am starting to realize that they were simply clueless and lost, as I am now. My grandparents were all rescued out of the Skin Clan nurseries and transformed to *domana* to fight their creators. They knew nothing of raising children. Neither my parents nor I could learn how to do it except by avoiding their mistakes."

All that Tommy knew about love came from his mother and aunts. He had always respected their strength to raise their children right despite the horror of their situation. He'd never considered it was because they themselves had benefitted from a loving home.

"I want to learn how to raise children properly," Jewel Tear whispered.

It was an odd goal but Jewel Tear had suffered so much, perhaps it was one that seemed obtainable after all the defeats.

Somehow Mokoto and Knickknack had been roped into shifting the children back to their rooms. It was not going well, because while Knickknack was human and fair-skinned, he was tall and male. That was enough in the children's minds to make him terrifying. The kids were running and screaming up and down the hallway as Knickknack tried to both corral them into their rooms and back away from the situation at the same time.

"Tommy!" Knickknack said, sounding slightly panicked. "I'm sorry! I'm really sorry."

"What did you do?" Tommy growled.

The boy burned red with embarrassment but plowed on with his apology. "In the last few months—since Mokoto told me that you're his...you know...p. i. m. p.... I've thought and said a lot of nasty things about you. I didn't know about all this." He waved at the chaos around him. "But it was stupid of me not to look at the evidence and see that everyone in your family were working together to protect each other. I mean...I was there, night after night, on Liberty Avenue. I could see Mokoto and Babe calling the shots. When to leave. When to stay. Which johns could be trusted and which ones couldn't. The few times you showed up, none of your family were frightened of you. If I had just opened my eyes, I would have seen that they all acted like you were a white knight riding in to save them but I just ignored that because it didn't fit into my head canon as to what was going on."

Tommy wasn't sure what the boy wanted out of him. To say that it was fine that the boy was a total idiot?

The children saved Tommy having to answer by running to him, crying. "Tommy, save us!" "Tommy! Save us from the oni!" "He's going to eat us!"

"He is not an oni, he's just tall." Tommy knelt, since the little ones were like kittens—they would scramble up the nearest adult when frightened. Some had sharp claws. Two even had cat ears, though not from his father.

They huddled against him, staring at Knickknack.

"If he was an oni," Tommy said, "then Mokoto would have killed him. Okay? Now, this nice lady is Jewel Tear. She's an elf, not an oni."

"Do elves eat people too?"

"No, elves do not eat people," Tommy said.

"Why do they keep saying that?" Knickknack whispered to Mokoto. "The oni don't...do they?"

"Some do," Mokoto whispered back. "The true bloods don't. They're not much different from humans or elves. But the lesser bloods...some of them are basically wild animals that walk upright and talk. They eat anything weaker than them."

Tommy ignored them, focusing on introducing Jewel Tear to

the children. "I want you to be nice to her. She needs to learn how to speak English. Can you teach her?'

Luckily the elevator dinged, announcing Kiki with a little cart of food. The ones with cat ears tilted up their heads and sniffed.

"Pork buns and egg drop soup!" they identified the incoming dishes.

"Knickknack, you're fairly good with Elvish." Mokoto nudged the boy. "Help Jewel Tear out."

The boy went wide-eyed with surprise. "Me? Sure! I've been dying to talk magic to a *domana!*"

"What was the fire that you were putting out?" Tommy asked once he and Mokoto were alone in the suddenly quiet hallway.

"When we were working on the backup generator, Knickknack found out that our electricity was patched into a building across the street. Basically, we were stealing power."

Tommy had been afraid that the power situation was something sketchy like that. The only good thing was that it seemed more likely that the greater bloods had abandoned the building completely if they weren't paying for the electricity.

"Why is she here?" Mokoto asked, pointing toward the kids' rooms.

"She needs a room."

Mokoto gave Tommy a long look that he didn't recognize. Was that anger or contempt or just worry? Maybe a mix of all three?

"I'll explain better when there's time," Tommy said. "She can't pay for a room so she's going to help out with the little ones for now since we're short adults."

"She's going to be a guest?" Mokoto asked slowly.

"Yes," Tommy said.

"So we're staying?" Mokoto said.

"Tinker has to pull off a win, Oilcan needs to stay alive, and we have to keep the electricity on—but yes."

Mokoto hopped up and down with rarely seen happiness. "Yes!"

28: FORGING NEW TIES

The storm tapered off as the twins arrived in Oakland on the back of hoverbikes. The heavy rain became a light drizzle. The streetlights flickered on, announcing the restoration of power. The gunfire had died down, although the smell of gun smoke still hung heavy in the air. Team Tinker wove through haphazardly parked pickup trucks and barricades made of rubble. In every hidden nook and cranny, wounded sheltered in little dioramas of pain and loss.

The hoverbikes split into two groups without a word being spoken between the adults. Axe Man and Gaddy headed into the night with wounded Law Monroe in the sidecar. The three hoverbikes with the twins and Crow Boy turned down a dark and spooky back alley behind some demolished buildings. Louise squeaked in alarmed.

"They're taking Law to Mercy Hospital," Abbey said. "The human doctors won't help your tengu friend but Moser's people should be able to patch him up."

Crow Boy was pale and quiet on the back of Tate's hoverbike. His bandages were alarmingly bloody. But then again, any amount of blood would be alarming. It seemed as if his bleeding had stopped, so he was in no danger of dying from blood loss, but his wounds still needed to be cleaned to prevent infection.

"We can take care of him," Jillian said with more confidence than Louise felt.

Abbey stopped at a big ironwood gate in the middle of the otherwise deserted back alley.

The twins had watched a video covering the invention of the hoverbikes—on another world, in what now seemed another life. Abbey had been in the background as part of Team Tinker, packing up after the races. Despite the fact Abbey had never been named in the documentary, the obvious friendship between the woman and Tinker made Louise feel safer being with Abbey.

"This is Oilcan's place." Abbey pushed the button on a wireless doorbell beside the gate. "I came to the back because there's so much chaos in the front. I'm not sure I could get them to open the other gate to let you in."

Louise hovered close as Tate got Crow Boy off their bike. Louise wanted to help but she knew from experience how difficult it was for the twins to move the taller, heavier boy when he was wounded.

Joy had been coiled around Louise's neck the entire trip. As they dismounted the hoverbikes, the little dragon stirred, sniffed dismissively at Crow Boy and suddenly vanished.

"Where do you think she went?" Jillian whispered.

"Maybe to go check on the babies," Louise guessed, and wondered if this guess was guided by her ability to see the future. How would she ever know when she was right and when she was just blindly guessing? It seemed dangerously easy to think all her guesses were right.

"Who's there?" came a frightened-sounding call from the other side of the wooden back gate.

"It's Abbey Rhode of Team Tinker!" Abbey called in English and then switched to Elvish. "Five flat cream puffs on a flat cream puff dish."

"What?" Louise asked.

"It's a password," Abbey said, shrugging. "I don't think it's supposed to make sense."

A spyhole opened, blue eyes looked out. "What's up, Abbey?"

"Oilcan sent these three with me, Floss," Abbey said in English. "The boy is hurt. They need to be washed, bandaged, given dry clothes, and something warm to eat."

"Oh! We didn't expect the children back so soon!" The spyhole shut again. A moment later the gate latch was drawn and the gate was opened only wide enough for a person to slip through.

"Hurry, the *indi* are out of their pen. I was trying to catch them to put them back in."

Louise and Jillian helped Crow Boy through the gate.

Floss was wearing a big straw cone hat and a straw cape that came down to her knees. Her black hair was braided into two long pigtails. The *indi* were lambs with coal-black faces and pure white coats of fluffiness. They were utterly adorable. They bounced around Floss, trying to take bites out of her cape.

"No, no, do not eat my cape!" Floss said in Elvish as she rattled a pail of dried corn that she was carrying. "If you go back into your pen, I will feed you."

Louise realized that the female was an elf. A real-live elf with pointy ears and everything. After latching the back gate, Floss lured the lambs to a little wooden shelter. There she locked the *indi* in with a gloating "Hee-hee-hee."

The twins followed with Crow Boy between them.

There were more elves in the big industrial kitchen. A pot of pork stew sat on the range and the females were taking fresh loaves of bread from the ovens so the place was warm, cozy, and smelling wonderful.

There was also a pair of calico kittens playing underfoot.

So much goodness in one space.

All three female elves were tall and willowy with long black hair. It meant that they were Wind Clan. Floss had a rustic feel about her but it could just be her pigtails and straw cape. The other two females seemed trendier, wearing stylish human clothes and with their hair woven into elaborate braids. The one wearing a Naekanian band T-shirt and blue jean short shorts seemed vaguely familiar. Being these were the first elves that the twins had ever met, it seemed impossible that they actually knew her.

"Who-who-who is this?" the vaguely familiar female asked while wiggling her finger back and forth between Louise and Jillian.

"They are Oilcan's kids, are they not, Briar Rose?" Floss said as she took off her straw hat. "Abbey brought them. They are the Stone Clan—oh, wait... they are not elves."

"They... they are Tinker!" Briar Rose whispered.

"We're Tinker's little sisters," Jillian said as the twins guided Crow Boy to a chair. "I'm Jillian."

"I'm Louise," she introduced herself. "He's with us. He's been hurt. We need to clean his wounds, rebandage them, and then cast a healing spell on him."

"I did not think Tinker *domi* had little sisters," the third female said quietly.

"It is Tinker we are talking about," Briar Rose said. "Anything is possible."

The three females gave their anglicized names of Briar Rose, Floss Flower, and Cat Dancing. Briar Rose seemed to be the one in charge. The elves could speak some English, so the conversation flowed in and out of the two languages.

Jillian gave a sanitized explanation of their presence as the females helped strip Crow Boy of his rain-soaked and bloody clothes.

"We don't have to take *all* his clothes off," Louise squeaked, turning around as the elves relieved Crow Boy of his pants.

"Humans and their fear of nakedness." Briar Rose shook her head. "There—a dry towel about his hips, and it is like he is wearing shorts."

"It's fine," Crow Boy murmured as they added a blanket wrapped around his shoulders even though he burned red with embarrassment. "They took off all my clothes at the Children's Hospital when my leg was broken."

The twins weren't in the same room at that time, but he had a point.

Crow Boy made faces as Louise and the elves cleaned his wounds. Louise couldn't tell if it was because the cleaning hurt or because Jillian was skirting close to outright lying to the elves as she explained that they were born on Earth, captured by the oni, escaped with the help of Crow Boy, and found their way to Elfhome.

"Ah, that explains so much!" Briar Rose said. "I have known Tinker and Oilcan for *nae hae* and they never mentioned you two."

Once the many thin slices to Crow Boy's arms and legs had been rebandaged, Louise dug out their printed spells. The healing ones used a sticky film that adhered to the skin. She pressed it to his upper arm and activated it.

"We might be able to find *saijin* to make it hurt less," Briar Rose said.

Crow Boy shook his head, "I do not wish to be drugged, especially not on a night like this. I will endure this."

There was a little restroom off the kitchen. While Cat Dancing ran warm soapy water in the sink for the twins to clean up with, Briar Rose slipped away to fetch them dry clothing. She came back with extra-large men's shirts that came down to the twin's knees.

"Naekanain band shirts?" Louise said in surprise as she tented hers out to examine the logo.

"Oilcan is opening a night club in the gym," Briar Rose said as she handed Crow Boy one of the shirts. "We are going to sell band merchandise on the side, so we moved all our stock up to here."

"Wait, Briar Rose? Naekanain?" Louise said. The sense that Briar Rose was familiar suddenly clicked. The twins spent untold nights looking at the few photos available of their favorite Pittsburgh band while listening to their albums on repeat. "Are you the lead vocal for Naekanain?"

Briar Rose grinned hugely. "Yes, I am."

"You live here with Oilcan?" Jillian asked with wide-eyed amazement.

The elves laughed.

"No, we do not," Cat Dancing said, waving off in the distance. "We live in the Strip District with Moser and the others. Our place does not have any magical defenses and only a handful of our people have weapons and know how to fight."

"We were too close to the front, so we came up here to hide," Floss Flower said. "Moser, Snapdragon, and the others who know how to fight are out fighting."

"After this, I'm having Moser teach me how to shoot." Briar Rose pretended that her right hand was a pistol and shot it. She finished by blowing across the finger muzzle.

"The other enclaves are full up because of the Harbingers," Cat Dancing said. "But also because we're a household of outcasts. We all came to Pittsburgh looking for a life that we could not live in the Easternlands. We thought that if we could get to Pittsburgh the households here would overlook our oddities and allow us to be who we wanted to be—but they wanted us to fit into the same narrow slot that our parents expected us to fill. So we drifted out into the city and teamed up with humans to survive."

"Oh, that is so sad, leaving your family like that only to get rejected," Louise said.

"We have made a new family here," Briar Rose said. "One that lets us be who we want to be. Our people might not accept us but the humans have."

Floss Flower nodded in agreement.

"Life would be easier if we were proper Beholden to Windwolf," Cat Dancing muttered darkly.

"We can see if we can make a pact with Tinker or Oilcan once things have quieted down," Briar Rose said. "We might even be able to talk to Windwolf now that Sparrow isn't running interference."

They served up bowls of stew and fresh warm bread and hot tea sweetened with honey. The twins hadn't had anything to eat since their bento brunch. The food tasted heavenly. One of the calico kittens climbed into Louise's lap and begged for meat. She knew that she shouldn't encourage such behavior but she fed it a piece of pork anyhow. Crow Boy ate slower and slower, wincing in pain every time he moved his right arm. After the last spoonful, he pushed away the bowl and laid his head on the table.

"We should get you settled down for the night," Briar Rose said. "If Oilcan was here, he would probably have put you up on the third floor. We are avoiding going upstairs, though, so you can crash with us in the gym."

"What's wrong with upstairs?" Crow Boy asked groggily.

"There are five very-freaked-out Stone Clan *sekasha* up there," Cat Dancing whispered in English. "They are all kinds of dangerous. We are trying to stay out of their way until they calm down."

"Forge is back awake, so that should be soon," Briar Rose said.

"Forge?" Louise echoed. "Our grandfather?"

The tengu at Haven had told them about Forge. Jillian's eyes went wide at the idea of meeting him. They had never had a real grandfather before.

The elves exchanged worried looks.

"He should be told," Cat Dancing whispered.

"Oilcan or Tinker should be the one who tells him," Briar Rose whispered firmly. "Otherwise he might think that they were lying to him when they really just did not know."

"The holy ones might think we are hiding them, though," Floss Flower whispered.

"He is up there doing wood sprite stuff," Briar Rose whispered. "When Tinker gets that way, it is like she has blinders on."

"What kind of wood sprite stuff?" Jillian asked.

"Who knows?" Briar Rose said. "He came down asking for paper and grease pens and other magical supplies in bulk. His people do not know the area, so he asked for us to do the fetch-and-carry. Maya is out getting them now."

Another name that Louise recognized. "Maya? Maya Hayes? Your keyboard player?"

"Yes, all the band members but Oilcan live at our place," Briar Rose said. "In all honesty, Oilcan and Moser started the band together but Oilcan has never liked the attention of being 'officially' part of it. He writes many of our songs under the name Orphan instead of using his own. He does not always play with us and when he does, he considers himself backup guitar."

That would explain why neither "Oilcan" nor "Orville Wright" had been on any of the albums' liner notes. They had noticed the name Orphan but thought the songsmith was an elf.

There was a ringing of a bell and a light went on over a sign that had BACK GATE labeled.

"That is probably Maya." Briar Rose made a shooing motion to Floss Flower, who put on her straw hat again.

A minute later, the undeniable Maya Hayes joined them in the kitchen. The band photos hadn't done her justice. She was a tall African-American woman with amazing espresso-brown skin and perfect teeth. Her black hair spilled down over her shoulders in ringlets. "Oh, geez, what a night! Everyone running around with guns, looking for something to shoot!"

"Did you find everything?" Cat Dancing asked.

"Yes!" Maya picked up a towel to dry her hair. "I had to track down my friend who's a grad student at Pitt for Magical Studies and we went over to her department's lab and ransacked the place. She really, really wanted to meet Forge and talk magic but I managed to convince her that today was not the day. I promised that if she couldn't get to talk to Forge she could have time with Oilcan. I really hope Oilcan is okay with that."

"He probably is," Briar Rose said.

Maya pulled off her rain poncho to take off a large backpack. "Barring that, she'll take time with a dragon—any dragon that won't eat her. I was willing to promise her the moon at that point but I'm not sure how I would deliver on a dragon, so I hope Oilcan comes through. Holy hell! Who are these two?"

She had looked up and saw the twins for the first time.

"I'm Jillian and this is my twin, Louise. We're Tinker's little sisters," Jillian introduced them as Louise eyed the things that Maya was taking out of her backpack. They were all supplies for casting magic.

"Those are for Forge?" Louise said. "Can we take them up to him?"

The adults—elves and human alike—all froze in surprise.

"I suppose it would be okay," Briar Rose said after a minute of silence. "His gossamer left, so he cannot take them and run."

"Poppymeadows said that he promised Tinker not to pull any more bullshit," Cat Dancing said.

"They should not be repeating private conversations like that," Floss Flower muttered.

Cat Dancing shrugged. "A lot of people were mad at Forge. Poppymeadows probably all thought that the information would help still the turbulent waters."

Louise realized that they were talking about a collection of elves who lived at the enclave, not an individual person. She glanced to see what Crow Boy thought but he'd fallen asleep, head down on the table.

"Good!" Jillian said as if a decision had been reached. She picked up as much as she could carry. "Forge is up on the third floor?"

"Second floor," Briar Rose said as Louise gathered up the rest of the supplies. "Go loud and noisy so his people know you're coming."

Once the twins left the kitchen, it became obvious that the building had once been a school. They went through a cafeteria filled with battered secondhand tables surrounded by mismatched chairs. In the front hall, there was a big staircase leading up to the second floor and third floor.

"Are you sure about this?" Jillian asked quietly.

"You said that there were only two shields that went up," Louise whispered. "Tinker's and Oilcan's. It means Forge was hit by the oni spell—and so were Windwolf and Prince True Flame. Forge is probably trying to figure out a counter-spell without knowing anything about the original spell that hit him. We have the Codex—which has all of Unbounded Brilliance's research on it—and the knowledge of quantum physics. The power is back on, which means we can connect with everything we left up and running at Haven. I think we're ethically bound to talk to Forge."

"I suppose if you put it that way, yes."

They stomped as loud as they could, calling, "Hello? We've got supplies! Hello?"

Oilcan had had two brown-skinned *sekasha* with him but the surprise of seeing elves who looked like them had been lost in all the overwhelming horror of combat. Up to today, they had thought all elves were tall and pale. The sole exception had been the youngest of Windwolf's *sekasha*, Pony. They only found a handful of pictures of him. His hair was black as all the others' and his skin was tan, hardly what you would call brown.

A male *sekasha* appeared at the landing of the second floor. He was noticeably shorter than any other elf that they had seen pictures of and even the females in the kitchen. His skin was darker than the twins' almond brown. His stern eyes were dark and his hair was a rich warm brown.

"You do not need to be that loud..." he started to say but then froze, mouth open. After a full minute, he backed up, staring. *"Domou?"*

That got another four *sekasha* to the landing, hands on swords, faces grim. They too looked surprised and dismayed for a moment and then set their faces to completely neutral. At least they dropped their hands.

"Who is it?" a male voice called as a second wave of elves arrived, these being noncombatants without weapons or armor.

Forge didn't look like a grandfather. He seemed too young, only slightly older than their dad had been. He looked like a middle-aged version of Oilcan. He was a shade stockier. A shade more brown. A shade more hair, as he had his dark brown hair up in a messy manbun. The lines on his face were more from laughing and grief than age. He wore a black apron over a white silk shirt and doeskin pants.

He stared at them, blinking in confusion. "I do not understand. They said there were not any more..."

"It's complicated," Jillian said, handing over the supplies that she was carrying to one of the noncombatants standing beside Forge.

"We were born on Earth." Louise gave her armful to another

underling. "Our mother and father—" She should have let Jillian repeat the story that she crafted in the kitchen. Louise didn't mean to start down that painful road. The words spilled out of her mouth and now needed to be explained. Somehow it felt important to continue walking that path. He needed to know what they'd been through. "Our mother and father were killed after Heaven's Blessing found out about us. He captured us and... he held us prisoner. But we escaped with the help of the tengu. We didn't arrive on Elfhome until a little while ago. Tinker and Oilcan didn't know about us until today."

"Oh, little ones!" he murmured from the heart and sank down to his knees. "I am so sorry for your loss. How glad I am that you managed to escape and find your way here."

Jillian sniffed back tears. "Honestly, I'm thinking we should maybe hide until everyone has been told about us. It's getting a little stressful having to explain over and over again about... *everything*."

Jillian's voice broke and honest tears started to flow unchecked. It made tears well up in Louise's eyes, burning like liquid fire.

"There, there, little ones, you are safe in this place." He gathered them into a hug. "This enclave has strong defenses and we will let no one harm you."

Forge smelled a lot like their dad's Old Spice with musk and cedarwood and notes of spices. It was close enough that something broke within Louise. It felt like a solid wall that she'd built up against all her fear during the day cracked and then started to crumble. She started to cry.

"It hurts to let it out, but it hurts more to keep it in," Forge murmured. "Cry all you need."

29: THE BATTLE BUT NOT THE WAR

His beloved had stopped fighting.

Wolf searched Oakland, worried as the night was still and quiet except for the distant crack of rifles. There were no calls to the Spell Stones. No shields. No flame strikes. Why had she stopped fighting? With all the warrior monks from High Meadow Temple in the city, he couldn't even pick out her Hand by their shields.

Everyone that he stopped and questioned sung her praises. She had been clever and fierce and unrelenting. Only they couldn't tell him where she was currently. They finally mentioned that she'd been with one of Forge's Hands, which let him track her by the unique mix of Wind Clan and Stone Clan shields collected into one tight knot.

Wolf found his beloved wrapped in a wool cloak, tucked into a sheltered entryway, being forced to drink hot tea. Little Horse and Discord were acting as shields as the rest of her people and Forge's First Hand stood guard as blades.

"They're getting away," Tinker was complaining. "Besides, I don't like hot tea. I only tolerate it as a medium for honey."

"The oni troops are too scattered for you to be effective," Little Horse murmured. "And Lemonseed knows how you like your tea. She has put honey in it."

Discord was more harsh. "You're about to go face down on the pavement. You still have not fully recovered from breaking your arm, you are dangerously chilled, and you had almost no sleep last night."

"Pfft, sleep is overrated," Tinker complained. "I bet the oni don't sleep."

"*Domou*," Cloudwalker said quietly to alert the others.

"*Domou?*" Tinker echoed, looking up in confusion. When she spotted Wolf, she gave a wordless cry. Hot tea, entangled cloak, and her own exhaustion forgotten, she tried to fling herself toward him.

Her Hand caught the teacup, the cloak, and their *domi* before all could end up on the ground.

Wolf swept her up and hugged her tightly, marveling at how small and fragile she felt. She'd taken on multiple horrors and a full army almost single-handedly. How could someone so tiny be so fierce?

"I was so worried!" she cried again and again, hugging him tightly. "I was so worried!"

"I was worried too," he admitted. "We left you all alone."

"I wanted to go to you but I needed to stay."

"You did well," he said. "I'm proud of you."

But he was still worried. Her Hand was correct in their assessment. She was soaked to the bone and shivering. Huddling in this damp, cold entryway was dangerous to her health.

"I was so scared," she whispered. "And angry. Mostly angry. But I was angry because I was scared."

He had to smile. That was his *domi*—fiercely protective of even a wounded stranger dropped into her lap. "I have been told by many of my teachers that that is the way of war. To be frightened for the things you hold dear. To be angry at those who threaten them."

She pressed a tear-stained face against his neck. "I don't know why I'm crying. I'm so happy that you're here. Safe. Unhurt. You are unhurt—right?"

"Yes, I am unhurt."

"I was afraid that I was going to lose you. Lose Oilcan. Lose everyone."

"It is over. We have weathered the worst of the storm." At least, he hoped this was the worst. Oakland was safe at the moment but his East Coast holdings might be under attack.

"What's our plan now?" Tinker asked. "Chase down the oni in the city?"

"No. We need to check the distant voices." Wolf headed toward a Rolls-Royce that he'd spotted earlier. Tinker must have abandoned it at some point. He was aware that the *sekasha* had spread out around them, keeping close enough to shield them but far enough out that there was an illusion of privacy. "We must see if there is news of an attack on our East Coast holdings. If not, we need to warn them that an attack is possible. I need to find out how my siblings fared during this, especially Starlight and Charcoal, who are at Aum Renau. Neither one of them is a fighter and the logical move for the oni is to take out the Spell Stones so that even if the queen sends reinforcements, the incoming *domana* will still be helpless."

"You're going to Aum Renau?" Tinker said, worry in her voice.

"As soon as I can. Not tonight, as our forces are scattered and in chaos. Tomorrow afternoon at the latest."

"Because Oilcan and I can protect the city?" she said quietly.

"I am sorry," he said. "I never meant it to go this way. I never wanted you to have to fight."

"I don't think you really had any choice in the matter," she said. "Between Vision, Pure Radiance, and my own stubbornness, it's all kind of beyond your control."

"Vision?" he said with surprise as the female was nearly mythical, born and vanished prior to the start of the Rebellion.

Tinker explained that the legendary female had been hiding in Pittsburgh, raising wood sprites and planning who knew what. "She gave me this riddle or clue or perhaps just a major distraction in the form of a chessboard set up with a Queen's Gambit. I think she wants me to do something—but I don't know what. I don't even understand what she's trying to accomplish. If the Skin Clan were hiding out on Earth for a thousand years or more, she probably could have taken them out without them even realizing she was there. And there's the whole thing about Dufae's box with the baby dragons inside the magical traps. Why didn't she find and open it? Why did she let the Skin Clan have it? It's not because she wants them back in power—she hates them with a passion. I think she's merely using them as a tool to make some change to the elves. Maybe she just wants to get rid of all the *domana*—she seems to think they're just as bad as the Skin Clan. But if it was as simple as all that, then what did she need me for? Why babysit generations of wood sprites and then try to keep me from falling under Pure Radiance's influence? And the lies she told me all of my life! What's that all about?" She dropped her head wearily on his shoulder. "It makes my head hurt trying to figure her out."

He paused to consider the question. He'd had to deal with Pure Radiance's odd directives his entire life. His parents' marriage and his nine siblings were all under her orders. She had foreseen that Pittsburgh would arrive deep in the virgin forest of an undefended continent, bringing the Skin Clan. He knew that he'd been born a tool to block the invasion.

Tinker's father had been the one who created the gate that delivered the city.

Wolf started to walk again. It could not be a coincidence. Vision raised generations of wood sprites until one created a gate to link the worlds. If she truly hated the Skin Clan, then why would she do such a thing? And why would she try to keep Pure Radiance from using Tinker to block the Skin Clan's attempts to take back the world?

Tinker had undone her father's work—which was done under Vision's guidance.

At the end of the first Oni War, Pure Radiance had directed all known gates between Earth and Elfhome be pulled down.

What if what Vision wanted was continuous contact between humans and elves?

All the elves within Pittsburgh were remarkably different from those who lived in his East Coast holdings. They were changed by their constant exposure to humans: Discord with her short blue hair and passion for all things human. Little Horse and Cloudwalker learning to drive the Rolls-Royce automobiles. Rainlily showing up on Discord's hoverbike, wearing blue jeans. Lightning Strikes had taken a human lover and fathered Blue Sky.

Dozens of elves were living with humans instead of in the enclaves—not that he had been aware of it until Sparrow was killed. From what he'd been able to gather since then, the outliers were elves who didn't fit into normal elfin society. There was no place for them except among the humans.

"You do not ask a child when he wants to go to bed," Wolf said.

"Hmm?" Tinker said.

"My mother loved babies but once they started to be able to talk back, she was more than happy for others to step in. In many ways, I'm much more Otter Dance's son than my mother's because of all the hours I spent with her, learning to fight. My training started before I could even walk by learning how to tumble without hurting myself. Otter Dance has always been leery of Pure Radiance. It was a caution that she had learned from both her father, Tempered Steel, and her mother, Perfection. By rights, the *sekasha* should rule us as they are the ones most holy—but they do not trust themselves. They know that the world is filled with shades of gray that they cannot see."

"They don't see gray?"

He was explaining this badly. "Morally speaking, no. The *sekasha* sees that, in every conflict, there is only right or wrong. They understand, however, that the world is more complicated than that. The *domana* have a better grasp of the grayness of morality. That there is sometimes no right answer and that the best you can do is the lesser of evils."

"Okay. What does this have to do with bedtimes?"

"There are certain traditions we follow that Tempered Steel has always complained against. One of them was the naming of children. There were others who he thought were wrong, such as the work appropriate for various castes. Some were in place prior to the start of the Rebellion. Others were developed while we were fighting to be free, and never revised. He approached the crown, asking for widespread reform. In the end, he had to choose only one—the banning of spell working—and appealed to his fellow *sekasha* whom Pure Radiance could not fully control."

"The evil lies with us, not the magic." Tinker paraphrased Tempered Steel's famous argument.

"Yes. When he first approached the crown, Pure Radiance blocked his reform proposal, saying that 'You do not ask a child when he wants to go to bed.' He was not swayed by this, saying that you teach a child wisely but in the end, step away and let it be guided by its training and its own heart. This is why the *sekasha* are by blood and sword. Yes, they were set upon their path by birth, but they must show that they understand what it is to be a *sekasha* and the desire to continue that path."

"They win their sword at a hundred," Tinker said.

"Yes, if they chose to fight in order to continue being one of the holy. If they decide not to try for their sword, then they are allowed to walk away from the path of the holy. I thought that Discord had always felt pressured to take the path of one of her parents. At first, she was sure that she needed to train as one of her mother's caste. Later, she chose her father's path. But was it truly right for her?

"In the Easternlands, there was no other road for her to follow. It did not exist. Within the cities, *laedin* are responsible for most duties that require knowledge of combat. No one would employ a *sekasha*. Those of the blood but not of the sword are considered flawed. They could live within the temples but always be looked down upon by the warrior monks. They end up in isolated areas, filling in where there is a need. Patrolling remote roads. Guiding pilgrims to mountain temples. Herding livestock to high summer pastures. It is an aimless life, drifting at the edge of society, one step away from being hermits. In Pittsburgh, there are no traditions that would lock Discord into one path. There was the freedom to make a road where there hadn't been one before. I urged her to explore different lifestyles. For a decade, she did."

"So Vision might be trying to dismantle the traditions that tie people into preordained paths?"

"I cannot say for certain but it seems to me there are vast changes to our people that Pure Radiance has not been willing to allow. I think I understand the problem because unlike other *domana*, I've always been given multiple paths to choose from. Will I be Wind Clan or Fire Clan? Do I chase the grandeur of my name? Even the choice of who I would take as my *domi* was never clear cut. I had freedom to choose anyone."

"I'm still amazed you chose me."

"You are the most extraordinary person I have ever met." He pressed his forehead to hers. "Time and time again you have done the utterly impossible. You amaze me constantly. I could not imagine anyone better suited for my life than you."

"Hmm, flattery will get you everywhere," she murmured and kissed him. "Why does it feel so comforting to be held by you? It's like you're emitting this wonderful drug that makes me feel so relaxed and peaceful."

"I think that is love," he said. "Because I feel it too. It is very nice after being so afraid of losing everything."

There were messages from all his East Coast holdings at Poppymeadows. All his siblings had dropped unconscious, triggering frantic queries to him and to the other holdings, which were automatically copied to him. No one on the East Coast knew of the spells to revive someone in the deep sleep after transformation. All his siblings were still asleep.

"Oh, this sucks," Tinker whispered, reading the messages with him.

"No word yet of an attack." Wolf tried to stay positive. "You should prepare yourself for tomorrow—it promises to be grueling. Take a hot bath. Eat. Sleep."

"Bath? Sleep?" Tinker complained. "Okay, a hot bath would be lovely but it doesn't seem right to sleep."

"There's nothing you can do now," Wolf said. "The trains are still tied up rescuing the royal marines and the Wyverns that stayed to support them. True Flame is awake but barely able to stand. All our people are exhausted, soaked to the bone, and scattered across the city. We cannot rush off either—not without food, water, and supplies. That way is insanity. It will take time to organize. If you push yourself to collapse, you will not be able to function tomorrow. The first rule of warfare as a *domana* is to stay alive."

She seemed to shrink smaller, as if she'd been held up by sheer anger and determination. "Being a *domana* sucks sometimes."

He felt a stab of guilt as he was the one who'd made her *domana*.

She kissed him and then let her Hand carry her off to the bathhouse.

"That applies to you too," Wraith Arrow murmured once they were alone.

"I'll eat and change to dry clothes," Wolf stated. "After that, I need to do what I can to make sure that Oakland is safe."

30: A HARD DAY'S NIGHT

It had been a long, hard day for Oilcan, starting with four talking mice and ending with a fight with his cousin's aunts. He felt battered and bruised in body and soul and chilled to the bone. He called Guy Kryskill as he wearily made his way to the gym's locker room, which was the only place in Sacred Heart with working showers.

"Everything's fine here!" Guy half-shouted over music playing in the background. He moved to someplace quieter to give a detailed report. "I started a fire in the fireplace, and broke out the camping equipment. We had chili out of cans, smores, and instant hot chocolate, which all went over big. Once the power came back on, I showed them the pinball machines and the jukebox. They're having a blast. Oh, and I called John Montana and let him know that Blue is safe with us."

"Oh, that's good," Oilcan said as he realized that he probably should let Tommy know that Spot was safe too. It sounded like Guy was pulling out all the stops to keep the other kids distracted. "How's Rebecca?"

"The spells that Thorne Scratch put on her worked amazing," Guy said. "She felt well enough to have some of the chili and then fell asleep on the couch."

"You're doing a great job, Guy," Oilcan said, painfully aware that it had been pure random chance that included Guy on the shopping trip. If Andy had had his pickup at Sacred Heart, Guy wouldn't have gotten involved. "Thank you for taking care of my kids."

"No problem," Guy said. "We have to stand together in fights like this."

"Things seem to have calmed down here," Oilcan said. "If things are still good tomorrow morning, you can bring the kids home."

"That's good news," Guy said.

Oilcan called Tommy to let him know about Spot. He woke the leader of the half-oni up for the second time in one day.

"I tracked down Jewel Tear," Tommy said sleepily. "She's pretty freaked out about not being able to cast magic. She's here at our place. She's going to be staying here, helping out with the little ones."

"Oh?" Oilcan hadn't heard that Jewel Tear had needed to be tracked down. He fumbled for the light switch for the locker room. "Okay. Thanks for taking care of her. Where is your new place?"

"William Freaking Penn Hotel," Tommy said. "Or I should say the new Chang enclave for humans, elves, and half-oni."

Oilcan laughed out of surprise. The William Penn Hotel? It made sense considering how many people Tommy had in his household. "Okay, I'll get Spot back home sometime tomorrow."

Oilcan stripped in the locker room, discovering mysterious bruises that he'd gathered during the day. Wrapping a towel around his waist, he padded to the gym's showers. He set the temperature to steaming hot, leaned wearily against the tile wall, and let the water pour down over him.

He hated the entire day. The images and sounds and feelings that he was never going to get out of his head: Rebecca lying wounded on the sidewalk with a flood of oni coming toward them. Ramming the sportscar with the flatbed. The wail of the horn after he reduced the car to crumpled metal. Seeing the rocket flying at Jane Kryskill and not being sure if he could save her. The knowledge that if he failed to kill the horror on the bridge it would plow through his friends. Finding the twins so small and terrified. The bloody tengu boy who could have been no more than thirteen or fourteen trying to protect them. Law lying unconscious and bleeding out. Danni falling to the ground, headless. He wished he could wash away the memories, the stark fear, and the hot rage. Especially the rage. He never wanted to grow into his father. His mother used to say that his father had once been a kind man but he allowed anger to become his default response to everything. The more his father let himself be angry, the greater his anger grew until he became a raging tornado of destruction. Until he killed everything that he cared about—his wife, the love of his child, his freedom.

Oilcan felt that monster rage while fighting. He hated it.

"That anger isn't a bad thing," Tommy told Oilcan after rescuing him. *"If I were you, I'd hold it tight and ride it, because you need it to be hard enough to do what needs to be done."*

What a razor's edge to walk.

"Domou?" Thorne Scratch called from the locker room door.

"In here!" Oilcan called back.

"I brought you clean clothes," she said as she came through the locker room.

She was naked when she joined him. He'd learned over the last few weeks that elves liked to share bathing. Being skin to skin was important to them. He'd started a true bathtub on the third floor but had been kidnapped before he could get it finished. The large shower room gave them space to be together, simply hugging each other, as the warmth washed over them.

He was glad that, while black and blue in numerous spots, she had no open wounds. She'd been so beautiful and fierce. She shouldn't have been fighting alone.

"When we last spoke about building my first Hand, I was reluctant," Oilcan said. "Today taught me much about grim reality. We needed Moon Dog. We were lucky he came with us."

Thorne Scratch nodded as she towel-dried her battered body. "Yes, the gods were kind to put him in our path."

"Do you think I should offer him Second?"

She lit up so much there was no mistaking her joy at the idea. But then, she caught herself and closed it down, hiding behind her warrior's mask. "That is between you and him."

Just a day or so ago—what seemed like a different life—Tinker had talked to him about her choosing which warriors she picked from Windwolf's four Hands. She had realized that Oilcan would need at least four more warriors. It was important, she said, that the members of a Hand were suited to each other for them to work as a unit.

"Does he ... fit ... with you?" Oilcan said.

She considered and then nodded. "Yes, I think we do. Nor is that surprising. Tempered Steel would only take one type of warrior as student: one who would be willing to walk his path, one who leads not to glory but to the adherence of a higher duty."

She ducked her head. "It is why I was considered dangerous to take into a Hand. With my cursed name and who I was trained by, I was the type that would cut down a *domana* who had strayed from the righteous."

She had beheaded Earth Son to keep him from killing the tengu who had been an important ally in the fight against Malice.

Oilcan felt he needed to make that right but didn't know how. He reached out and took her hand. She squeezed it tight, raised it up to kiss the back of his hand, and then pressed her cheek to his palm.

"In many ways, Moon Dog is like me," she said softly. "He will not shy away from a moral imperative. If he warns you, take heed."

"I will."

She whispered into his palm, "Are you sure this is what you want and not you attempting to make me happy?"

"Today, over and over again, I was glad that we had him with us," Oilcan said. "It made me realize the importance of having a full Hand. It seems stupid to ignore the perfect candidate right before me."

"The perfect ones are the dangerous ones," Thorne Scratch whispered.

She kissed his palm and let his hand drop. "That said, I am not totally sure he will say yes. I do not understand why he is in Pittsburgh. If he had been here merely to fight the oni, he would have gone with the warrior monks who accompanied the Harbingers. It almost seems that pure curiosity drives him and he was not aware that you have chosen to be Wind Clan. He still might not be aware."

"So make sure he's aware of that up front?"

She gave a small breathless laugh. "Yes, but I cannot advise you much more than that. He is a mystery to me."

They went in search of Moon Dog, starting in the kitchen as the rest of the building was dark and silent. The big industrial kitchen smelled of fresh-baked bread and was crowded with people. There were Moser and his household, half of Team Tinker, and a smattering of mutual friends of both groups. They went quiet as Oilcan came in, closely followed by Thorne Scratch.

"Something smells good," Oilcan said to break the silence.

"We've got meat!" Moser cried, throwing wide his arms. "You're eating with us!"

Oddly, it was the same thing that Moser said last time he saw him. Oilcan's stomach rumbled, reminding him that he hadn't had anything to eat since breakfast except the one half-abandoned ice cream cone.

"Sounds good," Oilcan said.

Everyone started to talk again as bowls of stew and slices of bread, still warm from the oven, were passed around. They spilled out into the dining room so that they could sit at tables like civilized people.

Moser settled across from Oilcan, flanked by Briar Rose, Geoffrey Kryskill, Snapdragon, Tenfold Clubs, and Gin Blossom. Jane Kryskill seemed to be commanding the militia, so Geoffrey was probably an officer in it too. The last three were all *laedin* caste, raised to be the foot soldiers of the elves. It seemed as if dinner was going to be a war council.

"Alton sold us a massive wild boar two days ago," Moser said, dunking his bread into the stew. "We just got done butchering it down and wet-aging it when the evacuation call came in, so we brought it with us, along with everything in baskets in our root cellar."

That would explain the thick-cut carrots and potatoes in the rich stew. Moser had an impressive block-long, walled-in garden in his backyard. The elf enclaves had similar setups. Oilcan was having trouble finding food. He was counting on Forge to bring in fresh produce during the winter. Fresh meat was going to require a different solution.

"Could you let Alton know that I'm interested in buying whatever he can provide?" Oilcan said. "I have cash to burn."

"Sure thing," Geoffrey said. "He can let the other foragers know that you're buying too."

Briar Rose updated Oilcan on who-all had taken refuge at Sacred Heart while he was out fighting. Briar had been acting as Oilcan's majordomo in his absence. It made sense since Oilcan had left with all the kids and Forge had sent most of his stonemasons to the Easternlands to gather supplies. Briar had made sure that everyone who had been allowed into the building was properly vetted, bandaged if needed, fed, and given a place to sleep.

The twins were on the third floor in elvish camping cots. (Oilcan wasn't sure how she wrangled cots but it seemed to involve shaming the other enclaves into not letting Tinker's little sisters sleep on the floor.) Moser's people and a select group of their trusted friends were in the gym in sleeping bags. Crow Boy had fallen asleep in the kitchen and been moved as gently as possible to the gym. Clothes had been provided for Bare Snow. She and Moon Dog had been settled on the second floor as proper "guests" of the enclave.

It meant that Moon Dog was probably already asleep. The conversation about offering him a place in Oilcan's Hand would have to wait until morning.

"We have set up a watch on the gates, so you do not need to worry about that," Tenfold Clubs said. "Get some sleep. You look like you are about to fall over. You need to attract some *laedin*, though, for the future."

Oilcan nodded. He couldn't expect the kids to protect the building.

"It should not be too hard to get some *laedin*," Snapdragon said. "There are always doubles reaching their majority and wanting something different from what they grew up with."

"They need to be able to fight," Moser said.

"Oh, not all want to drum like me!" Snapdragon drummed two spoons on the table. "Those born in cities like Court would like to hunt and forage but that's not possible in those areas. The land is tightly controlled by the *domana* other than their own."

Gin Blossom nodded. "And those who grew up in the countryside—like I did—usually just want to socialize with more than the handful of same old people that they grew up with. They head to the city while they are in their doubles, expecting to find a household there."

"Most households are not looking for more warriors," Snapdragon said. "In the city, out in the countryside, no one needs more *laedin*. Many of those who leave their birth household—either by choice or by need—find themselves homeless."

"We *sekasha* have the temples to take shelter in," Thorne

Scratch said, shaking her head. "The *laedin* have nothing. It is a growing problem."

"*Laedin* tend to be more prolific," Tenfold Clubs said. "There tends to be more of us than any other caste. Since we are warriors, we are considered expendable. When a household becomes overcrowded, the *laedin* children are the first ones driven out. My mother told me often as I grew up that she dearly loved me but that I would need to leave when I reached my majority."

"Most of the *laedin* here in Pittsburgh are from overcrowded households back in the Easternlands," Snapdragon said. "Windwolf put out a general call when he first founded Aum Renau that he and his Beholden needed *laedin*. That brought a flood of us to this side of the ocean. The first wave was picked up by Windwolf and his holdings on the East Coast, but not the later waves."

Tenfold shook his head. "That call was a century ago. We knew that chances were slim that we were still needed but we came anyhow."

"A few got lucky and got picked up by the enclaves on the Rim," Gin Blossom said. "Some headed back to the Easternlands on the next train. Some of us . . . well . . . drifted, kind of aimless, until we fell into something."

Tenfold shrugged. "It so happens that most of us who stayed were the ones who did not like fighting that much. We were looking for something else to do with our lives. Briar Rose has been teaching me gardening. Who would have thought?"

Snapdragon discovered that the stainless steel teapot in front of him could be used as a ride cymbal and wove it into his spoon drumming. "I talked with Jewel Tear's *laedin* before they fled back to the Easternlands. She had gathered the overspill from her parents' rural holdings. All big cities—Winter Court, Summer Court, Stone Haven—made her *laedin* nervous. Pittsburgh scared the living shit out of them."

"It is a lot to take in," Gin Blossom said. "I know it rattled me a lot when I first got here."

"With the war breaking out, more *laedin* might show up, hoping to be a replacement for someone killed in battle," Snapdragon said. "They will all be Wind Clan and will fit in with your neighbors."

"You could ask Forge to do a call out for Stone Clan," Gin Blossom said. "They will come in bigger numbers as they have not had anywhere to go before now. They might be desperate enough to change clans."

Briar Rose made a noise of disgust but didn't comment.

"Your best bet is to talk to Windwolf," Tenfold said. "He could make another general recruitment call. He will probably need to anyway, what with the battle in the forest, his holdings in the east might have taken a serious hit, and the *laedin* killed here in Pittsburgh the last few weeks."

"There is the royal marines," Thorne Scratch said, which earned her hard stares from across the table. "The Fire Clan has the only true standing army: it created a system to take their overflow of *laedin* and funnel them into royal barracks instead of households. Over the last thousand years, they have increased to a massive number. Tempered Steel expects the system to soon fail as it gives the marines no chance to opt out. They are next to slaves as they are now, barely educated past basic reading and writing."

"True," Snapdragon whispered, "but not a popular opinion to hold. It is not like the old days. They are well fed, never tortured or executed or forced to procreate, and are led by others of their kind."

"Does not make it right," Thorne Scratch said quietly. "But even Tempered Steel is not sure how to resolve the issue."

"There are thousands of marines in Pittsburgh right now," Moser said. "You could put out a call tomorrow."

All the *laedin* at their table shook their heads. "You need to be able to screen them. A *laedin* that is quick to anger or a bully in nature can be deadly—especially around those of other clans."

"I'll talk to Windwolf," Oilcan said since he didn't want to decide now. He was exhausted and raw from the day.

Briar Rose kicked Moser under the table.

Moser winced. "We were wondering: Considering how this year has been going...life would be easier if we were an official household."

"You're not official?" Oilcan asked. Moser and Briar Rose announced a few years ago that they considered their union a common law marriage. There was a party and everything. Elves didn't normally do marriages but Moser wanted to be sure that, in terms of human law, Briar Rose wouldn't be cheated out of anything if he died.

"We're not Beholden to a *domana*," Briar Rose said.

"Oh, oh, I see." Oilcan understood now where the conversation was going. He'd given Tommy—whom he barely knew but owed him his life—the protection of being a Beholden. Of course his close friends whom he'd known half his life would want the same. "Sure, we can work that out. I'm not sure what it requires other than us just saying 'yes' to it. So... Yes?"

"Yes!" Moser cried, throwing his hands up in the air.

Everyone in the room cheered. The elves were clearly ecstatic. The humans were happy because their friends were happy. It was not what Oilcan expected when he got up that morning, but considering all the day had held—the war, the fighting, the twins, the babies—it was a good thing.

31: STANDING DOWN

Since the moment that Jane had opened fire on the oni holding Boo captive at Sandcastle, she knew that she was in danger from the EIA. She'd killed an intelligent being. So many that she'd lost count. Yes, the elves would forgive her and even approve, but the United Nations had quietly changed the definition of "murder" within human laws. The wording now read "human, elf, or member of any yet unidentified sapient race." (Yes, she did discover the change afterward. No, it wouldn't have stopped her even if she knew beforehand.) Most likely the oni slipped the wording in just to tie the hands of humans. Many of her kills were head shots from a distance, so she couldn't claim self-defense. Worst of all, there been no formal declaration of war from any side.

Jane's team had nearly been arrested at Three Rivers Stadium after killing the *namazu* with her family's cannon. According to the EIA lieutenant who showed up with Sparrow and a Hand of Windwolf's *sekasha*, they had broken numerous human laws, starting with simply owning the cannon. What really put the lieutenant's nose out of joint was the fact that Jane had turned the first floor of the EIA's pristine crystal castle into so much broken glass. (She still wasn't sure what Director Maynard's take on the damage was, but he couldn't have been totally pleased.)

At the museum, Maynard would have arrested Jane's team except for the intervention of Queen Soulful Ember. He chose to accept their self-defense claim because only Jane was armed and the disguised oni warriors had opened fire on his men instead of surrendering. Since then, two NSA agents, Corg Durrack and Hannah Briggs, had acted as her unofficial overseers, checking in on her team often to make sure they weren't blowing up city landmarks. Jane doubted very much that the two weren't aware of her clandestine activities, but it was possible that they didn't feel the need to report them to Maynard. They were all about "truth, justice, and the American way," which included a heavily armed civilian population. The EIA was a United Nation organization. Jane suspected that the federal agents were willing to cooperate with the EIA—but only to a limit.

Jane had known when she started to build the militia in secret that she was heading for a confrontation with Director Maynard. It was said that Maynard had a strong sense of honor; it was why Windwolf demanded that Maynard head up the EIA after the treaty was signed. But Maynard would need to deal with the large percentage of humans who hadn't shown up to defend the city. Ambassadors. Embassy staff. Businessmen. Locals. All of them chafed at the restrictions that the elves had put on access to Elfhome's resources. All of them might believe that those restrictions would have been lifted by the oni. They might have even been promised peaceful trade for cooperation with the oni. They would want the letter of the law followed. They might demand that the militia be disbanded and its organizers punished.

She had known that, sooner or later, she was going to have to deal with Maynard. She just didn't want to deal with him first thing in the morning after the third-worst day of her life.

The night before, she had pulled the militia out as the royal marines flooded into Oakland. The chance for friendly fire from the elves was too high. There had already been a half dozen militia killed by the oni. All people she knew. All under thirty. Some of them had left spouses and children. All left family who would grieve them. Nearly a hundred more had been wounded, overflowing Mercy Hospital. The number of dead and wounded without Oilcan and Tinker fighting would have been staggering.

She and her team had retreated to WQED. Taggart, Nigel, and Hal had worked late into the night creating short news segments that would hopefully sway the people who thought that humans could stay neutral in the war. Each segment had two versions; one with Hal narrating and the other with captions explaining the action that could be used by the other television channels. They had also finished editing the footage for the *Monsters in Our Midst* episode on black willows.

Jane coordinated with her brothers and Yumiko. They pieced together what exactly had happened since the start of fighting. There had been a lot more going on in the city than she'd been aware of, some of it inexplicable, like Law Monroe spotting Kajo and a body double east of Oakland, Olive Branch charging back and forth across the city in a stolen truck, and Tinker's twin little sisters showing up at Allegheny Graveyard.

Around two in the morning, Jane and the men finished up their projects and slept on the floor in the Neighborhood of Make Believe studio. They woke up stiff and sore but glad to be alive. First order of business was to take Chesty out for a walk and to find something to eat. It was a typical autumn morning: chilly, clear pale sky, weak sun, colorful leaves drifting on a slight breeze. The Rim was surreal with barricades of debris, randomly parked vehicles of the wounded left abandoned, and the smell of gun smoke heavy in the air. Royal marines and EIA troops were scattered in pools of bright red and camouflage green.

Ellen's Tiny Deli was parked a block down from Poppymeadows, serving tea and breakfast to militia stragglers. She had eggs scrambled with roasted carrots and red peppers, fried onions, and goat cheese. She served them up with homemade wild boar bacon, sliced apples, and fresh biscuits.

"They all got turned around in the dark and rain." Ellen McMicking explained the stragglers to Jane. "They decided to hunker down under shelter instead of stumbling around lost. They've been trickling in since dawn."

"Thanks for taking care of them." Jane attempted to pay for their food.

"No, no, no," Ellen said. "Think of it as an early wedding present!"

Chesty rumbled a warning that someone was incoming with a weapon.

She didn't recognize Director Maynard at first. As a true military leader, he blended in with the other soldiers at the Rim, making him less of a sniper's target. He was in EIA combat gear instead of his typical elvish-styled flair. A Kevlar helmet made his long hair less noticeable. He had on a modular tactical vest instead of his normal elaborately embroidered waistcoat. His normal painted silk duster was missing. He carried a rifle with the ease of a soldier.

There was no missing, however, the intent on his face.

The first time they'd met at Sandcastle, he'd mostly ignored her, focusing instead on Nigel and Hal. He'd wanted a botanist to give him advice on the *namazu*. At the museum gunfight, he'd shifted to her as if he had guessed that she made the tactical decisions for the group. Today, he totally ignored the men.

"Ms. Kryskill," Maynard said in greeting. "We need to talk."

"Yes, I believe we do," Jane said, even though it was the last thing that she really wanted to do. Her mother would go on a rampage if Jane missed her own wedding because she was in jail.

"I had a long debriefing with Captain Josephson this morning," Maynard said. "If I understand him correctly, you're a close personal friend of Tinker *domi*?"

"I've known her for years," Tinker had said. *"I trust her completely."*

It hadn't been a surprising proclamation; Tinker was only ten when she met Roach, Geoffrey, and Andy. It was just a month or two after Boo's kidnapping. Jane's whole family had been extremely protective of the little orphan girl suddenly in their midst. They had given Tinker and Oilcan an open door to their homes and lives.

While it had only been two sentences spoken in the middle of a battlefield, it had acted like a blessing straight from God. Jane hadn't thought that its effects would last into the next day. She didn't trust it to last unless she was truthful about their relationship. (Especially with Hal nodding enthusiastically to the question.)

"Close friends? Me, personally? No. She's ten years younger than me. My entire family? Yes. My cousin is Team Tinker's business manager. Tinker and Oilcan have slept at my aunt's house more times than I could count. They've been over to my mom's place a couple of times. Tinker taught my little brother how to use magic and helped him build his carpenter's shop—which is just down the street from her scrapyard. The two are like extended family."

Maynard nodded slowly. "That would be enough for the elves, what with their households being mostly unrelated members acting as a family. Certainly they bent over backward to include her cousin into their clique. The humans...sometimes I wonder at the stupidity of the political beast."

Had all the politicians of Pittsburgh been raving at Maynard's doorstep since the fighting began?

"The existence of the militia has ruffled some feathers?" Jane guessed.

"The treaty limits the number and type of weapons..." Maynard started to quote law.

"Director Maynard, have you ever read over the actual Elvish version of the treaty? One that didn't come from Sparrow's hand?"

Director Maynard's eyes widened only slightly. He was probably good at poker. "Should I?"

"I would highly recommend it. The United Nations' English version has very bad translations of some keywords, especially in terms of what the elves consider 'natives.' Once you know that the elves meant to include humans born on Elfhome to be recognized as 'native' it becomes glaringly obvious. They would have used the word 'elves' otherwise—wouldn't they?"

He studied the boot toe that he ground against the pavement. "Sparrow was fluent in English, even more so than Windwolf at the time. She handled the translations of the paperwork. No humans knew Elvish yet. Since then, any human fluent in Elvish would have received an 'original' from Sparrow." He looked up sharply. "Where did you get a copy of the Elvish version?"

"My uncle saved one of Raisin Sauce's people from a saurus shortly after the first Shutdown." Jane waved toward Chesty. "He was given four elfhounds as a reward for his courage. He and his family have remained close with the entire enclave since then. I asked my uncle to see if he could get a copy from Raisin Sauce."

"But why did you even think to ask?"

"I guess Lieutenant Kukk didn't detail the discussion at the stadium after the *namazu* hunt. Dark Harvest said that the EIA misunderstood the terms of the treaty. I had reasons to suspect Sparrow's loyalty and that exchange got me wondering. It turns out that Windwolf personally gave each enclave an official copy. Raisin Sauce allowed us to take photos of his copy. Even before we started working with translators we knew we could trust, the differences were obvious. There are sections missing in the human versions. It seems that Sparrow left out pages that would have made the oni's invasion more difficult."

"Sparrow on one end, Chiyo on the other," Maynard said.

Taji Chiyo had been Maynard's administrative assistant who

had handled much of the paperwork on the EIA end, screening everything that he saw. She had been an oni lesser blood—a kitsune with the ability to read people's minds and create an illusion. Yumiko and the other *yamabushi* had been searching for the female since Tinker escaped from Lord Tomtom.

"I will have to get a new copy of the treaty from the Viceroy," Maynard said.

Jane would offer to email him a copy but it would be best that he secure a copy that he trusted completely to be authentic.

"Why didn't you let me know?" Maynard said.

"The work has been tedious and slow," she admitted. "It seemed fairly straightforward at first, but then we discovered that there is a fundamental translation discrepancy. The university-trained translators had been given different meanings to words in comparison to what locals had been taught in high school. Our teacher at Brashear was an elf who learned English in the Easternlands from elves that traded with England back in the time of Shakespeare. His day-to-day English had a lot of 'thee' and 'thou' thrown in. We thought at first that the differences in definitions were simply that English had changed in the last three hundred years. But then we discovered that Sparrow had been heavily involved in creating the Elvish coursework at Pitt. Even after we're done, someone is going to have to redo all our work to verify that Sparrow had deliberately sabotaged the Elvish language courses at Pitt—which is what all the Earth-based diplomats and businessmen use."

"God, what a nightmare," Maynard muttered softly.

"At that point we realized that it might seem as if we were purposely mistranslating the treaty. Certainly I don't see the university being quick to admit that everything it's taught for the last twenty years is wrong. It would be simpler for them to point fingers and say that we have a political agenda."

Maynard took out his phone and made notes on it. "For the time being, the less said about the militia, the better. I'll need time to get a correctly translated treaty that the political community can't deny."

Hal was going to be disappointed but Jane planned to stay out of the limelight as much as possible. According to Yumiko, Kajo wasn't among the known dead. The tengu were fairly sure that he was the one that cast the transformation spell that crippled the *domana*. They hadn't found the casting circle that he used. Law Monroe had tracked all but one of the eleven *nactka* to the graveyard. Oilcan had recovered them there without encountering Kajo. The assumption was that Kajo had been overseeing the magical attack while expendable subordinates had led both the defense of the forest camps and the Oakland attack. From what the tengu could piece together, Oilcan and his *sekasha* had fought and killed two women who looked like Chloe Polanski. The tengu were guessing that these were Kajo's Eyes.

The snake had been blinded but not killed. Until Kajo was dead, Boo could still be in danger.

"Since we can't talk about the militia," Jane said, "can we interview you on camera? You could answer a lot of 'what was the EIA doing?' questions for the viewers."

Maynard allowed a wince to go across his face to indicate that he wasn't completely happy with the idea, but nodded anyhow.

"Hal?" Jane turned to her team, who were still eating their scrambled eggs.

Hal all but flung his plate at Nigel to hold and literally bounced up to Maynard. He got hyperactive when he was tired and they were all running with too little sleep. "Director Maynard!"

On second thought . . .

Jane caught hold of Hal and hauled him back from Maynard. "Hal," she whispered, "I'm warning you: do not accidently blow up this man or set him on fire or shoot him."

Hal got that slightly guilty look that always indicated one of the three had been a possibility. "Accidents just happen."

He didn't have a visible gun. They'd decided that for neutral viewers, him not being armed would play better. It was unlikely that he could set Maynard on fire, even accidently.

"Give me the grenade," Jane said, holding out her hand.

Hal made an unhappy face. "How do you know I have a grenade?"

"I just do!" Jane curled her fingers into a fist warningly. "Give it to me!"

Hal surrendered the grenade and Jane gave him a push back toward Maynard.

32: BLUE MOON, YOU SAW ME STANDING ALONE

The kids arrived back at Sacred Heart shortly after dawn.

Guy had done a good job of distracting them; they were all happy and full of plans. Merry and Rustle wanted to find sheet music for the songs that they had heard playing on the jukebox. Barley wanted to learn more about the mysterious "Tex-Mex cuisine" and try to make his own chili. Cattail Reeds wanted to set up a game room next to the nightclub with pinball machines salvaged from across the city. Baby Duck had discovered the team's aquarium, filled with gleaming gold *pesantiki* won at countless street fairs over the years. Andy had scooped out a half dozen for her, transferring them to a large wide-mouthed pickle jar, cautioning her that she'd need to find someplace bigger to transfer them to quickly.

Oilcan asked Moser's people to find an aquarium with a pump and filter and then had a long talk with Baby Duck about *no more pets*. It was a dual problem of finding space for them as the number of people living at Sacred Heart increased, and finding food for the animals as the war dragged on.

"Quee," Baby Duck quacked while Blue Sky frowned at him and Spot looked nervous.

"You can keep the fish in your room, but please, don't bring anything more home until we're sure we can feed them, and don't have to eat them—because that would be very tragic."

"I promise," Baby Duck said in a quiet and solemn voice.

✧   ✧   ✧

The impending Noah's Ark temporarily halted, Oilcan moved on to Moon Dog. He wanted to make his offer to the male before Moon Dog drifted off in search of whatever had brought the holy warrior to Pittsburgh.

He caught Moon Dog in the foyer, coming out of the gym, looking clean and neat as if Oilcan hadn't dragged him to hell and back the day before. His brown hair was damp, so someone must have explained the showers to him.

"Moon Dog!" Oilcan trotted down the stairs to him, aware that Thorne Scratch was retreating to give him space. He was surprised how nervous he felt. His palms were actually sweating. He wiped them on his blue jeans as he struggled to put thoughts into words. "I...I...I wanted to thank you for everything you did yesterday."

Moon Dog beamed. "It was a good time! I have spent a hundred years training for battle, wondering if I would stay calm and rational and strike true and be everything that people expected of me. It was wonderful to know that it was all worth my time and effort—that I am all that I wanted to be."

"I am not sure what you know of me," Oilcan said. "Forge is my great-great-great-great-great-grandfather. His only child, Unbounded Brilliance, went to Earth and was trapped there during the Oni War. Unbounded Brilliance fathered a half-elf son with a human woman and was killed during a political uprising. For generations, my family has thought of themselves as human. Only a few days ago, Forge...Forge made me a *domana* elf."

"*Waya!*" Moon Dog said. "That explains much. You seem so at ease with all things strange to me."

"I was born on Earth and when my mother was killed, I was brought to Elfhome by my grandfather, Tim Dufae, and raised with my cousin. Earlier this summer, she became the Wind Clan *domi*."

"Ah, so the female who saved us on the bridge is your cousin," Moon Dog said. "She tapped the Fire Clan *esva* but held a Stone Clan shield and then did a Wind Clan spell."

"Yes, she has three *esva* but I only have access to the Stone Clan Spell Stones because Forge made me true to his son's bloodline. But...but that does not make me Stone Clan. I am Beholden to my cousin, Beloved Tinker of Wind. My household is Wind Clan."

Moon Dog tilted his head in confusion. "The children are Stone Clan."

"They were..." Oilcan wasn't sure how to explain without saying negative things about the Stone Clan. The children had been abandoned by their clan long before they walked away from it. "It has been a very intense and confusing summer for all of us. To those of us who were born human—mostly human—our choice of clan was based on sentiment, not genetics. We...My family has always seen ourselves as Wind Clan, because we were surrounded by elves of that clan when we were young. I know that it was a hard choice for the children, but we have decided to align with my cousin."

"Ah, I see. It is very sensible. Tempered Steel has always said that the clans were one of the worst things that we had done to ourselves. To willfully set ourselves apart from each other. It is a hatred of genetics that we should have never embraced. The color of one's eye should not determine love or hate."

"Yes, exactly," Oilcan said and then paused. Where was he going with this line of thought? How should he pose the question that he wanted to ask? "I am not sure of certain customs—because I was raised as a human. I was not even sure if I wanted to follow tradition and take a full Hand. Yesterday, though, I came to realize the value of having a Hand. We could not have survived all that the oni had thrown at us without you. I would like very much if we could be...if you would be...my Second?"

Moon Dog blinked a couple times, utterly silent. He finally said, "Could you repeat that?"

Oilcan carefully formed a clearer question. "Would you be my Second?"

"Ah, yes, that is what you said," Moon Dog murmured. He thought for a moment and glanced over Oilcan's shoulder. The only thing behind Oilcan was the front door. "I...I have something that I must do. I am not sure how it will go. I will return and say 'yes' when it is done."

After Moon Dog hurried away, Thorne Scratch came down the steps.

"What did he say?" she asked hesitantly.

"I think he said yes." Oilcan wanted to wait for Moon Dog's return but the male hadn't given him a time frame. He was an elf. His concept of time was vastly different from that of a human. Oilcan had too much to do to wait.

The next thing on his to-do list was to make sure the twins had more furniture in their bedroom than two elvish camping cots. The whole point of going to Once More With Feeling had been to present the twins with a viable place to live. He'd utterly failed to have a nice bedroom with a large workspace set up before they arrived. He could still salvage the situation if he delivered the furniture before the novelty of everything else in Sacred Heart wore off.

He would need help to get it done as quickly as possible. He didn't want to drag his kids back out of the enclave. Guy had managed to make yesterday a fun adventure. Oilcan was afraid to take them back to the South Side where they could plainly see how close to disaster they'd been. He headed into the gym to find Moser.

The night owls of Moser's commune had gotten to bed early and were—somewhat—awake. Their daylight counterparts had already gotten up, hung up their bedrolls to air, and were in the kitchen with Barley, starting breakfast.

"Hey, yesterday I bought a ton of furniture," Oilcan explained to Moser as the man sat up in his bedroll and scrubbed at his hair. "I need to go down to the South Side and pick it up at Once More With Feeling. I really could use a hand with the heavy lifting."

"Sure. Sure. No problem." Moser climbed out of his bedroll to stretch. "Geoffrey was out earlier, checking on how things stand. He says that there's still a shitload of oni scattered through the East End that the royal marines are mopping up. The EIA wants all humans to stay out of the area so there's no chance of friendly fire. We're stuck here until we get the all clear."

"And maybe another truck?" Oilcan had seen Moser's van outside last night but there had been cardboard and tools tucked under it, as if it had broken down beside the gate.

"My van is dead," Moser said. "Geoffrey's got his pickup here. He's in the kitchen. I'll grab him."

Moser's household was made up of fourteen adults—elves and humans. More, if one counted Geoffrey and any other stray they'd recently taken in. With Moser's people pitching in, getting the twins' bedroom furnished should be fairly quick.

33: MERCY

Law jolted awake to stare at an unfamiliar plain white ceiling.

What happened? Where am I?

She was in a bed with metal railings with various monitors attached to her and IV needles in both her hands. The big clear fluid bag on her right was half full, but the bag of blood dripping into her left arm looked nearly empty. Sitting up shot pain through every fiber of her body. Sunlight streamed through the window to the left of her, proving that it was daytime outside. She'd been unconscious for hours, if not days.

She was at Mercy Hospital. She recognized the styling of the room once she sat up: her grandparents had had multiple stays in the same kind of semiprivate room toward the ends of their lives. The bed beside her was occupied but the privacy curtain was drawn, keeping the myth of "semiprivate" alive. She could hear a soft beeping of monitors and some type of breathing machine.

The TV was on but muted. Hal Rogers was doing an interview with EIA Director Maynard. There was a banner reading OAKLAND FRONTLINE. Maynard seemed to be standing in front of Poppymeadows, and work crews were clearing rubble from the street. Other than that, there seemed to be no real sign of fighting.

What Law couldn't see was Bare Snow.

"Bare?" Law whispered, just in case the female was invisible for some weird reason. Normally, Bare Snow could walk around without her spell active and people still didn't seem to see her.

She apparently had spent her life judging people's line of sight and how to anticipate how others would turn to avoid being seen by a casual viewer.

Somewhere down the hall was the clatter of metal bedpans. No one answered her.

Fear started to set in. Where was Bare Snow? What had happened to her? They'd been alone against an army within the graveyard. How did Law end up at the hospital? Bare Snow wouldn't have known where the hospital was or what it was. She would have taken Law back to the Bunnies.

Maybe the Bunnies had brought Law to the hospital.

The thought was comforting for a couple of minutes—enough time to take inventory of her body. She'd been totally stripped; even her boyshorts underwear was gone. She had dozens of bandages on both legs and arms and random places on the very edge of her torso. She'd been lucky; no major organs seemed to have been hit by the puffball's darts. Major blood loss alone would explain the IV in each hand and being unconscious for hours.

The most chilling thing she found was the plastic bracelet on her wrist. It identified her as Monroe, Lawrie Earie. There were perhaps twenty people in the world who knew her full name: her parents, and the kids who were in school with her in first through sixth grades. Specifically the ones in her class when David Gillespie discovered what her middle name was and started to call her "Earwig." Every recess had her using her fists in an effort to get him to stop shouting the nickname. (Nearly twenty years later, she wasn't sure if he'd had some kind of death wish or actually had a secret crush on her. There was a good reason why she didn't like men.) Her driver's license only had her middle initial. After Lawrie graduated from high school, she shortened her name to just "Law." The Bunnies didn't know what Law stood for. She didn't know their real names. It was understood that they would never ask.

It meant that someone who actually *knew* her—but not the Bunnies—had brought Law to the hospital. If Bare Snow had been unhurt, why hadn't she come with Law and whoever transported her? Had Bare Snow been invisible and unconscious? Was she still at the graveyard, badly wounded and overlooked?

The worst of it was that Law hadn't thought to tell Bare Snow what to do if they got separated. The female might be roaming the city with no clue how to find Law or how to contact the Bunnies. Hell, just getting up to Mount Washington on foot wasn't obvious if you had only driven there.

"I'm a stupid idiot," Law whispered.

She climbed out of bed, wincing and swearing at the pain. Where were her clothes and boots and most importantly her phone? There was a little storage locker opposite her bed. She limped to it, dragging IV stands and monitors along. Her boots, soaked with blood—probably her own—sat at the bottom of the locker. None of her clothes apparently had been deemed salvageable—there was no sign of them. Her keys, phone, lockpicks, a handful of bullets, and a few other items that would have been in her pockets had been placed in a plastic bag and hung on the other hook. She'd left her wallet locked in her truck, so she didn't have ID or money.

She had turned off her phone when the city's network went down. She turned it on to discover that it was still at half power.

Usagi answered on the first ring. "Law! Are you okay? Where are you?"

"I'm at the hospital. Wounded. I don't know how I got here. Have you heard from Bare Snow?"

"Oh, dear God, no, I haven't. I thought she was you. I'll come get you."

"You don't have to..." Law started to turn Usagi down without thinking. She didn't like getting other people involved in her messes.

"I asked you to join our household," Usagi said. "That means I see you as family. Of course I have to come get you when you're in the hospital. That is what family does for each other!"

Law paused and actually thought about her options. She didn't have a lot of choices being that all she had to her name was a hospital gown and boots. Her truck was on the other side of the town—miles away. She felt too lightheaded and weak to hike to it. "Okay. I'm going to need something to put on. Can you bring some clothes? The whole works. Underwear. Socks. Pants. Shirt."

"Oh, Law!" Usagi said in dismay, recognizing that it meant that Law had been badly wounded. "I'll find some. My jeans would be too small for you. Clover probably has some that will fit you. I'll be there in ten minutes."

Law gave her the room number and said goodbye.

For Usagi to be able to drop everything and head to Mercy Hospital, it meant someone else was home to watch the kids. Probably Clover or Hazel. Usagi could maybe drop Law in Oakland but Usagi couldn't take her as far as the graveyard. It wouldn't be safe. Law wasn't sure where else to look for Bare Snow.

"Oh, fucking hell." Law leaned against the locker as her vision started to go dark. That's how she ended up passed out on the floor.

Law woke up the second time as Usagi and Dr. Nan Nuessle—who looked very sleep deprived—got her off the floor. They were both petite women, so it wasn't smooth going as they guided Law back to her bed.

"What the freak do you think you're doing?" Dr. Nan growled. "I don't have patience for this right now. Half the population of the city decided to play soldier yesterday. We've got wounded coming out of our ears."

"When you said 'wounded' I didn't expect to find you this hurt," Usagi said. "You look like someone used you as a dart board."

"Yes, basically, they did," Law said. "Which is why I'm worried about Bare Snow. Who brought me to the hospital?"

"It was all hands on deck last night in the ER," Dr. Nan snapped. "I was probably busy with someone else when you came in. No, wait, I did see you from across the room. Linda Gaddy brought you in."

That explained her middle name on the bracelet. Gaddy had been in her class all through grade school. They hadn't been close friends then and drifted further apart in high school. They hadn't seen each other since graduation.

"I need to talk to Gaddy." Law held out her right hand and started to pry at the tape holding in the IV needle. "I need to take these off."

"No! No, you don't!" Dr. Nan smacked Law's fingers. "You're not going anywhere. You lost a dangerous amount of blood. Until these bags are empty, you'll go face down every time you stand up. You might think that those IV needles will only smart a bit if you pull them out, but it *will* hurt a whole lot more when my nurses put them back in, and they *will* put them back in. Until the next Shutdown or Startup or whatever connects us back to

Earth, a wasted resource could mean the difference between saving a life or not. You've started those bags, you will finish them."

"How long will that take?" Law said.

"Another hour or two." Dr. Nan said.

"An hour or two?" Law wailed. "Can't I just take them with me?"

"No!" Dr. Nan said. "First off, when you came in unconscious, we put a Foley catheter in you. It has a balloon attached to it. That has to be removed by us. If you try to just yank it out yourself, you're going to learn a whole new meaning to the word 'pain.'"

Law was beginning to feel very violated. "How long will it take to remove it?"

"Depends on who is available," Dr. Nan growled. "Even with it out, you can't just waltz out of here. The fluid we've given you needs to equilibrate with the blood already in your body. We'll have to check your hematocrit an hour after the transfusion and again the following morning to ensure you're not bleeding internally."

"Morning?" Law howled. "As in tomorrow morning?"

"Oh boo-hoo, we're trying to save your life here," Dr. Nan said. "What part of 'almost bled to death' do you not understand?"

"I'm just a little lightheaded." Law said. "Do I need all these wires and stuff?"

"For now—yes! I'll tell my nurses to take out the catheter but everything else has to stay—like this cardiac lead." Dr. Nan indicated one of the wires taped to Law's hand. "It's connected to your EKG monitor. That's how I knew you were lying here on the floor. It's being watched by a sweet little old lady named Betsy. If you yank that off, your monitor will flatline, and Betsy will fall out of her chair and have a mild heart attack. Once she picks herself up off the floor, Betsy will call a code blue. People will come running from all over the hospital. They will come to your room to save your life! Only you wouldn't be dying—yet!

"After last night, my staff is overwhelmed and exhausted. Someone is going to throw in the towel and quit. Do you have any idea how hard it is to get good medical talent here on Elfhome? If so much as one staff member quits because of you, I will Hunt. You. Down!"

"I'll be good," Law promised. "You should try and get some sleep."

"After the transfusion is finished, we'll talk again about

whether you can leave or not." Dr. Nan stalked off, hopefully to get some rest.

"I brought you some clothes." Usagi held out a child's pink backpack with rabbit ears. "It was the only bag I could find fast. But I don't think you should leave—not until you're well enough to actually walk out under your own power."

"I need to find Bare Snow," Law said.

"I understand completely," Usagi said. "If it was one of my babies, I'd crawl over broken glass to find them. But I also know that it would be the quickest way of leaving them completely alone for the rest of their very long lives. It's why I started up my household—so there would be someone else who could protect my babies when I couldn't."

"I haven't really given you an answer," Law said, "on if I'm going to join your household or not."

"And I'm glad you haven't," Usagi said. "It means you're considering all the pros and cons rationally. That's what I would hope for, for such a large life decision."

"I know it would be good for Bare Snow," Law said. "And I really care for you all. But I'm not sure I could take the kids twenty-four seven."

Usagi laughed dryly. "I can't take it nonstop either. We all need to have some alone time with the door shut. None of us are getting it because we're squeezed in too tight. The place we have now was okay when it was just me, Babs and Hazel. When we picked up Clover, things started to get too tight upstairs. Poor Widget slept on the couch all last winter as her 'room' is just a lean-to on the roof. We've been shuffling the babies around all summer, trying to give Widget her own room that is weather-proof. There's no way to expand, perched on the cliff edge like we are. It would be nice if we had a garden and maybe some fruit trees and a few chickens, but there's no space for all that. And the heat is dependent on the gas and electric staying on. We don't have any backups. I'm not sure we can put in a wood stove safely in the main room. The one wall is all glass and the other wall has the upstairs overhang weirdness."

"Are you trying to distract me from leaving?" Law asked.

"A little bit," Usagi admitted. "I want you to think rationally. You're not all alone in this. You have a wealth of friends that you can reach out to."

"I don't have that many friends," Law said.

"Yes, you do. Every time I've had trouble in the past, you've always been like 'I have a friend that can help you.' What employer would hire illegals, no questions asked, but still be perfectly safe to work for. Who to call to get our furnace working last winter. Where to get a big table made that sits all of us. Every time I thought my back was to the wall, you found someone who could fix my problem."

"This is different," Law said.

"I'm assuming you don't know how to get hold of this Gaddy," Usagi pressed on. "Who would?"

"I don't know. In high school, her best friend was Lisa Mosteller but she went to college stateside and didn't come back—or at least, I don't think she came back."

"Would this Gaddy be part of Widget's resistance?"

"Maybe?"

"Let's find out what Widget knows," Usagi said, taking out her phone.

Widget answered her phone. "Hi, big sis, I think I've found us a cool place to consider."

"What?" Usagi said in surprise.

"You know how we talked about moving? I asked around and I think I found a place," Widget said. "Well, I didn't, a friend of mine did, but that will have to wait until later—the walls have ears and all that."

"We'll talk later. We've lost...a friend...someplace and we're trying to find her," Usagi stumbled through trying to talk code.

Law leaned in to say, "I'm looking for my other half."

"O. M. G." Widget actually spelled it out. "I heard you got taken to the hospital! Are you okay?"

"I'm fine," Law said. Usagi gave her a look that made her change it to, "Mostly fine. I'm not completely back on my feet yet. Did you send Gaddy to find me?"

"I wish I'd been that clever but no," Widget said. "Oh, wow, how am I going to explain this chaos?"

"Where is my other half?" Law repeated to keep Widget from wandering off in story-mode and code talk.

"I think..." Widget said slowly, as if she wasn't sure, "she's at Sacred Heart."

"Where?" Usagi said in surprise.

"The new enclave at the Rim?" Law said to be sure that they were talking about the same abandoned Catholic high school. There might be another one—somewhere—that Law didn't know about. The enclave was the last place she would have thought Bare Snow would have ended up.

"Yeaaah!" Widget said slowly. "Gaddy was playing backup for Oilcan when she picked you up. He...he was on a secret mission. At least, I think it was secret. I'll explain later—it's not important for you to know now. Anyhoo, there was a big fight there and afterward, everyone—but you—ended up at Sacred Heart. I think."

"Is there any way you can confirm that?" Usagi said.

"Um," Widget thought a moment. "Let me play Six Degrees of Kevin Bacon."

"Play what?" Law said. "Kevin who?"

"I'll explain," Usagi said.

"I'll call you back," Widget said.

Usagi had just finished explaining that it meant finding common links between scattered people to create a chain of relationships when Widget called back.

"Okay, Bow-Wow called Gin Blossom, who says that Briar Rose told her that Bare Snow is definitely at Sacred Heart," Widget said. "Apparently someone got the news to Briar Rose that you're going to be fine, so Bare Snow crashed in a borrowed bed there."

"Are you sure she's safe?" Law said. "Doesn't Oilcan have a dozen *sekasha* camping at his place?"

"One of the *sekasha* is 'standing as champion,' which is some weird thing that means no one can hurt her without going through him...so...I think so?"

Law's grandmother had graduated from Sacred Heart High School during the last century. She used to bemoan the fact that her alma mater had closed a decade before Law could have attended. Law suspected she and the nuns would have gotten on like gasoline and a lit match. Even her public school teachers called Law "incorrigible." She had thought a lot about her grandmother's nostalgia as she'd waded through the abandoned building shortly after the Wyverns had cleared it of oni. It had been a garbage-filled pigsty, riddled with bullet holes and covered with blood. Law couldn't decide if it was sad or ironic that the school known for ironhanded nuns had been taken over by animalistic lesser bloods. Any secret information that the dead oni warriors had on the Skin Clan was lost under the filth.

In the days following Oilcan's takeover of Sacred Heart, Law had rarely spotted people moving about the place. It wasn't too surprising as it was a large three-story building meant for several hundred students. Then suddenly, as if overnight, massive limestone walls had sprung up around the school, matching the height and width of the walls around the elf-made enclaves across the street.

As Usagi pulled into the parking lot between the Rim and Pittsburgh, there was a line of ants moving their nest into Sacred Heart. Not actual ants. A small mountain of household goods had been unloaded outside the new gate. Tables and chairs. Couches and love seats. Desks and bookcases. Bedframes and headboards. Even seven blazing white twin mattresses stacked up on blankets. The "ants" were people carrying furniture into the old schoolhouse. All four races were represented in the progression of goods: humans, elves, tengu, and one little dog-like half-oni.

Usagi rarely got out of the house, so she hadn't seen the defensive walls going up around the new enclave. "Wow, this place sure has changed in a few weeks' time!"

Law nodded. "That ironwood gate is new to me too."

Said gate was painted Wind Clan Blue despite the fact that many of the elves helping to unload the big truck were wearing Stone Clan Black.

The half-oni claimed a tall floor lamp to carry in. The humans paired off to handle the mattresses. The elves carefully lifted boxes of dishes off the back of the pickup. Four of the tengu picked up a dainty pink love seat and a tufted white settee. The line of ants marched into Sacred Heart. Law and Usagi followed.

The walls of the cavernous foyer had been cleaned, repaired, and painted a warm butter yellow. The floors had been scrubbed until they gleamed. The place smelled of roasting meat, fresh-baked bread, and lavender-scented cleaner. It was a stunning transformation since Law last saw the area.

A young female elf was directing the flow of traffic. She had the brown hair and dusky skin of the Stone Clan elves. She was even smaller than Usagi. She seemed to be only a tween but that could have been her braided pigtails, blue dress, rainbow leggings, and pink tennis shoes.

She eyed the tengu's load and pointed up the stairs. "Third floor."

"Of course! Our favorite floor!" one of the tengu quipped.

The female quacked nervously. "The pink settee goes in my room! Baby Duck's room. The white one goes into the little *domis'* room."

"'Once more unto the breach, dear friends, once more!'" the tengu quoted as they climbed the stairs. "'In peace there's nothing so becomes a man as modest stillness and humility.'"

"The mighty hero appears!" Briar Rose called as she came down the steps. "*Nicadae*, Law! *Nicadae*, Usagi Sensei!"

"*Nicadae!*" Usagi bowed in greeting. "Where did they get all the furniture?"

"Once More With Feeling," Carl Moser said as he jogged down the steps. "Oilcan bought out the store just before the fighting started. He and the kids were getting ice cream when they were attacked and had to leave everything behind. Good to see you upright, Law."

Moser continued out the door, leaving Briar Rose to explain the rest.

"Oilcan and Geoffrey have made three runs each to the South Side already," Briar Rose said. "Most of the big pieces had to go to the third floor, so we called in backup. Oilcan's other kids are upstairs making sure everything gets to the right rooms."

Four big wooden tables were carried in by another team of tengu.

"Cafeteria?" one of the males asked hopefully.

Baby Duck quacked, shaking her head. "Sorry, third floor. One for Cattail Reeds, one for Merry, one for Rustle, and one for the little *domis*."

"Third floor it is!" The tengu headed upstairs at a jog. Judging by the speed at which they were moving, the tengu were insanely strong.

Law hadn't expected the enclave to be so crowded. "I'm looking for Bare Snow."

"She's in the gym!" Moser passed them again, this time carrying a set of lamps. "None of the furniture is going in there, so it seemed the best place for her."

✧   ✧   ✧

The Sacred Heart gym reminded Law of the one at her high school—the gleaming hardwood floors, the high ceiling, the painted lines of the basketball court, and the wooden bleachers folded against the outer wall. Unlike Brashear High, one wall was a large stage. Rumors had it that Oilcan was going to turn it into a dance club with local bands performing on the weekends.

Moser and his people had fled their home for the safety of the Sacred Heart's newly constructed magical defenses. They'd arrived with their instruments, sleeping bags, and little else. They'd set up in an orderly fashion within the gym, but it still looked like a refugee camp.

In the far corner, Bare Snow sat holding the elfhound puppy she had rescued, once upon a time.

As Law approached, she was startled to see a tear trickling down Bare Snow's face.

"Bare? What's wrong?" Law said.

"Law!" Bare Snow stumbled to her. It was as if a dam had burst; tears started to stream down the female's face. "Law!"

"It's okay. I'm here. It's—ow, ow, ow!" This was because Bare Snow had hugged her tightly, hitting half a dozen wounds at once.

"Easy, Bare Snow!" Usagi said. "She's too hurt for that."

"I'm fine," Law lied. "What's wrong, Bare?"

"Moon Dog is *gaolata* me."

"He's what?"

"*Gaolata* me! He is going to try and force Wraith Arrow to abrogate the death warrant. I'm...I'm...I do not know what I am! I think I might be terrified."

Usagi gave Law a look that cried "What death warrant?" but said nothing.

"Cancelling the death warrant would be good?" Law said. "Wouldn't it?"

"Yyyeeesss!" Bare Snow sobbed. "My father's household knew nothing of my mother's sin. They threw me out simply because of my cursed name. That my mother was Wind Clan was merely an easy excuse. They were Water Clan; they had no obligation to care for a cursed child of another clan. They gave me coin enough to get to Court, telling me to find a Wind Clan household there to take me. Even if I failed, they said, I could go to the clan head and seek orphan rights. They did not know what it was that they asked of me! A child is fr...fr...free to choose a new household at a certain age. They did not know that the Wind Clan wanted me dead! I could not tell them—my shame was too great. And what would it have gained me? They already did not want me!"

Law understood the pain. Her parents had handed her over to her grandparents after they divorced, neither one wanting to have to act as single parent as they rebuilt their life. Before being bitterly angry about it, she'd been wounded to her soul.

"*I* want you," Law said.

"We all want you," Usagi said.

"I want to be able to say yes to the Bunnies!" Bare Snow said. "After I was turned down again and again in Summer Court, I just wanted to crawl into a hole and die. I had forever alone before me with no hope of ever being part of a household. I thought I would never be part of a family again. It is why I came to Pittsburgh—I had no hope. I sensed it was a trap even before I started to go from enclave to enclave, seeking a household that would take me. But I wanted so badly to be accepted that I was willing to risk everything."

"It's okay, baby," Usagi crooned. "We don't care about your clan or your name or anything your mother has done."

"I could not risk the babies!" Bare Snow sobbed. "I wanted so badly to say yes but I knew that it would put them in danger. And then...then...Moon Dog..."

And then she started a loud terrible ugly cry with tears pouring down her face as she made keening noises.

Law traced back through the conversation. Who was Moon Dog? What was he doing again? "He is going to force Wraith Arrow to abrogate the warrant?"

"I do not know if he can!" Bare Snow sobbed. "I want this so badly but I do not know if he can! He is temple born and he trained under Tempered Steel—the holiest of holy—but he is barely out of his doubles. He is only a few years older than me. To abrogate the warrant, he has to tell Wraith Arrow about me. Wraith Arrow! Howling's First. The killer of King Boar Bristle! Loser to only Cinder during the tournament that decided which Hand would lead us out of the Clan Wars. If Moon Dog can not force Wraith Arrow to back down, then the First of the Westernland's Wind Clan will know I exist and that I am here in Pittsburgh! He might tear the city apart to find me!"

"He's in the middle of a war right now," Law said.

"Today. Tomorrow. Next year. It does not matter. He will find me. I should have never told Moon Dog about my history. He guessed who I was and asked me kindly if I was well, and...and I was so alone without you! I could not help but worry about the day that you are not there for me. That if something happened to you, there is no one among the humans who so loves the edge as much as you. Once again, there would be no one, and I would be for...for...forever alone."

"Wraith Arrow hasn't said yes or no yet?" Law asked.

"Moon Dog went to find him," Bare Snow sniffed. "I do not know how long it will take him to get an answer. He might not even get an audience with the First. It is the not knowing that made me cry."

"Maybe we should leave—just in case he says no?" Law asked.

"I cannot abandon Moon Dog when he has put his life on the line to help me." Bare Snow wiped at her face. "I must wait to see the outcome."

"Okay. I need to fall down now," Law said as the world threatened to go dark again. She carefully lowered herself to the ground. "I'll wait with you."

There was literally nothing else she could do. The elfhound puppy eyed Law with concern as if it could tell that she wasn't well.

Law tried to pet the puppy but failed to lift her arm. Yup, literally nothing else she could do. "Usagi, I'll call you."

Usagi's face started to crumble as her desire to stay warred with the knowledge that she had to do what was best for her children. No matter how much she wanted to stay, she needed to keep a safe distance from whatever might happen. Tears started to stream down her face. "I-I-I shouldn't just..."

"Yes, you should," Law said. "If for no other reason than it might be days until he comes back. You need to go home."

"Law!" Bare Snow's voice quivered. "I am too frightened to be brave enough to tell you to go. I do not want to be alone if Wraith Arrow comes for me. I do not want to be alone for the end."

"You won't be alone," Law said. "You don't have to be afraid for me. Wraith Arrow has no reason to harm me and I cannot do anything but be here with you—to whatever end that comes."

34: PANTY RAID TAKE TWO

Tinker woke feeling betrayed.

The night before, everyone had acted like she was about to drop over from hypothermia. She had been forced to drink endless cups of hot tea and carried—*carried*—to the bathhouse. (Yes, soaking in the hot water was sheer bliss despite having all three males from her Hand in with her, Stormsong, and Rainlily. She still wasn't used to it. At least everyone used towels to keep naughty bits hidden for her sake.)

She thought about telling her Hand that she was to be woken up at dawn. She was sure that if she had said something, they would have complied. (But maybe they would have immediately chided her until she went back to sleep.) Part of her was sure that such an instruction wasn't necessary as they were in a state of emergency. Still, she had made plans in her head...and fell asleep in the tub before she gave any orders.

Worse, someone—probably Pony—decided that Tinker should be allowed to sleep in.

And then the killing blow on her good intentions: her own body decided that sleeping half the day away would be a good thing.

Totally betrayed from all sides!

"Oh, holy hell!" She sat up in bed, scrubbing at her hair. "What time is it?"

"An hour before noon!" Stormsong answered from the hallway.

She opened the door and strolled into Tinker's bedroom, giving the lie to Lain's claim that civilized people knocked. Stormsong had obviously been up for hours because she was fully dressed and her blue-dyed hair was neatly braided with a darker blue ribbon.

"Why didn't you wake me?" Tinker had been put to bed in a silky white nightgown that clung to her like a second skin, and no panties. (And she was glad about the panties part because she didn't want to think about someone wrestling a pair onto her while she was asleep.) She got up and started the ritual of trying to find the clothes that she had worn the day before. Since there were two gowns of fairy silk draped across the foot of her bed—one sapphire blue and the other ruby red—she suspected she wasn't going to find the blue jeans she'd been wearing. Once again, the staff must have decided that her outfit was beyond saving and made it disappear. "Did they burn my pants again?"

"Because you needed to sleep," Stormsong said. "And no, they're washing your clothes. They were covered with mud and ichor."

"Oooh!" Tinker swallowed down some curses. Poppymeadows did not have electric driers or any other method to speed up the drying of blue jeans. Depending upon the weather, it could be days before her pants would be dry enough to wear. Neither of the offered gowns had pockets and they went all the way to the floor. She was not going to wade into battle looking like a fairy princess! She tossed the gowns aside and stomped to her toilet as all that tea was hitting bottom. "Ichor? What's ichor?"

"Viscera of the horrors. Blood and guts. Not as much as you could expect, given the size of those we fought. It was more mud than ichor."

Tinker rolled her eyes while safely hidden by the closed bathroom door. She'd learned from experience that disdain expressed privately wasn't as private as she believed. "Gods forbid I wear muddy pants!"

"They still smelled vaguely like skunk oil," said Stormsong's muffled voice from the other side of the ornately carved wood door. "Lemonseed did not want that stench to seep into the bed linens and curtains. Also, some horrors have poisonous ichor so they might not have been safe to wear."

Tinker sighed. Defeated by totally valid points.

"Is . . . whoever . . . the laundry person . . . going to be okay handling them?" Tinker had been at Poppymeadows for more than a month but she still wasn't sure what anyone did beyond Lemonseed. The elderly female was the majordomo of Windwolf's personal household, organizing the work of all the others. Tinker had spent her time at Aum Renau thinking Lemonseed was just a bossy cook. The rest of the staff was all like ninjas, sneaking around, trying to be as invisible as possible. She was still struggling to learn names.

"They'll use cleaning spells to neutralize any poison and deodorize the fabric." Stormsong sounded like she had moved to lean against the bathroom's doorframe, probably so they didn't have to shout to hear each other.

Obviously the first order of business was to find clothes in which Tinker could handle anything life might throw at her today. Considering what her summer had been like, "anything" was mind-boggling in range.

What after that?

"Has Windwolf left for the East Coast yet?" Tinker attempted to quietly flush. One would think she wouldn't still be pee-pee shy after more than two months of living among the elves, but she had boundaries that she hadn't yet crossed. Lots of them. Probably more than she realized as there was so much about Elfhome, elves, and elf society that she didn't know (as she seemed to discover daily now that she lived in a house with them).

"No, not yet," Stormsong said. "He's at Prince True Flame's camp. The *domana* are having a meeting to coordinate prior to leaving. Pony is with him so he can stay abreast of the plans so that he can best guide you. He should be back shortly."

It meant that Tinker could consult with Windwolf before he headed out, although at the moment, she wasn't sure what she would talk to him about other than declarations of love and concern. What she wanted to be able to tell him was that she could reverse the damage done to the *domana*.

She washed her hands and then her face. Her hair was sticking in all directions as she'd been put to bed with damp hair. She looked like a crazed hedgehog. "I need...I need to fix things... somehow."

"I love you dearly," Stormsong said, "but I'm afraid this might be beyond even you to fix."

Hopefully, Stormsong was wrong about that.

"I need to borrow some more clothes." Tinker grabbed a towel to dry her hands and face.

Stormsong was leaning against the doorframe when Tinker opened the bathroom door. "What is mine is yours."

Stormsong headed to her room two doors down from Tinker's. It reflected its owner in all ways, from the manga on the night-stand—as though the female read them while lying in bed—to the candles that scented the air with amber and cashmere, to the dressers filled with human-made T-shirts, blue jeans, and lingerie.

Tinker started with the T-shirts, looking for something that wasn't a limited edition like the last one, which ended up being cut off her by the hospice workers. "It is possible that what Tooloo has been doing is raising wood sprites to connect Elfhome and Earth together in one mega-city instead of a lot of little, carefully guarded, caves. At least, I assume that the old pathways were guarded."

"Heavily," Stormsong said. "The caves themselves could not be altered or they would have lost their ability to connect to Earth. After the Rebellion, clans would build fortresses at the entrances as defense against anything from Earth coming out, and to limit who could get in. *Domana* would lead the merchants through the cave system as the path would sometimes alter course, depending on the phase of the moon. As the Clan Wars started, fewer and fewer merchants would be escorted through until the trading parties were only *domana* and their *sekasha*."

"Why was that?"

Stormsong shrugged. "My mother had all the pathways torn down before I was born. I can only guess. When we first found Earth, humans had just started to trade with one another. The world was unknown to them and we were accepted as just odd travelers. More importantly, they were not that much different from us. They used swords and spears and wore clothes of cloth. As time went on, they started to leap forward in technology. They developed metal armor and bows and chariots. They were outstripping us. I think when they invented cannons and guns, the end was drawing near anyhow. Humans knew more and more of their world and slowly came to realize that we should not be appearing within their lands with no ship to carry us from whatever distant place we came from."

"So the trading parties were limited because of the possibility that humans would do exactly what the oni did to Forest Moss?"

"That was the impression that Wolf and I got as we talked to those who used to trade with Earth."

"It's one thing to stop an object in motion," Tooloo had said. *"It's quite another to change someone's heart."*

What if the object in motion were the trading parties to Earth? Pure Radiance took down the natural pathways, closing off Elfhome from outside visitors. Tooloo, on the other hand, had set up Pittsburgh so it flooded the elves with new ideas and technology on a monthly basis. Pure Radiance countered by using Tinker to destroy the orbital gate.

Was the war in Pittsburgh between Pure Radiance and Vision with the Skin Clan merely being tools? It would explain why Tooloo hadn't attempted to kill off all of the Skin Clan while they were hiding out on Earth.

Was the entire plan to cripple the *domana* just a step meant to free Pittsburgh from Pure Radiance's influence, or was it a case of too many fingers in the pie throwing off Tooloo's careful planning?

And what was the chessboard all about?

Tinker picked out a cotton baseball jersey with blue sleeves and the word PITT embroidered on the left breast. She doubted it had sentimental value to Stormsong and certainly it wasn't a limited edition. "What would it take to change elf society?"

"Change it?" Stormsong blew out her breath. "I do not know if it can change. I still have a child's love of her mother, but it worries me sometime to know that Pure Radiance will forever sit to the right of any Queen or King who holds the throne and fill their ear with her vision of how the world should be. She was born within the slavery of the Skin Clan. While she guided us to victory, I think that her knowledge of how the world could be was stunted by her captivity."

Stormsong handed Tinker a pair of boyshort panties and a matching camisole. They were white so that the camisole wouldn't show under the thin white cotton of the jersey. "And it is not just her. In every position, high and low, our leaders are mostly of her generation. It is why we had the Clan Wars in the first place. Trust no one. Keep your secrets. Build barriers to the outside."

Tinker pulled on the panties, slipped out of her nightgown, and pulled on the loose camisole and the jersey. The shirt was too big but she liked that it came down to mid-thigh like a minidress.

Stormsong nodded to the outfit so far. "There are times I almost can see the shackles still on our people. Humans say that you cannot teach new tricks to old dogs. Certainly it seems as if my mother's generation cannot consider a new way of thinking. It seems too pervasive to be simply refusing to adapt. As we began to trade with humans, I was stunned at the things that the older elves could not accept as beautiful."

Stormsong dug through the pile of manga to find a strip of fabric that she was using as a bookmark. The background was rust red with a pattern of pale yellow, orange, green, and blue flowers and leaves woven into an intricate design. "I have been waging a war with Lemonseed for years. Decades. I would like new curtains of this fabric. I cannot get Lemonseed to see it as anything but garish."

"But it's beautiful!"

"Say you and I but Lemonseed cannot see the beauty in it. And it is not the first fabric sample I have brought to her. There have been a dozen at least. They are all fabrics that are made by humans. They are too foreign to her. And it is not just Lemonseed—the household is divided straight down the middle. Those who are young can see the beauty in it but the ancient ones—the ones who served Howling—think the colors are off and the design is too busy. Nor do the ancient ones like music like Oilcan plays. 'Loud noise' is what they call it."

"Huh." Tinker pulled open drawers, looking for shorts. Stormsong's pants were not going to fit—the legs would be ridiculously long on Tinker. (Yes, they could cut the jeans shorter but Tinker wanted to believe she was going to give the clothes back unscathed.) "Okay I'm going to make some wild guesses here. Tooloo is Vision but possibly like Jin Wong when Providence came to talk to me, is 'possessed' by her dead dragon soul, Clarity. I grew up knowing the dragon, not the elf, which is why Tooloo seems so weird when compared to other elves. Even as a newborn elf child, Vision would have known about multiple worlds and a vastly different society. On top of that, Tooloo has lived several hundred years on Earth as human societies shifted from monarchies to democracies. Pure Radiance, on the other hand, was born only knowing slavery in a society that had been beaten into one mold for thousands of years. One language. One religion."

"In terms of my mother, that is all true. I think your guess might be right about Tooloo. Vision was said to be unnaturally mature at birth. She spoke full sentences at a very early age and rarely cried."

Tinker plunged on, expanding her theory. "Clarity went to Elfhome with some kind of plan. It would help if we knew more about the dragons and how their society works—but if Clarity was anything like Impatience with a mind-bogglingly strong ability to see into the future, then maybe Tooloo's plan transcends being an elf."

"So, we are actually dealing with Clarity here, not Tooloo or Vision?"

"Perhaps," Tinker said. "She was the last dragon captured, so maybe this is some kind of wild, long-range rescue mission."

"What I have been told is, all the other dragons were dead before Clarity was captured."

"There's dead and then there's dead when it comes to dragons. Think of Providence." Tinker paused. "Yes, let's think of Providence. He's been around for thousands of years, protecting the tengu, even though he's dead. What if the problem is that even if Clarity rescued the other dragons, there were all the baby elves with dragon blood to consider?"

"Perhaps," Stormsong said slowly. "My mother said that Vision was more dragon than elf. Once she escaped the Skin Clan, however, Vision did not flee to Ryu."

"Impatience stuck around Pittsburgh to help out Oilcan's kids." Tinker held up her hand as pieces seem to fall together in her mind. "So what if the origin of the problem isn't on Elfhome with the freed elves but on Ryu with the elder dragons deciding that they had no right to interfere with the Skin Clan, no matter how evil they were? This doesn't sit well with the younger dragons and they come to Elfhome in an attempt to do something. They get captured and little half-breeds were made. It would be like Blue Sky. The Wyverns recognized that Blue was one of them even though he was half-human. Even though they didn't know Lightning Strike, they insisted something be done with Blue Sky to make sure that he was cared for after his human half brother died of old age."

"He is one us," Stormsong said in an "of course" tone of voice. "Regardless of who his mother was."

Tinker pressed on, chasing her theory. "Clarity couldn't save the original dragons but there were all the little pieces left over. She sacrifices herself in an attempt to save them only to discover that the little pieces have a twisted idea of what being saved would entail."

"Blue Sky didn't want to be taken from his brother," Storm-song murmured. "Even though, in the long run, it would be healthier for him."

"Exactly! What if all this—this insane crazy summer—has been Tooloo gathering up all the little pieces in one place and trying to do what is right for them? She's got Impatience and Joy and Providence here and Oilcan's kids and all the elves and tengu and even all of Forge's kids in one place."

"You might be right. Certainly it seems unlikely that Oilcan's kids and your siblings and the tengu would come from worlds apart to show up here at the same time."

Their logic seemed solid but it still didn't explain what Tooloo wanted her to do with the chessboard.

Tinker pulled on the pair of shorts that Stormsong handed her. "Let's just forget Tooloo and the chessboard and everything. I'm going to focus on undoing what the Skin Clan did in crip-pling the *domana*. I need to talk to Windwolf, then, to make sure we're coordinated. I don't want to take him out when I cast the cure on the other *domana*."

35: BIRD IN HAND

-♦-⧫━○━⧫-♦-

Olivia had never been to a hotel before. Were they all this nice? The William Penn felt rich and luxurious. The rooms looked like something out of a magazine. The bed was massive—bigger than anything she'd ever seen. It had a half dozen pillows stacked up like a snowy mountain range. A throw blanket lay across the foot of the bed, its dark chocolatey brown in sharp contrast to the creamy tan of the comforter. There was a big overstuffed armchair in the corner. The windows had heavy drapes that reached the floor. Art hung on the walls. It was the biggest, nicest bedroom she had ever seen.

Her childhood attic bedroom at her grandmother's had only been big enough for a twin bed and a nightstand that doubled as a bookshelf. She shared her first bedroom at the Ranch with all her unmarried stepsisters. They slept in three sets of triple bunkbeds, stacked up like firewood. Even after she got married, as the third wife she only had a double bed with a sagging mattress and two threadbare pillows, one of which her husband claimed on the nights that he was with her. On Elfhome, she'd been sleeping in her kitchen on a futon until Forest Moss blew down her house. From there, they'd squatted in whatever place she could find. The Phipps Conservatory had showers in the employee locker room and an equal lack of privacy in the area that they set up cots in.

After the day that she had had, she needed the pampering that the room promised.

345

Forest Moss was soaked to the skin, dangerously cold, and bone weary after being struck down by the oni spell that stole his powers.

"Sit him in the armchair," Olivia told the royal marines carrying him. "Aiofe, can you see that the troops are settled into their rooms? And make sure that they know that the half-oni are not to be hurt?"

She needed to strip the wet clothes from Forest Moss. Olivia really didn't want Aiofe to be part of that. The elves saw nothing shameful about being naked—she knew from firsthand experience with the marines—and Aiofe was a good bit older than she. Still, the girl was sweet and naïve for her age. Seeing a male naked would be troubling to Aiofe. Probably. Maybe Olivia was wrong about that. What did she know about the Irish? The elders at the Ranch went on and on about how the rest of the world were immoral and sinful. Maybe the Irish danced naked in the streets. (Although she doubted it greatly.)

To be totally truthful with herself, Olivia wanted peace and quiet. Since early morning she'd been surrounded by people, forced into dangerous or uncomfortable situations again and again. She wanted a locked door between her and the outside world and all the responsibilities that came with being Forest Moss's *domi*.

"Yes, I can do that." Aiofe seemed more than willing to flee the room, suggesting that Olivia's first guess was the correct one.

Olivia shooed everyone out of the room and locked the door. Immediately she felt a little lighter, as if a huge weight had been lifted.

"You look worn," Forest Moss murmured as she stripped off his clothes. He seemed barely able to move.

"I'll sleep soon enough." She toweled him dry and wrapped him in the throw blanket.

There was a private bathroom attached to the bedroom. Another first in her life. Over the sink was a massive five-foot-by-five-foot mirror. In that wide reflection, she discovered that sometime during the day, she'd gotten blood splashed across the skirt of her gingham sundress. Blood itself wasn't distressing—she'd ended up covered in worse during slaughtering days at the farm. There was the fact that the dress was the only thing she had to wear until they got back to the Phipps. But more distressing, the blood probably came from a human. She really shouldn't have shot Jonnie Be Good or the EIA officer whose name she could no longer remember.

She started the tub to fill with warm water, and then stripped off her sundress.

"Our heavenly Father, forgive me for what I've done today." She sluiced the dress skirt through cold water, hoping a quick rinse would get the bulk of the dried blood. "I shouldn't have shot Jonnie Be Good—slimeball that he is, I am not fit to judge. Nor should have I shot . . . what's his name? The oni mole. Lieu-tenant Something. I really should at least remember the names of the people I got killed. Shooting him was what was needed to be done—but I should have known that the elves would take no prisoners."

The stacks of oni dead that had littered the sidewalks of Pittsburgh all summer should have been enough for her to learn that lesson.

Much of the blood had been rinsed away, but some remained soaked into the dress. There were tiny bars of soap and little bottles of shampoo next to the sink. She opted for the shampoo. She pulled the sink plug, poured in a little of the shampoo over the stains, and pressed the wet fabric into the water as the sink filled.

"It's so hard, Father. I tried to do the right thing. Save the Undefended. Save Duff and Widget. I could only do that by stealing the truck. To save Forest Moss and the others, I had to steal the train. But . . . doing the right thing led to so much death. I know that I should feel awful right now but the truth of it is, I found slaughtering day more upsetting. Animals are such helpless things. The chickens will run right up to you, expecting corn, not to be grabbed and killed. It always felt like a betrayal of trust. Today didn't feel like that. If anything, we were the chickens. We thought that everyone had agreed to play nicely with each other. I wouldn't have brought my unborn child to Pittsburgh if I'd known that the oni were about to attack. Peace only works if both sides agree to play fair. If one side attacks, the other must defend itself."

The tub finished filling. She checked to be sure it wasn't scalding hot. Leaving the dress to soak in the sink, she went to get Forest Moss.

"Humans have such tiny tubs," he complained as she led him into the bathroom. "I wish to bathe properly with you."

"Someday," she promised.

Once he was warmed up, she got him out and dried off and into the bed. She showered longer than she should have. It felt wonderful to clean the day off of her.

The soak in the soapy cold water had done the trick. The dress was innocent of blood. She wrung it out in a towel and hung it up to dry.

She turned off all the lights, said her prayers, and crawled into the massive bed. The sheets had been freshly washed and were a higher thread count than she'd ever experienced. It felt wonderful to climb in.

The wise part of her whispered like an old crone that she should be leery of the room and its luxury as she wouldn't want to leave it when it came time. She hugged the softest pillow and whispered firmly, "I will enjoy this now. Leaving is a problem for the future me."

A knock at the door woke her late the next morning. She sat up and glanced about the room in confusion. Where was she? Oh, yes, the William Penn Hotel. Alita Chang had offered her family's place as a refuge for the night. Her stomach roiled, reminding her that she hadn't eaten since the sandwich on the train. If she didn't eat soon, morning sickness would wreak havoc on her.

Forest Moss lay beside her, still deep asleep.

There was another knock at the door.

"Coming!" she called in English without thinking as she climbed from the bed—and realized that she was naked. She hurried to the bathroom to check her dress. It was still very cold and damp to the touch. The idea of pulling it on made her skin crawl.

A third knock, a little louder.

"Who is it?" she called out in Elvish since it was most likely one of the marines.

"Dagger!" came the reply. "We have fetched breakfast!"

Olivia didn't really want to answer the door wrapped in a towel or sheet but if she didn't eat, she'd be throwing up shortly. Besides, she'd seen all of the marines buck naked more times than she could count. Dagger wouldn't see anything wrong with Olivia answering the door wrapped in a towel.

"Hold on." Olivia took the biggest towel and wrapped it around her torso. It covered everything a sundress would but she still felt ashamed. The Ranch had stamped its will on her no matter how hard she fought it. She unlocked the door and forced herself not to use it as a shield against the marines.

Luckily, only Dagger was in the immediate vicinity, carrying a stack of wooden lunch boxes. For days the marines had been showing up with the bento-like containers with meals from the main encampment of the Fire Clan.

"You've been to the camp?" Olivia stepped back and waved Dagger in. She wanted to shut the door quickly. The marine was female, although she was a full foot taller than Olivia. For some reason their difference in height made Olivia feel younger than when she was around the male elves.

"Ya!" Dagger brushed past Olivia to carry the boxes to the room's minimalist desk. Her redcoat uniform looked spotless. She had her sword at her side but she'd left her rifle someplace else. Today she had her long, brassy red hair up in a ponytail that swayed side to side as she walked.

Olivia shut the door, puzzling over how the marines had gotten to Oakland and back. They had ridden on the bus yesterday but it seemed unlikely that the marines figured out Pittsburgh's complex bus system with that one trip. She hadn't made a point of explaining the street signs indicating what bus picked up where.

Oh God, what if they'd just flagged down a passing bus and demanded to be taken to Oakland—ignoring the fact that the predetermined route had been in the opposite direction?

"How did you get out to Oakland and back?" Olivia said.

"We asked the little one, Alita, what we should do about food. She said that they are too low on food to give it out free. We told her if we could get to the Fire Clan camp, we could pick up food there, so she got a *pickup truck* to drive us out there."

"Pickup truck" had been in English and said as if Dagger had carefully practiced the words. Olivia guessed that Alita had used her Resistance contacts to arrange the ride. She wasn't surprised that the Changs couldn't feed twenty-three unexpected guests in a few hours' notice. The supermarkets were picked bare. The only places with reasonable supplies were the ones that dealt with local farms.

Dagger also had her diaper-changing bag filled with baby clothes and a large travel pack. The female undid the ties of the canvas bag to hold out a bundle of clothes. "I thought that we should go to the glass palace and gather your things."

"Bless you!" Olivia took the light blue maternity dress with white flowers off the top and ducked into the bathroom to strip off her towel and pull on the clean dress. Only when she was safely dressed did she realize that Dagger truly meant all her things. She owned very little since Forest Moss blew up her house. She had picked up some clothes while shopping at Kaufmann's with Jewel Tear but not much more than underwear, socks, and three maternity dresses with expanding waistlines.

While she was glad for the change of clothes, why had Dagger brought every single thing? Even the baby clothes? Did the female think Olivia was staying at the hotel forever?

"Thank you for the clothes," Olivia started cautiously, "but why did you bring everything?"

"Glaive Smites the Sun asked where we had spent the night. I told him it was a human enclave run by Wind Clan Beholden." Dagger repeated what Aiofe must have told the marines, changing "hotel" into "enclave." The two probably were quite similar—Olivia wasn't sure. This was the first time she had stayed at either one. "The holy one said that we should stay where we were. Oakland is still quite dangerous. The crystal palace is not safe enough since its defenses have not been completed, especially with Forest Moss unable to call the Spell Stones. The enclaves out there are overcrowded already, even the new one. The Wyverns will instruct the Stone Clan that they have ordered the expense, so Alita's household will be paid for our stay."

Dagger was grinning, as if all this was good news. Olivia supposed it was. It felt like a defeat. The Ranch had been a hard lesson that there was little in the way of charity—everything had a price.

Yet Glaive was thinking of the safety of them all. If they were attacked at the Phipps, the royal marines would put themselves between Olivia and the oni. It would be selfish of her to risk their lives when there was a safer option.

"You like it here?" Olivia guessed.

"Oh, yes, we all like it greatly!" Dagger's smile grew wider. "It is very much like the Cathedral. There are so many interesting things to find. There is the television, which is very fun. The others are watching it now! The beds are nicer than our cots.

There are more latrines than we are used to and they do not smell. Everything washes away. Human latrines are wonderful. The soaps are pleasant."

Dagger sniffed the back of her hand and then held it out to Olivia. "Smell how nice it is. It is like fruit. Ox thought it was some kind of candy and tried to eat it. Aoife stopped him."

They were like toddlers. Tall. Deadly. Toddlers.

"Prince True Flame will be sending some of the marines back to the East Coast," Dagger said. "We will be staying with you. We're very glad at that. But it made us think. When this war is done, we will go back to the barracks, never to return to the human city and that makes us sad."

"Never?" Olivia said.

"This is Wind Clan territory with two undeveloped Stone Clan holdings. It is doubtful that any Fire Clan households would set up here. Even if they did, they would not have *laedin* such as we. Royal marines are born in the barracks and will die in the barracks. We do not know the life of a normal household. One would think we are mad dogs, frothing at the mouth.

"Before we came to Pittsburgh, we were happy with our lot. The barracks was all that we knew. We never even interacted with the *laedin* who lived within an enclave. Coming here, though, has shown us what we are missing.

"And there is this." Dagger pulled the tiny onesie from the diaper bag. "If we do happen to spawn children among us, they would be fated to the barracks too. It is a circular trap."

Olivia heart went out to the female. "If you want to stay, can't you?"

"We need to be part of a household. Our elders would not allow us to leave the royal marines to drift in a city held by Wind Clan. In Fire Clan lands, yes, but not here."

Olivia sensed where the conversation might be going. She and Forest Moss were a household of *domana* level with the money and land to make a go of it in the city. The marines might own their weapons and the clothes on their backs. It was possible, though, that the weapons belonged to the crown. Certainly when an American soldier was honorably discharged from the army, he didn't keep his rifle. Even if the royal marines were allowed to stay in Pittsburgh, they might not be able to survive with winter setting in. Yes, there were houses to squat in, but the marines had no idea how to get them heated and the water running. They would be limited to food they could hunt—perhaps without actual weapons.

A small selfish part of her couldn't ignore the fact that she and Forest Moss would benefit greatly by teaming up with the royal marines. The last few days, however, had taught her that the relationship wouldn't be equal. Elves expected underlings to be completely loyal and obedient. She hated the idea of escaping the Ranch only to become the head of another zealot commune.

"Will you be our *domi*?" Dagger asked.

But she hated more the idea of refusing to help another person who was trapped in a situation that enslaved them to a future that they didn't want. "Okay, I will."

36: FORCE OF NATURE

⋖⋗⟶⟵⋖⋗

Tinker always moved like a force of nature now, because it was never just her going from point to point. She had her Hand and random strays who attached themselves to her. There were tengu darting overhead, keeping watch for snipers. There were EIA guards holding reporters from various news agencies at bay. There were members of Team Tinker hanging out, pretending that they weren't part of the militia. Royal marines still flooded the area and at least one set of Wyverns herded some of the red-coated marines after Tinker in the name of extra protection. She decided to walk to Prince True Flame's camp because it was such a short distance that it seemed silly to drive. It felt like the world shifted with her as she came out of Poppymeadows and headed toward the sea of white canvas tents where the Fire Clan had camped under the massive Wind Oak trees.

Everyone watching and waiting for her to do something.

She controlled the urge to do cartwheels or juggle to justify the intense focus. Pittsburgh was rattled by a full-on attack—complete with giant monsters. There was no reason to make light of their fears. If she was feeling helpless with everything that she had at her command, then the average person—human or elf or tengu or half-oni—was probably feeling utterly powerless.

Walking with *sekasha* was an odd learned skill—especially when you didn't know where you were going and they did. Tinker hadn't completely mastered it.

"Just walk in front of me!" she snapped at Stormsong. "All I can see is backs and shoulders."

Stormsong shifted forward with Cloudwalker flanking her. The two plowed through the sea of red-coated royal marines.

Windwolf had planned to make the grove of large ancient Wind Oaks into their Pittsburgh-based palace. Tinker had worried that the place would always be tainted by Sparrow's ambush. Now, it barely looked like the same place. All the trees but the oaks had been cut down and used as either firewood or rough timber. The tents of the royal marines had taken up the entire area like a sudden explosion of giant white mushrooms. Round patches of grass marked where some of tents had been taken down. The month of occupation had beaten down everything else into pathways of hard-packed dirt. It was obvious at a glance that half of the royal marines were going to be leaving Pittsburgh while a large number of them would remain.

Stormsong suddenly made a hard right, detouring them around the edge of a large tent. The structure was larger than the one where she first spoke with Windwolf's cousin and made of sturdier white canvas. The furniture within was the same. A teak folding table, richly carved chairs, a map chest, ornate rug, although this time everything was set on a wooden riser to make everything more weatherproof.

They had dodged around the west entrance to come in via the east entrance. The reason for the detour was immediately clear: the Stone Clan *domana* were heading out of the west opening, fighting among themselves.

"Spare us your endless childish whine, Cana Lily," one of them was saying. "I have decided on a course of action and you will obey me. That my decision benefits the Wind Clan is immaterial. Get your people to your gossamer. If you are of a mind to ignore my order, I strongly suggest you have a long private conversation with your First."

Tinker was glad that they had avoided the Stone Clan *domana*.

It meant, however, they collided with Prince True Flame. He wore wyvern-scale armor with a massive sword strapped to his back. His golden hair was woven into a tight, plain *sekasha* braid. His First, Red Arrow, was one step behind him.

Bow. Stormsong signed in blade talk as she shifted back to her normal position one step behind Tinker.

Tinker bowed to the prince, thinking of Tooloo's war against her daughter. Pure Radiance set up True Flame's grandfather as the first king of the elves. Was this merely a war over the gates to Earth or did Tooloo want something more democratic for the elves? How deep did this go? Did Tooloo want to disband the clans too?

Prince True Flame smiled warmly at her. "Beloved Tinker, I am heading for the East Coast via the train. We will be at Brotherly Love by midnight. We leave Pittsburgh to you, our little goddess of war. You did well yesterday. The Wyverns were impressed."

Behind him, Red Arrow nodded.

Tinker blushed as she'd been wondering what the elf society would be like if they got rid of the royal family. "Thank you."

"May the gods watch over you." Prince True Flame gave a slight bow in farewell.

"May the gods watch over you," Tinker echoed and returned the bow, this time without a reminder from Stormsong.

Prince True Flame walked away, calling out orders to the royal marines.

"I am glad you rested well," Windwolf said in greeting to her. "The Harbingers understand the peril and are united with us but Cana Lily is still lost in the Clan Wars. He felt the need to debate every detail of our plans. This took twice as long as it needed to."

"I would have been disappointed if you had already left." Tinker hugged him, still afraid that she might lose him. Yes, the others would be going with him to the East Coast but he was the only one able to fight as a *domana*.

"Because of Cana Lily, it was decided that the Stone Clan would load their gossamers first." Windwolf waved toward the airfield far to the west of the grove. Several living airships hovered in the pale blue autumn sky, framed by the vivid crimson of the Wind Oak leaves. The gondolas that the translucent beasts carried were black, edged by red or green, marking them as part of the Stone Clan. They bristled with weapons and had sawtooth prows that could work as rams against enemy ships. Windwolf's smaller gossamer was a distant shimmer in the western sky. Tinker knew that it was unarmed. Until recently, there was no airborne enemy in the Westernlands to fight beyond one nesting pair of wyverns. Even then, a human with a rifle dealt with those, not the gossamer.

"So, when they're done, you will leave?" Tinker hugged him tighter.

"I must go and protect our East Coast holdings and make sure that my brothers and sisters are safe."

Tinker nodding, knowing that if it were Oilcan, helpless and alone, nothing would stop her from saving him. She was glad that Windwolf had made her a *domana* at the start of summer. Even with all her cleverness, she would have lost so much if she hadn't had the power of the Spell Stones to call on.

Had Tooloo wanted the *domana* helpless? Surely not. It was one thing if they were alone on their world, but humans were just one sidestep away. Even if they didn't know how to make a gate now, they knew that Elfhome existed. They would find a way. Worse, the Skin Clan might still have forces on Earth. They might be marshalling forces even as the elves stood helpless.

History showed—again and again—what humans would do to natives unable to match their firepower.

"I need to reestablish the *domana* link to the Spell Stones," Tinker said. "Oilcan recovered the *nactka* last night. We can use one of them to cast a *mei*-wide spell to repair the damage done."

Concern flashed across Windwolf's face. "Spell-working is very delicate stuff. I spent decades learning it."

Tinker shook her head. There was no way she was casting a spell of her own design that could kill or maim all of Windwolf's brothers and sisters. "Forge will be the one who designs the spell. He's been working on it since yesterday. I'll help how I can."

How could she help? She knew next to nothing about spell-working. All those spells had been edited out of her copy of the Dufae Codex—probably because her curiosity would make them irresistible despite the danger.

"We'll need to be able to communicate so we'll know when it's safe to cast the spell," Tinker said.

"It will only take me a few hours to reach Aum Renau. At that point, we can use the distant voices."

"You'll need a copy of the shield spell for yourself," she realized. "Since the first didn't seem to change you, there's no telling what trying to reverse it would do."

She had printed off the shield spell at the tech center but hadn't thought to print more than one. She had the original email but Windwolf didn't have a computer. She could send a tengu with him. The simplest solution would be to print off the spell. She didn't have a printer at Poppymeadows. Oilcan might have one.

"I'm going to Sacred Heart." If there wasn't a printer there, she'd send the tengu out to find her one. "I'll have one of my Hand bring you a copy of the shield before you leave."

They stood a moment, silent, wrapped in each other's arms.

"I love you," she said.

"I love you," he said.

She didn't want to let him go but the clock was ticking. Once the Stone Clan was loaded and the airfield was clear, he would call his gossamer to the field and leave.

Forge's Second Hand were guarding Oilcan's newly constructed front gate. They opened the door to Cloudwalker's knock and allowed Tinker and her Hand in, cutting off all the people following in her wake.

Briar Rose greeted her in the foyer, smiling widely. She bowed and said, "*Domi*, welcome. Oilcan is not here at the moment. The kids are rearranging their new furniture. How can I help you?"

"Is Forge here? Awake?" *Healthy?*

"He's up on the second floor with the two little ones doing wood sprite stuff."

Two little ones...? Oh! The twins! She'd forgotten about them.

For one brief flash of terror, she considered turning around and fleeing back to Poppymeadows. She could get the tengu to find her a printer from there.

Courage! They're just little girls. Insanely clever little girls, unafraid to do the impossible. But little girls nonetheless.

She went up the stairs to find her grandfather and sisters.

Forge had taken over one of the second-floor classrooms as his bedroom. It had been painted rich forest green. The far wall was all windows from the waist up. They stood open to let in the autumn breeze, billowing out gauzy white curtains. Since Forge intended to stay a hundred years or more, he'd shipped in beautiful handcrafted ironwood furniture from his Southern holding. A massive armoire—eight feet high and ten feet long—created a room divider, cutting the big classroom into two defined areas. (Windwolf had brought such a piece from Aum Renau that broke down into a dozen individual pieces—a bit like wooden Lego blocks—so it could be moved easily.) The back of the room held a big four-poster bed with drawers for storage underneath and white drifts of mosquito netting hanging from a canopy tester. In the front of the room, there was a big round table with six sturdy chairs, a drafting table with a simple stool, a map cabinet, a set of tall bookcases, and a big secretary desk with a fold-down writing surface and a host of little drawers making up an upper cabinet. Under the deep sills of the windows were a dozen three-drawer campaign chests with metal fittings to protect the corners and legs. It felt very homey and permanent. It certainly explained why every time she saw Forge, he was wearing a different outfit.

Today he wore a loose white-cotton poet shirt and black pants of some soft denimlike fabric, styled on the same lines as carpenter pants. His long brown hair was up in a ponytail with writing tools tucked behind each ear and forgotten. He looked like he might be thirty-five at the oldest, not several thousand years old.

He leaned over the table, bracketed by two little girls in adult T-shirts worn as dresses.

Tinker hadn't been sure what "wood sprite stuff" meant. She guessed that Briar Rose meant the odd magical and technical things scattered everywhere one looked. The chalkboards were covered in diagrams of spells and mathematical formulas. There was a big plastic ice chest floating by the door. There were four luggage mules, which Tinker instantly coveted, roaming the old classroom. She had always wanted one but they were insanely expensive. How in the world did the twins get four? Why were the mules picking their way around Forge's room instead of wait-ing for the twins to move? Wasn't their default mode "conserve energy when user isn't in motion"?

On the top of the campaign chests was a large, obviously damaged, partially dissembled robotic dog. Beside it was a 3D printer making what Tinker assumed to be replacement parts. The robot was less coveted (she had access to elfhounds after all) but again was insanely expensive. Judging by the Team Tinker stickers on the printer, it was from her salvage yard, which meant Oilcan or Riki had moved it for the twins' use. She was leaning toward Riki because Joy was sitting beside it, eating rugelach cookies as if wallowing in decadence. *Little Miss Pocket Dragon gets anything Little Miss Pocket Dragon wants.*

If the tengu had gathered all this equipment—luggage mules, hovercarts, and 3D printers—then there was probably a printer nearby that could print off spells. Somewhere. Just not in Forge's space. Maybe upstairs...

Tinker was distracted by a miniature racecourse set up throughout the room. Jumps made of books and chunks of limestone. Banking turns and even a tiny loop-the-loop made from scrap lumber. Four white mice on little floating carts were zooming around the racecourse. Three of the mice had different colored scraps of fabric around their necks like scarfs that fluttered in the wind. All four were making fake engine noises as they raced through the jumps and turns. "Vroom! Squeal! Vroom-vroom!"

The distraction level was so high that it took Dark Scythe a full minute to realize that Tinker was standing at the door, taking in the chaos.

Fleeing might have been the correct choice.

But then, Tinker noticed that there were spell orbs whizzing around the girls' heads, threatening to bean Forge if he got too close. Where did the twins get the spell orbs? From Forge? Why didn't he give ones to her and Oilcan? She had secretly wanted one since she saw the pair that Jewel Tear had. Or had the twins made the orbs?

Tinker had expected identical twins and that she would have trouble telling them apart. But one looked more like Oilcan. Something about the nose and eyes. The other twin made Tinker realize for the first time Lain's family contribution to her. It was very much Lain and Esme's determined jawline.

"Hey, it's Tinker!" one of the mice squeaked in a little girl voice.

"And Pony!" another one squeaked.

The mice abandoned their race and came zooming toward Tinker and her Hand.

Her Hand did not cope well. Not surprising as she was a little freaked out herself.

"It's okay!" Tinker threw out her hand to block Pony from pulling his *ejae*. "They're not..." She parsed through options. *Real? Mice? Dangerous?* "Hostile."

Pony took his hand from his sword.

Of Forge's two Hands, only his First, Dark Scythe, was in the room. He had started visibly at the sight of Tinker and then locked eyes with Pony. They did the silent communication thing that Firsts did when *sekasha* collided. It was hard not to think that Dark Scythe was saying "help" or "not her too." The rest of Tinker's Hand drifted back out of the room, apparently satisfied that the area was safe and now fleeing the chaos under the disguise of giving Tinker privacy to be with her "family." Tinker wanted to ask them to stay but it was probably better to limit the number of weapons floating around.

"Tinker! Pick me up!" one of the mice demanded as all four scrambled off their floating carts.

She knelt down to eye the mice closer. They were tiny little robots, only crudely made, but they still projected so much personality that she could guess some of their names. The timid one in the back was probably Nikola. The one loudly demanding to be picked up, its right ear torn and dirt streaked across its face like war paint, had to be Chuck Norris. She picked up Chuck, surprised at how fragile the mouse felt. Chuck waved at Tinker enthusiastically.

How were they doing this? They weren't even born yet!

All four mice squeaked, talking over each other. "We made mini-bikes." "We can race just like you!" "We've seen videos of you racing!" "It was so cool!" "Vroom! Vroom!"

Tinker realized that some of her fear of her siblings was because she had been feeling somehow responsible for their very existence. That because she was born, they had been born, orphaned, running for their lives, and doing crazy, insane things. But there was no way that she could be blamed for whatever these mice siblings were. It was all set in motion before she was even born. She was not responsible for this insanity—and so her siblings felt a little less terrifying.

But only a little less.

"You're Chuck?" Tinker asked the mouse she was holding.

"Yup! Chuck Norris! Always was! Always will be!"

"I'm Scarlet Overkill!" Scarlet wore a red gingham scarf.

"I'm Nikola Tesla." He had a blue scarf and a voice that sounded like Christopher Robin. "Pleased to meet you."

"I'm Hunter Green!" Her scarf of green velvet was starting to fray at the ends.

Tinker was glad for the scarf color-coding because otherwise she wouldn't have been able to keep track of who was who as the mice moved around.

"Hey, guys?" the twin who looked like Oilcan called. "Weren't you racing? Did someone win?"

"Busted!" "Oh no, the race!" "Put me down! Put me down!" "Team Mischief, Go!"

Tinker put Chuck Norris down. The mouse ran to her tiny floating cart and took off at full speed.

"No fair!" Hunter Green cried and the other three followed.

The twins watched Tinker walk toward the table with guarded expressions. They seemed as leery of her as she was of them.

Tinker had never thought of herself as beautiful—probably because of the number of times that people had thought she was a boy. Roach's entire family. Windwolf the first time he met her. She realized now that it was merely that they took cues from what she'd been wearing and the shortness of her hair. The twins were pretty and they looked only slightly different from her at that age. A lot less dirt. Better manners. Not prone to cursing or saying snarky things. When they got older, and got dressed up nicely, they would be beautiful. Which made her wonder how she could still look in a mirror and think of herself as plain.

She was fairly sure the twins knew who she was. It had to be fairly obvious—unless she had even more sisters that she didn't know about. She wasn't sure what she should say, so she defaulted to simple manners. "Hi. I'm Alexander Graham Bell, but everyone calls me Tinker. Sometimes Beloved Tinker—although I'm not sure why. Something about Tinker being too short a name."

"I'm Louise Mayer," said the twin with Lain's chin.

"I'm Jillian Mayer," said the twin who reminded Tinker of Oilcan. "We have extra tablets, so we're giving one to Forge with a copy of his son's journal."

Forge took out a handkerchief to dab at tears welling up in his dark eyes. "It is a wonderful, wonderful thing. I feel so blessed. When Unbounded Brilliance vanished, his mother and I had so many questions. Had he been murdered somewhere nearby, buried just under our noses? Had he been slain by a monster that we had not hunted down and killed? Or had we somehow wronged him so badly that he fled our home? It is comforting to know that he had found a cause to dedicate himself to—one that could save our people from our ancient enemy. Yes, it is still tragic but at least his life meant something. He left something behind. While his life was short, he found love and had a child that he adored with all his heart. That is precious beyond words. I only wish my beloved could have read this before she was so cruelly betrayed."

Tinker felt another stab of guilt. "I'm sorry that I didn't... didn't manage to shield you from the spell. I assumed that Oilcan was in Oakland..."

"It is what it is," Forge said. "You cannot protect everything dear to you during a war. A stray arrow. A random horror attack. Treacherous mud. A flash flood. A chain breaking from metal fatigue. Disease running rampant through a camp. Even things that you think are within your control rarely are."

Tinker felt as if Forge had just listed ways he'd lost people he cared about. If she protested, saying that she should have known to send a copy of the spell to Oakland, it would be like saying that Forge was responsible for all those earlier deaths. She nodded, struggling to let go of her guilt for his sake. They should be able to reverse the spell and this was only a temporary problem. Right?

Tinker really hoped Forge knew how to reverse the spell as her knowledge of biology and healing was almost nonexistent. "How do we fix this?"

Forge shook his head. "Much as you wish to rush, we cannot immediately revert everyone. There must be a period of recuperation for anyone affected by the initial spell. The drain on the body is similar to a deadly disease. To attempt a second transformation spell now would put them all at serious risk of such things as organ failure."

Tinker flinched with the knowledge that she would have cast the spell instantly last night if she had had it on hand. "How soon, then?"

Forge pulled down the neck of his shirt to show that he had an active healing spell inked onto his chest. "Given the correct precaution, tomorrow morning at the earliest. This is one of the most basic of our recovery spells, so all should be familiar with it. I have advised Wolf Who Rules Wind to have his siblings' people know that it should be placed on the affected. I have let Oilcan's Beholden know that we need to track down Forest Moss and Jewel Tear and make sure their recuperation is accelerated in this manner. I have also contacted my holdings to the south. They will deal with the Stone Clan *domana* there."

Tinker wondered where the two Stone Clan *domana* ended up the night before that they needed to be tracked down. She'd warned that redheaded girl that the Phipps wasn't a secure place— where had she gone after that? Thorne Scratch had refused to allow Forest Moss to stay at Sacred Heart. Did she need to tell the tengu to find the girl and make sure she was okay? Where had Jewel Tear gone? Shouldn't she be upstairs someplace? Tinker thought casting the spell on the Pittsburgh-based *domana* was going to be the easy part of fixing the problem. They couldn't transmit the complex spell via the distant voices. She'd discovered that limit while picking the lock on the spell-locked box from the whelping pens. To hit Windwolf's siblings and whoever was in the Stone Clan holdings in the south, they were going to need to use a wide-area spell like the one that the Skin Clan used. At least Oilcan had managed to secure the *nactka*. The magical devices would allow Tinker and Forge to reverse the spell in one go. At least...hopefully they could.

"Can we reverse it?" Tinker asked.

"That's what we're trying to figure out," Jillian said.

"I am glad that you are here," Forge said. "I can teach you three what is safe to pass on."

"Safe?" Tinker, Louise and Jillian all echoed.

Forge laughed. "I am sorry, it is not a subject to make light of but I delight in your youthful curiosity."

"There is nothing more dangerous than a curious wood sprite," Dark Scythe murmured.

Forge indicated Dark Scythe standing behind him. "My people will trust you. I suppose the Harbingers' Hands are well used to us too. I worry about the others who do not know that our curiosity is checked by our love of others. All spell-working was outlawed after the Rebellion. Because of Tempered Steel, we were allowed to improve crops and do limited work on animals that could be otherwise considered disabled. For example, we were allowed to cure fainting goats."

"Fainting what?" Tinker asked.

"Fainting goats!" Louise said. "They're goats with congenital neuromuscular disorder that makes them appear to faint. It's not a true faint, where they would lose mental awareness, but a sudden muscle stiffness that makes them topple over when startled. Earth has them too. They're said to be easier to keep fenced in because they can't jump over fairly low barriers, so farmers continued to breed the animals despite the defect. I think it's cruel, though, as it makes them unable to run away from true danger."

"That is the general opinion of those who would otherwise ban spell-working," Forge said.

"Will they allow the spell to be reversed?" Tinker asked.

"They who?" Jillian asked.

Forge turned to his First. "What will the Wyverns rule in this?"

"We convened and discussed it late last night since the answer to that question would be needed in short order. The Wyverns will allow it. All those who lost their link to the Spell Stones were born with the connection. It would not be a sin to return them to the way that they were."

"Excellent!" Forge said.

"For real?" Jillian muttered in English. "They had to debate that?"

"They're touchy on the subject," Tinker answered in English. "The Skin Clan did a lot of horrible things to the elves when they were their slaves. They see any spell-working as a slippery slope, so they're careful."

"But you and our cousin...?" Louise murmured, avoiding Oilcan's name.

"Don't try to apply logic to it—you'll only hurt your brain," Tinker said quietly.

Forge gave Tinker a querying look.

"It's good that we're allowed to fix those who have lost their ability," Tinker said instead of admitting what the conversation had really entailed.

The twins nodded solemnly as if that was *totally* what they were discussing. Was she that good at looking innocent? It was impressive and terrifying at the same time.

"How do we do it?" Tinker asked, trying not to think of the future when she was going to be responsible for heading off her little sisters. Were the other four going to be this sneaky too?

Focus, Tinker, focus!

Forge was sorting through papers and thus didn't notice her sudden panicked thought. "When we set up the stones, we gave out copies of the spell that could be used in cases like yours, where a *domana* wanted to give a person who they had marked with a *dau* the ability to access the *esva*. The stones represented a huge tactical advantage. We had thought all of the command positions would be given access to them. All four clans, though, only spell-worked a few thousands of their people during the Rebellion. We started to be concerned that it meant that the *domana* were hoarding their power."

"Or they were afraid of their Hands," Tinker said.

"Hmm, that *is* possible." Forge pulled out a giant piece of paper with a complex spell drawn out onto it. "Only *domana* overseen by *sekasha* are allowed to promote someone into their caste."

Tinker recognized the general design of the spell as being similar to the one that Windwolf had used to change her into an elf. His had had a few embellishments, probably to deal with the fact that she was human—mostly human.

Forge stepped back to let the twins study the paper. Tinker wasn't sure if he realized that they were taking pictures of it. He continued with his magic lessons. "The idea of the Spell Stones came to us after the warlord Death complained that most offensive and defensive spells on the battlefield were dependent on ley lines. You could build a fortress on a *fiutana* but if you marched to meet the enemy, attempting to expand your area of control, you had to make do with whatever level of magic was in the area to tap. Protective spells like those of the *sekasha* can fail if the area has too little power to support them. We discovered that magic could be jumped from one point to another up to a *mei*. We considered creating a talisman of some sort, but to be honest, that seemed too simple—trite—to us."

Given the level of mechanical technology that the elves had now, Tinker doubted that any handheld device would have had even a fraction of the versatility. She hadn't studied the Spell Stones closely while at Aum Renau: after she disassembled the laundry machines, she was actively discouraged from going anywhere near the Spell Stones. But even with her casual examination, she could tell that they could be easily expanded. It would be like plugging another board into a computer. The finger positions and key words gave a mind-bogglingly wide range of triggers. She'd been impressed by the highly ingenious design. It tickled her now to know that it had been her family that invented them.

The conversation detoured into Forge explaining to the twins what the Spell Stones looked like and how they were constructed. It was impressive that the two girls took turns listening intently and then making detailed notes. A lifetime of joint building meant that the twins could tag-team the process that Tinker always tackled solo. More than once, the twin making notes would make a slight noise or utter a single word, and the other would back Forge up to a previous point for clarification.

Forge's description featured elementary magical construction principles that Tinker had already deduced from her brief inspection. The Spell Stones were basically vertical casting circles with the spells permanently inlaid onto them. Around the stones was the vast circle of the "operating system" that decided which spell would be triggered. Tinker would need to nail Forge down later for a more in-depth discussion. They were getting lost in the weeds.

"What we need to know is how the *domana* are linked to the Spell Stones and how the Skin Clan broke the connection and how to repair the broken . . . part." Biology was not Tinker's strong suit; she didn't like the arbitrary nature of it. Evolution. Mutation. Resistance. It was all too-random chance instead of good concrete numbers. The only reason she knew anything at all about how cells worked was a lifetime of interactions with Lain. There was a reason she hadn't known how to heal Windwolf other than slapping a randomly picked spell out of the Codex onto him.

"Ah. Where to start?" Forge considered a moment, scratching his chin. Her grandfather, Tim Bell, had the same habit. Tinker hadn't thought that such a thing was biological. She eyed the twins, wondering what quirks they might share.

"Magic etched itself into our genetics long before the Skin Clan enslaved us," Forge said. "It is woven into our very warp and weft. It is the same with all creatures born on our world, some more imbued than others, but none have been untouched. Without magic, most of the creatures of Elfhome would die. It is why the transfer of this city—to and fro, between the two universes—has never triggered an ecological disaster on either world. Humans and elves are among the few creatures that can live on each other's worlds. Even the dragons, if stripped of magic, will eventually die. Every creature of Elfhome is harmonized to a different spectrum of magic, depending on where its ancestors evolved."

"Like with the monster call whistle?" Jillian asked.

Monster call whistle? Riki had used some kind of whistle to pull Impatience off Tinker shortly after she had turned Turtle Creek into blue soup.

"Yes, exactly," Forge said. "When the Skin Clan would vanquish a nomadic tribe, they would attempt to erase it completely by scattering the members far and wide. The thing is that they rarely would move their slaves beyond their home continent. It meant that in any one region, all the slaves shared the same harmonization even though they came from countless different tribes. When we designed the Spell Stones, it became clear that the various clans wanted devices that only they could use. At that time, it made sense tactically, so we cooperated."

"But wouldn't the Skin Clan of that area be able to use them too?" Tinker asked. Pony had been sure that the enemy wouldn't use a general death spell since they were too close biologically to their slaves.

Forge seesawed his hand. "Evolution is a messy thing. Random tosses of the dice and then never throwing anything away, just in case it would be useful again. Even before the Skin Clan started to play with our genetics, at least eighty percent of it was bits and pieces of ancient architecture. A bit here from when we were fish in the sea. A fragment there from when we scuttled about on four limbs. The Skin Clan were invaders. They were from a section of the world where none of their slaves had crawled out of the sea and swung about the trees before becoming proper elves. It is entirely possible that they were originally humans or oni who had gotten lost in caves and ended up on Elfhome. We have no way of knowing what their origin was as they erased even their own traditions to merge us into one race."

"I thought it was related to the ability to see magic," Tinker said and then remembered that Tooloo had been the one who told her—wasn't she? Or was it Lemonseed, who prefaced her story with a disclaimer that she didn't know everything related to the events? Neither one was a reliable narrator.

Forge shook his head. "We did require that every *domana* have the last improvement that many of the Skin Clan were adding to themselves—the ability to sense magic. It was vital to detecting the results of the scry spells and determining range and even judging if you're connected to the Spell Stones—but no, it's not the genetic factor that determines who can call the stones.

"It means that even you"—Forge tapped Louise's nose playfully—"have the ability to call the magic from the Spell Stones despite not being able to see the magic."

Tinker probably could have used the Stone Clan Spell Stones before her transformation if she had known the initialization spell. Her grandfather had edited it out of the electronic edition of the Dufae Codex that he'd given her and Oilcan. It had handicapped them as children but it also meant that the Stone Clan had remained unaware of them until that summer.

"What determines the ability, then?" Tinker asked.

"The harmonization that we spoke of. It is a tremble in the ether. The *domana* only needs to pluck the string, so to speak. Nor is the ability an on-or-off thing like those switches for the lights overhead. We had to use multiple identifiers to make sure all the *domana* could call their stones—not just for our generation but the generations to come."

Louise fumbled through the Elvish. "So it's a... dominant gene?" She did a quick sketch that biologists used to represent genes. They always looked like worms to Tinker. "That is to say, a child receives a version of each gene from their parents. We call them *alleles* in English. If the *alleles* of a gene are different, then only one is expressed. The one that is expressed is dominant. The other is considered recessive; it is masked by the dominant gene."

Forge gave a surprised laugh. "I'm simplifying the science. The Skin Clan has taught us very many harsh truths about what the cells in our bodies can do. They are much more fluid than one supposes. A frog, for example, starts out as an egg, becomes a tadpole without any legs, and ends up as a four-legged creature. That process is not controlled by genetics alone but also by processes within the cells. There is a parasite that invades tadpole bodies and triggers the 'grow a set of legs' process in the cells, causing the adult frog to have six or more limbs."

"Why would it do that? How can it do that?" Tinker asked, disliking biology even more.

"The affected frogs are slow to evade predator birds, which are another host for the parasite in their lifecycle. Evolution can be as cruel a master as the Skin Clan."

"How does 'too many legs' relate to our problem?" Tinker asked.

"As I said, there are many trash pieces of old genetics in our system, most of which are not active. They are from the periods of time when we were closer to frogs than apes. Trust me, you do not want to know how we came to realize this."

Dark Scythe sighed. "Now they will surely want to know."

His First was completely right. The twins' eyes gleamed with curiosity. Tinker had seen the whelping pits—she didn't want to know. Besides, that was all messy biology.

Forge ignored his First. "We have retained much of the genetic trash at the same level as 'elves have two eyes, ten fingers, and ten toes.' For example, citrus has a certain vitamin in it necessary to ward off sickness. Most animals can produce it within their own bodies via an enzyme in their liver or kidneys. We elves have the genetics to do so but for some reason, we lost the ability."

"It was lost in humans too," Louise said. "It's nonfunctional gulonolactone oxidase pseudogene. We have the gene within our DNA but it doesn't actually work."

"Fascinating," Forge said.

Of course the one with Lain's chin was into biology. The messy nature of the science must not annoy her little sisters as much as it annoyed her. It was one big difference between them.

"Wolf Who Rules Wind is a rare creature in that his parents were *domana* from different clans," Forge said. "It was unusual during the Rebellion and unheard of during the Clan Wars. Any one of his siblings could have inherited both sets of identifiers from their parents—but sometimes families only have girls or boys. That Wolf Who Rules kept his ability to call both sets of Spell Stones is an important clue to exactly what the enemy spell did."

"How so?" Tinker and Louise and Jillian all said.

Okay, that was spooky, Tinker thought.

"We thought that *domana* like Wolf Who Rules Wind would be much more common over time. It meant that the initialization spell needed to be slightly different for all four clans. Setting it up that way meant that you could hold two spells from different *esva*."

The twins looked to Tinker for confirmation. Tinker nodded slowly. She had been aware of it but hadn't actually considered it from a design angle. She had only been able to pull the trick in space because the Wind Clan and Stone Clan initialization were on different hands. Fire used the same hand and fingering as Stone but different activation words. She could only assume that Wind and Water were likewise tied together. Having the foresight to set it up that way was pure genius.

"Fingering is always the same, no matter the *esva*," Tinker explained to the twins, holding up both hands with the fingers molded into the correct position. "The activation words are different."

Forge launched back into his lesson. "Our enemy has had thousands of years to analyze what we have done. What they have had to study, though, were *domana* who were born to single clans. Wolf Who Rules was the first person who could use multiple *esva* and he has been under Pure Radiance's watchful eye since she named him. Our enemy obviously did not realize how deeply we layered the ability to call the Spell Stones. Someone like Wolf Who Rules would have natural redundancy."

Which was why Pure Radiance encouraged his parents to spit out kids until one of them had both *esva*. It weirded Tinker out to know that she "harmonized" to three different continents. That was practically half the planet.

Joy suddenly appeared on the table as if teleported. She made the *sekasha* stiffen as she came within biting range of their *domana*.

"It's okay!" Tinker was slightly dismayed that the twins echoed her a heartbeat later. Was this now a thing? That sharing genetics put them on the same wavelength? *Surely not. Surely. Right?*

"All gone," Joy announced, tossing the cookie bag to Jillian.

"You promised to be good if we gave you cookies," Jillian said.

Joy made a rude noise. She marched across the tabletop to Forge, making Dark Scythe take a step forward, intent on the baby dragon. Forge merely looked interested. Joy ignored the *sekasha* to rear onto her back legs and extend her front paws to Forge. She made a grabbing gesture.

Like approaching a strange dog, Forge curled his fingers into a protective fist and held out the back of his hand.

Dark Scythe was obviously trying not to show that he was dying inside to keep Forge from doing anything stupid, while at the same time letting his *domou* do whatever he thought was wise.

Joy caught hold of Forge's hand with both of her front paws and turned it this way and that, eyeing it closely. "Just Brilliance. Not mine."

She let go of his hand. Turning, she eyed Tinker.

Oh, shit, Tinker thought. It was her turn. She had a thing about getting her hands near dragons, no matter their size.

Joy waddled over, still on her back legs, to do the "give me" gesture again. When Tinker didn't move, she made another rude noise and this time snapped her fingers impatiently.

Pony had shifted forward. He didn't bother to disguise the fact that he was not happy with the idea of her trusting Joy.

"She won't hurt you," Louise whispered. "She only attacks people trying to hurt us."

"It's fine," Tinker murmured to Pony and copied Forge's "strange dog" approach.

Joy's paws were like a kitten's. Soft pads with needle-sharp claws that lightly pricked Tinker's skin. Tinker expected the same brief inspection. Instead, Joy swarmed up her arm to perch on her shoulder and press nose to nose with her.

"Joy!" Louise cried and lunged across the table to grab the baby dragon.

Joy, however, had anchored herself firmly via Tinker's ears and a tail wrapped around Tinker's neck. "Hmm. Brilliance..."

"Let. Go. Of. Her," Louise growled, tugging gently.

Joy ignored Louise, still nose to nose with Tinker. "Clarity. Junk. More Junk. Still mine."

The baby dragon let go. Louise staggered backward.

Pony picked up Tinker and backed away from the table.

"I'm fine! It's fine! Everything is fine!" Tinker beat on Pony's arms until he put her down.

"I'm sorry!" Louise cried, backing away with Joy still in her hands. "I'm really, really sorry! Maybe it would be better if she wasn't here."

One of the laptops on the table made a loud noise, drawing the attention of everyone in the room.

"Oh! The timer! I forgot I set it!" Jillian said loudly as she jumped to turn it off. She typed on the keyboard and then closed the laptop before Tinker saw what she had entered. "It means that the final piece for Tesla should be almost done."

The mice popped their hovercarts up onto the top of the campaign chests and raced over to the printer. They dismounted to dash around the printer and the half-dissembled robotic dog, talking excitedly.

"What's so important about the robot?" Tinker asked.

"Tesla?" Jillian looked surprised. "It was the last present our mom and dad gave us. They got a nanny robot to protect us as we went to school. We couldn't have saved the babies without him."

"I broke Tesla trying to save Louise from Yves," Nikola said sadly. "I nearly got us all killed."

"You were brave." Jillian stroked the head of the timid mouse who was somehow their baby brother. "And you did save Louise. Yves would have killed her if he'd got in a second shot."

Tinker felt a flash of rage at Lain's older stepbrother that only cooled with the realization that the man was probably dead. At least, Esme seemed sure of it. The more Tinker heard about Lain's family, the less annoyed at Lain she became. With Yves and Sparrow both in Pittsburgh during the first Startup, the Skin Clan would have been able to easily keep track of Lain's every movement.

Tinker suddenly realized that only three of the mice were dashing around the robot. One of the mice was missing, as was Louise with Joy. She glanced around the room, feeling uneasy about the three disappearing.

"Tinker?" Jillian called her attention away from the missing siblings. "We asked the tengu for a printer. They said that you had one that you weren't using and that we should ask Oilcan about it. He said that it should be fine to borrow it. 'Should be' and actually is—that's two different things. Is it okay that we borrowed it? I know that it's a little late to be asking now but... sorry?"

"It's okay." Tinker didn't care about the printer being borrowed. She'd seen the grief that Oilcan had gone through when he lost his mother and—by default—father. Strangers had cleaned out his family's rented apartment, throwing away everything he hadn't packed into one suitcase. He'd treasured every little thing that he'd managed to bring with him. "Print as much as you need."

Tinker turned back to Forge. "I'm going to work up an action plan of what needs to be done to fix this mess. First and foremost, I'll need to make sure Windwolf has a copy of the shield that the twins developed."

"I can print off copies!" Jillian edged toward the door, pointing upstairs. "The tengu moved all our gear over this morning. I can run up and be right back with them."

All our gear? Tinker had been hoping that the twin had a printer nearby but she hadn't expected that they had already moved lock, stock, and barrel to Oakland. Had they decided not to stay in Haven? Did that mean that they meant to stay at Sacred Heart? With Oilcan as their guardian, or Forge? Or did they assume that they would be living with her?

Focus, Tinker, focus!

"Good," she forced herself to say. "Thank you."

Only after Jillian disappeared did Tinker realize that the girl had taken the remaining mice with her. The room suddenly seemed very empty. How did such small souls take up so much space?

She pushed on with her plans. "I'll have one of my Hand get the spell to Windwolf. We'll be able to communicate with him via the distant voices, so we'll cast the counter-spell when... when we get it ready...and the time is right?"

She felt an odd spark of magic from somewhere above her. She ignored it as Sacred Heart was full of elves, any one of which could cast some kind of minor spell.

"So the important questions are: how soon can we get the spell ready, and when will the time be right?" *And maybe something about a game of chess with monkeys?*

A second spark of magic made Forge lift his head to stare upward.

"Odd," Forge said.

"You can still feel magic?" Tinker asked as a third spark went off.

"Yes, I've lost connection to the Spell Stones so I can't tell when someone is tapping them, but a magical device used within the same building still sparks against my senses."

"Magical device?"

Oilcan's kids had almost nothing to their names except human goods that Oilcan had scrounged out of thrift stores. Were the twins using something? Did they invent something?

"A very elaborate spell..." Forge murmured as a luggage mule picked its way past him.

It suddenly hit her. The twins, the mice, and one of the luggage mules were gone—as well as the floating ice chest by the door. Those little brats! They created as much chaos as possible in order to sneak the *nactka* out of the room!

"Shit!" Tinker growled as the fourth spark rippled over her. "Shit!"

How many baby dragons were locked in the *nactka*? Ten? More like six now!

Tinker started to run.

37: I LOVE IT WHEN A PLAN COMES TOGETHER

The plan had gone flawlessly.

Louise and Jillian had talked the tengu into ferrying all their tech toys from Haven to Sacred Heart. It required a handful of handwritten spells to float the bigger pieces like the luggage mules, but with twenty thousand tengu on call, the items arrived within an hour of their request.

The rule "people believe the stupidest things if you deliver the story while bleeding" seemed to apply. Crow Boy was the one who was covered in blood and still asleep, but the fact that a *yamabushi* nearly died while retrieving ten baby dragons made anything that the twins did credible. The tengu stacked the thrifted furniture without asking many annoying questions. They arranged the beds, nightstands, desks, chairs, love seat, bookcases, and other random pieces of furniture into a Jenga puzzlelike fortress with a secret inner hollow core.

Then—just like the twins planned—they set up the most chaotic mess that they could imagine without the adults losing patience, untethered the floating ice chest, and guided it upstairs.

Stealing the chest behind Forge's back had been a little scary as he was one of the original gangster wood sprites, creator of the Spell Stones, and wicked smart. He didn't know technology, though, so he'd been easy to distract, especially when he went off into teacher-mode.

The plan became terrifying when Tinker arrived. She was wood sprite smart but she might also have the ability to see the future like Louise. Luckily, they had created a big enough chaos field that their older sister hadn't figured out what they were doing.

It was, however, only a matter of time before the adults realized what they had done.

Ten of the delicately etched monster-sized eggs sat inside the ice chest. Relief washed through Louise. They had lost only one of the eleven baby dragons trapped inside the magical devices. She had been afraid that there would only be one or two *nactka* inside the chest. She loaded them onto the luggage mule and directed it into their fortress of furniture. There was so little space that she needed to stack the *nactka* carefully into every nook and corner. Once the *nactka* were hidden deep within the pile of furniture, she had the luggage mule back up and close the tunnel so only a child could crawl into the pile. She threw a blanket over the luggage mule so it was less obvious how to undo their work.

Jillian dashed into the room, carrying the four babies. "It worked! It worked! I can't believe it!"

"Not for long." Louise crawled into the secret hollow within the furniture. "We need to hurry!"

Jillian put the babies on the floor to crawl in after Louise.

It was dim within the space but light filtered in from dozens of breaks between the furniture. Joy bounced around the tight space excitedly, pausing often to rear back onto her haunches and clap her hands. The babies were talking all at once, each wanting a turn to open a device.

"I hope they're friendly," Jillian whispered, reminding Louise that Joy had been angry and scared when she was released.

"Joy is here to explain things," Louise said with more confidence than she felt. Joy was not the most dependable collaborator. Still, the baby dragon had managed to keep the *sekasha* hyper focused on her as Chuck had the luggage mule undo the restraints on the floating ice chest and towed it away.

Jillian spoke the keyword to unseal the first *nactka*. The dome of the device cracked at the lines and unfolded like a flower, as if the cream-colored shell was on hinges. The baby dragon inside had been curled up as if asleep. It uncurled and yawned deeply. It was a very pale cream color—so pale with just the barest blush of yellow to suggest that it wasn't a pure white.

"Finally," the baby dragon said in Elvish as if it was bored waiting.

The now-empty *nactka* took up unneeded space. Louise pushed it down the tunnel and out of the fortress without bothering to close the device up.

Chuck Norris opened the second *nactka*, revealing a beautiful little dragon that was a rich purple shade.

"Oh, I didn't expect them to be all different," Louise whispered as she cleared the second *nactka* away. For some reason, she thought that the baby dragons would all be twins to Joy.

The purple dragon eyed the girls suspiciously but Joy launched into a speech in the dragon language. (At least Louise assumed that it was the dragon language as it sounded the same as when Joy had spoken with Impatience and Providence.) The purple dragon relaxed, grunting as if just annoyed with the situation.

Louise opened the next *nactka* to reveal a nut-brown dragon with a diamondback pattern. It eyed her with curiosity and was told firmly "Mine!" by Joy.

This got a raspberry blown at Joy by the nut-brown one and a long discussion started by the pale cream dragonet. Louise shoved its empty prison out of the fort.

Jillian opened a fourth *nactka*, revealing a stunning iridescent turquoise-colored dragon. There was a sound of running footsteps coming up the stairs.

"Oh, crud! They figured it out!" Louise grabbed another *nactka*. "Open faster!"

38: FORTRESS OF FURNITURE

Ten empty *nactka* sat in front of a furniture tower in the middle of the twins' bedroom. There was no sign of the twins.

Oh, dear gods, have my little sisters run away into a city filled with oni? Tinker stopped at the door, fully aware that ten *sekasha* had charged up the stairs with her. She put out a hand to keep the warriors from pushing into the room.

They're just little girls! Well, little wood sprite girls with eleven baby dragons and four impossible-to-define babies.

"Louise?" Tinker called—trying not to snap. "Jillian?"

No answer.

She hoped that they were still in the room, just hiding, perhaps on the other side of the furniture. They could even be invisible. "I'm not angry." *Much.* "I am...upset. You should have discussed this with me before letting them all out."

"You were going to use them!" Louise's little-girl voice came from somewhere inside the tower. Correction: fortress of furniture. It seemed haphazardly stacked until you realized that it created a solid barricade with little spyholes.

"Yeah!" Chuck Norris squeaked. "We can outsmart you! We have you outnumbered!"

"Chuck!" Louise yelped.

"You didn't actually need the baby dragons!" Jillian shouted. "You can just do the spell regularly. Get everyone together. Bammo!"

"Surely we can think of some other way," Nikola called out, the voice of reason.

"She's going to have to," the two other mice muttered together. "Now that we let them all out."

This was life with herself. Karma. Tinker grumbled, remembering similar scenes from her childhood where it was Lain arguing with the child who was sure that she was right.

"I'm hoping that you're right, but we can't know that—not now. We don't know where the main force of the oni are and what they plan to do and if we can get to the East Coast to where Windwolf's brothers and sisters are unconscious. Six of his brothers and sisters are at his other holdings—all currently helpless. We might not be able to get to them. We certainly can't get to them quickly. Even with a gossamer, they're over a full day away. And that's just Windwolf's siblings. There's Stone Clan Spell Stones to the south with who knows how many *domana* who are currently helpless, and while we're trying to get to Windwolf's holdings, we're not going to be able to go save them!"

"We'll find a way!" Louise called back. "With Forge, there are four of us."

"Eight!" Chuck Norris squeaked.

No wonder many of her visits to Lain ended with Lain having a headache.

"Yes, we'll find a way," Tinker said. They now had no other choice.

39: DOWN THE RABBIT HOLE

It was as if Tristan had fallen down a rabbit hole into a totally different world. His sisters had taken him to Lain's house on Observatory Hill. They fed him Mickey Mouse sugar cookies and put him to bed in a room with the changeling's name literally written all over it. (What was this obsession of marking things in crayon? Judging by the wobbly child printing on the most unlikely of places, she had settled on her nickname early.)

There were no weapons in the bedroom, nor anything that could be made into one. Perhaps because it was used to house an inventive child, such things had been long stripped out. He considered trying to sneak out but the room also seemed tactically set up to make that difficult, if not impossible. What kind of wild monkey had his niece been as a child?

He kept his phone hidden but close at hand, set to vibrate. He tried out excuses to tell Lucien, trying to decide which one would be safest for both sides of his family. Near midnight, Lucien called.

"Yes?" Tristan whispered into the phone.

"Are you safe?" Lucien asked quietly.

Lucien didn't know that Tristan was with Lain and Esme if he was asking that.

"Yes." Tristan braced himself for Lucien asking where he was and why he wasn't with Adele. He still didn't have a good excuse as to why he left Mount Washington that didn't involve Lain and Esme. Times like this, it was best to wait for a question instead of offering up information.

"The key in your bag is to a business office on Fifth Avenue Place," Lucien said. "Hyde Enterprises. Ninth floor. The other offices on that floor are short-term leases—you should be able to come and go unquestioned. You'll find clothes, food, and money there."

Tristan knew that Lucien had many safe houses scattered around Pittsburgh. The building on the corner of Liberty and Fifth Avenues downtown was centrally located. His coming and going probably would attract less attention than some suburban house.

"Okay," Tristan whispered, still giving nothing away.

"Stay safe," Lucien said and hung up without asking anything more.

Tristan played the short conversation over and over in his head. Why hadn't Lucien asked about Adele? What had happened when Lucien got to WESA? All the tengu had left the radio station, so Tristan had assumed that Boo had also left. Why hadn't Lucien asked more about her? Had he captured her? Or had something else happened that put her on the backburner—if such a thing was possible...

The sudden lack of focus and information made him feel like he was freefalling.

My mother is dead. Bethany is dead.

It was a deep, dark rabbit hole.

Lain had taken charge of the baby chicken, keeping it warm, dry, and fed. It was cheeping in the corner of the kitchen as his sisters made him bacon, eggs, and pancakes. Esme arranged them into a smile on his plate before putting it before him.

"I am not a child anymore," he complained as she added whipped cream for "hair" on the pancake face.

"Yes, you are." Esme settled into the seat across from him and added whipped cream with gusto to her pancake. "We might have missed all the clues when we were younger but we know better now. You are a half-elf—or maybe more like seven-tenths elf."

They believed the old female's claim of their mother being part elf.

"I'm not a child-child," Tristan stated firmly while indicating the food art. Did he even enjoy this when he was five or ten? Maybe he did. It was so long ago. His memories of before his father took over his education were dim.

Lain eyed his plate and gave their sister a disappointed look. "He's right about that."

Lain sat down beside Tristan. She only had a mini-pancake on her plate and one egg. She was eating like an old lady concerned about her weight. It bothered him to see even more evidence of her age.

Esme shoveled into her breakfast with gusto. "He needs to relearn the joy of being a child. That freedom of not worrying about whether you remembered to pay the electric bill, or if you have clean underwear, or the leftovers in the fridge will give you food poisoning."

He flinched as he remembered the first time he ended up on the bathroom floor, feeling like he was about to die and having no idea why. No one had warned him that food could go bad. There was no one there to tell him to drink fluids to keep from getting dangerously dehydrated, nor to explain that electrolytes were nearly as important as water. He was afraid to bother anyone when it started and by the time that he was full-blown sick, he was too weak to find his phone and call for help. He thought he was going to die in that bathroom. The worst thing about it was that he didn't make the connection between the bad food and being sick the first time. He suffered through a second bout before he realized why.

"Why are you doing this?" Tristan asked.

"Because you're our baby brother," Lain said.

He made a noise and picked up his fork to smear the whip cream across his pancake to destroy the impression of a face. "I'm my father's son."

Esme made a rude noise, and said something with her mouth full that he couldn't translate. It was probably obscene by the way Lain frowned at her.

"Our mother loved children," Lain said. "Two was not enough to fill her heart. She wanted more. She would have gone to a sperm bank if your father hadn't cooperated. She glowed through her pregnancy and was radiant when she could finally hold you in her arms. You were always full of smiles when you saw us. Our names were your first words. We helped you take your first steps. How could we not love you?"

He'd felt that way with his secret baby sisters. They would toddle toward him, calling, "Tris! Tris!" They would demand hugs and attention, desperate for any adult affection.

If only he'd told their mother about them. She would have

loved his baby sisters. She might have been able to save Britany. Their mother, though, hadn't been able to keep herself and his older sisters safe from his father. Heaven's Blessing had maneuvered her into a marriage that was cold and loveless. She might not have been able to do anything to save the Eyes from his father's plans. But maybe she could have. If she had, she wouldn't have died completely alone.

"We know about Chloe," Lain said gently as she took a piece of jewelry out of her pocket and put it on the table. "Since she had Mother's necklace, we're assuming that you boys know—knew about her."

Oh, poor, proud Chloe.

"I gave the necklace to Chloe before she left Earth," Tristan admitted. It had been the last time he'd seen Chloe. "Mother never wore that piece so I didn't think she'd miss it. Chloe was fixated on her. I...I thought it was because she wanted to meet Mother. But after I came to Pittsburgh...it seems like the girls were jealous of how much Mother meant to me and Lucien."

It might have been why the Eyes thought Boo was dangerous even from the beginning. Boo had the nearly white-blond hair that their mother had.

"Girls?" Esme latched onto his slip. "Exactly how many children did your father steal from her?"

"All of them—even you, in the end," Tristan said.

"Tristan." Lain sounded like their mother in her firm and disappointed tone.

Ancient history should be safe enough to confess to.

"There had been five at one time," Tristan reluctantly started. "Father didn't create them immediately after the eggs being harvested. He planned to wait until Mother was older and less able to carry out her duties. All of Father's plans changed when the hyper-phase gate project fell into our laps. He wanted his own *intanyai seyosa* to deal with Pure Radiance and the rest of her caste. He hired surrogate mothers, all in New Jersey."

Esme snorted. "New Jersey. Thick with thieves."

"Mother must have realized at some level that someone in New Jersey had the girls," Lain murmured. "It would explain why she suddenly hated the state so much. I thought it was dementia setting in early."

"It took decades for everything to come together on the gate, especially after Dufae was killed. The girls were just graduating from high school when the Chinese turned the gate on for the first time," Tristan said. "Yves investigated Pittsburgh and set up contacts to smuggle Lucien and the girls into Pittsburgh."

"Good God!" Lain whispered. "Lucien looked like he was a grade school student when he was eighteen. You could still pass as a middle school student and you're...what, forty? Your father has to be insane, sending a child into a war zone."

"He needed people he could trust..." Tristan started to defend his father out of habit.

"You mean he wanted disposable tools," Esme said. "If he valued his children, you wouldn't have been running around in the middle of the night with a good chance of being killed."

"I was perfectly fine," Tristan said.

"You were not!" Esme snapped. "How do you think we found you? We had been talking about you and Lucien all day and I got a sudden feeling that you were in imminent danger."

Tristan deflected the statement with a question. "Why were you talking about us?"

"Tinker came to see us about her siblings."

The female elf claimed that the twins were on Elfhome. *Charging into danger even as we speak.*

"Are they okay? Louise and Jillian? There was this crazy elf who said they were in some kind of trouble."

Lain and Esme exchanged worried looks.

"I only had one dream of the children," Esme said. "They were all playing in a sandbox but Tinker's sisters kept taking all her toys. It seemed harmless."

"You should go check on them," Lain said. "I'll stay here with Tristan."

"The female elf also said I need to give the chick to Tinker with a message," Tristan said quickly, trying to squash the idea of him being left behind. If the twins were in trouble, he wanted to know and be able to do something.

"I can take the chick with me," Esme said.

"She said it had to be me," Tristan said. "It's all *intanyai seyosa* nonsense. The messenger might be the important part."

Esme growled with frustration and exchanged looks with Lain.

"We'll all go," Lain said.

✧   ✧   ✧

Tristan had spent the last few weeks hidden away in the forest of Elfhome. Father had had him smuggled in and dropped at the edge of the city and then ferried by boat to Lucien's camp downriver. Tristan had missed all the most famous landmarks, from the glass castle EIA offices to the Cathedral of Learning, to the Rim in Oakland with human businesses on one side of the street and the fortified enclaves of the elves on the other.

Said Rim was swamped with royal troops who should have been trapped deep within the forest and wiped out. Had their trap utterly failed?

Esme had driven Lain's SUV to the Rim. He had thought it was because Lain was crippled but instead it was because their vehicle had been stopped multiple times by Wind Clan *laiden* who recognized Esme as their *domi*'s mother and waved her through.

Esme paused in front of one enclave but then continued down the street until they got to a large brick building that looked like a century-old high school.

"Makes sense," Lain said mysteriously. "Go around to the back gate."

"Yeah, we're not getting in the front door," Esme added.

Esme made her way to a narrow back alley and parked in front of an ironwood gate. There was a spyhole slot at elf eye-level, which put it nearly a foot over Tristan's head.

"Hello?" Lain knocked on the gate.

The spyhole slot opened. For a moment there seemed to be no one there and then a boy jumped up to glance through the hole before dropping back to the ground.

"Hi, Lain," the boy called from the other side. "Are you looking for Oilcan? He's not here right now."

"I'm here for Tinker, Blue Sky," Lain said. "It's important to talk to her."

"I think she might still be here," Blue Sky called back.

There was a rattle of locks and the gate swung open to let them in. The area had been a small parking lot at one point with basketball and tennis courts on either side. The space had been converted into a barnyard with ramshackle animal pens.

Blue Sky was a male half-elf in blue jeans and a T-shirt that read TEAM BIG SKY. If the boy recognized Lain on sight, then he might be a friend of the changeling. Blue Sky was with a young, dusky-skinned female elf. Tristan hadn't realized that there were any Stone Clan children in Pittsburgh. Had she come with the Harbingers? Most confusing of all, there was a little lesser blood oni male with them. The three children had been in the middle of feeding a flock of six chicks that looked like slightly older models of the one in his hand, a pair of indi, a piglet, and an elfhound puppy.

One or more of the children obviously lived at the high school, which been turned into an enclave.

There was so much that Lucien hadn't told Tristan.

Blue Sky eyed Tristan with suspicion. He opened his mouth to ask questions. "Who is—"

"Blue!" the little female cried out and then shouted out in Elvish, "Shut the gate! Shut the gate! Quee!"

The piglet had escaped out of its badly made pen and was heading for the open gate.

Lain took advantage of the distraction to head them into the high school. There were several doors into the back of the building. They took a set of double doors that led into a wide shadowy hallway that reminded Tristan of the schools he had attended in the past. To the left were kitchens leaking out the clatter of dishes, sounds of running water, laughter, and the smells of breakfast.

The hallway led to the front foyer with doors leading to cafeteria, library, gym. A grand staircase headed upward to floors above. At the foot of the steps was a male Wind Clan *sekasha* who nodded to Lain and Esme.

"Mother. Mother's sister," the male said in Elvish, identifying the two women in their relationship to Tinker. "*Domi* is upstairs with Grandfather. Second floor. Last door on the right."

"Thank you, Little Egret," Lain said.

The place was thick with *sekasha*. Tristan counted over a dozen as they walked up to the second floor and down the hall to the last room on the floor. Most of them were Stone Clan. Obviously any attacker would have to go through all the warriors to get to their *domana*. Tristan hadn't considered how thin his protection was. On Earth, children could meander into the most restricted areas with simple lies like "I was curious" and "I'm lost" and be safe from harm. His age would not protect him here if his lineage came out. At least, that's what his father always claimed. His sisters marched up to Forge's room as if there was nothing to fear.

And there she was—an older version of the twins. She wore a Pitt baseball jersey and short shorts and a pair of boots, looking extremely human if you missed the pointed ears and almond eyes.

She glanced up from the papers covering the table and winced. "Oh gods, now what?"

"Has anyone checked on my other children recently?" Esme asked.

"Now you ask!" Tinker growled softly. "We could have used you last night. They were behind the enemy front line, duking it out with horrors and such. I sent Oilcan to go fetch them. You could have taken them home with you so that they couldn't trip me up this morning. The damage is done, now, everything is over except the crying."

"Are they okay?" Lain asked.

"They're fine!" Tinker snapped. "But, thanks to them, we're totally screwed!"

"Ah," Esme said. "So they did take your toys?"

"Yes!" Tinker snapped. "They did! Lain, I think I need to give you some kind of wonderful present for putting up with me for eighteen years. One day in and I'm ready to drown them all."

"But they're okay?" Lain asked again.

Tinker waved her hand over her head. "They're upstairs printing off copies of their shield spell for Stormsong to deliver to Windwolf."

She paused to squint at Tristan. She pointed at him. "Is this... is this who I think it is?"

Tristan froze as fear spiked through him. He resisted the urge to look at the male *sekasha* standing behind Tinker. Did the male speak English? What did Tinker and her people know about him? Did they know who his father was? Surely not. Lain and Esme hadn't realized that he and Lucien were half-elves. While his sisters knew now that his father was an elf, they didn't know that he was Emperor Heaven's Blessing. Nor did his sisters know that Lucien was the warlord Yutakajodo.

He took a deep breath and calmed himself with the knowledge that Tinker probably only thought of him as Lain's little brother.

"Yes, this is Tristan." Lain skipped past the introduction to get to why they were there. "He had a conversation with Tooloo last night—or at least we think it was Tooloo. 'Crazy old female elf spouting a mix of secrets and illogical comments' doesn't describe many other people."

"What did she say this time?" Tinker asked.

Tristan held out the baby chick. "She told me to give this to you. She said to tell you to remember your chess moves. It will be important."

Tinker growled in frustration as she took delivery of the chick. She inspected it closely, looking under its stubby wings and at its feet. She found nothing unusual about the chick. "*Anything* else?"

Tristan considered the conversation. It had been mostly about his dead family members. He didn't want to share any of that. "No."

Tinker visibly struggled not to scream out loud. She handed the chick to the male *sekasha* behind her, distracting him. "You should really get Tristan out of here before Stormsong comes back. I'm not sure if any of the others realize all the connection points. She was there for the whole half-sister conversation and she's still pissed at Esme about the dream stuff."

Tristan struggled to look innocent. Half sister? Tinker suspected that he was in league with Chloe? Certainly it seemed as if the *sekasha* would make that assumption.

"Noted," Lain said.

Esme was looking upward as if she had X-ray eyes to see through the ceiling to the floor above. "She's already headed downstairs. I would like to go up and meet my daughters."

Tinker blew a raspberry. "Go. Meet them. See if you can talk them into living with you. Whatever. I asked Oilcan to be their guardian but now that I've met them, I don't think he's going to be able to ride herd on them. Maybe the three of you have some hope."

Tristan had been surprised that Tinker knew exactly who he was and what he might be, yet still kept him from harm. Even more surprising and somewhat alarming was that she was going to let him meet with the twins. Surely she should be more protective of her little sisters! Children should be protected. Then again, he knew how hard it was for a child to raise younger siblings.

It reminded him that despite all the hateful things that the Eyes had said of Tinker, she was just eighteen and could be considered still a child. Certainly, she was half the age or more of the Eyes.

The third floor was much quieter. Doors stood open to the big classrooms done up as huge bedrooms. More Stone Clan children shifted pieces of furniture around as if the entire building had just taken delivery of several truckloads of bedroom suites. The young elves were laughing and talking in excited happy tones. It was a serene, bountiful feeling.

In the last room on the hallway, there was a mountain of furniture still stacked up, awaiting deconstruction. With the exception of a light scattering of computer equipment, printers, and luggage mules, there was no sign of the twins or anyone attempting to help them unpack from the disorganized mess.

Part of him was deeply annoyed that his mother's beloved granddaughters were being treated this way. Their older sister was angry with them, their cousin was missing in action, and none of the elves were helping them.

"Hello?" Esme said, walking into the room as Lain and Tristan paused at the door. "Girls? You don't know me but I'm—"

"Esme!" Louise cried from within the mountain.

"Esme!" Jillian echoed.

And then a bunch of squeaky voices joined in.

A wave of bodies suddenly came out of the furniture mountain: two child-sized, eleven the size of house cats but covered in scales, and four mice. The girls grabbed hold of Esme, hugging her while talking excitedly. The lizards circled Esme, then Lain and then Tristan to grab hold of their legs and stare up at them, saying, "Mine? Mine?"

One suddenly appeared on Tristan's shoulder. It grabbed his cheeks and stretched them out. "Mine? No. All Clarity! Not mine!"

"Mine?" one of the other lizards cried in surprised happiness. It swarmed up Tristan to perch on his other shoulder even as the other lizard suddenly disappeared as if it teleported elsewhere. "Ah, yes, all me! Mine!"

Surely this was what Alice felt when she landed in Wonderland.

40: DISTANT VOICES

"What is it that you want for yourself, my little wolf?" his cousin, Queen Soulful Ember, had said over a hundred years ago. It was an endearment that she only used for him when they were alone—when she could act as his cousin and not as the queen.

She had asked once before: in her throne room, on the day that he'd reached his majority. On that day, she called him Wolf Who Rules Wind and accorded him no more favor than their cousin Earth Son of Stone. Wolf requested then that she give him time to marshal his forces. He'd gone straight from that very public audience to High Meadow Temple to corner Wraith Arrow and the others of Howling's First Hand. He'd spent two decades after that, gathering up another strong Hand, a hundred *laedin*, dozens of households, and waiting for Discord to win her sword.

Only when he'd done all he could prepare, he waited for a chance to meet with the queen on her first day at Summer Court on the Emerald Island. If she said yes, it put him a quarter of the world closer to his goal just as the last hard frost of spring gripped the place that the humans called "Hudson Valley." He'd begged for a private audience, so no one could steal a march on him if she asked him to delay his plans because of his young age. She had agreed to meet him in the lush greenness of her conservatory with only Pure Radiance and her First, Sword Strike, in attendance. In that sheltered space, the lilacs were blooming early, filling the air with their sweet lushness.

She had forgone all trappings of power. She wore a simple red fairy-silk dress. Red armeria flowers were woven into her golden hair instead of her ruby-studded circlet. The look in her vivid blue eyes said "Impress me."

Wolf spread out the human map that his older sister, Starlight Singing in the Wind, had given him. "This is a western continent, beyond the island that my brother Whiskey was given. The humans had just started to explore it when the gateways were closed to Earth. I have spoken with my father and he is willing, as head of the Wind Clan, to fund a set of Spell Stones. I have considered all that was known by the humans and decided on this landing, just north of where this river meets this large bay. It would provide a large protected harbor with plenty of level farmland. I did some initial surveys of this area last summer and found a strong *fiutana* at the edge of this palisade. I would set my Spell Stones here."

She had her head canted in the way that meant that she was thinking deeply. She tapped her chin with her fingers. "I see why you needed time before you made your request. I assume that you have things ready, waiting just for my word."

"Yes." He'd gambled that she'd agree and had sunk much of his last funds into the purchase of a young gossamer. The crossing by ship would be too slow and perilous. He needed the speed of the airship. "Since it was uncharted by elves before the time of the Reckoning, it's also unclaimed and thus property of the crown. You alone can award it to me."

She continued to tap her finger. "Oh, how the others will yelp 'unfair' that I give you such a thing. Who else, though, could make use of it? One would need to be free from other obligations and with at least two Hands, scores of *laedin*, and a dozen households—which you have gathered."

She turned to her right where Pure Radiance waited. The female stood silent as a statue, the red blindfold of her caste in place, which announced loudly despite her silence that she was there as her queen's eyes.

"What do you see?" Soulful Ember asked.

Pure Radiance leaned down to run her hand over the map. "Truly he is Howling's grandson. This is the place that you need your wolf to guard. Be generous. His reach needs to be wide."

At the time, joy had jolted through Wolf, blinding him to

implications that there would be something to guard against and that it would be a distance from his initial settlement at Aum Renau. Later, he would spend the winter months surveying all that the queen had given him, making plans that came to nothing when Pittsburgh appeared at the far edge of his holding.

If he'd known...

But what could he have done? No matter what, there needed to be holdings in the east to allow for trade. Pittsburgh had several strong *fiutanas* but none comparable to the one at Aum Renau. Building on the coast had been fairly simple—pushing deep into the forest to reach Pittsburgh had been a struggle. His people had needed those seventy years of ease to build up something that could hope to withstand the oni.

If wishes were horses, as the humans said, *beggars would ride.*

The path to this moment was so convoluted that he'd never imagined that Pure Radiance had been pushing him down it. She had convinced the heads of the Clan to marry into the royal family. She was responsible for his many brothers and sisters, whom he loved dearly; he could not hate her for that. It galled him, though, that the events she set up led to him asking them to protect his East Coast holdings. All the things he would have done differently if he had just known that the oni were in Pittsburgh. That Sparrow would betray him. That there were horrors in the forest. Like his *domi*, he must wonder why he wasn't simply told of the danger.

"We'll be there soon enough," Wraith Arrow said quietly, guessing the direction of Wolf's thoughts. "The distant voices have been quiet."

Wolf could only pray that it meant that his brothers and sisters were well—not that they'd been vanquished after yesterday's frantic messages.

The plan was that he and the Stone Clan *domana* would take their airships to Aum Renau while Prince True Flame took the train to Brotherly Love.

Wolf's young gossamer had been bred from merchant stock. It was much smaller, faster, and less aggressive than the Stone Clan beasts. Until their ships had departed, his would not come near the airfield. The Harbingers' gossamers were well used to each other and could be moored together. Since Wolf wanted to make sure his people in Pittsburgh were organized and braced for a possible second attack, it made more sense for the slower beasts to use the airfield first.

"Maynard," Wraith Arrow murmured, announcing the arrival of Wolf's old friend and ally.

Director Maynard looked much the way he had when they first met, decades ago. He wore chest armor over a crisp green uniform, a rounded helmet, and multiple weapons tucked into holsters and pockets. The only change was that he looked worn and old.

"Wolf Who Rules Wind." Maynard bowed. "Are you well? We have heard some disturbing rumors."

"Director Maynard." Wolf bowed in return. "I am well. I hope to continue to be well, but that is not a given. I have heard how your people supported my *domi* without reserve. Please pass my thanks on to your warriors. I must leave for my East Coast holdings. What are the EIA plans?"

"My men have blockades on all the bridges out of the city," Maynard said.

"You are trying to trap them within the triangle?" Wolf questioned the wisdom of this since the wedge of land between the Allegheny River and the Monongahela River was Pittsburgh's most populated area.

"We're finding it difficult to coordinate with the royal forces," Maynard admitted. "They do not know the city but they're suspicious of anyone who is not an elf. My advance squads were unable to direct them in any meaningful fashion. My intelligence reports say that the oni landed at Herrs Island and crossed into the Strip District via the Thirty-first Street Bridge. I've managed to set up barricades at Twenty-ninth Street so that they hopefully funnel back to the island. That's where I'm hoping to trap them. There are only two bridges off the island to the North Side and we have them heavily blockaded. So far it seems successful. The royal marines are driving the enemy back toward the island. The oni shouldn't be able to escape safely. Personally, I'm hoping that they'll try swimming for it."

Windwolf nodded as he pictured the area. The next bridge down from the Thirty-first was the bridge at Sixteenth Street. The Strip District lay between the river and the high cliffs of the Hill District. The busway with its many barriers sat at the foot of the cliffs, making another barrier to the oni escaping that way.

Maynard's strategy might work, especially if the oni were lacking leadership. The problem was the royal marines. He turned to Blade Bite. "See that the royal marines understand this tactic."

Blade Bite bowed and jogged off.

Maynard changed the subject, almost hesitantly. "The young humans born on Elfhome and some of the young elves not affiliated with any of your enclaves have banded together to make an unofficial military group. They're the ones who kept the oni from reaching the enclaves yesterday until Oilcan and Beloved Tinker *domi* could get to the front line. They were also the ones who helped Olive Branch Over Stone get the train safely through the front line. They don't have a standard uniform, which means that the royal marines will have a difficult time telling the humans from disguised oni. I have some influence on the leaders but not complete control over them. They promised me that they would stay out of the triangle if they're allowed to patrol the areas outside of it. It seemed like a good compromise."

Wolf had heard that there were many humans out of uniform fighting alongside the EIA last night, but his people couldn't identify them beyond that Tinker *domi* had vouched for them. With the EIA stretched thin, it seemed wise to allow the improvised group to continue. "Very well."

Wraith Arrow shifted forward to give a report on details he'd learned since the *domana* meeting.

"The tengu report that a large number of the oni fled out of the city proper." His First motioned to the towering ironwoods that edged the wide grassy airfield. "The tengu are sweeping the forest beyond the Rim. They have found and eliminated pockets of oni but so far have found nothing of note. What fled north have continued in that direction. The tengu will pursue, whittling the oni down. Unless the enemy converges with a large hidden force, the oni who fled into the forest should not pose a threat."

"Any word from the tengu that went east to the camps?" Wolf asked.

"The camp that we attacked is empty," Wraith Arrow said. "It is a burnt shell. The camp immediately south of it has been abandoned. The scouts are pushing on to the camps east of them. They have the human version of the distant voices, so we should hear shortly what they find."

The camps were over a day's march away. With the tengu

keeping watch, Pittsburgh should have plenty of warning if that force advanced on the city. It was somewhat comforting news.

Darkness finished loading his people onto his massive gossamer. The horn to loose the mooring lines sounded and the airship drifted upward, trailing ropes that were being rapidly hauled up.

"That is one away," Wolf said.

Maynard listened to something on his earpiece. "Information has come in that the oni command had a large camp downriver. The tengu have dispatched people to see if there might be more forces being held in reserve. We won't hear back from there for several hours, if not days, since the oni employ cloaking spells to hide their camps."

Wolf nodded uneasily. "It has been like fighting shadows."

"Tactics of cowards," Wraith Arrow growled.

Tactics of someone who knew that they had an entire world braced against them. If they managed to take out the Spell Stones at Aum Renau, then only the Stone Clan could fight against them in the Westernlands.

You can only hold what you can protect.

At least his beloved and her cousin would be able to protect Pittsburgh if he failed at Aum Renau.

Cana Lily's gossamer was departing when a young Stone Clan *sekasha* came striding up in a way that spoke of purpose. Instantly, all of Wolf's Hands went on alert.

"I need to speak to you, First," the stranger said to Wraith Arrow, giving a bow that acknowledged him as a senior of another clan but of the same caste. "I am The Hound that Races Alongside Death's Midwinter Moon Over Mountains of the Enemy. I was born at First Bastion. At the time of choosing, I took myself to Cold Mountain Temple and trained under Tempered Steel."

The young warrior looked as if he was newly out of his doubles.

"On what matter do you wish to speak?" Wraith Arrow asked in a tone that said he would not tolerate a test of skill. It was common for young *sekasha* who came to Court to seek out duels to show off their fighting abilities. They wanted to prove that they weren't just Vanity Hand material. Wraith Arrow was often a target of these since he had served Howling as First during the Rebellion and the Clan Wars, but failed to protect his *domou* from assassination. Wraith Arrow's failure and his retreat

to High Meadow after Howling's death made him highly attrac-
tive for such tests. Those duels, though, were Wind Clan versus
Wind Clan during peacetime.

"I wish to speak of the death warrant on the House of Death
Wind for the assassination of Howling. I believe it was unjust
and wish for you to abrogate it."

"The House of Death Wind is no more," Wraith Arrow said.

"It is not completely," Moon Dog stated. "A child was born
since the warrant was put forth. As the child is orphaned and
homeless, the child remains part of the household of Death
Wind. It is completely unjust that a child not even born during
the time of the events should be held responsible for the acts of
the household."

"Hate can be learned from the breast of the mother," Wraith
Arrow stated coldly.

"Sparrow Lifted by Wind has been proven a Skin Clan mole
within Howling's household. It was she who planted the lies of
Howling's intent to kill the holy warriors of his household to free
himself if the Wind Clan was not chosen to lead our people."

"You speak of things that you cannot possibly know."

"Perhaps. Because of the ill omens in my name, I sought out
the Wind Clan First when she came to visit her father at Cold
Mountain Temple. We spoke at length about how she came to be
First. She was quite open with me—perhaps because I was still
in my doubles or because I was first candid with her. Howling's
assassination was just one step in that journey but one vital to
her ascent. In that knife stroke, she went from a lowly half-breed
of a young landless *domana* to the head of her caste in the Wind
Clan. The battles that she had to fight to prove her worth and
her loyalty to her *domou*'s clan were countless. I would wager it
safe to say that no one was more vested in knowing the truth
about Howling's assassination than she."

"I stand corrected," Wraith Arrow murmured. He had to, else
it would seem that he was speaking ill of the Wind Clan's First.

"While Otter Dance on Wind had no proof, she always suspected Sparrow Lifted by Wind. Otter Dance believed that the
assassination was part of the Clan Wars' hatred of others. She
obviously did not suspect Sparrow's connection with the Skin
Clan. Sparrow's opposition to Longwind's marriage seemed to be
more of the same—thus was she exiled away to a minor holding.

If Otter Dance had anything more concrete than suspicion, I believe she would have warned Wolf Who Rules not to take Sparrow into his household."

"My blade mother had warned me against Sparrow," Wolf admitted. "She believed, though, that Sparrow's fervor came from a love of the Wind Clan, not an ill will toward it. Her caution was that if I took Jewel Tear as *domi*, I would most likely have to put Sparrow aside. Since Jewel Tear refused to respond to my proposal, I did not heed Otter Dance's warning. Her treatment of my Beloved Tinker seemed more of the same."

"Otter Dance believed that Sparrow manipulated the issuing of the death warrant and the speed at which it was carried out," Moon Dog said. "None of the Death Wind household was ever captured and questioned—Sparrow could not allow the trail of evidence to lead back to her. Not even the children were spared. Centuries of faithful obedience ignored to wipe clean all traces of the household. It was ruthless and shameful, an act worthy of our creators—but not us."

"Otter Dance never spoke of this to me," Wraith Arrow said.

"How could she? Longwind was not the clan's first choice as head—young and unproven in battle. You were still First of Wind Clan while the debate on Howling's successor raged on. By the time that Otter Dance became First, the Death Wind household was thought all dead. You retired to High Meadow, satisfied that the guilty were punished, and she had to deal with Sparrow by herself. Anyone with proof of Sparrow's guilt was long dead by a *sekasha*'s blade by your orders. It was a battle that Otter Dance had not the resources to spare for."

Wraith Arrow glowered at the young warrior. "You say there is a survivor who makes this conversation necessary? A child?"

"One still in their doubles," Moon Dog said.

"That young?" Wolf said in surprise.

Moon Dog nodded. "The mother had been a child herself at the time of Howling's assassination. Yet this innocent double still has the death warrant over its head."

"Has it been trained?" Wraith Arrow said.

"What does that matter?" Moon Dog said with a look full of innocence. "Cleansing is the way of the Skin Clan—not ours. Those who plotted against Howling are all dead. Let the living be judged on their own actions. If I need to battle to right this wrong, I will, but my hope is that my caste proves itself worthy of the praise heaped upon it."

Wraith Arrow glanced toward the airfield where Sunder's last gossamer was in final stages of loading. Wolf could only guess his thoughts. Everything that the young warrior said was true. There was also the problem that if Wraith Arrow refused, it would require combat to settle. The youth had just crossed half the world to bring the issue before Wraith Arrow. "Later" would not be an acceptable answer.

Wraith Arrow breathed out and raised his hand. "By blood and sword as a *sekasha*, I recognize that unborn children cannot be held accountable for the actions of their household. I lift the death warrant on the Death Wind household."

Moon Dog bowed deeply. "Thank you, elder. It gladdens me that one that I respected all my childhood would prove worthy of that esteem. I hope that we will have chance to spar in the future."

"The Stone Clan loads even now," Wraith Arrow pointed out.

Moon Dog glanced across the airfield with a sad look. "Ah, I will not be Stone Clan after today. I will accept Oilcan's offer to be his Second. I will stay in this fascinating city."

Wraith Arrow looked shocked for a second and then recovered, managing to wipe all expression off his face. "Very well."

Moon Dog bowed and took himself off toward Sacred Heart.

"How did that one end up with Cousin?" Wraith Arrow murmured once the youth was out of hearing range. "It has been only a few days—a scattering of hours—since the Stone Clan arrived in force! All from Cold Mountain Temple had been with Sunder during the battle in the forest. When would the child even have time to meet Cousin?"

"We will find out later," Wolf promised.

Discord arrived just as Wolf's gossamer drifted in over the now empty airfield, unfurling ropes to tie off at the mooring anchors.

"There are ten copies of the shield spell in each binder." Discord handed him two leather binders. "You should only need one but it seemed safer to cover all possible situations. We put them in two binders in case *domana* arrive from the Easternlands prior to Forge and *domi* being ready to do the spell working. I sent a third to the train station to catch up with Prince True Flame."

"Good." Wolf gave the second binder to Wraith Arrow to protect.

Discord continued her report. "You should be warned that *domi*'s younger sisters are at Sacred Heart. They opened all the *nactka* containing the baby dragons."

"All of them?" Wolf managed to say after a moment of surprised silence.

"Yes, eleven very small, very annoying—but mostly harmless—dragons are now flitting about the enclave, sticking their noses into everything. It is sheer chaos. The *domi* is attempting to stay focused. It has set her back, however, as she had planned to use one of the *nactka* to reach the full *mei* to the East Coast."

"She will figure it out." Wolf had confidence in his *domi*.

A runner came running from Poppymeadows. "*Domou!* A message from Aum Renau!"

He took the paper as his heart dropped in his chest. It could only be bad news.

What a mess! the note read. *Glad I didn't wait for you to answer. You've got enemies on your doorstep. Big brother will clean this up for you. Jay Bird.*

41: WHEN A CHICKEN IS NOT A CHICKEN

⊹⟞⟾◯⟿⟝⊹

Tinker watched the chick walk across the paper-strewn table, pecking at crumbles dropped by the twins and Forge. (Apparently they had a working breakfast.)

Remember your chess moves.

She didn't scream in frustration when Tristan relayed that, merely because people tended to get beheaded when she screamed.

What in the world was it supposed to mean?

She pulled out her datapad and called up the photos of the chessboard.

Tooloo knew that the oni spell was about to be triggered, so the Queen's Gambit had nothing to do with saving the *domana*. If everything since Unbounded Brilliance breaking into Iron Mace's spell-locked box had been Tooloo's doing, then the chess game was a clue to Tooloo's grand scheme. Or at least, what she was trying to manipulate Tinker into doing without knowing cause and effect.

Tinker had already played that game for most of the summer. She was sick of it.

Some of the symbols were obvious. The five Minnie Mouse and one Mickey Mouse figurines were literally the four babies and the twins. The monkeys were Chloe, her sisters, and maybe Lain's two younger half brothers. It depended on how many sisters Chloe had.

Tinker had to assume that the real live chick that Tristan

handed her was a reference to the two black rooks. Tooloo had set up chicken figurines in place of the game pieces. In terms of "chess moves" the rooks moved in a straight line or, under certain conditions, could be essentially "swapped" with the king. In exact terms, the king moved toward the rook two spaces and the rook "jumped" over the king to a protective flank position. One could quibble since they didn't move to the exact same position that the other piece formerly occupied that it wasn't a swap, but essentially it was. Anyone planning to attack the king would suddenly find themselves face-to-face with the rook instead.

But what and who was being swapped with what?

The black king on the game board was a bottle of Heinz ketchup. She had assumed that it represented the city of Pittsburgh. (She couldn't imagine it being Windwolf. There was nothing ketchuplike about him.) Even if it was supposed to be the Heinz factory where the condiment was made, how did you "swap" that with a chicken? Especially since the presence of the chick seemed to indicate that Tooloo meant a literal chicken.

This exact chicken, or Box—who had been the literal chicken at the game board when Tooloo showed Tinker the layout?

Box was a huge, buff Orpington rooster, fifteen pounds of pure golden-orange fury. Tooloo had other Orpington chickens since Box was as randy as he was large and fearless. Nor was he the first Box. The first one that Tinker remembered had taken on a bear that attempted to raid Tooloo's chicken coop when she was nine. While the rooster had chased off the bear, it had been wounded to death.

Tinker had been conflicted over the death of the original Box. She'd known him her entire life at that point. He had been like a faithful dog, loyal to Tooloo but less tolerant of Tinker. He was not above bullying her if he thought she'd stepped out of line.

A few days later, Tooloo picked out a newly hatched chick much like the one currently strutting about the tabletop and named it Box.

"Again?" Tinker had complained at the time. "How could you give his name away? And what kind of name is that for a rooster? Wouldn't it be better to name it Sir Crowsalot? Or Duke? Or Grandpa?"

"I call him Box because he's a box," Tooloo said. "He holds an old fierce soul that routinely miscalculates what he can survive."

There's dead and then there's dead when it comes to dragons.

Wait! Had the original Box somehow swapped his dead body for a living one?

Tooloo had a bed made of dragon bones. Esme had said that she had found Tooloo because of a dream of a female elf with a golden dragon the size of a mountain behind her. Stormsong had said that her grandmother Vision had been guarded by a golden dragon named Vigilance. The Skin Clan had sent Vigilance after Vision and neither had ever returned.

What if Vigilance had died but his spirit clung near to his bones, possessing one chicken after another, much like Providence possessed Jin Wong's body when the tengu brought him to talk to Tinker? Chickens were, after all, little dinosaur descendants.

Was this entire chess riddle just to tell Tinker: *Swap the bed and Box for one of the baby dragons*?

"Oh, you've got to be kidding!" Tinker shouted. "Why didn't you just say it?"

42: A ROSE BY ANY OTHER NAME

"Sunny" was not a word that Law would normally use to describe a *sekasha* but it was the first impression that she got of Moon Dog. It was the first time she'd ever seen one of them grin ear to ear. Normally they were expressionless and radiated menace that you could feel. It was like a coiled rattlesnake inches from your bare leg, projecting "move wrong and you're dead."

Moon Dog was shorter than the Wind Clan *sekasha*, as smolderingly handsome as a Bollywood actor, yet beaming sunshine and flowers. The most surprising thing about him was that his wyvern chest armor and the tattoos up his arms were all Stone Clan black.

Law had fallen back to sleep so missed any explanation of how Bare Snow ended up being championed by a *sekasha* from another clan.

Moon Dog gracefully sat on the floor beside Bare Snow. "It is done. I have spoken with Wraith Arrow and he has seen the error of his ways and lifted the death warrant."

Bare Snow squealed and flung herself on Moon Dog from her sitting position. "Oh, thank you! Thank you! This is wonderful."

"It was only right that this wrong was corrected," Moon Dog said. "I am glad to have had the chance to fight alongside you and to have seen your wonderous skill."

Bare Snow blushed, bouncing in her seated position, smiling. She looked to Law, obviously wanting to fling herself on her and containing herself only because Law was wounded.

"Do you need a place, child?" Moon Dog asked. "Or have you found a home with the humans?"

"I have found my place!" Bare Snow put out a careful hand to Law. "There is a home and a purpose and children to raise. It is a wonderful life now that I am free to live it without fear."

"I am glad for you," Moon Dog said. "I believe I have found the life that I was seeking. Long has my name defined me, regardless of what I wanted for myself. I have taken a new name, one that is truly me, and not a fate that I could not escape."

"That's wonderful!" Bare Snow said. "I too have a new name, given to me with love. I am Bare Snow."

"I am Moon Dog."

"I am Law," Law said as she realized she too had chosen a new name, abandoning the Lawrie that her parents had saddled her with.

Moon Dog stood with the same grace of a dancer as he had used to sit. "I must go and find my new *domou* and let him know that I am free of all burdens."

Bare Snow carefully hugged Law. "This is so wonderful. I had no hope that this would ever happen! I have no fear now that my presence will harm the children."

It meant that she probably hoped that they would join Usagi's household. Law was willing, especially if the Bunnies found a larger place. She had come close to leaving Bare Snow adrift in a world without a place that would take her. The Bunnies' new home wouldn't be cool like her barn but winters were close to torture, with the windowless old sheep pen being the only place that could be heated. Plus the Bunnies' home would come with lots of love and comforts like well-cooked meals.

Law smiled at Bare Snow. "I'll call Usagi to come pick us up."

43: THE JENGA TOWER OF DOOM

Oilcan had just returned to Sacred Heart with the last load of furniture when Moon Dog came out of the building to greet him.

"You've returned?" Oilcan called in greeting as he climbed out of the flatbed. Maybe he misunderstood what the male said earlier.

"I have cleared my conscience of moral obligations," Moon Dog said. "I can now say yes."

"Oh, good! Thank you!" Oilcan wondered if there was more to it than that. It seemed that there should be but there hadn't been with Thorne Scratch.

"Third floor?" Floss Flower asked as a collection of humans, elves and tengu lifted his newest purchases off the truck.

"Yes. Please. Thank you!" Oilcan grabbed his tablet from the flatbed's cab and followed the furniture up the staircase. "Okay. We've got a couple empty spaces on the third floor. You can choose one of them to be your private room."

Oilcan had had Moser's people move Jewel Tear's furniture down to the second floor. He hadn't been entirely happy that Jewel Tear claimed a room on the family floor, but he'd let her stay as there seemed to be something going on between her and Tommy. Since she had moved to Tommy's new enclave, Oilcan wanted the space to revert back to family only.

It gave them three very large classrooms on the family floor. There were also five mystery rooms—offices or storage rooms—that could be respectable-sized bedrooms. Assuming he could get the twins to stay, he planned for them to share one of the classrooms. The twins were asleep when he'd headed out for the first load of furniture. He'd asked Briar Rose to make sure that the twins got breakfast, picked out which of the three rooms they wanted, and see that their incoming furniture got delivered to it.

He planned to reserve one of the classrooms for the four babies—once they got born. (*When are they going to be born? Soon? Half a year from now? Scratch that, any time would feel like too soon. Don't think too long on it. Oh, I forgot to look for cribs and such.*)

He paused to make a note. *Four cribs. Find out what else babies need. Find someone who knows about babies.*

Oilcan continued up the grand staircase with Thorne Scratch and Moon Dog following him in semi work mode. If he'd counted right, it left them with only one big room and the five smaller ones. He wanted his Hand to have their own private rooms, someplace to call their own. He would probably also need some space for the babies' caregivers. Esme? Gracie? Both of them? An entire platoon of women?

Was the tengu *yamabushi* boy staying with the twins? He'd slept in the gym the night before simply because Moser's people didn't want to jostle the wounded boy by carrying him up two flights of stairs. He might need a separate bedroom.

When Oilcan first came to Pittsburgh, the old hotel felt too big and too empty for him. It reminded him too much that he was a world away from everything he knew. Everyone that he'd cared about. That his mother was dead. Tinker guessed that and would often crawl into bed with him. The twins might feel safer if the boy shared their room. Certainly it was big enough to create a private space with bookcases and wall hangings.

Oilcan wasn't completely comfortable with the idea though. "Sleeping together" was one thing with a grieving ten-year-old cousin being raised like a brother and quite another with a fourteen-year-old male who wasn't related to the girls. Those four years made a big difference.

Oilcan also wanted to set up a living room like a typical American family had, so that the twins had neutral ground to interact with the other kids, all of whom were older than them, but not as clever. The smaller rooms wouldn't be able to handle a dozen or more people at once, so he'd told Briar Rose to put the big sectional in the classroom that the twins didn't pick.

He felt like he was quickly running out of space. It was a claustrophobic feeling, like he was being backed up against a wall.

You're not alone. Everyone will help out. Tommy's family knows about babies. Forge can help control the chaos. Moser's people could bridge the gap between humans and elves.

"I got you a bed." Oilcan forced himself to focus on the immediate problem of getting Moon Dog settled in. Oilcan had bought a double bed for Moon Dog, as the male was much taller and wider than his kids. It was just a mattress and frame, not a full true bed. He hadn't picked out a headboard or any other furniture, thinking that Moon Dog might want to choose his own things.

"I wasn't sure what you would like in terms of furniture," Oilcan explained. "There were so many choices. We can go back to the store—tomorrow or later—and pick out anything that pleases you. We could even hire a woodcrafter to make something, if you would like something more Elvish."

"Oh, no, I would like to see what the world has to offer before choosing," Moon Dog said. "Yesterday, there was a bewildering array of furniture that I did not know existed. I might want a chair that moves but I am not sure. It might just be the novelty of it. I will have to meditate on the question."

Still, Oilcan felt a little bad. They hadn't touched the smaller rooms yet. They all needed to be deep cleaned, the many bullet holes in the plaster patched, and then painted. Well, Moon Dog could pick out the room he wanted and then stay temporarily in the classroom designated as the nursery.

"Forgiveness, but things will be haphazard for a while," Oilcan said as they reached the top of the stairs. "This summer has been hectic and unplanned. Things will all be temporary until work can be done."

"It is wonderful!" Moon Dog sounded like it was. "At the temples where I grew up, everything was literally set in stone. Nothing could be changed—especially the style of fighting. I'm hoping that the Wind Clan will spar with me so that I can learn more about how they fight."

"*Domi*'s Hand is quite welcoming." Thorne Scratch spoke for the first time. She was quietly radiating happiness at the situation.

Oilcan led the way to the first mystery room, feeling somewhat better. He hadn't considered that Moon Dog would welcome things being chaotic.

Oilcan's bedroom was at very right of the stairs, guarding the other rooms. Merry, Rustle, Cattail Reeds, Barley, and Baby Duck had rooms strung out beside his. To the left had been the empty classrooms. The first was set up as a living room as he planned. The large sectional attempted to dominate the center of the room and failed, as even it was not big enough. Someone had donated a big-screen TV and got it hung on the wall. The area needed work to be homey.

He took out his tablet and made notes to get area rugs, a coffee table, at least two end tables, and more artwork for the room.

Across the hall was the first mystery room. He was surprised to find it cleaned, repaired, and freshly painted. Someone was a step ahead of him. Moser's people? The tengu? The elves? It was hard to say. The mystery painter had used the paint leftover from the kid's rooms. The main color was a warm tan called Honey Oak that Barley had picked, but one wall was Rustle's deep green.

It was a nice room, around fourteen feet by twelve feet, though a little uneven as the door was off-center and the walls jutted out or in to account for the neighboring restrooms. It had one big window in the back, looking over the kitchen courtyard. It had no closet, so it would need a dresser or armoire to hold clothes.

"This is one of the private rooms for you or Thorne Scratch." Oilcan reminded himself that since he'd grown up in a hotel, the space felt small but it was larger than the spare bedrooms of his old condo. The smaller of the two had been a tiny eight feet by ten feet, not counting its closet.

"I will take this one, if First allows," Moon Dog said. "It is near the stairs, so I'll be able to hear anyone coming or going."

"I will allow it," Thorne Scratch said.

"It's not too small?" Oilcan asked as it was the smallest of the mystery rooms.

The two *sekasha* laughed.

"This is three times what we are given at the temple," Thorne explained. "Many had no windows."

Oilcan couldn't imagine. Even his small bedroom in Boston had a window.

"No window was sometimes a blessing in the winter," Moon Dog said.

Winter! Did the room have heat? Yes. There was a heat vent by Oilcan's feet.

"If you don't like the colors, they can be changed," Oilcan said as he made a note to look into the heating system for the building. He remembered that it was up to date but that didn't guarantee that it actually worked. The first hard frost would be in a matter of weeks.

"I like the colors," Moon Dog said. "They are quite welcoming."

On the other side of the restrooms was a slightly larger mystery room, narrow and long with three windows on the right-hand wall. It was only eleven feet wide but nearly eighteen feet long. Like Moon Dog's room, the wall jutted out and in as they detoured around neighboring rooms. It had been cleaned, repaired and painted as well. The paint from Oilcan's bedroom had been used: a cream yellow and a rich brown called Weathered Oak. The color scheme had been flipped, making the brown the accent instead of the main one.

"I will take this one," Thorne Scratch said.

"There's a bed for each room." Oilcan looked around. He'd seen them being carried up the stairs.

The twins had claimed the bedroom across the hall. The door stood open, showing off a mountain of furniture piled up in the center of the room like some kind of Jenga game. There was no sign of the twins, the mice, or the baby dragon.

"Oh no," Oilcan whispered.

He hurried into the room and circled the tower, trying to figure out what piece to take down first without toppling the entire pile.

"Why would they do this?" he said out of sheer frustration. How do you clean, patch, and paint two rooms to perfection and then do this craziness?

"Because we told them to?" Jillian said from within the furniture mountain.

Well...yes, that sounded like something Tinker would do.

The twins climbed out of the pile. They were wearing Naekanain T-shirts like dresses and tennis shoes—because he hadn't realized that they didn't have any clothing with them. Scratch going back to Once More With Feelings tomorrow or the day after, he should go back tonight and buy out their girls' clothing section. Maybe. Assuming that the twins weren't leaving.

"Is it because you want to go back to Haven?" Oilcan guessed. With Tinker, the furniture tower might be because of something that simple or part of some weird plan to steal a bulldozer or sneak out to a street fair after being forbidden to travel that far by go-kart.

"No!" Jillian gave a honest sounding cry of dismay.

"While Haven is charming—" Louise started.

"And isolated," Jillian added.

"—the tree houses are simply magical," Louise continued.

"And painfully rustic," Jillian clarified even further.

"And terrifying to get down out of," Louise added.

Jillian gave her sister a surprised look. "No, that's the coolest part. The needing someone else to fly you up and down is what sucks."

Louise cut to the chase. "We really don't want to live there."

"And we don't want to live with Alexander," Jillian said firmly.

"She's scary," Louise added quietly. "In a cool way, but . . . we don't think we would get along with her, day to day."

"We'd butt heads like mountain goats," Jillian muttered darkly.

Oilcan wondered what had happened during the day that triggered this impression. "The Jenga tower?"

"Has served its purpose," the twins said in unison.

They stared at him in silence for a minute. The twins didn't want to explain.

"Okay," Oilcan said. "We can take it down?"

The twins nodded without adding anything.

"And you want to stay here?" he asked.

"Yes," Jillian said.

"Please," Louise added.

He didn't want to rush them. His grandfather did that to him—although much of it was purely political. His grandfather had been just a photograph and a voice over the phone every few months. Almost a total stranger, he showed up at the doorstep of Oilcan's foster home just days prior to Shutdown. He'd spent most of the month working through red tape to make sure Oilcan could cross the border legally. Without much introduction or explanation, they'd driven to Cranberry and camped in the sprawling parking lot at the edge of the quarantine zone, waiting to cross. Oilcan didn't know where they were going (the hotel at Neville Island) or who all waited for them (no one until the next morning when Lain brought Tinker home). The big, dark, empty hotel had been like something out of a horror movie. Already unsettled by his grandfather's grieving silence, the place terrified him.

The last thing Oilcan wanted was for the twins to feel uncomfortable at Sacred Heart.

Oilcan started to carefully dismantle the tower. People drifted in to help. He shooed away anyone who tried to steer the twins into setting up the room. For some reason they just wanted everything clustered haphazardly in the center of the room— and that was fine. They had their world taken away from them. They should be given control over as much of their life as they needed to heal.

While the elves might want the guardianship of the twins cleared up quickly, Oilcan didn't see the need to force the girls to choose one yet. The twins didn't want to stay at Haven. Whether or not Gracie could shift from the tengu village to Oakland was unclear. Neither the twins nor Tinker wanted them at Poppymeadows. Lain's house was big but it still didn't have the room for six children, no matter what Esme wanted. It meant that regardless of who they picked, they would stay at Sacred Heart.

If Sunder wanted to make it political, then they would fight that battle when it happened. Until then it would be best for the twins if they could float along, unofficially, until they knew what their hearts needed to heal.

44: WHEN A BOX IS NOT A BOX

The OPEN sign in Tooloo's shop window was swinging back and forth. Tooloo must have flipped it seconds before Pony pulled the Rolls-Royce into the parking lot. It meant that Tooloo had known that they were coming.

Tinker wasn't sure if this was good news or bad. It meant that she didn't need to break in and steal an old woman's bed with possible interference from her morally superior Hand, but at the same time, she would have to actually talk to Tooloo. She expected Tooloo to be Tooloo: noncooperative, insulting, and possibly lying to Tinker's face.

Tinker stared at the swinging sign and wondered if she should tell her Hand to stay outside. It would be bad if the *sekasha* snapped and took a swipe at the old bat. Then again, if Tooloo was Vision, it was unlikely that they would land a hit. Still, annoying as Tooloo was, she was the closest thing to a grandmother that Tinker had.

Wait. Does this mean Stormsong is my cousin?

Stormsong noticed Tinker jolting in surprise as the connection was made. *"Domi?"*

"I'm fine, it's nothing, let's go," Tinker said hurriedly and got out of the Rolls-Royce.

In the space of three months, she had gone from just Oilcan as her only family to having relatives coming out of her ears. Loving husband. Crafty lying grandmother. Overprotective grandfather.

Time-traveling mother. Secretive aunt. Murderous undercover half aunts. (Was half aunts even a thing?) Child uncles. Twin younger sisters. Impossible baby siblings. Now a very distant cousin. What was it with this summer? Was there a fire sale that no one told her about? Buy one relative, get a dozen free?

Riki pulled in beside her, driving the flatbed from her salvage yard.

Tooloo's dragon-bone bed was a big wonky thing. It wasn't going to fit in the Rolls-Royce. Tinker had debated driving the flatbed herself since none of the *sekasha* could drive manual transmission. In the end, she decided that having a morally flexible tengu in tow would be a good thing. She had dragooned Riki into driving the salvage yard's flatbed. (Oilcan had been using it all day so they had to stop at Montana's gas station to fill it up.)

"Huh," Riki said. "I've never seen this place open before."

Which could only mean that Tooloo had been hiding from the tengu. It was probably better that Riki didn't go in with them. The fewer innocent bystanders in the mix, if it all boiled over, the better.

"Stay here," she told Riki.

It was the same dimly lit, dusty shop full of random treasure that she remembered from her childhood. Some of the items had sat unmoved on the shelves her entire life. She thought that she knew the store well. Every time she'd been in there that summer, though, she saw it with new eyes.

Today was no different. She had built forts under the big bed as a child, crawling under the bracing of pale yellow "wood" that made up the frame. For the first time she looked at the bed and recognized the bones for what they were. Rib cage. Femurs. Hips.

What's more, the dragon shown coiled on the kitchenette's tile mosaic was the same orange-gold color as Box.

"Silly beast died without the magic," Tooloo had claimed the first time Tinker visited as an elf. *"I was tempted to burn my bed after the Pathway reopened, but waste not, want not, as the humans say."*

Was that a lie? If it wasn't, then Tinker should be able to take the bed without a fight. Right?

Tooloo was sitting in the same armchair as Tinker's last visit, holding a delicate china teacup full of fragrant Earl Grey tea. Tooloo didn't even raise an eyebrow at the sudden invasion. She was wearing a different worn fairy-silk gown—the rose one with delicate threadbare needlework—but her normal red high-top tennis shoes. Her white hair was braided into a thick cord that came down over her chest to pool in her lap. Now that Tinker had Lain, Esme, and Louise to compare her to, she could see the family resemblance in the determined chin. The chessboard had been banished from the table without a trace. That was fine with Tinker; she'd never liked the game anyhow.

"I'm here for the bed and the chicken," Tinker said.

Tooloo raised her teacup, took a sip, and then eyed Tinker over its rim. "Have you brought me a replacement bed? You don't expect me to sleep on the floor?"

"I'm not taking the mattress." Tinker waved at the lumpy queen-sized mattress strewn with warg skins. "It can sit on the floor until I find a replacement frame."

"I did not think I raised you to be inconsiderate to a little old lady," Tooloo said.

"You're not little and you're not a lady," Tinker snarled. Tooloo was nearly a foot taller than her. She stomped back to the front door to shout to Riki. "Go find me a queen-sized bed frame. Oilcan only got twin-sized ones from Once More With Feeling, so there might be some there."

"Yes, *domi*." Riki started up the flatbed to make it so.

Tinker returned to Tooloo. They had at least half an hour before Riki had any hope of returning with a bedframe. "Why the puzzle with the chess pieces? Why not just give me the bed when I was here last time?"

"I didn't want to sleep on the floor." Tooloo took another sip of her tea. "Besides, it wouldn't have fit in that fancy car you came in and you had better things to do, like win a battle."

Tinker flailed her hands with all the points she wanted to scream. "Why not just tell me?"

Tooloo shook her head. "It's like trying to explain composing a symphony to someone who can barely pick out "Chopsticks" on a keyboard."

Tinker knew about the song only because she was an occasional roadie for Naekanain. "Chopsticks" was the tune that idiots liked to play on Maya's keyboard to show off that they knew "how to play too." Since Maya had a strict "no touch" policy for her instrument, this did not go over like the idiots thought it would.

"I do not play the keyboard," Tinker said.

"Yes, that's been obvious since you were born," Tooloo said.

"For once, can you just explain what it is that you want?"

"Will it make any difference? Won't you just go off and do whatever you think is for the best?"

This was how Tinker expected the conversation to go. "Can you at least explain to me what Pure Radiance wants so I don't help her out again? She basically tossed me to the oni and let me figure it out on my own. Why did she have you bound hand and foot with a dragon guard dog? Is it because she wants Elfhome to be isolated from the other worlds?"

"The thing that my daughter failed to understand was that despite being broken down and scattered to the four winds, our genetic donors would never abandon any little part of themselves that remained. Trying to explain it to her would have resulted in her just gathering up the shards of our antecedents and finding some way to end them completely. Pure Radiance has always been wholly elf with all the frailties that implies."

"So all this madness—the last two or three thousand years— has been about the twelve baby dragons trapped in the *nactka*?"

Tooloo snorted into her tea. "If our antecedents would listen to reason, none of them would have come to Elfhome in the first place."

"Couldn't you just send them home?"

"The shards? Just wait. You'll soon see how difficult they are to deal with."

"But...but...the gate and Pittsburgh? It has nothing to do with anything?"

"Oh, that was all key to my plan. The society that my daughter crafted will not be acceptable to the dragon children who came to Elfhome. It's too rigid. Too unfair to the individual in the name of protecting the masses. Ironically, it echoes the confines of the dragon society that the children were rebelling against on Ryu."

"Clarity came to Elfhome as an angsty teenager pissed at her parents?"

Tooloo made a dismissive noise. "I—She told the antecedents it was too dangerous. Nirvana was first to ignore Clarity, wanting to spread hope to the captive elves. Brilliance charged in to save her, always sure that he could outthink any problem. Honor trotted behind, sure that Brilliance will find a way, blinded by love. Even Solitude and Muse eventually joined in. It was cascading into a disaster across multiple worlds. As it was, Onihida was lost when the Skin Clan started to step across worlds. Earth would have slowly been won over despite the lack of magic. Ryu would be invaded by its own twisted grandchildren. Worlds that you have yet to hear about would follow. The evil needed to be stopped on Elfhome."

"The whole chessboard thing?"

Tooloo smiled slyly.

"What? Did you do that just to tease me?"

"No, of course not," Tooloo said—still smiling. "I needed to compose a symphony. Don't mistake your plinking on a keyboard as understanding the process. There was much more to the music than your little 'Chopstick' solo."

Tinker gritted her teeth, mindful that even Stormsong looked slightly annoyed. Rainlily looked outraged. (Did they ever explain to Rainlily who Tooloo really was? Surely Pony and Stormsong had filled her in.)

Tinker seemed to have guessed right on the bed—or at least, Tooloo was letting her believe that she had. It made too much sense. There was the ley line that flowed through the living space, pooling in a strong warm presence that brushed over Tinker's bare legs. There was no really good reason for Tooloo to camp on a ley line except to keep the dragon bones seeped in magic.

"Box is the dragon Vigilance?"

Tooloo sniffed. "I suppose you could call Vigilance a dragon. He is not a shard, per se. Our cruel creators were starting to realize how strongly the antecedent's personality would influence the derivatives. They expected infants who would be easy to manipulate. What they got were echoes of the antecedents."

Tooloo waved a hand toward the bed. "Vigilance was an attempt to strip off the base personality from a genotype. It would be like stripping a human back to what you call the 'primitive reptile brain.' What they got was a four-claw dragon. The Skin Clan might have seen me as an elf, as did my idiot daughter, but other dragons know what I am. I am a five-claw dragon. No four-claw dragon would ever dare to harm me."

Malice had been a four-claw dragon. Impatience was a five-claw.

"Impatience said that he couldn't take Malice in a fight," Tinker said.

"He said that he couldn't fight Malice," Tooloo said, "in that he had been forbidden to fight by our elders. He could do nothing more than save his own life if it was in immediate danger. He's done what he can within the limits of the edict but it's allowed him very little wiggle room. If he did more, he would not be allowed to return home. The loss of one's home world to an immortal is soul crushing. Centuries of longing for what you can never have again."

Tooloo had talked about years of lying in her dragon bed, too depressed to move. She understood the pain that Impatience would face if he were exiled from Ryu.

"How would the dragons even know?" Tinker complained. "They don't seem to be paying any attention to what's happened to their children beyond Impatience and Providence. Even Providence's mate seems unconcerned over what has happened to their child."

Tooloo laughed dryly. "What a monkey answer. Your curiosity is endless. The reasons why Providence's mate has done nothing are none of your concern. Believing that others are not acting outside of your awareness is how Brilliance got himself killed. Remember, just because you are not aware of the world does not mean that it doesn't exist."

"So, the dragons are paying attention but not doing anything?"

"Yes. Sight is a dragon's gift. There are those who can peer between the worlds. Just because you can see the falling tree, however, does not mean that you realize it's about to take out your house. Otherwise intelligent beings can convince themselves and others that they are above cause and effect. They knew that the Skin Clan was deadly but they were sure that they could contain the evil to one world. Onihida was lost because of that belief. Ryu would have been lost too if Clarity hadn't acted—but she's been condemned for her actions instead of praised."

That had to burn. To give yourself up to be torn apart and turned into enslaved twisted versions of your true self—and then cast as evil for that sacrifice.

Oh, damn, she's making me feel like a hypocrite for being mad at her.

To escape her feelings, Tinker stomped outside to capture Box. He made it easy. As if he'd forgotten their entire nine-year history with each other, he came at her like she was a complete stranger out to steal eggs and hens.

"Ow! Ow! No, don't kill him! We need him alive! Box! Rainlily!"

✧   ✧   ✧

They escaped half an hour later—once Riki returned with a replacement frame and headboard—with one ugly bone bed and one pissed-off rooster.

There. She'd solved the chess puzzle. Forge could cast the spell and fix the *domana*.

But that didn't seem like it addressed what Tooloo wanted to do.

If Windwolf had been right, then the fight between Pure Radiance and Tooloo had been about the structure of the elf society. Certainly Tooloo had brushed over that at one point.

That Tooloo was allowing Tinker to fix the *domana* probably meant that undoing the power structure of elf society completely wasn't her end goal. Perhaps it was nothing more than to make everyone aware that the war was won not by elves like Cana Lily—clinging to old roles—but Windwolf, Tinker, and Oilcan, who forged new alliances. The young elves coming to Pittsburgh had been desperate for a new life. They arrived just to find that the new land held to the same old structures where they had no place. They survived only because humans had reached out in friendship.

But the locals could only do so much. The Skin Clan had made it difficult for humans to stay on the planet if not funded by an Earth-based company. They limited education, technology, equipment, and visas that would have expanded Pittsburgh's ability to maintain its human population. Her grandfather learned of her Aunt Ada's death one month but couldn't leave until the next. Oilcan had drifted between foster homes for nearly three months before being rescued from that system. Tinker had been handed over to Lain for the thirty-plus days it took for her grandfather to queue up for leaving, get Oilcan, and then come back to Elfhome. One mishap at the border would have meant it would have taken two months for him to return.

Pittsburgh was barely working for anyone prior to this summer. She would wait for days or weeks for Shutdown to put in an order and then wait another month or two for it to be delivered. Everyone she knew struggled against a system that seemed built to work against them. Blue Sky could never see his mother again. Half the kids they grew up with left Elfhome for colleges off-world because the education system in Pittsburgh was so limited, and didn't return because there were no jobs. Sean Roach had left Elfhome at eighteen and then fought with red tape for an entire year to be allowed to come back home. Moser's band had to jump through hoops to sell their albums on Earth. Geoffrey Kryskill struggled to export his furniture. All the scientists who came and went on Observatory Hill spent years working through red tape to be allowed less than thirty days of research.

Pittsburgh didn't work. It was probably all Pure Radiance and the Skin Clan's fault. No one on Earth would benefit from making it as difficult as it was to travel between the worlds.

Tinker had started plans to make Squirrel Hill Tunnel into a gate but she'd abandoned it. Yes, some of it was because she was afraid that she would open up a hole to the oni army on Onihida, but mostly because she didn't feel like she had a right to decide the future of the world on her own. (Okay, because she'd ripped the orbital gate out of the sky without asking anyone, she had been sitting back and waiting for the Queen or someone to give her permission.) Well, screw that. This was Pittsburgh and she was its *domi.* Pure Radiance wasn't going to give her that permission, so she was going to have to take it while the female was distracted by the war.

At least with Forge, the twins, and a dozen dragons underfoot, she should be able to get lots of help to do it quickly.

45: LEMON-LIME JEL-LO

The twins had pulled down the furniture tower with the help of everyone at Sacred Heart but left the pieces as an island of clutter at the center of the room. The beds were made up to sleep in, side by side, but the twins had resisted putting any of the other pieces into place. They wanted to plan the layout of the furniture before shifting the pieces but didn't know what they wanted in a bedroom.

Esme's room at the Fortress of Evil had been a lesson in what was possible in self-expression. Fake windows that looked at imaginary landscapes. A bed that raised and lowered. A secret room. Steampunk elements that looked cosmetic but hid a message sent through time.

Their room at Sacred Heart was a big classroom with hardwood floors, a wall of windows, and a chalkboard at one end. Oilcan had gathered all the furniture that they could want: beds, nightstands, desks, chairs, dressers, bookcases, tables, and even a cute love seat. Still, the pieces seemed very little when compared to the size of the room. Their entire house in Queens, New York, had been only slightly bigger.

The question was: what did they want in a bedroom? Did they try to create zones by scattering the pieces of furniture? Create a "living room" around the love seat? Do a meeting room with the table and desks? Did they want to sleep with the twin beds two feet apart like they grew up doing or pushed together to make one big bed like all the beds that they'd shared since their parents died? Or would they go halfway and have bunk beds?

"We could even put a divider in the middle," Jillian said as they lay in the sun on the warm wooden floor. The babies were amusing themselves down the hall, watching a Chuck Norris movie. The baby dragons were off exploring. It was finally just them with no epic quest looming in front of them. It was strangely peaceful. "If we split the room in half, we both could have our own private space."

"Maybe later," Louise said as the idea of being that separated from her twin created pangs of anxiety. "Do you like the color? It's cheery enough. Oilcan said we could pick a different one—all the other kids did."

"I like the yellow," Jillian said. "It's a little like sunshine and lemons. We could do a green accent wall."

Louise followed Jillian's idea. "Because we are Lemon-Lime."

"Yeah." Jillian raised her hand to sketch a line across the back of the room. "The ceiling is high enough to build loft beds."

"Like the one in Esme's bedroom?"

"Less mobile, but yeah. It would free up space on the floor."

"What would we need all that space for?"

Jillian snorted. "To make videos! Lemon-Lime JEl-Lo has fans to please! We'll have to create a backlog for when we reconnect Pittsburgh back to Earth."

"You really think we can build a gate?"

"We're wood sprites—we can do anything. But I don't think we'll have to—Tinker is probably going to make one before long. She's going to have to get enough food, toilet paper, bread, eggs and milk for the city. The stores are like a winter-long blizzard is coming. We should be ready to roll the moment Tinker gets a gate up and running. I figure we should set up a bank account here in Pittsburgh so we have somewhere to transfer in the money we stole off Ming. Also we should make a shopping list of things that we want from Earth. Cameras. Computers. Microphones. Soundboards. Barbie dolls."

"And we have to let Aunt Kitty know we're okay," Louise said.

"Definitely. Oh! We could get the pets that Mom and Dad would never let us get! You know—a gerbil or a hamster or a guinea pig. Maybe something bigger. I wonder if we could get a kuesi. The tengu probably know where to find one."

"Oh, wow! A kuesi!" Louise breathed. Considering how the tengu had fulfilled all their whims so far, they might even be able to talk them into getting a kuesi. She knew it was wrong to think that way; she struggled with temptation. "I don't think there's room for one here. They're bigger than African elephants. Besides, there's already so many pets here: the puppy, the kittens, the indi, the piglet, and the chicks."

"Yeah, but those aren't ours."

The kittens didn't seem to have a bias between them and Baby Duck but the elfhound puppy did. It would play nicely with them but was firmly bound to the little elf female. "I think... I think I would like a toad."

"A toad?" Jillian said with surprise.

"Or a turtle or a salamander. I think they're really interesting and they wouldn't eat much." She didn't add that they were pets she always wanted. She couldn't understand why they weren't allowed them until they discovered that their father was deathly afraid of snakes and such beasts.

"I don't know about a toad, but a turtle would be cool," Jillian said. "I still think a kuesi would be cooler."

"Yeah," Louise agreed quietly. She knew that their mother would be mad at them for asking for something like that, knowing that it would cause so much trouble for Oilcan. It was like when they let the python loose in their father's office. "So, what is our next video going to be about?"

"How Prince Yardstick meets his one true love?" Jillian suggested. "We kind of missed the mark with the Valkyrie and the weird putt-putt golf course. Or we could do Tinker falling off the planet and finding Esme? I wonder what the anthropology ninjas thought of all that. Turtle Creek all blue and cold and then 'pop' there's a spaceship standing there."

"Oh, I know! 'Invasion of the Baby Dragons'!" Louise said. "Prince Yardstick and his faithful First trying to be all serious and having a war conference while attempting to totally ignore the eleven baby dragons going, 'Who is this? Are you mine? Ohhh, cookies!'"

"Is that where they all are?" Jillian asked.

"Oh, I don't know! I doubt it... but they could be." Louise still wasn't sure what was "knowing" and what was just creative thinking.

"Oh! 'Queen Soulful Ember Meets the Baby Dragons,'" Jillian said.

"Blast them all!" Jillian and Louise both said, hands over their heads, fingers wiggling.

They giggled for several minutes, imagining the reactions of the royal court—as they depicted them in their videos.

"Do you think we'll ever meet her?" Louise said. "Queen Soulful Ember?"

"Oh God, I hope not," Jillian said. "I don't think I could keep a straight face."

46: STORM FURIES

Tinker had hoped, since the last step of the spell-casting would be at the tech center, that it would be less like the three-ring circus that Sacred Heart had been for the last day and a half. Unfortunately, the madness came with her in the form of Oilcan, the twins, eight of the draconic shards, all four of the unborn Dufae babies, and six *sekasha*. Roach was there as backup along with his big elfhounds Pete and Bruno—much to Louise's delight. The dogs and the white-canvas tent protecting the casting circle lent to the circus feeling.

Tinker had no idea where the other three pocket-sized dragons were or how the Dufae babies were there at all as they were somehow projecting their mouse bodies instead of riding inside the little robotic ones. Tinker couldn't wait until they were born and became somewhat spirit-locked in their own bodies. *Oh please, gods, don't let them be able to dream walk after they are born.*

Their caper to save the baby dragons aside, the twins turned out to be surprisingly quiet, polite, well-behaved children. They said "please" and "thank you" and "may I" in a way that Lain had never been able to beat into Tinker. Their range of interests was staggering, from making clothes to writing music to obscure Earth food culture. For some odd reason, they were also fascinated by Queen Soulful Ember and her court. Or at least Jillian was—she had been asking questions all morning about the queen of the elves.

"But does she have a sense of humor?" Jillian was asking Pony.

"I do not know the queen well enough to say that," Pony admitted. "While I grew up in the house of the Wind Clan leader, and thus spent most of my life at Court, I rarely saw her beyond occasional family visits to her sister—Wolf's mother. Stormsong would be a better one to ask."

"Do not get me involved in this discussion!" Stormsong said in English from the grid of camera feeds on the twins' laptop. "If I am going to answer questions about her, I want to be face-to-face and behind closed doors."

Tinker hadn't been sure how to keep all the various parts of the casting coordinated. They needed to sync up half a dozen locations scattered across the Westernlands, from the tengu village to Aum Renau. The twins had suggested the camera and monitors. Apparently the camera thing was something that they did routinely on Earth. It was called video teleconferencing and it let people see and talk to each other from two or more locations. It was very cool but made Tinker feel like some uneducated country bumpkin for not knowing about it.

In theory, Tinker was setting up the shield spell to protect the Dufae kids: herself, Oilcan, and the twins. In practice, everyone was helping out in the tracing and the double-checking. It made for quick work. Everyone had been given copies of the spell to carry with them just in case something unforeseen happened. (Considering the summer so far, "unforeseen" boggled the mind.)

Tinker had leaned heavily on her and Oilcan's Beholden to pull this off. It gave her access to a wide range of tengu, elves, and humans. Stormsong had Blue Sky and Geoffrey Kryskill working with her to coordinate the Pittsburgh-based casters with the East Coast holdings via the distant voices. Blue and Geoffrey handled the computer end while Stormsong interacted with the highly protected "magical telegraph" devices. (Geoffrey had officially joined Moser's commune because the elves wanted that clarification of "us" vs. "them.") The monitor at Forge's location showed Moser sitting back, strumming a guitar, chilling until showtime. Maya and Gin Blossom were somewhere off camera. The tengu were setting up the shield spell on the woman or women carrying the Dufae babies at Haven. (Tinker really needed to nail down how many women were pregnant. Every time she thought to bring up the question, the conversation would suddenly get derailed by the pale yellow baby dragon.) At the moment, there was only Jin Wong and Riki in camera range. Scratch that—Joy suddenly eclipsed the tengu to make faces at the camera.

Tinker sighed and went back to checking the spell tracings for a third time.

The twins remained fixated on the queen.

"Has anyone ever, like, done a play or something about Soulful Ember? Something with music and songs—and silliness?" Louise asked.

"Silliness?" Pony echoed as if he wasn't sure what the word meant even though the question was in Elvish.

"Music and songs?" Thorne Scratch fielded the query. "Like an opera? They are usually tragedies. The queen has not had a tragic life."

"The Fire Clan have a temper," Stormsong added from the monitor despite her earlier comment. "No one would dare to face the queen—and, by default, my father..."

Whatever Stormsong was about to say was cut off as the baby dragon Einstein shut down the teleconferencing program—probably because of Joy's taunting.

"No, no, don't do that!" Louise cried. "We need to keep this up."

Luckily, Tinker had foreseen that the insanity of babies—Dufae and draconic alike—would be at her end. Moser and his gang were overseeing the computer that hosted the teleconference meeting. They were manning the setup for Forge at the University of Pittsburgh casting circle.

While Louise picked up Einstein, Jillian got the connection back up.

Tinker had been fixated on go-karts and robots at the twins' age. Somehow the difference between her and them made the twins far less frightening. It was kind of fun playing big sister and teaching them the finer details of magic. She explained using the big casting circles as they scrubbed clean the spell she'd laid down a few days earlier. They could have just used it again, but she hadn't traced it out with multiple uses in mind. Many of the tracings had been damaged by the power of the spell pulsing through it. She'd been lucky that she hadn't had a flare out. It was safer to clean off the stone and start fresh.

"I don't see any flaws," Tinker said after examining the new spell tracings for a third time.

"Everything looks good," Oilcan said. "I'm still a little nervous about putting all our lives on one cast but with this many eyes on it, it should work just as well as it did last time."

"This is a lot more scary..." Louise murmured.

Jillian nodded and finished the sentence. "When you've actually met all the people who could be hurt by getting it wrong."

"It worked the first time. It will work this time." Tinker turned to face the camera. "Is everyone ready?"

Jin Wong came to the camera and confirmed the statement with, "We're ready here."

"Wolf is standing by," Stormsong said with Geoffrey Kryskill and Blue Sky at Poppymeadows. "He and Jay Bird have the spell scribed at Aum Renau and are waiting for your signal. Prince True Flame at Brotherly Love is in a safe position. Wolf's siblings at New Haven are also ready. The Harbingers and Cana Lily report that they're standing ready. They say that the *domana* at the Stone Clan holdings in the south have been warned."

"Forge says that everything is good," Moser said from the university casting circle.

There was a loud crowing from behind Moser.

"Is that our star?" Tinker asked.

Box's interactions with the baby dragons had been sad to watch. He was used to being the only dragon in a flock of chickens. It was obvious that he wanted to strut about Sacred Heart as if he owned it but any time he got near a baby dragon, he visibly drooped. It did not help that the baby dragons seemed to see him as a clever dog, something to pat on the head and then ignore.

It reminded Tinker that Tooloo had once said that Box was never fully happy as a rooster. He wanted to be bigger and mightier. At the time, Tinker thought it was just an analysis of the chicken's behavior. She realized now that Box was suffering from a major downsize as a rooster.

How long had he been a rooster? Since Unbounded Brilliance left Elfhome? Before that? Even if it was during the French Revolution, one was talking hundreds of years. Being that chickens only lived ten or twelve years—if not killed by attacking things like bears and wolves—that could be pushing two dozen lives as fifteen pounds of muscle-bound fluff.

No wonder Box always seemed annoyed.

Maybe he'd spent some time as a parrot. Some of those lived

for decades. Tinker could see Tooloo swaggering about like a pirate with a foul-tempered cockatoo on her shoulder.

At some point Box had discovered the chick that Tristan had left and decided he could impress it with his size and grandeur.

After the literal pain she had gone through to catch him, Tinker hadn't been feeling bad about his fate. Watching him with the chick, she couldn't help but feel sad about what she needed to do to protect all the holdings on the East Coast.

"He seems to know that he's the star of the show." Moser rotated the camera to show that Box was perched on the tightly packed bones at the center of the university's casting circle.

Box flapped his wings and then posed, neck feathers puffed up.

Yes, that was Box in full-of-himself mode.

Did he understand what was going on? Was he sick of being a chicken? Did he want to do one last big thing?

"Okay, let's do this," Tinker said. "Stormsong, let Windwolf know we're about to start, once we know he has his shield up. Jin Wong, cast your shield now. I'm going to cast ours."

She motioned to Oilcan and the twins. "Let's get into position. Roach, you're up."

Roach shifted forward to take command of the laptop since it couldn't come into the circle.

"Go, go." Louise waved to the spirit mice, who popped out of existence like soap bubbles.

She and Jillian held hands as they hurried to Tinker. They huddled close to her and Oilcan.

"It will be okay," Oilcan murmured.

Our fragile little family, Tinker thought. She really hated that everyone that she loved was on the line. If they messed this up badly, they would all be powerless and the *domana* dead. If the Spell Stones fell to the oni, there would be no Wind or Fire *domana* coming to the rescue from the Easternlands.

She felt the shield rise in Haven. The tengu had successfully triggered their spell.

She spoke the key word. The tracings all gleamed as the spell came to life. The ghostly shield rose around her. It pushed the walls of the tent out, bulging almost to the point of breaking. In the background, she could hear Box still crowing.

"Okay! We're set!" Tinker shouted at the camera. "Jin, you're set, right? Stormsong, is Windwolf ready?"

"Windwolf has the special shield up," Stormsong reported.

"We're ready here, domi," Jin Wong reported.

"Okay, Moser, tell Forge to let it rip!"

There was a flare of power toward Oakland. Almost instantly their protective shield flashed to blinding light as it deflected the transformation spell.

"Oh! Oh!" Moser shouted. "Was Forge supposed to faint?"

Tinker winced. In the confusion she must have forgotten to warn Moser. "Yeah, that was expected. He didn't get hurt—did he?"

"His people caught him," Moser said. "I just wasn't expecting it."

"The babies seem fine," Jin Wong reported needlessly as the mice popped back into existence when Tinker dropped the tech-center shield. They hopped up and down beside Roach, squeaking and clapping.

"Wolf is reporting that his shield worked," Stormsong added.

The twins looked like they were about to burst into tears. At first Tinker didn't know why but then she realized that the crowing had abruptly stopped. Box was gone.

"He seemed proud that there was something only he could do," Tinker said quietly, hoping that would ease the pain.

"He was so brave," Jillian said as tears started to pour down her cheeks.

Louise scrubbed away the danger of crying. "Did the transformation spell work?"

"We won't know until Forge's Hand can get him up," Tinker said. "Moser, can you guys scrub clean the casting circle? We want to wipe out all traces of what we used."

"Will do," Moser said. "Are we done otherwise?"

"Yeah, everyone, we're shutting down!" Tinker called to all the remote groups.

"Now what?" Louise asked quietly once it was just them. The camera was stored away and the laptop powered down.

"Now," Tinker said, "we have a gate to build back to Earth."

It took less time than Tinker expected. A baseball team's worth of wood sprites, a dozen dragons counting Impatience, more magic-wielding tengu astronauts than you could shake a stick at, and one "borrowed" massive 3D printer made short work of what had taken her three weeks to build before.

They made a small prototype to test first. It reminded her of the dream she had at the start of summer where she made one the size of Hula-Hoops. In the dream, foo dogs, crows, Riki, the NSA agents, and Windwolf all jumped through the magic Hula-Hoops until the foo dogs ran off with the magical toys.

They drove to the end of the Parkway West. It ended halfway up a steep hill. Temporary ROAD CLOSED signs stood where the pavement abruptly stopped at a wall of towering trees. Autumn leaves littered the abandoned highway with brilliant reds and yellows—a reminder of how desperately Pittsburgh would need food for the coming winter. During Shutdown, the signs would be shifted to the berm and steel plates laid down to connect the Pittsburgh side to the roads of Earth.

Forge and the twins were fascinated for different reasons. Forge was impressed with the road design and engineering. The twins closely studied the clean line where the Rim cut through metro Pittsburgh, shifting everything from Earth to Elfhome.

Tinker pointed at the forest. "If the prototype gate works right, the first thing we'll see is the quarantine zone outside of Monroeville roughly where Churchill used to be."

"Six lanes of highway should be fairly hard to miss," Oilcan said.

Tinker continued with the plan so that they were all on the same page. "If we see that, we power down the prototype, back up to Squirrel Hill Tunnel, and set up the big gate. If we see anything else, we cut power and go back to the drawing board."

"Why don't we set the big gate up here?" Jillian asked.

"The tunnel creates a natural chokepoint," Tinker said. "It means we can better control who comes and goes from Earth. Also there's electrical power, offices, restrooms for checkpoint personnel, and everything set up at the tunnels. Also it creates less road for us to maintain, which is especially important during the winter. This hill is a bitch in the snow."

Oilcan nodded. "We wouldn't come out here in the winter with our tow truck if someone called us. The chances are too high that we'd get stuck on the wrong side of the Rim as the EIA-controlled exit gates are clear back at Monroeville."

"That's scary," the twins both said at the same time. It suggested strongly that they didn't want to go back to Earth. It would be a step down, as they were currently surrounded by seventeen of the best warriors on the planet and a host of heavily armed trusted adults. On Earth, they'd be alone.

Tinker couldn't blame them for wanting to stay on Elfhome. "Let's see if this works."

The prototype was only sixty-eight inches in diameter, shorter but slightly wider than a normal front entranceway. The twins called it a hobbit-hole door. They set it up on an asphalt road, made sure all possible metal debris was swept clear of the area, and then turned it on.

The six lanes of empty highway climbed the hill like an optical illusion against the backdrop of virgin forest.

"Oh, that's so cool," Louise murmured.

Jillian took out her phone, took a picture, and then stared at the screen a moment. "Oh, God! A signal!" She started to tap on her phone. "Oh, how I've missed you, Earth internet!"

"Sweet!" Louise took out hers and checked the screen. "You know, if we made a tiny one of these gates, we could have internet twenty-four seven!"

In Tinker's dream, she'd shrunk the gate down to wedding ring size.

"You still have to pay for the internet connection somehow," Oilcan said.

Tinker nodded. "That was the biggest pain about Shutdown: the Earth internet was there but you couldn't access it directly without buying a device that was useless twenty-eight days of the month."

"Money is not a problem," Louise said, as Jillian said, "We've got money coming out of our ears."

Tinker glanced at Oilcan, who shrugged. "Once we get the big gate up, you can connect as much as you want today and then we'll work on a ring-sized gate for internet service."

The twins bounced with happiness and unexpectedly hugged Tinker. "This is so cool! We have so much to upload!"

Over the last few days, Tinker had heard more about the twin's rescue of the tengu children, how they had figured out how to create the new shield spell, and even what led them to charge across the forest to face the oni at the graveyard. Oddly, it washed away all the fear that she had of them. She would have made the same decisions. Yes, they could be wicked clever like her—but then again, she always tried to do what was right.

Tooloo might not have wanted Leonardo's gate destroyed, but it was the right thing to do. Yes, it stranded Pittsburgh on Elfhome, but it shut the gate to Onihida and took the control of the pathway away from the Skin Clan. The right thing to do now was create a limited access but full-time pathway that would let Earth and Elfhome exchange goods and ideas. Ultimately the elves needed a goddess of war to sweep through and change their society. They needed to keep their people—like Oilcan's kids—from falling between the cracks and disappearing. They needed the flexibility of the humans. And according to their own legends, the goddess of war did not ride alone. She rode with storm furies.

The End